Olive oil, pancetta, bay leaves, red peppers, olive oil . . .

BANG! BANG! BANG! BANG!

Carly stopped, pencil hovering over the page for a minute before she frowned and crossed the repeat offender off her shopping list. For God's sake, how was she supposed to get anything done with all that racket going on outside? Not to mention the racket her libido was making every time the man she swore she'd avoid crossed her line of sight.

Looks like there's something inside *the house that needs fixing. Betcha he's got all the right power tools for the job.*

Carly sent a panicked look around the room, as if her dirty subconscious had broadcast the unexpected thought out loud. It wasn't her fault that no matter where she went in the bungalow, Contractor Guy ended up in her line of sight, hard at work. And she could forget turning a blind eye, because staring at the man was just a foregone conclusion. Carly might still be irritated that he'd embarrassed her, but let's face it: she was aggravated, not dead. And Contractor Guy was 100 percent red-blooded man.

Read all of Kimberly Kincaid's Pine Mountain series

Gimme Some Sugar

Turn Up the Heat

The Sugar Cookie Sweetheart Swap
by Donna Kauffman, Kate Angell, and Kimberly Kincaid

Published by Kensington Publishing Corporation

Some Sugar

KIMBERLY
KINCAID

ZEBRA BOOKS
KENSINGTON PUBLISHING CORP.
http://www.kensingtonbooks.com

ZEBRA BOOKS are published by

Kensington Publishing Corp.
119 West 40th Street
New York, NY 10018

All Kensington titles, imprints, and distributed lines are available at special quantity discounts for bulk purchases for sales promotion, premiums, fund-raising, educational, or institutional use.

Special book excerpts or customized printings can also be created to fit specific needs. For details, write or phone the office of the Kensington Special Sales Manager: Attn.: Special Sales Department. Kensington Publishing Corp., 119 West 40th Street, New York, NY 10018. Phone: 1-800-221-2647.

Zebra and the Z logo Reg. U.S. Pat. & TM Off.

First Mass-Market Paperback Printing: June 2014
ISBN-13: 978-1-4201-3285-4
ISBN-10: 1-4201-3285-7

First Electronic Edition: June 2014
eISBN-13: 978-1-4201-3286-1
eISBN-10: 1-4201-3286-5

10 9 8 7 6 5 4 3 2 1

Printed in the United States of America

To my three girls—
thank you for cheering me on
while I pursued my dreams.
Mommy's heart
(and her sanity!)
is all yours.

ACKNOWLEDGMENTS

So many people contribute to the joyful and grueling process that is writing a book, and this story in particular would've never been the same without the following people and their unending support.

To my editor, Alicia Condon, who encourages me and challenges me at the same time, and my agent, Maureen Walters, who fields my emails with such finesse, thank you both so very much for believing in Pine Mountain. Also, to Vida Engstrand at Kensington and Elizabeth Radin at the Curtis Brown Agency, having you two on my team makes life so much easier. You are both amazing!

To my literary besties, Alyssa Alexander, Tracy Brogan, Robin Covington, Avery Flynn, and Jennifer McQuiston, there are not enough words (or enough wine) for me to thank you properly for all your support. I adore you all.

Huge thanks to Dr. Daniel Roper for all the medical advice on TIAs and strokes, and to Chris Kulak and Jeff Romeo, for answering endless questions about paramedic procedure for head injuries. All the knowledge belongs to you three, while all mistakes are definitely mine. Likewise, much gratitude goes to my lovely cousin, Joy Paulson, for her deep well of patience in helping me with the Italian phrases found in this book.

To Bella Andre and Wendy Corsi Staub, who have always been so supportive and patient in their encouragement of my career, thank you so much for reading this book and loving it enough to say so out loud. You are the best.

To my husband, who makes my life a living embodiment of happily ever after (and luckily has a vast knowledge of deck building), words don't touch my love for you. And to my three girls, I am so grateful that you love Cheerios. Now we can have a "real" dinner.

Lastly, to both sides of my loving, amazing, warm, and wonderful Italian family, but most importantly to my grandma Frances. I know you're proud of me. Hope you're reading from heaven.

Chapter One

"If there's a serial killer out in those woods just waiting for the cover of a creepy storm so he can kill us, I'm going to be pissed."

Carly di Matisse snickered as her best friend Sloane Russo's wild imagination got the best of her . . . again. Carly stopped short on the floorboards of the cozy mountain bungalow they'd shared for the last six months, undoing the top button of her chef's whites and tossing her keys on the counter.

"You watch too many horror movies. It's just a little storm. Look, I'm barely wet." Carly raised her arms up as proof. As if offended by her nonchalance, the storm flashed a split of silvery light outside their living room window, immediately chasing it with a crack of thunder to rival the shrieking wind.

Sloane arched a brow in Carly's direction from her perch on the couch before shooting a wary look at the windows. "That's because we have a garage, smartass. I swear it doesn't rain like this in Brooklyn."

Okay, fine. So Sloane had a point. The wind sure didn't shake the bricks of Carly's New York brownstone with its gusting and groaning, and you could forget about being able to hear it from the deep recesses of any big city kitchen. Raindrops crashed over the bungalow with even more force now, like handfuls of angry marbles being pelted at the logs.

Things were definitely different in the middle of the Blue Ridge Mountains, AKA the middle of nowhere. And the spectacular weather wasn't the half of it.

"Yeah, yeah. We're not in Kansas anymore, *cucciola*." Carly hoped her homesickness didn't permeate her voice as much as it did her chest. God, she hated being so far away from home.

Sloane's head snapped up. "Oh, Carly. I'm sorry. I didn't mean—"

"I know." Lightning streaked the sky, and a near-simultaneous clap of thunder ripped through the night. "So you want a cup of tea? I was going to give that new vanilla chai a whirl, see if it's any good."

Not the slickest subject change in the world, but it'd do. Carly didn't want to talk about the reasons she'd left New York any more than Sloane wanted to tangle with that imaginary serial killer.

"It's after midnight. Aren't you exhausted?" Sloane eyed Carly's sauce-splattered chef's whites, the product of a typical Saturday double shift.

"Weird hours are an occupational hazard. Especially since it's just me in the kitchen now." She flicked on the overhead light in the kitchen, her Dansko clogs whispering over the hardwood as she moved to find the teakettle.

"Weird hours. Don't I know it." Sloane closed the laptop propped over her pajama-clad knees with a mutter. "If I don't get these pages to my editor before I leave on Monday, I'm going to be ankle-deep in a bad situation. Speaking of which," Sloane paused just long enough for it to be noticeable. "Are you sure you're going to be okay all by your lonesome for a whole week while I'm at my conference?"

Carly tested the water rushing from the kitchen faucet,

her answer as steady as the stream under her fingers. "In the twenty years you've known me, have I ever not been okay?"

Sloane held up her hands to concede. "Point taken. You *are* everyone's favorite tough cookie." She padded over to the breakfast bar separating the kitchen from the living room, flinching at a particularly loud clap of thunder as she went.

"I come by it honestly," Carly said, coaxing a burner to life with a turn of her wrist. Her profession dictated she wear a certain amount of toughness on her sleeve. Current circumstances took things one step further, pushing her to wear the rest of her fortitude like a suit of armor.

"Yeah, about that." Sloane winced, tucking the dark swath of her bangs behind one ear. "Travis called while you were at work. Said it was important."

Carly's stomach did a full gainer due south. "Did he say what he wanted?" It figured she'd get hit with this when she was trying to unwind. Travis had always known how to wreck a good thing.

Sloane made a rude noise and a face to match, propping her elbows on the granite counter at the breakfast bar. "You should be so lucky. He just said he needed to talk to you ay-sap. His cheesy expression, not mine."

"Well, shit." This was about as eloquent—and polite—as Carly got when it came to her ex. While she could run a high-pressure kitchen without feeling an ounce of stress, dealing with her soon-to-be former husband was another story altogether. The man was the living embodiment of ulterior motives.

"Personally, I think you should ignore the call and let your lawyer have at him. He's just trying to rile you up. Now that you're not there in person, he's got no choice but to phone it in."

Carly reached for two mugs, dropping a tissue-thin tea bag into each one. "Travis wouldn't spend the energy unless he wanted something. This is a man who manipulated his way into a head chef's job by way of my coattails, then schmoozed everyone in the five boroughs into believing *he* was the true talent behind our husband and wife team. Never mind that I'm the one who created the menu at Gracie's from pot to plate while he just stood there looking pretty and taking the credit."

Her voice gave a slight hitch over the name of the restaurant where she'd spent over four years as co-head chef, only to be ousted by the owner when she gave him the either-Travis-goes-or-I-go ultimatum. Of course, the fact that the owner's daughter, Alexa—who also happened to be the restaurant manager—was completely smitten with Travis probably went a long way toward making the decision easy. Carly often wondered if the owner would've felt the same way if he'd been the one to catch Travis and Alexa having sex in the back office after hours. Not that it mattered now.

Sloane rolled her baby blues. "Please. You're so much better off out here."

"Am I?" The question crossed Carly's lips before she could tamp it down. "It's not as if Travis had to leave the city to get out from beneath *my* shadow." She should've known better than to tie herself to him so inextricably in the first place. Everything they'd done in their five years of marriage had been a joint endeavor, with his name headlining. God, with all his sweet talking and that confident trust-me smile, he'd had her convinced it was all just a part of their happily ever after.

More like a bushel full of poison apples, each one stamped with his conniving name. The only way to salvage her reputation among the tight-knit kitchen circles in the city was to hope that out of sight truly did mean out of mind.

And running a kitchen in the Pennsylvania boondocks certainly qualified as out of sight.

Sloane interrupted Carly's thoughts. "Yes, but Travis

wasn't offered the once-in-a-lifetime chance to revitalize a restaurant at a beautiful mountain resort. Pine Mountain's executives courted you alone, darling, and with good reason. Once the reviews come in and La Dolce Vita takes off like the superstar it is, you'll be able to write your ticket to any restaurant in New York." She gave a look that dared Carly to argue before adding, "*If* you even feel like going back."

"You're kidding, right? I'm a born-and-raised city girl." New York was the Promised Land in the restaurant world, and she wanted her place back as a rising star. Badly enough to wait things out in Mapdot, Pennsylvania.

Carly pasted on a smile, forcing herself to ditch the pity-party. "We did get a nice review in the *Travel Times* on Monday. I guess a local travel guide is a good place to start." In truth, she was learning a ton from running a kitchen solo, and it was good experience while the gossip mongers on the New York restaurant circuit grew tired of churning out her sullied name. "Anyway, the food is what matters most. The kitchen here is on the upswing, and it's only getting better."

"That's the spirit!" A loud burst of thunder took the edge off Sloane's grin, and Carly went right into distraction mode.

"So how are your pages coming along?" Steam curled from the teakettle in thick tendrils, wrapping around Carly's fingers as she poured hot water into each oversized mug.

"Not bad, actually. My editor loved the outline. She said it's shaping up to be my sexiest work yet," Sloane said, waggling her eyebrows.

"Well, it's a good thing you write romance novels. I don't think I'd know sexy if it fell into my lap."

"Oh, that's a load of crap. Those clogs don't fool me, Chef. There's a dirty girl under those dirty chef's whites. You just have to find the right man to share her with, that's all."

"Sloane!" Carly laughed in a quick burst. "Don't be ridiculous. Men are way more trouble than they're worth, both for me and my career. And trouble is something I am definitely not interested in."

"Jaded, party of one, your table is now available." Sloane's laughter softened under the warm glow of the kitchen lights. "Come on, Carly. Not all men are lying slime like Travis."

Carly shrugged, unconvinced. "Let's get realistic here. Any man who's not in my field probably isn't going to understand the weird hours and backbreaking work of it. And any man who is, is competition. The odds of me finding Mr. Right somewhere in the middle don't look too good. And I'm definitely not risking my career over a man. Ever again."

"Well, yeah, but maybe—"

A hard shot of wind rattled the window panes, capturing both women's full attention. Though she was grateful for the interruption, the ferocity of the gale made Carly pause. She narrowed her eyes on the sliding glass door connecting the living room to the deck on the back of the house. "Wow. That wind is really nasty."

"I thought you said it was just a teensy little storm," Sloane protested, knuckles blanching over the handle of her mug.

"It is. Don't tell me you're scared." Carly bit back an amused smile. Tree limbs whipped high over the roof, whistling eerily in the merciless wind, but she remained undaunted.

"Hell yes, I'm scared!" Lightning forked in jagged, steely lines, illuminating the yard beyond the sliding glass door in a blue-gray glow, and Sloane cranked her eyes shut. "Doesn't *anything* freak you out?"

Carly's smile escaped despite her best efforts to spare her friend's pride. "There's nothing to be scared of." She walked to the door and put her palm to the glass. "See? It's just a—"

A gust of wind smashed into the side of the house, gluing Carly's unfinished sentence to her throat. The floorboards vibrated under her feet, and her eyes flared at the staccato snap of breaking wood followed by the surreal groan of moving earth.

Before Carly could release the scream gathering in her chest, one of the tall, proud oak trees lining the property came crashing toward the house.

Somewhere amid the jangly throng of eight-penny nails in his tool belt, Jackson Carter's cell phone was making one hell of a racket. He slid his hammer into the fraying loop on his hip and palmed his phone, grinning at the caller ID.

"Hey, Luke. What's doing?" Jackson wiped his brow with a bare forearm. Man, this weather was a far cry from the storm they'd had a couple days ago. Although considering June was almost over, it was really about time for some heat.

"You tell me. How's Mrs. Teasdale's fence coming?" his boss replied.

Jackson took a step back to double-check his work, inhaling the crisp scent of the pine boards he'd been hammering into place for the better part of two days. "Your timing is perfect, actually. I just finished the build. All it needs is stain and seal coat, and it'll be good to go."

"I'm going to send Micah out there to finish it. I need you on another job, and it looks like a doozy." The unspoken apology hung in Luke's voice, and Jackson fought the urge to groan.

"Why does that sound like a disaster right off the bat?"

"Because it probably is. I just got a call from old man Logan about that bungalow he rents out. You know the one, off Rural Route 4?"

Jackson had lived in Pine Mountain since the beginning of his double-digit days, plus he'd done local contracting work for Luke for nearly a decade. If Jackson didn't know every property in Pine Mountain by now, then shame on him.

"Yeah. It's the log cabin-looking place, right?" He walked the length of freshly built fence to make sure he hadn't missed anything before doubling back to the front of Mrs. Teasdale's aging cottage.

"That's the one. Well, apparently that storm we had the other night was a bit too much for one of the old oak trees on his property, and the wind actually uprooted the damned thing."

Jackson let out a stunned whistle as he popped the locks on his pickup truck. "Did it hit the house?" Those trees had to be sixty feet tall. Oh, man, this job was going to suck.

Luke snorted. "Relax, I'm not sending you on a demolition. The tree fell across the backyard, but it wiped out part of the deck in the process. The arborists just got done hauling away the last of the tree, and now that we can get a good look at the damage, Logan wants us to see if anything can be salvaged. I told him not to get his hopes up, but if anyone could do it, it'd be you."

"Thanks for the vote of confidence." Jackson grinned and slid into the driver's seat. At six foot four, fitting his large frame behind the wheel wasn't an easy job. "Tell old man Logan his deck is in good hands. Or what's left of it, anyhow. I'm on my way."

One of the beautiful things about living in a small town was that it was just that, and the trip out to Rural Route 4 took less than ten minutes. Jackson pulled up to the tasteful little bungalow and got out, inhaling the fresh summer air as he sauntered to the front of the house to ring the bell.

The strains of some old R&B song were clear from the porch, even through the firmly closed front door. Jackson rang the bell anyway, but after the second try, he gave up. Clearly, someone was home and having the Tuesday morning of a lifetime. He chuckled, picturing some hard-of-hearing old lady getting her Motown groove on inside the house. Far be it for him to interrupt a good time, he thought as he ambled around toward the backyard. All he needed to do was to take a look at the damage, anyway. In and out, no problem.

"Huh," Jackson murmured, realizing that the muffled music was decidedly clearer back here. He recognized the song blaring through the open windows as an oldie his sisters used to sing along with on the ancient boom box in their bedroom. Right, yeah. Kind of a girl mantra, something about being a natural woman. He whistled along with the song as he approached the deck, most of which was thankfully still attached to the house.

"Well, at least it's ground level." He shrugged and examined the deck with a practiced eye. Although much of it was still intact, the tree had taken out the entire far row of railings and pickets, along with a good couple feet of floor boards, clipping what had once been a square into a rectangle with one hell of a rough edge.

The three stairs leading from the yard to what remained of the deck were still anchored in place, and Jackson mounted them easily even though the far side of the deck had sustained enough damage to make it a bad idea. It was the only way he was going to get a good enough look at the point of impact; plus, if the boards ended up giving way, it wasn't as if he'd fall more than a foot or two.

He was crouched down low to examine the missing boards and busted railing when the most horrific attempt at song filtered loudly through the screen door.

"Ouch." Jackson winced at the spectacular racket over his shoulder, biting back a laugh. It was absolutely wrong to eavesdrop on a client belting out oldies in the privacy of her own home, even if she *was* doing it with nothing but the rolling screen that accompanied her sliding glass door between them. The woman's voice was an audio train wreck, and his curiosity jumped like a trout at daybreak. One peek wouldn't hurt, would it?

As soon as he caught sight of the woman through the screen door, all bets for a quick look-see were off. The image of an old lady went up in smoke, replaced by a curvaceous, dark-haired woman in a skimpy bathrobe. Her eyes were shut tight, pretty face turned up to the living room ceiling as she wailed out the song with all her might. Common decency dictated he step back from the house and pretend he hadn't seen her. He needed to walk away, and he needed to do it pronto.

Nope. Not happening. This woman was fucking *beautiful*. Even if she did sound like a bag full of pissed off kittens.

Jackson stood, mesmerized, as she moved in place to the slow beat of the music. She was a little slip of a thing, but an air of strength belied her size. Muscular calves tapered gracefully into slim ankles, nearly covered by a pair of floppy yellow socks. A handful of dark tendrils came loose from the knot on top of her head, perfectly framing her Mediterranean features. She stood in the middle of the living room, eyes squeezed shut to serenade God knows who, and propriety be damned, he couldn't rip his eyes from her.

Every time she undulated to the sultry rhythm of the song, the belt on her bathrobe slipped lower over her hips, loosening it just enough to reveal the thin tank top beneath. The cotton stretched over her chest as she swayed, and she crooned again to the climbing music.

"You make me feel, you make me feel, you make me feel like a natural womaaaaaaan!" With each breath, the generous curve of her breasts pressed against the fabric, clearly outlining the woman's tight, shadowy nipples.

For a split second, all Jackson could think was *oh, hell yes*.

But then his decency kicked in, hard and fast. He averted his heated face, raising one hand to knock on the metal door frame of the screen. In that same instant, a blood curdling scream ripped through the air over the music, followed by a string of curse words that made Jackson wonder if he should cower in fear or be hugely impressed.

"Whoa, whoa, whoa. Hold on!" Jackson hollered, holding his hands up. He opened his mouth to tell her who he was and why he was there, but before he could form the words, she snatched something up from the side table and flung it at him with freakish accuracy.

"Wait!"

Too late.

Out of instinct, Jackson shielded his face with both arms and stumbled back as the offending object smashed into the frame of the screen door that separated them, right where his face had been. His heel caught on a gap between boards, wrenching the loose plank from its place, and the sudden tilt in balance sent him ass over teakettle.

Jackson's breath shot from his lungs in a hard *whump* as he crashed, elbow first, to the remaining boards of the deck, mere feet from the jagged drop-off into the yard. Pain streaked down his arm in a snap, heating his fingers with a nasty tingle courtesy of his pissed off nerve endings, and the deck groaned in protest under the sudden shift in weight.

"Ow! Take it easy, lady. I'm your contractor." At least the damaged boards had withstood his crash-landing. He pulled himself to a sitting position, taking his throbbing elbow into his opposite hand for inspection. Damn, that funny bone was so not funny.

"Get out, you fu—whaaaaat?" The woman stopped, midtirade, at the screen door, the frame over her head now skewed at an awkward angle. Her dark eyes narrowed with a mixture of anger and confusion. "What did you say?"

"I said I'm your contractor. You know, to look at your deck. Or what's left of it, anyway," Jackson said loudly, pointing to the boards beneath him. "So could you do me a favor and keep your throwing arm to yourself?"

The pain in his elbow pulsed along with the end of the song, and he flexed it a couple of times to make sure everything was where it belonged. The woman's eyes widened until they resembled two coppery-brown pennies, flashing with sudden understanding.

"I'm so sorry!" She whipped the screen door along its track and stepped out onto the deck, wearing a panicked expression. "Are you okay?"

"Stop."

The word came out harsher than he'd intended, a fact that became even more apparent when the woman put both hands on her hips and shot him a feisty look. The deck shifted subtly beneath his body at the additional weight, and he jack-knifed to his feet. "You can't be out here."

"It's my yard," she intoned over the music.

Jackson shook his head and tried to shoo her back into the house. "I know," he returned, just as forcefully. "But it's not safe with all the damage. You could get hurt."

"I'm barely a foot from the door," she said, refusing to budge. Man, she was infuriating.

"The deck isn't structurally sound. Ma'am, please—"

The woman rolled her pretty brown eyes. "If that's the case, you'd better get off it too." Her sarcasm rang through like church bells on Sunday. Too bad for Jackson, she was right. He'd been pushing it to walk on the deck in the first place.

"Okay." Jackson turned toward the wooden steps to get to the yard, but the now-loose part of the deck he'd upended with his boot stood smack in his path. He started to tiptoe around it, but the adjacent boards gave an ominous groan under his weight.

"Oh, God." The woman's eyes went wide, as if she'd realized all at once that he wasn't just blowing smoke. She motioned toward the house, the sleeve of her bathrobe flopping around her elbow. "I thought you were exaggerating. Okay, come this way. Don't fall through the boards or anything."

Jackson covered the newly damaged space in one long stride and followed her into the living room. "Thanks. That was more eventful than I'm used to," he said, fighting to be heard over the still-pumping music.

"What?"

"I said—"

But she cut him off midsentence, moving toward the radio to silence it with a swift crank of her wrist.

Jackson's ears rang in the unexpected hush. "What I said was, that's more eventful than I'm used to."

The woman frowned and crossed her arms over her chest, pulling her chin up to look at him. "You shouldn't sneak up on people like that, you know. It's not very polite."

She had to be kidding.

"I rang the bell, twice actually, before coming around here to check out the damage." Jackson took a step toward her, noting that she only came up to his chest. "I can't help it if you were a little hard to miss."

"I . . . I was listening to the radio!"

Note to self: the blush? Insanely hot.

"Yeah, I got that." Okay, so he was messing with her a little. It couldn't be helped. "Whatever that was is probably toast." Jackson gestured to the mangled black shrapnel at her feet. Despite her tiny stature, she sure packed a wallop.

"Huh? Oh." The woman danced up to her tiptoes, sock-feet pressing into the edge of the area rug beneath them. "That was the remote for the stereo."

"Here, let me help you." He lumbered toward the hard-wood at the exact moment she bent low to retrieve the broken pieces, and their foreheads knocked together with a startling *clunk*. Her hands flew to her head, and she wobbled for a second before falling smack on her butt in the middle of the living room.

A slice of panic streaked through him from conscience to chest. "God, I'm sorry. Did I hurt you?" Jackson reached for her instantly, cradling her elbow in his palm even though the pain in his own was still banging away like a nine-pound hammer. "Are you okay?"

"I think so." She blinked, and both her focus and her quick frown suggested she was indeed in top working order. "Are you?"

Relieved and dazed, Jackson bent lower to try to regain some clarity. The scent of something earthy and fresh filled his nose, like the flowers in his mother's garden, and he blinked as he breathed it in. In her tumble to the carpet, the woman's bathrobe had fallen all the way open to reveal that infernally sexy, nearly see-through tank top. As his eyes raked lower, Jackson couldn't help but get an eyeful of her white cotton panties. The no-frills fabric hugged the fold where her tanned legs met her body, showing off the curvy flare of her hips with just enough suggestion to spike his blood.

Forget trying to focus. Now he just wanted to keep from passing out.

"You, uh . . . your, you know . . . bathrobe is kind of . . ."

Okay. While he might earn a point or two for being a gentleman, he sure as hell wasn't going to score high in the suave category. Not that he was trying to impress her or anything. Christ, he wasn't still seeing stars, was he?

"Close your eyes!" Her head-to-toe flail might've been amusing if Jackson's head wasn't now pounding as hard as his elbow, but at least she was okay. He turned his face to give her a chance to cover up, and the rustle of fabric being yanked into place told him she'd taken full advantage.

Time to use a little humor to wrap this up, since she'd clearly recovered and he still had a job to do. "I'm going to stand up now. I just wanted to give you fair warning. You know, so we don't bang into each other again."

She double knotted the belt on her robe, her blush creeping all the way to her ears. "You're the one who smacked into me."

Guilt pumped through him, staying his smile. "I really am sorry. Are you sure you're okay?"

"Oh . . . well, yes, of course."

"Okay, then. You're not going to toss anything else at my head, are you?"

"I only did that because I thought you were a Peeping Tom," she argued, scrambling to her feet. "You scared me half to death."

"Guess I deserved it, then," Jackson replied without skipping a beat. "I'll be here for a little while to assess the damage to the back of the house and take some pictures, but I'll do my best not to interrupt you. Oh, and I'll fix your screen door after I'm done. Free of charge, of course."

"But the tree didn't hit the house. There's nothing wrong with the screen door."

Man, he'd bet she was feisty even in her sleep. "If you say so." Jackson trundled the door along its track, the dent in the metal frame as clear as his hand in front of him. "Have a nice morning."

He clamped down on his laugh as she gasped from behind him, but he didn't turn back toward the house. It got kind of dicey when the gasp turned into a muttered curse, but when the cursing went from English to Italian, he had no choice but to bury his face in the crook of his elbow and let the laughter in his chest have its way with him.

Chapter Two

The sharp sound of a horn knocked Carly from the distracted fog she'd been unable to shake all day, and she gave the car behind her a guilty wave before proceeding through Pine Mountain's only stoplight. Her cheeks prickled with warmth as she shamelessly let her mind zero back in on its new favorite subject.

The Contractor Guy had her in the world's weirdest tizzy.

In her defense, that Aretha Franklin song begged to be turned up loud and sung along to. Still, that didn't change how totally mortifying it was that Mr. Fix-It had caught her warbling her little heart out. And it *definitely* didn't change his being as sculpted as a freaking Michelangelo, or his breathtakingly blue eyes which crinkled around the edges when he smiled. Even though that smile had been 100 percent at her expense this morning.

Well, you know what they say. You never get a second chance to make a first impression. Not like you'd need one after that.

Oh, Lord. The mere thought of it was going to ruin that song for her forever. At least she could hide out in the kitchen until the new deck was done.

She pulled off the main road and onto resort property, grateful for the first reassuring thought she'd had all day.

As much as Carly missed the bustling sights and sounds of New York, she had to admit that the grounds of the resort really were beautiful. The main lodge was set against the backdrop of the Blue Ridge skyline, with entrances on both the east and west sides of the stone façade. La Dolce Vita sat nestled on the west side of the building, which gave her the full advantage of a gorgeous mountain sunset to boost the restaurant's cozy atmosphere.

Carly had been pleasantly surprised to discover Pine Mountain Resort wasn't just a tourist draw during ski season, which meant there was no terrible off-season lull in the summer. The sizeable lake and extensive hiking trails made Pine Mountain an attractive warm-weather vacation spot, and the new full-service spa at the resort added elegance and upscale appeal. With the rejuvenation of the main restaurant, courtesy of Carly's hard work and vision, the resort was sure to become even more popular in the upcoming season.

Which was a good thing, because the more buzz she got, the easier it would be to prove her worth and snag a primo job in New York.

She made her way to the kitchen on cat feet, snapping on the overhead lights and giving each station a quick once-over. With the exception of the faint buzz of the walk-in fridge and freezer lining the rear wall, the kitchen hummed with eerie silence. Carly shut the door to the back office with a snick and squared her shoulders, giving the desk phone a wary look before scooping up the receiver. As much as she didn't want to call Travis, the fact of the matter was that their divorce was still in red-tape purgatory. Until they both signed on the dotted line, she'd have to suck it up and return his phone calls.

"Travis Masters."

Was it her, or had his voice gotten even more unctuous since she'd last spoken to him a few weeks ago? "Hi, Travis." Carly cradled the phone between her shoulder and her ear and imagined herself on a beach in Tahiti. "Sloane said you left a message the other day. What can I do for you?"

"Carly." Travis's voice was as thick as clotted cream. "How's it going at the resort? What's the name of that little place you've got up there again?" He paused for maximum condescension. "It's so far off the beaten path, I can never remember."

Carly's radar flipped into overdrive at Travis's niceties, in spite of the veiled dig. "La Dolce Vita," she said, trying not to grit her teeth. "You're awfully pleasant today."

"What? I'm not allowed to be nice now?" His wounded tone peppered tiny holes in Carly's carefully constructed defenses before he continued. "Just because we're getting divorced doesn't mean I don't care about how you are."

She frowned. Maybe she was being a touch cynical. After all, not all of their five-year marriage had been set on stormy waters.

"Sorry. You just took me by surprise, is all." Carly twisted the phone cord between her fingers. "Everything here is great. Our soft opening in the spring was successful enough that we were able to do the grand opening in time for Memorial Day. So far, the early summer crowds haven't disappointed, even though the weather's been on the cool side."

"Well, that sounds like a nice little payoff for you, although I have to say, I'm surprised you left our stomping ground. You must miss the city something fierce." Travis's voice folded over the words with a little too much concern, and Carly's unease shimmered like waves of heat on summer pavement. Travis could get as cordial as he wanted. No way was she tipping her totally homesick hand.

"It's actually lovely out here. I can't complain." Carly paused, unable to keep her mounting wariness at bay. "Look,

Travis, I'm sure you didn't call me for a game of catch-up, and I've got a tasting menu to prep for my dinner staff. So is there something you need?"

"Still straight to the point, I see." His voice took on a sharp edge beneath the smooth demeanor. "Winslow called me a few days ago about the show. He wants us back for another season."

Carly barked out a laugh in a total knee-jerk reaction. "You're serious."

In the flurry of favorable reviews that had followed Carly and Travis's debut at Gracie's a few years ago, she'd been approached to host a cooking show on a local cable channel. The original deal had been for her to do the show solo, but as usual, Travis had other plans. One dinner meeting and half a case of pinot noir later, he'd schmoozed both Carly and the producers into believing that *Carly in the Kitchen* should be *Couples in the Kitchen*, and thus, their first and only cable season had been born.

"Of course I'm serious," Travis continued in his saccharine-sweet voice. "We garnered great ratings last season in the northeast market. Winslow and the other producers don't want to scrap the chance at another run, and frankly, neither do I. They're even willing to overlook the longer than usual break we've had between tapings."

God *damn* it. She should've known better than to ignore her instincts. How had she not seen this coming?

"Winslow never called me about this," she said, still trying to get over her shock. Of course Travis was locked and loaded with a cool reply.

"The producers called me late last week, but I told them just to let me tell you. What's the big deal? The show is great PR. And no offense, but you could really use some right now."

Carly clenched her jaw so tight that her ears popped. "I hate to break it to you, Travis, but it's kind of hard to do *Couples in the Kitchen* when there's no couple."

He humored her with a patronizing chuckle. "We wouldn't have to actually be a couple in order to tape the show. Come on, Carly. What do you say? Another season for old time's sake wouldn't hurt, would it?"

"Uh, yeah," Carly replied with sarcasm so thick she could've sliced it up and served it with basil and olive oil. "In case you haven't noticed, I have a kitchen to run. I can't just up and come to the city to tape a show. Not that I would."

God, Travis was so freaking smug! And Winslow was eating right out of his hand. She made a mental note to call the cable network first thing in the morning to personally set the producer straight. She'd rather take a leisurely stroll through Times Square in her birthday suit than spend five minutes with Travis, never mind put on a happy face for the sake of boosting his livelihood. Again.

Travis exhaled audibly. "Look at it from a business standpoint, Carly. Coming back to New York to do the show would be a boon for your career, one you need. I'm trying to do you a favor. You can't hide out in the middle of nowhere forever."

To think she'd once been a sucker for that sexy-smooth baritone. Carly took a deep breath to try to keep her voice from shaking in anger. "I'm not hiding from anything. I have my own kitchen out here. I didn't need any favors from you to get it, and I sure as hell don't need any favors from you to keep it. Thanks but no thanks on the show. I'm not interested."

Travis's tone flipped from lovely to Lucifer in less than a breath. "I really think you should reconsider." He paused before slithering in for the kill. "Otherwise who knows how long our divorce settlement could take."

An icy fist slipped around Carly's gut and gave it a sick twist. "Are you threatening to drag out our divorce if I don't come back for this?"

Her heartbeat slammed beneath the thick cotton of her chef's whites. Travis had done some pretty underhanded stuff in the past, but come on. He couldn't be serious.

"I'm just saying I think it would be a smart move all around for you to come back to New York and do the show. Who knows? You might even be able to get a job as somebody's sous chef if you're really lucky."

Something ugly snapped in Carly's chest, shoving the words right out of her. "Oh, I'll be back in New York, but it'll be when I'm good and ready and not a minute before. Until then, I'm going to have to call your bluff."

Please God let it be a bluff. Was it too much to ask to just get on with her life?

"Fine." Travis's voice wrapped around the word like a dirty dishrag. "You're not good enough to hack it in the big leagues anyway. Have fun committing career suicide out in the sticks, Mrs. *Masters*."

Before she could work up a reply, Travis hung up the phone.

Carly pinched the bridge of her nose between her thumb and forefinger. "It's Ms. di Matisse, you asshole," she told the dial tone before replacing the receiver on the cradle. She'd never gone by Travis's name in her life.

After a quick round of deep breathing, Carly turned her attention to the clock. She didn't have enough time to call her divorce attorney, who would likely have a field day with Travis's threat. Plus, Carly wanted to be levelheaded when she made that call, and right now, that wasn't happening. She needed to breathe, to think, to cook. And maybe to pound something while she was at it.

Yeah. Veal cutlets would make an excellent special.

A familiar sound made its way through the thin walls of the office, and Carly propped the door open to lean into the frame. Even though her arms were crossed and her mood was for shit, a smile brewed on her lips at the sight of the man in front of her.

"Someday, when I'm awfully low . . . when the world is cold . . . hey, Carlsbad! You look pissed," Adrian ventured gleefully, mid-Sinatra.

Adrian Holt had been Carly's sous chef, right-hand man, and confidant for five years. Well, technically, for four and a half of them, he'd been Travis's sous chef, too, but Carly didn't feel like splitting hairs.

"I hate it when you call me that." Despite her mood, a smile bloomed on her lips at the sight of her ginormous sous chef singing golden oldies in his chef's whites and a backwards Harley Davidson baseball cap.

"I aim to please. What's got your knickers in a knot?" Adrian's singing morphed into a buttery hum as he rolled his sleeves to his elbows and moved through the kitchen to start checking the stations. The wide expanse of his shoulders bunched and released beneath his white jacket with each movement, lean muscles flexing over the tattoo covering his right forearm.

Carly expelled a breath and fell into step next to him, comforted by the routine of prepping for the night. "Travis."

All Adrian needed was the two-syllable punch to understand her sour mood. "Sorry." His hazel eyes clouded over with a swirl of emotions Carly knew all too well. Adrian's forehead creased, drawing the stainless steel barbell through his right eyebrow down in a slash. "Everything all right?"

"Yeah. I'd rather not talk about it." As it was, the mere presence of Travis's name on her tongue made her want to go brush her teeth.

"No skin off my nose, Chef." Adrian paused for just a fraction too long before moving down the line to the last station.

"Do you regret it? Leaving, I mean."

His head jerked up, the rest of him completely still. "No."

"It's not permanent. I know you went through a lot to come here. And I know you miss home," Carly whispered, melancholy threading through her chest.

"We'll go back when you're ready. Until then, I'm good here. *Capice?*" Adrian's eyes flickered over hers, his gaze gone before she could read it.

"Well. Dinner staff will be here in less than thirty. Let me grab the book and we'll talk specials." Her eyes rested on his for just a fraction of a second longer, but Adrian had slipped right back into business as usual.

Good. Business as usual was what Carly was made of.

But the memory of the phone call lingered like stale smoke, and as she headed for the office to grab the leather-bound notebook that held her handwritten recipes, it was the first time she could remember being in the kitchen when her mind was somewhere else.

Jackson tipped his crew cut at his little brother, Dylan, who sauntered from the back porch onto the fresh carpet of green grass. The phrase "little brother" was rather ironic when the man in question was six-three and weighed in at a linebacker and a half. Then again, it wasn't as if either of the Carter men could be labeled as anything other than pretty damn big. The expression "big brother" was actually fitting, considering Jackson outshadowed his brother by a good inch.

"Hey, you want to tell Mom these are almost done?" Jackson gave one of the burgers on the ancient charcoal grill in front of him a nudge with a spatula. Another minute, and they'd be perfect.

His brother eyeballed the back of the house where they'd grown up and shook his head. "Are you kidding? I came out here to *avoid* the horde of women in that kitchen. Here." Dylan passed over a bottle of Budweiser, still frosty from the fridge. He shifted his weight under the sunshine filtering through an umbrella of oak leaves.

"Don't let Autumn and Brooke gang up on you," Jackson replied, although it was so much easier said than done. Dealing with one older sister was bad enough. Trying to handle two at once was just courting disaster.

"Easy for you to say. You're out here."

"When the shift at the firehouse ends in a bit, we'll even out the score." As soon as Jackson's brothers-in-law arrived from their shifts at Pine Mountain Fire and Rescue, the male-to-female playing field would be just about level. Until then, he and his brother would have to tough it out with the estrogen brigade.

Jackson popped the top off of his beer, and the bottle hissed in approval. "Damn, that sounds like summer," he mused, taking that first perfect swallow.

"Whoa!" Dylan jerked his chin at Jackson's upraised elbow. "That looks like it smarts. How'd you get it?"

Jackson lifted the bent limb a little higher for inspection. A bruise about the size and color of a plum bloomed just above his elbow joint. "Oh, that? It's not so bad. And you wouldn't believe me if I told you."

His mind shifted to how the bruise came to be. Something about Jackson's exchange with the fiery mystery woman had lingered with him all day, whispering to him enough to jostle his concentration.

Damn those white cotton panties. The way something so demure could cover up something so wicked just turned him on like runway lights. It was almost unfair.

"Anyhow." Jackson cleared his throat and pushed the image of the woman—and her underwear—from his mind. "These are done. I hope you're hungry, little brother."

Dylan fidgeted in uncharacteristic nervousness rather than moving toward the house. Any time a Carter man didn't jump at the chance to eat, something was definitely wrong.

Jackson narrowed his eyes at his little brother. "What?"

"I'm getting married."

A burger slipped off the plate in Jackson's hand as it dipped in response to his shock. Otis, the family's geriatric black Lab, loped over to take full advantage of Jackson's party foul, while Jackson struggled to gather his wits.

"Get out of here!" he finally sputtered, still completely floored by Dylan's admission.

An ear-to-ear grin spread over his brother's face, paving the way for a creeping flush. "Yeah. I asked Kelsey last night. We've been together for a year, and . . . well, she's the one. So we're getting married."

"Congratulations, man." Jackson slid the plate of burgers onto a rickety picnic table to clap his brother on the back. "Wow, my baby brother, getting married." He laughed, shaking his head. "Wait a second . . . does Mom know?"

Amidst his happiness for his brother, Jackson's gut double-knotted. When their mother was done with the requisite shrieking over the prospect of yet another legion of grandbabies, Jackson was going to be on the frickin' hot seat.

Again.

"Not yet." Dylan rolled his eyes, but kept his grin in place.

"You know you're making me look bad," Jackson said, only half-joking. Their mother had been after all four of them to fall in love, settle down, and have babies ever since Jackson could remember. And now everyone was on board except him.

Of course, he was the only one who knew firsthand why that version of happily ever after was as impossible as moving the moon. He might've discovered it ages ago, but he'd have to be dead in the ground to forget why staying out of love was the smartest thing he could do.

And the safest.

"I know the nagging gets old, but Mom means well. She only wants all of us to be happy." Dylan's eyes grew a shade more wary as he ventured into touchy-topic territory.

Ironic that Catherine Carter wanted all of her children to find happiness through marriage when the only way she could find it herself was to end the one marriage she'd ever had.

Stuffing down the sudden flash of bad memories, Jackson worked up his trademark easygoing smile. He sure as hell didn't want to go down that road, especially not in the face of Dylan's good news.

"I'm already happy," he pointed out, draining his beer. "Come on. Let's eat these burgers before they get cold."

It seemed that Jackson's low threshold in the satisfaction department was going to come back and bite him square in the ass. It wasn't his fault he never really got the love-of-my-life thing. No disrespect to women, mind you—after all, his mother had raised him right. Still, was it such a big deal that he was happy just being single? It wasn't like he never dated. He was terminally unattached, not terminally stupid.

"Oh, it's about time! If I didn't know any better, I'd say you two were dawdling out there." Catherine drew a sharp brow inward, but there was a twinkle behind her sky blue gaze as she waved her sons into the house. The kitchen bustled with premeal activity, both of Jackson's sisters chasing their respective children to the bathroom for a good hand washing as the last of the side dishes found a home on the already crowded table.

"I don't dawdle when food is involved. Where do you want these burgers, Ma?"

"Right there is fine, honey. Oh! Let me grab these baked beans out of the oven, now."

Fitting the platter into the only empty spot on the worn farmhouse table, Jackson retreated to the fridge for another beer. He had a feeling he was going to need it, a hunch that was cemented in place when Dylan cleared his throat with purpose as soon as both of his sisters made their way back to the kitchen with their kids in tow.

"Before we eat, I have an announcement to make." The room fell uncharacteristically quiet, the only sound coming from Brooke's youngest daughter cooing to her spoon in her high chair. Jackson's pulse popped through him as if it was being directed by the conductor of a marching band. What the hell was *he* nervous for? He wasn't the one getting hitched, for Pete's sake.

Dylan's expression fell into a boyish grin, and Jackson was struck by the fact that his brother barely looked old enough to buy beer, let alone get married.

"Last night, Kelsey did me the honor of saying she'll be my wife."

Time hiccupped for just a fraction before the pandemonium of joyous squeals split the stunned silence of the kitchen. Thankfully, everyone in the room descended on Dylan and Kelsey, leaving Jackson to sneak to the edge of the room like a commitment-phobic Ninja.

"Oh! Oh, sweetheart, I'm so *happy* for you," Catherine gushed, her eyes glistening. "This is just wonderful news!"

Jackson's gut jangled with guilt. Okay, so it was good to see his mother happy. God knew those moments of undiluted goodness had been too few and far between for her, raising the four of them by herself. Jackson watched from the periphery as everyone hugged the happy couple, then finally started to move around the table to fill their plates. Another Carter wedding wouldn't be the worst thing in the world. After all, he'd survived both of his sisters' weddings, as well as his cousin Lisa's, without too much damage. Surely he could handle this.

Just so long as he wasn't next.

"We'll have a party to celebrate, next Saturday night," Jackson's mother declared, dabbing her eyes with a tissue.

"Next Saturday is the Fourth of July." Dylan's complaint fell flat when Catherine shook her head, resolute.

"All the more reason for us to have a party. It's about time we had everyone together, anyway."

"Ma, we're all here now," Dylan protested, but he was clearly outnumbered, and Jackson wasn't dumb enough to jump on a sinking ship. Plus, considering there'd been a foot of snow on the ground the last time he'd gone on an official date, the less attention he got with the old marriage spotlight flying around, the better.

"Oh, but we should include all the cousins. And it wouldn't hurt to invite the Griffins . . . and of course, everyone from Kelsey's family. It'll be our first gathering with the new in-laws. How exciting!" Catherine's eyes lit up like Christmas morning, and Dylan promptly caved.

"Well, I guess it wouldn't be too bad to see my cousins." His reluctant agreement sent everyone with a uterus into full-on planning mode. Jackson surreptitiously made his way to the table to fill a plate while the women chattered and laughed, but it wasn't like being six-four made stealth a natural asset.

"Guess you're the only one left now, hmmm?" His oldest sister, Autumn, reached up to pinch his ear with a sassy grin.

"Yeah. I'm thinking of it like the Marines. The few, the proud. That kind of thing." Jackson heaped enough macaroni salad onto his paper plate to make it droop under the weight.

Brooke, his second-in-command sister, clucked her tongue and bent down to punch a straw into her three-year-old son's juice box. "Try *the only.*"

Jackson's defenses stirred around in his gut like a lion shifting in its cage, prowling for a way out. "But living vicariously through you is so much fun." He parked enough baked beans to sink a ship next to the macaroni salad on his plate, and if he didn't know better, he would have sworn the damned thing actually groaned.

"You know, it wouldn't be the worst thing in the world for you to meet a nice girl," his mother said, looking up from the table.

"I know lots of nice girls." He grabbed another paper plate, shoving it beneath the one in his hand to keep it from collapsing over his work boots.

Why was he suddenly so irritated about the whole thing? If pressuring him to meet a nice girl and settle down was the Super Bowl, his mother had achieved MVP status ages ago. He prided himself on the fact that, while it was sometimes aggravating to dodge her good intentions, his mother's scrutiny never rattled his composure.

Until now.

Catherine lifted her delicate brows in Jackson's direction. "Really." The word wasn't an accusation, but it definitely wasn't a question, either. "I don't seem to recall you seeing anybody for quite a while."

A strange heat crept up the back of his neck, and the image of the bathrobed woman flickered across his mind for a split second before he spoke without thinking. "As a matter of fact, I'm seeing somebody now."

Whoa! Where had that whopper come from? And why, of all people, had he thought of the stranger from this morning before he'd spouted it? Jackson didn't make it a habit to lie, and *definitely* not to his mother, but the strange and unexpected frustration of being put on the spot must have forced the words right out. Oh well. It wasn't like the indiscretion was going to kill him.

Catherine beamed. "You *are?* How wonderful! You'll have to bring her to the party then."

Okay, so he stood corrected on the it-might-not-kill-me thing. *Shit*.

"Oh, uh, I only just started seeing . . . this girl, Ma. She might be, you know. Busy or something." *Way to go, slick. Open wide for that size twelve. You big dumbass!*

His mother's expression flirted with disappointment. "Well, it's not going to be anything fancy, just a barbecue here at the house. After all, we'd really like to meet your girlfriend."

Oh, Jesus, now he had a girlfriend. Jackson opened his mouth to tell his mother it had been a misunderstanding, that there was no girlfriend; hell, there was no girl, period. But then he caught the look on her face, so full of rare happiness and hope, and the next words were out of his mouth before he could stop them.

"Sure thing, Ma. What time should I bring her by?"

Chapter Three

Carly covered her yawn with a haphazard hand as she filled the coffeepot with extra grounds. She sighed into the sleeve of her bathrobe while she waited for it to burble to life, catching a familiar flicker out of the corner of her eye. The answering machine blinked steadily, desperate for attention. Carly had been too exhausted to check it when she got home last night, and she braced herself as she pushed the button, the memory of her nasty conversation with Travis still all too fresh in her mind.

"Carlotta, it's your *mama*." In spite of the fact that Carly was thirty-one years old, her mother's brisk tone halted her midstep across the kitchen floor. Damn it, guilt before coffee was so *not* how Carly wanted to start her day.

"Dominic tells me you're busy at work, but you had the time to call him and say so. I worry about you out there in the middle of nothing. You should be here in the city, working things out."

Carly winced. Her brother had probably meant well when he'd told their mother Carly was busy at work. She pressed the FORWARD button, making a mental note to call her mother back when she had more stamina.

"Hey, *cucciola*. It's Dom."

Carly chuckled as she pulled a mug from the cupboard. The guilt must be catching.

"Mrs. Spagnolo went to dinner at Gracie's the other night and saw Travis." Her brother paused to mutter a couple of choice Italian curse words into her machine before proceeding. "Anyway, you know how the gossip goes. *Mama*'s a little riled up over it, so look out. And give me a call, yeah? She's been acting weird lately. It's probably nothing, but . . . well, give me a call. Love you."

Carly shook her head. Considering the circumstances, there weren't a whole lot of things in the world weirder than her mother actually wanting Carly to reconcile with Travis. Then again, as a devout Catholic, her disdain for her only daughter's failed marriage had been a source of contention between them for months. The sanctity of marriage was no small potatoes in the di Matisse house. Never mind that Travis had broken it by cherishing Carly's career and talent more than anything else.

The machine *beeped* with another message, and she braced herself. Please God, let it be a telemarketer, just this once.

"Oh, hello there, young ladies." Her landlord's gentle voice filtered through the kitchen, causing Carly to both heave a sigh of relief and break into a tiny smile at being called a young lady. Mr. Logan was eighty if he was a day.

"I have a bit of bad news. Unfortunately there's enough structural damage to the deck that the whole thing has to be taken down and replaced. The contractor assured me he'd be as quick as possible, but the work will probably take about a week."

She groaned. So much for never seeing Contractor Guy again. Now she had to spend a whole week with him right outside her window? And with Sloane gone, Carly was the only point of contact, at least for a couple more days. Still, he'd be outside pretty much the whole time. Maybe she could avoid him.

"Anyway, give me a call if you have any questions. The contractor should be there first thing tomorrow morning, so don't be alarmed when you see him." The machine *beeped,* signaling the end of the message, and Carly creased her brow in slow-motion thought.

"Wait a second . . . this message is from yesterday . . ." The implication started to trickle in, like water slowly filling each pore of a sponge.

The doorbell rang.

She whirled around to stare at the door, eyes widening in panic as she raced toward it, pressing her body against the cool wood to look through the peep hole. Sure enough, there stood Mr. Fix-It, his eyes just as crinkly and breathtaking as yesterday.

And once again, she wasn't wearing any pants.

"Oh, come *on!*" Carly cursed, hurling herself toward her bedroom while snatching the robe from her body. She jammed her legs through a mostly-clean pair of jeans, barely pausing to zip them before donning a bra and whipping through her dresser for a clean shirt.

No dice. The only thing she'd had time to wash in the last couple of weeks were her chef's whites, which stood at attention in her closet. Her hand closed around the only clean item in the drawer, a New York Islanders T-shirt her brother had bought for her at an Eastern Conference quarterfinal game in 2002. It was barely a step away from dust rag territory, and every time Carly laid eyes on it, she was tempted to toss it, but she could never manage to do the deed because despite its horrible state, the damned thing was beyond comfortable. She shook her head. There had to be something else. There had to be . . .

The doorbell rang again.

"Goooooood enough." Carly yanked the holey old thing

over her head, certain she was testing the limits of the ancient fabric with her less than gentle maneuvering. "Coming!" As much as she wasn't looking forward to coming face to face with this guy again, at least this time she wasn't in her underwear.

Carly swung the front door open and tried not to gasp for air. "Hi." It was all she could manage without passing out.

"Morning." His eyes zoned in and settled right on the Islanders logo emblazoned across her chest. "Hey, nice shirt."

Carly bristled. God, he was so unnervingly smart-assed! If she hadn't been totally out of breath, she'd have flipped back one of the glib comments rattling around in her brain. As it stood, she could barely stay upright without wanting to collapse.

Contractor Guy's perfect-summer-sky eyes traveled up to her face, and his smile shifted, dropping slightly. "You look . . . uh, different."

She finally caught her breath. "I'm dressed." Carly heard the naughty inference only after the quip had crossed her lips. "I mean! You know, I'm not in my bathrobe." Flushing all the way to her ears, she made a mental note not to speak again until more oxygen had reached her brain.

But instead of continuing to make fun of her, Contractor Guy cut her some slack with an easygoing laugh. "No, it's your hair." He motioned toward his shoulders, mimicking the way her hair spilled over her own shoulders. "I guess you had it pulled back yesterday."

"Oh." Carly's hand shot up subconsciously, and she tried to smooth the tangled mess to no avail. Nine times out of ten, she braided it to keep it out of her way, but in her haste to find clothes, she'd forgotten all about it.

"Ah, anyway." He shifted his weight. "I just wanted to let you know I'm here. I usually start early, but I had to get some tools together for the demolition, so today was an exception."

Her brows paved the way for her frown. "It's early now."

"It's after nine," he replied teasingly. Wow, his eyes were stunning, the same piercing blue of the cornflowers in her grandmother's tiny garden plot back in Brooklyn.

Carly blinked, rattling herself back to reality. "Uh-huh." She tipped her head in an easy translation of *I fail to see your point.* "How early do you normally start?"

"I'd like to shoot for seven-thirty, if it's okay with you."

Carly couldn't help it. She laughed. Out loud.

"That's not early. It's cruel and unusual."

"Nah." He shrugged, the wide expanse of his shoulders rising and falling with casual ease. "Cruel and unusual is trying to do manual labor outside in the dead heat of a summer afternoon. It's easier to start early and end early. Unless that's a problem."

She shook her head. "I'm not the one who has to be out there with the roosters. Be my guest." After all, it would make it a whole lot easier to give him the slip if she was nestled in her bed clear on the other side of the house.

"Okay then. I guess I'll get to it."

As Carly replaced the door in its sturdy oak frame, she turned to cast a glance at the sun-filled windows on the rear wall of the house.

Yup. She could steer clear of those. Forgetting he was there was going to be a piece of cake.

Olive oil, pancetta, bay leaves, red peppers, olive oil . . .
BANG! BANG! BANG! BANG!

Carly stopped, pencil hovering over the page for a minute before she frowned and crossed the repeat offender off her shopping list. For God's sake, how was she supposed to get anything done with all that racket going on outside? Not to mention the racket her libido was making every time the man she swore she'd avoid crossed her line of sight.

Looks like there's something inside *the house that needs fixing. Betcha he's got all the right power tools for the job.*

Carly sent a panicked look around the room, as if her dirty subconscious had broadcast the unexpected thought out loud. It wasn't her fault that no matter where she went in the bungalow, Contractor Guy ended up in her line of sight, hard at work. And she could forget turning a blind eye, because staring at the man was just a foregone conclusion. Carly might still be irritated that he'd embarrassed her, but let's face it: she was aggravated, not dead. And Contractor Guy was 100 percent red-blooded man.

She inclined her head at the sliding glass door, pretending her pulse wasn't doing the skip-to-my-lou in her veins at the sight of him at work. His thick arms were already burnished from having been exposed to the sun all morning, tanned muscles standing in relief against his white T-shirt. Carly nibbled on the end of her pencil, letting her eyes trail over the hard planes of his chest, clearly visible beneath that snug, light cotton.

Just think. You're stuck with him all week, you lucky girl.

"Oh, shut up." She tuned out the suggestive little voice in favor of the grocery list on the counter. Carly didn't care how good his butt looked in those jeans when he bent down to rip up the old deck. She needed a man like she needed a tax audit, and plus, he'd laughed at her twice now. Although considering the circumstances surrounding both of those scenarios, it would have been nearly impossible for him not to laugh at her a little.

BANG! BANG! BANG! BANG!

Olive oil . . . no, wait . . .

Carly tossed her pencil in disgust. Okay, yes, he'd laughed at her, but he hadn't really been mean about it. Not even when she'd made an honest attempt to knock his block off like a raving lunatic. A really foul-mouthed raving lunatic. Wearing underpants circa the Clinton administration.

She eyed the sunshine pouring in through the windows. Yeah. Maybe apology lemonade was a good idea. Nothing said "I'm sorry for hurling insults and electronics at you" like a nice tall glass of summer, right?

Christ, she really was an idiot.

Carly padded to the bowl of Meyer lemons and limes on her countertop, rifling through it to pick out the prettiest specimens. She put a saucepan of water on the stove to boil before turning her attention to juicing the lemons. While there was an electric juicer hidden in the depths of her cupboards, she'd always been partial to doing the job herself. Something about the cool, imperfect exterior of the citrus just felt right under her hands, and she worked with quick, efficient strokes to get the job done.

She measured the sugar for the simple syrup just like she measured everything in the kitchen—with her eyes. People usually fell into one of two camps when it came to lemonade, but if she split the difference between tart and sweet, she'd probably come up with a winner. After all, it was the thought that counted anyway, right?

Yes. I made you some lemonade. Please forgive my complete lack of social graces and oh, by the way, I'd love it if you'd take off your shirt while you work.

Snappy sexual tension aside, she really needed to apologize and forget it. Her track record with all things male was abysmal on a good day. Carly didn't have the time or energy to deal with anything that would sap her concentration from the restaurant, thus lessening her chances to move back to New York on the buzz of great success. If she got distracted and La Dolce Vita failed, she'd have no way to regain her good reputation. So, while Contractor Guy provided quite the view, as soon as she was done with the

apology-and-lemonade thing, she was going to put her
nose to the grindstone and get some work done.

With the blinds drawn.

Sighing, Carly filled the belly of a gallon-sized infusion
jar with ice, then added the ingredients to come up with a
not-too-tart, just-sweet-enough batch of lemonade. She
tossed in some lemon slices for good measure and gave the
whole thing one last swirl before locking the spigot so it
wouldn't all leak out. All that was left to do before embark-
ing on her little peace offering mission was to exchange her
T-shirt for one that wasn't impersonating Swiss cheese.

Except Contractor Guy had noticed her threadbare
wonder earlier, enough to make a snarky comment about it.
If she changed now, surely he'd notice that too, and the last
thing she wanted was for him to think she'd changed because
of his little remark. She glanced down at the garment in
question, only to notice she'd managed to dribble coffee
along the bottom hem at some point during the course of her
morning.

Lovely. She picked up the infusion jar with a grumble,
heading toward the back of the house before she could
change her mind.

As soon as Carly peeked through the sliding glass door,
she realized that walking through it wasn't an option. In ad-
dition to the damaged board from yesterday, all of the railings the storm had left intact had been removed. The broken
down railings and accompanying pickets littered the yard
like discarded toothpicks, and power tools dotted the wreck-
age in a sprinkling of scary-looking machinery. Contractor
Guy was down by the side yard, hauling a long beam of
wood away from the house.

Right. Time to put an OUT OF ORDER sign on the ol' sliding glass door until further notice.

Dappled sunlight filtered through the leaves of the soaring oaks and poplar trees that lined the property as Carly

made her way from the front door around to the side yard. Other than the obvious clamor from the demolition of the old deck, it was terribly quiet out here. No sirens breaking through the flurry of activity on a busy street, no voices floating by from people going out for a bite to eat. The quiet weighed on her, pressing against her eardrums as if she were under water and sinking fast.

"Hey. Just so you know, I'm behind you. I want to cover all my bases for personal safety."

Carly whirled around, only to find herself face-to-sternum with Mr. Fix-It.

"Oh! You startled me. Again." Damn! He must've made a whole loop around the house rather than doubling back as she'd expected.

"Everyone's good at something, I suppose." He chuckled, a low rumble that managed to reach into her belly. He was close enough for her to catch the clean scent of soap mingling in with a masculine layer of sweat and freshly cut wood. All of Carly's plans to play it cool took the hand basket route straight to hell.

He gestured to the infusion jar awkwardly balanced on her hip. "Here, that looks kind of heavy. Do you want me to take it?"

Carly nodded, and he slid the cumbersome jar from under her arm just as easily as if it were the daily mail. "Thanks."

"So, what is this?"

She blinked and craned her neck to look up at him. Man, he must have eaten his veggies as a kid.

"It's lemonade." Carly thrust out the glass she'd grabbed from the cupboard in an awkward peace offering.

His good-natured laughter plucked all the way down her spine, and he took the cup with a lopsided grin. "No, I meant the jar thingy. I'm pretty familiar with lemonade."

Could she be any more graceless? "Oh, right. It's, ah, called an infusion jar. See the spigot on the bottom there?"

She pointed, and his muscles flexed as he turned the jar beneath his tree trunk of an arm to take a look.

Holy. Moly.

"Oh yeah! It's kind of like the thing football players use to dump Gatorade on the coach after the Super Bowl. Only yours is smaller. And nicer."

Carly's laugh escaped before she could temper it into a mere smile. "Yeah, it's exactly like that. I figured you might be thirsty, and it's less likely to spill than a pitcher, so . . ." She trailed off, clasping her hands in front of her and wiggling her thumbs.

"Wow. That's really nice of you . . ." He shifted his weight, but didn't move to put the infusion jar down. Finally, she registered his raised eyebrows and expectant look, putting two and two together to come up with the sum of *duh*.

"Carly! I'm Carly."

"Jackson Carter." He lowered the lemonade and glass to a soft patch of grass and extended his hand, which outsized hers three to one. "I'm not bothering you too much with the noise, I hope." He dipped his chin in order to look her in the eye, and she noticed the slightest cleft in his clean-shaven skin.

"Um, no. Not too much," Carly clarified with a sardonic quirk of her lips. "Anyway, I wanted to apologize. You know, for yesterday." Her face flushed, but she pressed on, eager to get the apology over with. "I shouldn't have thrown the remote at you. It was a stupid thing to do."

"No it wasn't." He cocked his head at her, blond crew cut glinting in the sun.

"Excuse me?"

An all-American smile took over his features, causing the heat that had bloomed on Carly's face to migrate down her neck.

"It wasn't stupid. For all you knew, I was some stranger

sneaking around your property with bad intentions. I'm glad the screen door was shut, though. You've got a killer arm."

She resisted the urge to wince. The remote had been so far beyond repair, she hadn't even bothered trying. "Still. I feel bad about your elbow," she said, twisting a small patch of grass under the toe of one flip flop.

"What, this?" He flipped a thickly muscled arm up, pointing his elbow at her with a grin. "It doesn't even hurt."

Carly gasped at the sight of the three-inch bruise staring her in the face, and her gut settled into its new home somewhere around her knees. "Oh, God. It left a mark?"

"Hey, seriously, it's no big deal. I'm just glad I didn't hurt *you* when we bumped heads."

His expression suggested he really meant it, but her embarrassment took over nonetheless. She was about to make a hasty retreat into the cool haven of her kitchen when Jackson caught her with his now-familiar boyish smirk, and the twist of his lips rendered her legs useless.

"So you're an Islanders fan, huh?" His eyes flickered to her shirt, and Carly automatically smoothed her hands over the front to hide the coffee stain.

"Well, seeing as how there's probably a permanent imprint of seat 14 in section 102 at Nassau Coliseum somewhere on my butt, I'm going to go ahead and say yeah. I'm a fan."

Annnnnnd now there was no way he wasn't going to look at her butt when she walked away. God, she should just not speak.

"Wow. And I thought driving into the city from all the way out here a couple of times a season was devotion," he drawled, his half-smile melting into something a touch more reverent.

"It's a four-hour drive, at least," Carly replied, confused.

"Only ninety minutes, actually. But I think we're talking about different cities."

As far as she was concerned, there were no other cities. Carly pictured Pine Mountain's location on the map in her mind's eye, letting her focus travel outward past the Blue Ridge . . .

"Oh, hell no. Please tell me you're not a Flyers fan." Great pecs or not, Jackson was gonna have to go.

The kick of his lips returned in all its hot-man glory. "That I am."

Carly groaned. "Well, everyone has their cross to bear, I guess."

Silence settled between them for a noticeable beat, and it pressed her to go back inside. She'd offered her apology, he'd accepted in his own weird and flirty little way. Said, done, pick up your parting gifts at the door.

Wait, was he flirting with her?

Carly mashed down on the thought. Travis had flirted with her, too, in the beginning, and just look what that had gotten her. Keeping her mind on the kitchen was the only thing that was important here. Getting warm and fuzzy over the contractor was just plain stupid.

"Well, Jackson, I'm glad you're okay, and sorry again for yesterday. Enjoy the lemonade." The absence of her trademark composure was really starting to get under her skin, and she turned to make her long overdue retreat.

"Hey, Carly?"

She stopped to look over her shoulder. "Yes?"

"I was wondering if you'd like to go out with me next weekend." Jackson paused for a second and blinked, almost as if he'd been surprised to actually hear the words. "If I promise not to make any sudden movements," he tacked on with a smooth chuckle that made her cheeks burn.

Carly's pulse ricocheted through her veins. The word *yes* tasted sinfully good as it formed in her mouth, and for that split second, she actually considered saying it. But the memory of her phone call with Travis threaded through her brain, weaving over the *yes* with a whole bunch of reasons why she'd be nuts to say it. She'd come to Pine Mountain to run a kitchen for a little while and leave just as quickly. Men—even crinkly-eyed ones with traffic-stopping muscles— weren't part of the deal.

"I don't think that would be a good idea. Not that I'm not flattered. And not that you're not . . . well . . ." She trailed off, closing her eyes as she exhaled. "I've just got a lot going on with my job that keeps me pretty tied up. So I'm sorry, but I'll have to pass. Thank you, though. It was nice of you to ask." Carly had never babbled in her entire life, but boy was she making up for lost time.

"No problem. Sorry if I was out of line." Jackson took a step backwards even though there was plenty of space between them.

"No, no. It's fine. Just . . . yeah." Ugh. How fast could she get back to the house?

"Well, thanks again for the lemonade. I'll make sure to leave the infusion jar on the front porch when I'm done, if that's all right with you." Jackson nodded toward the jar at his feet, but she noticed that his smile had lost some of its zing.

"Oh, thanks. And, I guess . . . you're welcome."

The walk back to her house had never taken so long.

"Okay, so I need some help with a little problem, and it's kind of a weird one." Jackson sat back in his best friend Shane's tiny kitchen, his chair creaking in disapproval at the seconds he'd had for dinner. Shane's girlfriend Bellamy was training under some fancy New York chef at the Italian restaurant in Pine Mountain Resort, and she took her job seriously with a capital S. Whenever they hooked up for dinner, seconds were a foregone conclusion. Thirds were an even fifty-fifty.

"Oooh, this ought to be good." Bellamy propped her elbows on the table and leaned forward to listen, green eyes sparkling with interest.

"Screw good. This scares me," Shane quipped, draping his arm over the back of Bellamy's chair.

She rolled her eyes, blond lashes sweeping up and around in a familiar gesture. "Ignore him, Jackson. What do you need?"

"I need a nonexistent girlfriend."

Shane's mouth popped open. "You need a huh?"

Jackson released a long breath. "Either that or the mother of all believable excuses. Take your pick."

"Um, okay. I'm not really sure I follow," Bellamy prompted, brow drawn tight over her confusion.

He gave a slight grimace. "I kind of shot my mouth off over at my ma's the other day. It was an act of self-preservation, I assure you," he added quickly. "But now she's got this wild idea that I'm bringing a date to Dylan and Kelsey's engagement party on the Fourth, and I don't have one."

"I don't get it. If you need a date, why don't you just ask somebody?" Bellamy wondered out loud, but Jackson cut her off with an emphatic head shake.

"I don't want a bona-fide date. Any woman I ask to a family event is going to read way more into it than she should, and not wanting a girlfriend is what got me into this mess in the first place."

Except that you asked someone just this morning, didn't you, Romeo?

Jackson's inner voice had niggled at him all day, even though he'd done his best to stuff it down. Asking Carly out had been impulsive at best, and even now he couldn't peg exactly why he'd done it. Except she'd looked so unassumingly pretty with her dark hair framing her face, and who could resist a girl in a lucky T-shirt, of all things? The softness of her beauty offset her fiery demeanor in a way that made him want to pull back all of her layers to find out where the two met. Something about her had whispered to him, and he would've thought for sure that he was losing his mind if the words hadn't made so much damn sense.

Feed her, the voice had said.

Not that it mattered in the long run. Of course she'd said no, and why wouldn't she? The notion that a total stranger would want to go to his brother's engagement party with him skirted the edges of pretty fucking ridiculous.

But not as ridiculous as how badly he'd wanted her to say yes.

The edges of Bellamy's lips twitched upward in just a hint of a smile, and she got up to slide an apple pie from its perch on the countertop. "Do I even want to know why you're anti-girlfriend?"

Jackson shook off his strange thoughts of Carly for the umpteenth time. He exchanged a nanosecond's worth of a glance with Shane, but then resorted to his default easy-going shrug-and-smile combo. "It's nothing personal. I'm just happy being single. I mean, can you really see me picking out china patterns?"

Bellamy tipped her head in a nonverbal *you may be right* as she put the pie on the table and went back for plates. "Okay, fair. What about a stand-in? You don't know anyone who would be willing to fake it for you, just for one night?"

Jackson and Shane both snorted. "Babe, that is so *not* something you should say to a guy. Ever," Shane emphasized on a laugh.

"Oh, for the love of . . . I'm being serious!" She put the plates on the table and swatted Shane's arm, which only made him laugh harder. "Stop being a smartass and cut this pie, would you? I mean it, Jackson. Maybe there's a girl out there who would be sympathetic to your cause and wouldn't mind a little acting."

"Eh, I'm not so sure that's a good idea. The cloak and dagger thing isn't really my style," Jackson pointed out.

"Would you rather be thrown under the relationship bus? It doesn't look like you have a whole lot of options," she replied with a tart grin. "Unless you want to come clean or bring a real date."

Shit. How come women were so frickin' smart? "Good point. But it's not like I can go to Rent-a-Girlfriend or something. How am I going to find a date who's not a date in four days?"

"How about Molly O'Brien?" Shane asked.

Jackson shook his head. "She's going out with Marcus Lawrenson."

Shane made a face like he smelled something rotten. "Never liked that guy. Michelle Pierce?"

"Went out with her last year. She asked me to meet her parents on date three."

"Okay, that's a *no*. Come on. There must be somebody." They sat in silence for a minute, both of their faces bent in concentration. Finally, Jackson had to admit defeat. As much as he wasn't crazy about telling his mother the truth about his bachelor-and-loving-it lifestyle, he wasn't really wild about telling another out and out lie, either. Coming clean was the only way out of this mess.

"What about Jenna?" Bellamy asked, and Shane smacked the table in a *that's perfect!* manner.

Jackson considered the possibility. He'd met Bellamy's friend from Philadelphia a handful of times, and she'd always been fun to hang out with. The fact that she lived a hundred miles away was a bit of a bonus—he could always blame a fake breakup on the distance. No harm, no foul.

Then why didn't it feel right?

Jackson hedged. "Do you think she'd do it?"

Bellamy sat back in her chair wearing a triumphant grin. "She might. You want me to call her?"

The whole web of deception thing had a way of back-firing the minute it got past the little white lie stage, and Jackson was clearly crossing the line with this charade. He should just forget it and tell his mother the truth. He was an adult, after all. And she'd get over the disappointment eventually.

Except he'd done nothing but disappoint her so far in this arena. And she had really good reasons for wanting to see him happy. Ones he didn't want to contemplate.

In the grander scheme of things, how many ripples could one fake date really cause?

Jackson blew out a breath and pasted a smile to his face. "That would be great. If she's willing to come out for the weekend, I'd love to take Jenna to the party."

Chapter Four

After trying everything from covering her head with both bed pillows to playing one of the meditative CDs Sloane swore by for relaxation, Carly bit the bullet and got out of bed. The banging coming from her backyard wasn't horribly loud, but the source of the noise seemed to vibrate within her like the hum of a tuning fork.

A really sexed-up tuning fork. Whose titillating thrum reminded her that almost a year had passed since she'd experienced an orgasm that hadn't been self-inflicted.

It was way too early for this.

Carly pulled a pair of yoga pants and a freshly-washed T-shirt from the top of her clean laundry pile and put them on. No way was she going to get caught without clean laundry—or worse yet, without a major article of clothing—again. She'd spent her few spare hours before work yesterday separating darks from lights and letting the detergent do the talking. Sadly, it had only taken three loads to wash just about every stitch of non-work related clothing Carly owned.

She padded out to the kitchen, grateful that she hadn't been in too much of a bleary, post-work haze to set the auto timer on the coffee pot last night. Although things were really starting to gel at La Dolce Vita, the process of bringing the restaurant from vision to reality had had its share of growing pains. As a result, Carly had been popping off fourteen-hour days like Pez since the New Year. Even then, most of her precious little at-home time was spent in the sunny kitchen of the bungalow, ideas and recipes rattling through her head in various stages of readiness.

But she loved every self-affirming second of running the back of the house at La Dolce Vita, of having her name and her name alone on the kitchen, even if said kitchen was in teeny-tiny Pine Mountain. That success, combined with being far away from Travis while their names untangled, was enough to make putting a whole lot of hustle-and-go into a small-town restaurant worth it. Plus, if she was too busy to even take a bathroom break, then she'd definitely be too busy for those little pinpricks of loneliness that slipped past her defenses when she drifted off to sleep at night.

"Ugh, knock it off," Carly muttered, wiping the sleep from her eyes. She wasn't exactly a pity-party kind of girl, and living in Pine Mountain was only temporary. Plus, she had a kitchen. Her *own* kitchen, one she'd worked incredibly hard for.

So why did she still feel like a square peg trying to shimmy into a round hole?

As Carly poured herself a cup of coffee big enough to do the backstroke in, her eyes shamelessly skimmed the bank of windows on the rear of the house. Jackson's sun-kissed head was barely visible through the glass, and she creased her brow in confusion. Either he'd shrunk about three feet overnight, or something was seriously amiss in her yard.

What the hell? Carly's confusion gave way to pure surprise as she moved closer to the sliding glass door for inspection.

The entire deck had been cut away from the house, leaving a drop off of a couple of feet between the sliding glass door and the bare, damp earth below it. Three stout-looking wooden posts jutted up from puddles of long-hardened concrete, the furthest one from the house sporting a huge split down the center. Jackson maneuvered a shovel around the edges of the old concrete, trying to loosen the packed dirt from the murky gray edges, but it barely budged.

Carly watched, captivated. His sinewy shoulders tightened and flexed beneath his T-shirt, which clung to him in just enough places that she had a flash of envy for the cotton and stitching. His face was bent in concentration, yet still so open, that she had the strange urge to memorize him and keep him for later . . . until she belatedly realized he'd stopped what he was doing to wave at her through the glass.

Oh, *crap*. Now she had no choice but to open the door and face her bustedness full-on.

"Hi. Sorry to disturb you. I was just, ah, checking out the progress." Carly's inner voice high-fived her quick wits, making a genuine smile more manageable. "It looks like you've been busy." She gestured down to the yard with one hand, watching the sunlight scatter as a lazy breeze ruffled through the trees.

"Yeah, but I can't take all the credit. One of the guys I work with was out here with me for the better part of the afternoon yesterday. As a matter of fact, I'm waiting for him right now. Seems whoever put these posts in originally wasn't planning on their ever being replaced. 'Fraid I'm going to have to jackhammer them out of here."

The mention of heavy artillery quickly chased away the heat of Carly's less than discreet staring. "Are you serious?"

Jackson's doleful nod played against his mischievous grin. "Yeah, sorry. I was going to knock to warn you, but I didn't want to wake you up until my buddy Micah got here."

"Well, thanks for that," she laughed. "Somehow I'm guessing I'd have been up either way. Is a jackhammer as loud as I think it is?"

His boyish excitement was obvious, and it zinged a bolt of heat down her spine, finishing with a deep tingle right between her hips.

"Louder."

Oh. Lordy.

"Do you want to have a cup of coffee while you wait?" Carly blurted out the invitation before she could stop herself. Okay, fine, so it kind of turned the whole avoiding-him plan on its ear, but there was one small fact she just couldn't get past.

It was in her nature to feed people, and she wanted him to say yes, plain and simple.

Jackson's sandy brows popped up in surprise. "Sure."

Before Carly had enough time to acknowledge the are-you-nuts message pumping from the rational part of her brain, Jackson had disappeared around the side of the house. Come on, surely she was overreacting. There was nothing indecent about a cup of coffee and fifteen minutes of small talk.

The doorbell rang just in time to snag the not-so-rational part of Carly's brain from imagining how many indecent things could happen in fifteen minutes.

She blanked her expression so it wouldn't betray the naughty images she'd just conjured up, then swung the door open, gesturing inside. "Hi. Come on in."

Jackson bent to unlace his work boots, shucking them on the brick threshold of the porch before padding into the bungalow on sock feet. "Thanks. My last cup of coffee was ages ago."

"Okay, you do know it's only 8:45, right?" She pulled a mug that matched her own down from the cabinet, inhaling the deep, earthy scent of the coffee as she filled it. Jackson followed her into the kitchen and leaned against the rectangular butcher block island in the heart of the room, giving her a grateful nod as she passed him the mug.

"I've been up since six."

"My condolences. Milk?" Carly popped the fridge open, feeling in her element surrounded by food. While she might need work in the social graces department, feeding someone was definitely something she could do with seamless ease.

"Please," Jackson replied. "So you're not a morning person. Is that a personal preference or an occupational hazard?"

Her snicker was unavoidable, and it snuck out as she passed him the milk. "Both. I've got some scones if you want a couple. Are you hungry?"

She'd been fiddling with a recipe for basic scones for the better part of two weeks, looking to add something versatile to the Sunday brunch menu. The results of her experimentation currently overflowed from the enormous cookie jar on the counter.

"Well, I wouldn't want to put you out . . ." he started, a sip of coffee washing down the rest of whatever he was going to say.

Carly put a hand on her hip. "Is that a yes?"

Jackson held up his hands as if to cry uncle, a drawl tilting the edges of his lips upward. "You are direct, aren't you?"

"Sorry." She edged past him to put the milk away, but he caught her forearm with a brush of his fingers so gentle, it belied both his strength and his size.

"It wasn't a criticism. I'd love some scones."

"Oh." Carly blinked up at him, unable to make her feet move. Okay, make that unwilling. *Damn* his hand felt good on her skin, to the point that not even getting him something to eat could make her put one foot in front of the other.

But then he let go, clearing his throat and taking a giant step to the side so she had more than enough room to get by him. "So, ah, what do you do?"

Carly paused for a moment too long, trying to make heads or tails of the passion-fried circuitry that had replaced her brain. "Oh! What do I do, right. I'm a chef at La Dolce Vita, the restaurant at the resort." The refrigerator door squeaked on its hinges as if startled by her cursory jerk of the handle. "Ginger peach or lemon blueberry for the scones?"

"You pick." Jackson propped a sun-bronzed arm on the counter and looked at her. "My buddy's girlfriend works as a line cook over at La Dolce Vita. She's got some crazy skills. Makes the best apple pie you ever had. Even better than the new bakery down on Main Street, and theirs are no joke."

"Really?" Carly pulled a couple lemon blueberry scones from the jar and replaced the lid, popping them into the microwave for a quick spin just to warm them up. "Who is she?"

"Bellamy Blake. Do you know her?"

Ah. That figured. Adrian had culled Bellamy from a long list of hopefuls looking to move up the ranks, and so far, she'd been one of the brightest spots in La Dolce Vita's kitchen.

"Mmm hmm. I'll have to ask her about the pie."

Jackson made a *so good* face before continuing. "Yeah, she's training under this fancy chef from New York who's allegedly the best thing since pockets. You probably work for her too, come to think of it." His forehead creased in thought. "I can't remember her name to save my life."

Carly's laughter tasted incredibly good as it bubbled up from her chest. "Chef di Matisse."

"Yeah! That's it," Jackson nodded, eyes bright. "What's so funny?"

"Bellamy's the only one formal enough to call me that. Everyone else just calls me Chef Carly."

He jerked his coffee cup to a stop halfway to his lips. "*You're* the fancy chef from New York?"

"At your service."

"Oh, shit. I mean!" Jackson scrambled to apologize. "Sorry about that. I just pictured her—you, I guess—kind of, uh. Differently." He gulped his coffee, clearly chagrined.

"It's okay. We fancy chefs from New York are normal people, I promise. Well, most of us anyway," she amended, leaning against the counter. The buttery smell of the scones tickled her senses as she pulled them out of the microwave, and she took a deep draw of air, savoring the smell.

"I guess it's not really fair to judge a book by its cover. Or where it comes from, in this case."

Carly rummaged through a deep-bellied drawer for a sifter. "Things are a lot different out here in Pine Mountain." God. Was she ever going to stop feeling so homesick? It wasn't like she was never going back.

"Pine Mountain's not so bad." Jackson's voice was suddenly stiff.

"I didn't say it was," Carly replied, shocked at her lack of defensiveness. "But I grew up in the city, and I lived there all my life. It's hard not to think of it as home. I miss it."

Whoa! Where had that come from? Not that it wasn't true or anything, but still. Spilling her guts to a veritable stranger was definitely not her MO.

"Oh." His response softened with understanding, and he leaned toward her. "Well, every place has its advantages, and Pine Mountain has tons of them. Who knows? Maybe someday you'll think of this as home."

Carly shook her head. "To be honest, I'm not planning on being here for the long haul. I got a great opportunity at the resort, but eventually I'm going back to New York. Nothing personal."

Jackson shrugged. "Mmm. Well, I'm happy to point you

in the right direction if you want some good places to check out while you're here. Just a little food for thought."

The corners of her mouth ticked upward into an involuntary smile, washing away her sudden melancholy. "Nice food reference, slick." She rolled her eyes and reached for a box of powdered sugar in the pantry.

Jackson waggled his eyebrows, which only kicked her smile up another notch.

"You like that? I can come up with another one if you want. Piece of cake."

Carly's groan fought with her laughter, both escaping her lips together. "Boo! You're going to have to do better than that."

Jackson's blue eyes sparkled like ocean waves under the midday sun. "What? That one didn't cut the mustard?"

"Argh, you're getting worse." But still, her laughter didn't let up.

"Come on. You're not going to make me sing for my supper, are you?"

Ouch. The subtle jab at her Motown performance made her wince, but she kept a straight face and sifted a fine dusting of powdered sugar over the warm scones like softly falling snow.

"You know what they say. There's no such thing as a free lunch." She paused for just a beat before adding the pièce de résistance. "Honey."

God *damn*, Jackson thought with a shake of his head. Who knew kitchen banter could be so sexy? All it took was one look from Carly's chocolate-brown eyes and a hot little kick of her lips as she spoke, and he'd all but forgotten about the food.

All things considered, that was a pretty big deal.

"I suppose you think that one should count double." His

attempt at a frown was a poor disguise for the amusement lurking beneath it, a fact he was sure Carly could sense.

"Of course." She slid the plate with the scones across the island. "Here, you don't even have to sing for them."

Jackson paused, even though his mouth watered at the sight of the two thick triangles of flaky goodness in front of him. "Aren't you going to eat?"

Carly shook her head, propping her elbows on the butcher block as she leaned across from him at the corner of the island. "Nah. I usually eat a little later in the morning, closer to when I leave for the restaurant."

"Wait, I thought the restaurant was only open for dinner during the week. When do you go in?"

"Well, now that we're pretty established, most days I start around eleven, but it depends. Some days I meet with the restaurant manager, which is impossible to do while we're open because he and I are both slammed during a service. Other days, I like to supervise food deliveries to make sure everything's fresh and we have what we need." She shrugged, as if the laundry list of daily tasks was as easy as a stroll down Main Street on a cool Sunday morning. "Oh, and I have to hook up with my sous chef to talk shop before the kitchen opens, review specials, plan food orders, that kind of stuff. Then there's the tasting menu to consider . . ."

"Whoa. I had no idea it was so involved," Jackson replied, struck not just by what Carly was saying, but how her face looked when she said it. She looked so totally relaxed and in her element that he didn't want her to stop talking, so he said the first thing that popped into his head. "What's a tasting menu for?"

Her face softened even further, pretty eyes animated with a glowing excitement that hit Jackson like a boulder on a downhill slide.

"Every night before a shift starts, my sous chef Adrian and I make a couple of regular menu dishes and at least one of the specials family-style, and the staff all sits down together to eat. That way everyone can experience what they're bringing to the patrons firsthand, whether they cook it or serve it. It helps everybody get to know the food, if that makes sense," Carly said, dropping her chin into one palm. "Then everyone has an idea of how the flavors go together, why the colors and textures of each dish are important, and how it all makes the food more than just a meal."

Jackson scratched his head. "I don't get it. How can you make the food more than a meal?" He was all for good eats and everything, but this just didn't make sense.

"By turning it into an experience." Carly swept her hair off her shoulders and gestured down at his plate. "Here's a perfect example. See how the powdered sugar is so fine on top of the streusel here? Two different textures, and that's before you even get to the scone itself, which adds yet another layer."

Her brown eyes sparkled like liquid amber. "The colors do the same thing. Break one in half, and look at the blueberries against the dough."

Huh! Hell if she wasn't right. The colors *did* make it look mouth-wateringly good, and the crumbly piles of brown sugar-laced topping seemed to fade right into the fluffy cake of the scone. "Wow. That's pretty cool," he murmured, lifting the plate for a better look.

"Now keep it right where it is and breathe in."

Her face was wistful as he inhaled. Jackson was no stranger to breakfast pastries, but he was utterly unprepared for the bold knockout punch of the scone's aroma, a combination of lemony tang and heady butter that made his mouth water and his tongue demand not just a taste, but a bite that would fill him entirely.

"All that and you haven't even taken a bite." Carly smiled, as if she'd just shared a secret with him. "So even though those things are subtle, they build anticipation. Add to it things like smell and presentation, and you have yourself an experience."

Jackson blinked. "And I thought I was hungry five minutes ago." His stomach sounded off like a car with a busted muffler, which made both of them laugh.

"By all means, complete the experience. Eat," she encouraged, burying a smile in her coffee cup. She didn't have to tell him twice.

The first bite sent so many flavors and textures through Jackson's gray matter that he couldn't pick one and stick to it. Tender, flaky dough melted against his tongue, leaving behind the signature salty-sweetness of both the butter and the sugar, and the grainy crunch of the streusel balanced out the soft, almost jelly-like quality of the blueberries in every bite.

"Mmmf." Jackson tried to slow down, he really did, but the flavors were so intense and incredible that both scones were gone way too soon. "Man, those are insane." The lingering taste of brown sugar played on his tongue as he brushed the crumbs from his hands, following the deep, caramelized sweetness with a sip of savory breakfast blend.

Carly's laugh was humble and soft, yet it drove right into him all the same. "Thanks."

The conversation had smoothed into silence while he ate, but Carly didn't seem to be pushing for him to go, so Jackson took another wild stab at easing more laughter out of her. "So, are you fluent in Italian? Or do you only know the curse words?"

Her head sprang up, bouncing a few dark locks off her shoulders. Although he'd swear her olive skin pinkened just slightly, she pinned him with a bold stare that canceled it out. "Well, my brothers all delighted in teaching me the curse words first, but yes. I am actually fluent in the rest of the language too."

Jackson's fascination went from a flicker to a steady

stream, and something odd snapped to life deep in his gut. "Okay. Impress me."

"You want me to curse at you in Italian?"

"You've already done that," he reminded her. "Why don't you mix it up this time?"

"So, what? Just say whatever pops into my head?" Her expression was a combination of wariness and amusement, suggesting that she thought he was losing his marbles a little bit. Hell, considering how badly the unnamed force in his head pushed at him to keep her attention right now, he probably freaking was.

Not that it was going to stop him.

"Go for it," Jackson drawled, dishing up a smirk to provoke her. "Anything you want."

Carly tipped her head at him, the warmth in her eyes turning fierce. *"Tu sei l'uomo più bello che abbia mai visto."*

The sexy velvet of her voice wrapped around each intonation, and even though he had no idea what she was saying, every last one of Jackson's nerve endings smoldered at the sound of the words.

"Anything else?" he asked, the low tone of his voice shocking him. He knew he should take a step back, that daring her like this was going to lead to trouble and he should stop. But then her lips parted, and the words that rolled out seemed to pulse through his blood with each hypnotic inflection.

"Amo il modo in cui mi guardi. Mi fa sentire bella."

Jackson's eyes flared, and he closed the space between them without realizing he'd done it. "Are you going to tell me what any of it means?"

"No." The single syllable fell from Carly's lips on little more than a throaty sigh, but she raised her chin in a defiant lift, turning her back on the counter to face him.

Christ, the heat coming off of her was incredible, and all he could think was *more*. He reached down and caught one of the strands of hair tumbling over her shoulder, sliding his fingers all the way down to the ends before tucking it back behind her ear. "No?"

"It was nothing, really," Carly breathed. "Mostly gibberish."

"Mmm." His fingers brushed her cheekbone, and he stared down at her, not giving an inch. "Say it again."

Her eyes dropped to his lips, but she didn't hesitate with her words.

"Tu sei l'uomo più bello—"

Jackson captured her words midsentence, his mouth brushing hers in a hot, unyielding stroke as her lips parted over a sigh. His fingers tightened in her hair before he moved his palm to cradle her face. The kiss was like a low fire, begging to be stoked, and Jackson obliged on nothing but impulse.

His tongue mingled with the supple sweetness of Carly's bottom lip, testing the way and drowning in the magnetic pull of her as he deepened the kiss. Her mouth vibrated against his as she released another small sigh, and it tore through him like an avalanche, prompting his hands up into the thick fall of her hair. Christ, she tasted so sweet and yet so sinful, pushing enough hot need under his skin to tighten his fingers against her nape. With a demanding stroke of his tongue, Jackson searched her mouth with even more intensity, until . . .

A loud tap on the glass of the back door made the two of them scatter like leaves in a brisk fall wind.

"Oh!" Carly crossed one arm tightly over her chest and covered her mouth with her opposite palm, staring up at him with wide, holy-hell eyes. Micah, who Jackson had totally forgotten was on his way with the jackhammer, stood with his hands in his pockets outside the sliding glass door. Although his vantage point had been somewhat blocked by the new drop-off created by the missing deck, the uncomfortable way he stuffed his hands in his pockets and refused to look through the glass told Jackson all he needed to know.

Micah had seen everything.

"Carly, listen, I'm really sorry. I don't— "

"It's okay, really." Her raspy voice was suddenly level and cool. She inhaled a slow breath, and the swell of her breasts beneath the pink cotton of her T-shirt did nothing to improve the how-*you*-doin' status of Jackson's hard-on.

She continued. "I think it's probably for the best if we agree to forget that that happened."

Not bloody likely! His inner voice snapped to life, but his rational side countered fast. There was no denying that it hadn't been a run of the mill kiss. Okay, fine, it had come within inches of being a life-altering experience. But wasn't that all the more reason he should forget about it?

A girl like Carly couldn't be good for him if he wasn't interested in anything serious, because everything about her was *seriously* addicting. Walking away wasn't just a good idea.

It was absolutely necessary. For both of them.

Jackson cleared his throat and ran a hand over his barely-there crew cut. "Okay, sure. But I really am sorry."

"Not at all." Carly replied quietly. "So, we're good?"

"You bet."

Jackson tasted that lie for the rest of the day.

Chapter Five

Carly couldn't tell which was more surreal—the fact that a jackhammer was going full-bore six feet from her kitchen or that the guy behind it had just kissed her senseless over an impromptu language lesson.

Well, what do you expect when you tell the guy how much you love the way he's looking at you and that it makes you feel beautiful? Carly scowled at the dishes in the sink, giving them an extra swipe with the sponge for good measure.

Okay, yes, technically she *had* said that, but it wasn't as if Jackson knew it. There was just something so enticing about the way he'd asked her to speak a language she'd known for most of her life that the words she never would've dared to say in English simply poured out without her permission. The way his eyes glittered, darkened to navy blue, had only been gasoline to the flame of her words, and kissing him had been a foregone conclusion.

And, oh God, that kiss. Far from being one of those awkward, first-kiss-out-of-the-gate deals, this lip-lock had been on its own level entirely, generating enough electricity within Carly's body to power up a small town. The intensity of it, even in hindsight, was enough to send a flush of warmth all the way to her earlobes.

Or maybe that was just sheer embarrassment over Jackson apologizing—not once, but twice—at having kissed her in the first place. As in, sorry for the slip-up, my mistake, have a nice day. Carly brushed her fingers gently over lips that still tingled in the aftermath of Jackson's sexy little wake-up call. Just beyond the sun-filled windows, the jackhammer's insistent *rat-tat-tat-tat-tat* made the floorboards vibrate beneath Carly's bare feet, rattling her nerves in a steady pulse.

Forget this. She needed her kitchen. She needed to breathe.

Carly made quick work of showering and packing her chef's whites neatly into her bag, averting her eyes from the goings-on in the backyard as she hustled out the door. The stress of Travis's ridiculous threat coupled with the go-go-go of her grueling workdays and her lingering homesickness must have gotten the best of her, and she'd given in to a silly impulse. Between the underpants thing and the forgive-and-forget kiss, Carly had fulfilled her embarrassment quota for the foreseeable future, and what's done was done. All she needed now was to get her body to her kitchen, channel her energy into the food, and her mind would be good and straight.

The rest of her would follow suit. Memory of that kiss be damned.

"Uh-oh. You've been here for a while." Adrian's voice had more gravel to it than usual, and he eyed Carly with suspicion as he sauntered into La Dolce Vita's kitchen. "What gives?"

"I had a meeting with Gavin at noon to do the weekly rundown," she replied, not looking up from the stockpot on the burner in front of her. The hearty aroma of tomatoes and garlic wafted up from the mouth of the pot like a breath being slowly exhaled in satisfaction.

"That soup smells like ten-thirty to me. Eleven at the latest," Adrian flipped back, arching the dark brow sans piercing. "You want to try again?"

Damn it. She should've figured Adrian would know better. "Nope. You want to taste this?"

"You're fucking kidding me, right? Fork it over." He waved his huge hand, palm up, at her in a *c'mere* motion. "Your peasant soup is like nectar of the Gods, baby."

The laugh that unwound from her chest was just what the doctor ordered, and the remaining stress from Carly's morning—hell, from her whole week—began to jog loose and scatter. "Glad you think so, 'cause it's the specialty soup this week. I thought we'd play with some of the summer vegetables now that the season's in full swing. They came from the farmer's market in Riverside. The tomatoes are practically a work of art."

Her mind caught on the triangle-shaped slivers of zucchini, skin as bright as emeralds as they bobbed through the stockpot on a sea of light, tomato-tinged broth. The tiny, perfect circles of ditalini played off the wedges of zucchini in both color and shape, and both danced in the fresh broth to form a soup that was neither too strong nor too heavy for a summertime menu. When the cooler months came, she'd play with different vegetables to make it heartier, but to Carly, the soup always signaled warmth regardless.

Adrian didn't waste any time putting the spoon Carly passed over to good use, ladling it deep into the belly of the pot for a taste. "Yeah, well they taste like one, too. Way better than the crap we get through the distributor." He paused to make a face, then took another bite of the soup to erase his stubbled grimace. "Simplicity through ingredients, complexity through taste. Man, that's good."

"Yeah, I'd love to figure out a way to use some of the

locally grown produce on more of a regular basis. The closer our source, the fresher the food, you know? Plus, it doesn't hurt the local economy." She stirred the soup one more time, swirling the satiny broth.

"Sounds like a win-win. Maybe you should bring it up with management." Adrian leaned back against the stainless steel counter.

"Yeah, they might go for that. Riverside is close enough to spin a locally grown campaign. I'd love to have fresher produce, and management would probably eat up the PR." She shrugged, not moving her eyes from the pot.

Adrian's eyes may have been with hers on the red-gold broth in the stockpot, but his focus was entirely on her. "Hey, are you okay? You usually make this as a comfort food thing."

"Not always." Her protest was casual, barely there, but Adrian seemed to register it all the same. He tilted his platinum head at her, and she could practically hear the gears of his brain grinding away at full-tilt. Oh, to hell with it. Carly had never been any good at lying, mostly because she never saw the point. "I just miss New York a little, that's all. It'll pass."

Adrian nodded once, his thick shoulders pulling tight as he reached for a stockpot of his own and took it to the sink to fill it with water. "Maybe you should go back to the neighborhood for a couple of days. See your *mama* and your brothers."

Hearing Adrian's hard New York accent curl around the Italian pronunciation of *mama* sent a pang through Carly's gut, for more reasons than one. She hadn't forgotten her mother's message on her machine, or the reasons behind it, either.

"No." The word was clipped enough to snap at her ears as she spoke it, but she didn't back down. "I'm not leaving my kitchen just because of a little wistful yearning, Ade.

It's stupid. I'll be fine." God, how had she managed to skip breakfast and still wind up with heartburn? Carly rubbed the heel of her hand between the twin rows of buttons spanning the length of her jacket.

"She's not going to stay mad at you forever, Carly. She's your *mama*, you know?" Adrian slipped a handful of potatoes into his stockpot and cranked the burner beneath it to life.

As much as she loved her, having to deal with her very Catholic mother's disdain for her only daughter's failed marriage and subsequent divorce was about the only thing Carly didn't miss about being in the city. Plus, there was always the danger of running into Travis in their neighborhood, and considering his recent threat, nothing good would come of a chance encounter.

"You're clearly underestimating the power of the di Matisse resolve," she said. "My *mama* will probably give me grief over this until I'm eighty."

Adrian laughed in a gruff rumble. "Uh, I work with you every day. Believe me when I tell you, I'm well-versed in the di Matisse resolve." He jutted his chin at her, dark stubble gracing his sturdy jawline. "All I'm saying is that if you need a dose of home to get you good and straight, then maybe you should go."

Carly fought to keep her tone light, but it was calm water over a rip tide. "I don't need to be anywhere other than here. This is where my kitchen is." It didn't escape her that she couldn't utter the phrase *this is home*. "You're right. My mother will forgive me eventually, plus, I'd just as soon give Travis a wide berth. With the shit he's been pulling lately, the last thing I need is to run into him by accident."

Adrian grunted, letting Carly shift the subject while he pulled a container of flour from one of the open-air shelves outside the pantry. "What did your lawyer say about his threat over the show?"

Carly managed a genuine smile at both the distraction from her homesickness and her lawyer's response. "When she was done laughing, she said she didn't think it would be a problem. The contract for the show was for one season only, and it was fulfilled. I spoke with Winslow personally to let him know that there was no way in hell I'd work with Travis again. Any future projects he wants me for will have to be solo. Of course, he was surprised, because Travis had given him the impression that things were amicable."

She paused to do the wince-and-eye-roll maneuver that was synonymous with all things Travis before continuing. "Technically, Travis can still drag his feet over the divorce if he really wants to, refusing to sign anything or agree to any reasonable terms. But in the end, my lawyer can file a motion—something about defaulting, I think. It basically says that he's being difficult and I still want out. And then the divorce will be finalized anyway, even though it might take a little longer. So I doubt he'll keep up his tantrum for long."

The added *I hope* was silent, but it rang through as clear as Prosecco in a fine crystal goblet.

"I hate what he did to you." Adrian's hands were fluid motion, measuring flour with green-gray eyes as hard as glass. His brusque quiet belied something louder beneath the surface, something Carly had only seen once but would never forget. Her chest tightened, but her steadfast will overruled it.

"I do, too, but we have a job to do here. I can't afford to get upset over it. Plus, soon enough, I won't have to worry about Travis. I have this restaurant, and I have you and Sloane. It won't be long before we can all go back to New York. I don't need anything else." She put a hand on his thick forearm, interrupting him midmotion. "So don't worry." Carly's words were soft, a direct contrast to her sous chef's troubled expression.

"Carly—"

Nope. Not going there. "Look, I promise that once the summer rush is over and all of this stuff with Travis simmers down, I'll think about going to New York for a couple of days. But really. I'm fine."

Adrian narrowed his eyes, but surprised her by letting it go. "Okay. If you change your mind, just let me know. I've got you covered."

Carly nodded, reaching for one of the loaves of rustic bread she'd pulled from the pantry. Peasant soup and garlic bread were the Italian version of tomato soup and grilled cheese, and her need for comfort food just wouldn't be quelled without the hand-in-hand combination.

"I will. Thanks."

The thing was, neither the city she'd left nor the place she lived now currently felt like home. So no matter how homesick she got, Carly didn't have a place to go.

Jackson eased his truck onto Rural Route 4, Carly's bungalow receding behind him in the rearview mirror. Nine hours of straight-up manual labor had always been just the trick to knock even the most persistent thoughts out of his head, but the image of kissing Carly in the sunny warmth of her kitchen proved to be the exception to that rule. The familiar comfort of the road home became a quick afterthought in the wake of his brain's ping pong match between *hell yes* and *are you out of your goddamn mind?* Team *hell yes* was outscoring its opponent two to one.

On the one hand, he didn't really know what Team *are you out of your goddamn mind* was bellyaching about. Okay, so locking lips with a client he barely knew wasn't exactly his speed, but come on. Four syllables into Carly's sexy Italian monologue and all bets were off. With the way her voice rode the rich curves of the language, any man in his right mind would've caved. Never mind the fact that he'd probably kissed her for saying something like, "You're a gaping Neanderthal" or "I can tell you haven't showered today."

So all things considered, Jackson should probably file the whole thing under the category of *no harm, no foul* and get on with it. It was one mutually exclusive, impulsive as hell kiss, prompted by some sexy banter that would've made a dead man wake up and take notice.

Except now that he'd taken notice, he couldn't stop noticing, which was the crazy part. Unable to help it, he replayed the sensual slide of the words again in his mind, the memory of Carly's full, provocative lips moving around each sound, drawing him in and making him want to . . .

Jackson's phone knocked him out of his bilingual reverie, and he jumped in the seat of his truck like he'd been goosed with a red-hot cattle prod. Breathing a mixed sigh of relief and frustration, he fumbled for the hands-free device, finally managing to pop it in his ear.

"Hello?"

"Hey man, it's about time. Don't you check your messages?" Excitement tinged Shane's voice in a Christmas-morning kind of way.

"Sorry. I got caught up in this little thing called work. Ever heard of it?" Jackson's crack carried every ounce of the good-natured tone he'd intended, especially since Shane was one of the biggest workaholics he knew.

"Go ahead, be a jackass. See what you miss out on."

"Okay, I'll bite," Jackson laughed. "What's up?"

"You won't believe what I'm looking at right now."

He creased his brow, making the turn to wind his way up the mountain. "This isn't a trick question that's going to get me into trouble, is it?"

Shane barked out a laugh. "You wish. Remember the guy

with the '67 Camaro I met at that auto auction outside of Carlisle last month?"

"Oh, yeah. He had connections close to here. Bealetown, right?" Jackson asked. Shane had inherited Grady's Service Garage from his grandfather when the old man decided to retire six months back, and Shane was looking to expand it to include his love of restoring and remodeling classic cars. He'd gone to more than a few auto auctions and car shows over the last few months, and Jackson had been happier than a pig in a puddle to tag along and help make contacts.

"Yeah, that's him. Well the guy he knew out our way has a pristine 1968 GTO, and he's been looking for someone to rebuild the engine. He gave me a call at lunch and asked if he could bring it out so I could give him an estimate. The thing is frickin' *sweet*. He liked what he saw at the shop and we agreed on a price, so I started to work on it a couple of hours ago."

Jackson shook his head. "I know you work your ass off, but I swear you have all the luck. Those GTOs are off the rails."

"Yeah, no two ways about it. Just thinking about the thing kinda gives me a hard-on," Shane said over a laugh.

Hell if that wasn't dangerous territory for Jackson right about now. "Well congratulations, man. Only you would land a rebuild on a GTO as your first really big resto job. Outside of your Mustang, I mean."

Shane's 1969 Mustang was the best kind of bad, all sleek metal and hard lines. The fact that he and Grady had restored it by hand from frame to fender didn't hurt.

"Yeah. Bellamy's working tonight, so I was going to mess around with it for a while. You want to come out and give me a hand? I could use your muscle when I pull out the old engine block."

Jackson pondered it for all of two seconds. "Sure." What

better way to get back to normal than a badass distraction on wheels. "I'll be there in ten."

"Cool. Oh, hey, I almost forgot. Congratulations on striking gold in the girlfriend department."

Jackson's breath jammed in his lungs, and he pulled back with a start. "Dude, it was only one kiss!" Okay, so the kiss had been knock-your-socks-off good, but let's get serious. One kiss, even a really good one, did *not* a girlfriend make.

"Uh . . . when did you kiss Jenna?"

Recognition slapped Jackson upside the head just in time for him to fill the totally awkward buzz of silence coming over the phone line. "Oh, crap. You meant for the party next week."

"I did, but clearly you've got someone else on the brain. So, who's your mystery girl?"

Shane's knowing grin was practically audible through the phone, and although his tone suggested he wasn't going to drop the topic without either an answer or an argument, Jackson hedged. The kiss had been a one-time-only thing; plus, Carly was Bellamy's boss, which ranked high on the awkward-meter. He doubted Bellamy would gossip, but still. He and Carly had agreed to forget about it.

Not that he was holding up his end of the bargain there.

"I, ah. I kinda had breakfast with the woman renting the bungalow out on Rural Route 4. I'm rebuilding her deck. The kiss was accidental." Jackson cranked the dial on the air conditioning. Man, it had to be the hottest day of the year so far.

"How do you accidentally kiss someone? It's not exactly like tripping over the dog. Unless . . . oh, please tell me you didn't trip over this girl."

"You're an ass, you know that?" Jackson had to laugh, which was actually a good thing, because he was in serious danger of taking this Carly thing way too seriously. "Of course I didn't trip over her. The kiss was just an impulsive thing, that's all. In hindsight, it was a bad idea, but it's really no big deal."

"So do you maybe want to ask this girl to the party instead? I'm sure Jenna would understand," Shane said.

Hell if Jackson hadn't put the cart before the horse on that one. The big, fat negative that Carly had offered up in response to his invitation rang in his memory, and it hammered home the fact that this whole thing had gone far enough. Getting torqued up over a woman was a bad idea anyway. A woman he barely knew? Even worse.

"No, no, no. I'm still in for taking Jenna to the party. Like I said, this morning was just a mistake. Nothing doing."

The untruth tasted like a mouthful of motor oil, but Jackson stuffed it down. The only way he was going to get back to business as usual was to man up and actually forget about Carly, the sooner, the better. He swooped in for the full-frontal subject change before Shane could get another word in edgewise.

"Listen, I'm going to stop by Joe's Grocery and grab a sandwich or two on my way there. You want me to grab something for you?"

After Shane had taken the bait and given him a short dinner order, Jackson hung up and tossed his earpiece and phone onto the passenger seat. He'd done his best not to think about taking Jenna to Dylan and Kelsey's engagement party, but the reality was it would be way easier to pull off a one-time-only girlfriend charade than to even consider bringing a real date. An odd tingle of unease worked its way up his spine, and he shivered before it dissipated.

Yeah. Once this party was a thing of the past, everything in Jackson's world would be right back to normal.

Just like he wanted it.

Chapter Six

Sloane turned her Tom Ford sunglasses up to the dappled sunlight in the backyard and preened, wiggling her fresh pedicure as she propped her feet up at the end of her chaise lounge.

"I gotta admit it. While there might not be a Starbucks within a forty-mile radius of this place, the Zen going on out here is totally first rate. There's something to be said for lolling around outside in your pajamas on the Fourth of July. It's like a whole new version of Independence Day."

Carly inhaled a breath steeped in Saturday-morning sunshine and let it percolate in her veins before releasing a sigh of agreement, about both the Zen and the pajamas.

No two ways about it—the new design of the yard was something else. Rather than jutting off the back of the house in a ho-hum square like its predecessor, the upgraded deck took both the footprint of the house and the feel of the yard into consideration. Thick, honey-colored boards ran the length of the modest bungalow, making the deck look like a seamless extension rather than the tacked-on afterthought it had previously been. The new structure, partially shielded by a verdant canopy of gold-veined oak leaves, allowed plenty of room for two chaise lounges and small side tables on either end. With finishing touches like Carly's potted herb garden and the delicate wind chimes Sloane had discovered in a flea market clearance bin in Bealetown, the whole setup was nothing short of beautiful.

Kind of like the man who'd created it.

"I'm going to remind you that you chose Zen over Starbucks the next time you bitch that there are no baristas to flirt with way out here in God's country," Carly replied, smoothing over the image of Jackson in her brain. She padded across the sun-warmed planks to the chaises where she and Sloane had been drinking their morning coffee ever since the seal coat on the boards dried four days ago. "And speaking of coffee, here you go."

Sloane took the mug Carly offered and blew her a kiss of gratitude. "Mmm, I do miss having a luscious little barista on every corner. And that sizzling hot pastry chef at the new bakery on Main Street? Totally taken." Sloane's pouty moue melted away in favor of her bright-idea expression. "Oooh, maybe I'll have to write my next book about a hero who works in a coffee shop. You think Starbucks will let me use their name?"

"Doubtful." Carly plunked down on the chaise next to Sloane's and took a long draw from her coffee mug. "Unless your hero wears the Starbucks logo throughout nine-tenths of the book."

"If I had my way, he'd be naked throughout nine-tenths of the book. Helllllooooo, barista." She jounced her inky black brows.

"Maybe you could give him a tattoo of the Starbucks logo in a very strategic place." Carly tucked her feet beneath her, and Sloane lifted one shoulder in a demi-shrug.

"Or maybe I could just get laid and stop obsessing over imaginary baristas."

Familiar, needful heat seeped downward from Carly's belly, making itself at home between her thighs. "Either that or you could seduce a contractor and have the best of both worlds." Yeah. Thick, corded muscles, a chest that could make retaining walls green with envy, and a mouth lush enough to make a girl want to—

"Don't you mean a barista?" Sloane laughed.

Carly snapped to attention, eyes widening. "That's what I said."

"*Au contraire*, my friend." Sloane paused, leaning in to examine Carly with growing interest. "You're looking a little flushed over there, sweetheart. Have you got something going on that I should know about, or is it just wishful thinking? That contractor guy *was* pretty smokin'."

Carly's neck prickled. "No! And no."

Yes, yes, and more yes. Generously drizzled with a reduction sauce of hell yes, and topped with a lovely garnish of oh-by-the-way-I-kissed-him.

Well, that settled that.

"Come on, Carly. It's okay to admit you're human. Getting horizontal with a nice, hot bene-friend might be good for you." Sloane's lips gave a devilish twist before parting on a dreamy smile. "Unless you're looking for a swan."

"Are you even speaking English?" Carly knotted her arms over the chest of her Islanders T-shirt. Despite its raggedy state, she'd become weirdly attached to wearing the damned thing this week. "I don't understand a word you just said." Five years of being out of the dating loop and the terminology had gone off the deep end.

Sloane didn't skip a beat as she turned to Carly with the translation. "A bene-friend is just that—a friend with benefits. Think of it as mutually agreed-upon, no-strings-attached sex."

"No offense, but I'm not really a one night stand kind of girl." Carly said with a frown. She might've been out of things for a while, but she wasn't *that* desperate.

"No way would I steer you toward a one night stand. Hello, stranger danger," Sloane replied with a snort. "What I'm suggesting is totally different. Think of it as an agreement between acquaintances to share all the physical benefits of a relationship without the other stuff. It's completely casual, but without the skank factor."

Carly's hair fluttered over her shoulders as she shook her head, and she pulled it back into a thick knot. "It sounds kind of contractual."

"Believe me, sweetheart. If you play it right, the last thing you'll be thinking about is legalese." The wicked smile on Sloane's face made it perfectly clear what would be on Carly's mind—and her other parts—if she found a good partner for the job.

She let out a breath, hoping it would extinguish the heat spreading over her cheeks. "Okay, fine. What about the other thing? The flamingo, or whatever?"

Sloane's laugh carried over the morning breeze wafting through the yard. "Not a flamingo, a swan—you know, white feathers, long neck. Swans are one of the only species that mate for life. So when you find The Guy, it's like he's your swan."

Okay, clearly her best friend had lost her faculties. "What guy? Jesus, Sloane. You're not making all of this up as you go, are you?"

Sloane flipped her sunglasses to the crown of her head, turning to look Carly in the eye as if this were very serious business. "Not *the guy*, as in, little *t*, little *g*. I'm talking capital letters, sweetheart. *The Guy*. The one who makes you feel like you've got raw electricity in your veins. The one whose laundry you want to steal because it smells like him. The one who would do anything just to have you, and that you would return the favor for, bar none. The Guy."

Carly's brain zeroed in on the scent of clean soap and freshly cut wood, and she shook her head, wondering where the hell it had come from. "Wow. The only thing I ever noticed about Travis's laundry was that it was usually all over the floor, and I was married to him for five years. Are you sure about this guy thing?"

"Oh, please." Sloane clucked her tongue in disgust and lowered her mug. "Travis is a swine, not a swan. I'm talking about someone who can curl your toes from halfway across the room, someone you never want to be without. The Guy is the living embodiment of your happily ever after, honey. Riding off into the sunset is optional."

"Okay, definitely not Travis." Carly sighed. "And I don't think that's my thing. I barely have time to do my own laundry, much less worry about The Guy or the ostrich or whatever he's called."

"The swan," Sloane corrected. "So you need a bene-friend, then. Someone to give you a little sugar."

"I don't *need* anything." Carly scanned the emerald-green carpet of summer grass flowing out into the yard to meet the grove of trees on either side of the property, while every last inch of her skin tingled at her big, fat lie. The kiss she'd shared with Jackson had been an all-too-startling reminder of what she'd been missing by being alone. Not that Travis had ever kissed her like that.

"Look, if I'm past due for a little between-the-sheets lovin', you must be in fucking foreclosure over there. The last person you laid lips on was your ex, and that is just a *travesty*," Sloane said with a cluck of her tongue.

Carly coughed out a laugh. "Thanks for the reminder."

Only the last little bit wasn't exactly true. Not that she wanted to cop to her steamy little escapade, especially since she and Jackson had held true to the whole bygones thing. In fact, she'd barely seen him for the duration of the project after he'd hightailed it out of her kitchen.

So yeah. Definitely bygones. Casual or not, the last thing

she needed was a man who'd probably end up duping her like Travis had, anyway.

"Sorry. I suppose you've been busy at work, so I'll cut you some slack," Sloane said, a feline smile tugged at the corners of her lips. "But still. All work and no play makes Carly a dull girl."

"Sorry to disappoint you, but seeing as how there's a definite shortage of candidates willing to polish me to a shine, you may just have to live with dull Carly for the time being. I'm not sure anyone in Pine Mountain would be willing to . . . what was it you said? Give me some sugar?"

"You'd be surprised. The best men for this kind of thing are usually right under your nose." Sloane paused in thought. "Take the deck guy for example. He'd have been perfect for this. Maybe you can get his number from . . ."

"No!" Carly jerked up so fast that her coffee sloshed over the death grip she suddenly had on her mug handle. "Uh, I mean, I'm not so sure the deck guy would be a good idea."

Sloane arched an eyebrow so high that it breached the top rim of her glasses. "Why not? Did you see the man's biceps? I had to fight off the urge to swoon when he knocked on the door and asked me to do the final walk-through with him. That man definitely had second helpings of muscles marinara, if you know what I mean."

"Oh, I know what you mean, all right," Carly muttered, blowing out a hot breath.

"Okay, you're acting very weird. What gives? And don't even think about saying *nothing*. It's insulting."

Carly forced herself not to fidget. What was the big deal, anyway? It wasn't like it was ever going to happen again. "Okay, fine. Last week, before you came home, I kind of . . . kissed him."

Sloane choked on her coffee. "I thought it was just a fantasy thing that prompted that verbal slip! You actually kissed muscles marinara? Where?"

"On the mouth," Carly said obviously.

"No, I meant where were you when it happened," she replied, starting to giggle. "Not where on his anatomy. Although . . ."

"The kitchen, the kitchen! We were in the kitchen." Carly's cheeks flamed, but it was hard to tell whether it was over the memory of the clandestine kiss or the thought of all the other places that kiss could've gone.

"You little minx. Why didn't you say anything?" Sloane's baby blues went as wide as ultramarine nickels. "Are you going to see him again? Please, I'm dying over here!"

"No, I'm not going to see him again." She tried to take a deep breath, only to be denied access to anything even remotely calm. "And I didn't say anything because we agreed to forget about it. Plus, he likes the Flyers, for God's sake."

Her awkward attempt at humor thudded around between them like a giant boulder of trying-too-hard, and Carly finished the last of her coffee so she'd have something to do. Other than revisit the whole biceps-scones-hot-kiss scenario in her head.

For the tenth time. This morning.

"And why is it that you'd want to forget about it, crazy hockey fetish notwithstanding? Was it a bad kiss?" Sloane served Carly with a look that suggested she'd lost her mind, but Carly refused to bite.

"No. Yes. I mean—" Carly broke off and took a deep breath. "No, the kiss wasn't bad, but I barely know him. Add to that the fact that I'm not even technically divorced, I have a career that dominates most of my waking hours, and oh by the way, I'm leaving Pine Mountain at the first available opportunity, and I don't think the odds of me getting to know the contractor are too good. Even if it is for . . . you know. Sugar-getting."

Carly's chest filled with resolve, and she held up a hand to stave off the protest she knew Sloane was working up. "So while it's nice in theory, in practice I just don't think that whole friends with benefits thing would work out. Plus, I'm never going to see the guy again, anyway. So that's why I didn't say anything."

Sloane let out a slow sigh, like a balloon with a soft leak. "I hate to see you lonely. But I know better than to mess with you when your mind is made up." She tipped her head like she was going to say something else, but didn't. "Well, I guess I'd better get online. Fifty bucks says that wading through the fine print for Starbucks logo rights is going to take me a couple of hours."

"Yeah, I have to get to the restaurant anyhow. I know we're only open for limited service today since it's the Fourth, but if Adrian beats me to the punch, I'll still have to listen to him gloat." Carly swung her feet to the sun-warmed deck, and the image of Jackson's steady, strong hands as he nailed the boards into place flashed through her mind with startling clarity.

What if . . .

No. Jackson Carter, with his broad, beautiful chest and those sapphire-blue stunners that crinkled extra when he laughed, was not a possibility, not even in the casual sense. Carly tamped down the memory of his lips on hers, hot and rich and oh-so-good, for the last time. No more thinking about what-if, she decided with a sad nod.

It was time to start thinking about what was.

"You're lucky I liked you when we started this whole mess." Shane's expression suggested he was only half-kidding as he slid Jackson a wary look before stepping back to eye the canopy posts scattered on the lawn. "Are you sure you know what you're doing here?"

Jackson scoffed, feigning insult. "This is the same tent we used last summer for the family reunion. Once we get the frame together, getting the canopy on it is a piece of cake." The food reference echoed for a second longer than normal in his head, but Jackson shoved it aside. This tent wasn't going to pitch itself.

It had been over a week since he'd decided to put the pedal to the metal and concentrate on the job in Carly's backyard rather than the heat in her rare-but-sexy smile. The whole thing should've been easy, since he'd only caught shadowy glimpses of her through the windows here and there as he finished the job. He hadn't even had to worry about facing her for the final walk-through, since Carly's roommate, a tall, willowy girl who looked like she'd sprung from the catwalk of some upscale runway, took care of it instead. So really, Jackson should be breathing a sigh of relief that Carly hadn't slugged him for being so forward. Getting jacked up about a woman—even one who kissed well enough to curl his toes—wasn't on his agenda.

It couldn't be.

So why couldn't he get her out of his head?

"I thought this was supposed to be a small family get-together. How is it you suddenly need a canopy tent that takes up half the yard?" Shane's question jogged Jackson's thoughts back to the here-and-now of his mother's backyard.

"Two words: Brooke and Autumn. I swear my sisters could make a three-ring circus out of a trip to Joe's Grocery." Jackson picked up the metal bars that made up the corner post and started fitting them together, waiting for Shane to mimic his movements with identical parts for the opposite side before continuing. "This thing surpassed 'small family get-together' last week. Now it's a full-blown epic event. My ma's been getting food ready nonstop since yesterday morning, and I doubt she'll take a breath until people start flooding in through the back gate."

At least there was one thing Jackson couldn't complain about. Given his mother's track record for gatherings like these, the food at this not-so-little shindig was going to be off the rails, and he planned to take full advantage of the down-home spread. Between the barbecue and the beer, he'd be all set.

Don't forget about the fake girlfriend. He rubbed a hand over the sudden unease parked on his sternum like a Buick and measured Shane with a careful look.

"You know, I've been thinking. Maybe this Jenna thing isn't such a good idea. Maybe . . ."

"Jackson? Are you and Shane okay out there?"

If Jackson didn't know any better, he'd swear his mother could hone in on his indiscretions from fifty feet. He clapped his mouth shut, trapping the thought inside.

"Absolutely. We should have this thing put together pretty soon."

His mother leaned out the back door wearing a food splattered apron and an ear-to-ear smile. "Okay. I should have some of this chicken salad ready to go in a bit, in case you two are getting hungry. Just come on in when you're done."

Jackson's stomach gurgled in a spasm of joy as she retreated to the kitchen, which had to be bursting at the ceiling joists.

"Well, at least we'll be eating well for the next week or so." Jackson shrugged, letting his unease over the party melt into the background of his thoughts as he maneuvered his half of the tent posts into order.

"Tell me about it. Bellamy's made four pies in the last twenty-four hours, and had two more in the works when I left. It's total kitchen insanity over at my place, too." Shane finished putting together his half of the metal skeleton and stood back to examine his handiwork. "So, you were saying something about Jenna?"

"You know what? I'm probably blowing it way out of proportion. We'll all hang out, have a good time. No big deal."

"Bellamy asked me about it. After you left the other night." Shane's eyes skipped over Jackson's for a brief second before he turned his attention back to unfurling the canvas for the canopy.

Jackson exhaled through his teeth. "What'd you tell her?"

"That you have your reasons for not wanting to get serious with anyone." He yanked one edge of the cream-colored canvas over the corner post of the tent frame to fasten it in place, and the action gave Jackson a minute to decide how to proceed. He opted for the standard, easygoing approach that was as much a part of him as the swirl of his fingerprints.

"Look, I don't have anything against the concept of serious relationships. I mean, other people fall in love and get married all the time. It's just not my thing." Jackson gathered the opposite end of the canvas, attaching it to the posts on his side with a series of efficient tugs. In this case, *not my thing* roughly translated to *no way in hell*, but it wasn't as if Jackson could really say that out loud. Christ, his buddy was the poster boy for MEN SICK IN LOVE.

Shane didn't lift his eyes from the tent. "At the risk of getting my ass kicked for saying so, you're not your father, you know."

Jackson stopped short, a fistful of canvas twisting in his palm. His answer shot out before he could reel it back.

"Well, nobody really knows that, do they? After all, I look exactly like him. It probably wouldn't be so bad, except from time to time, my mother flinches when I walk into a room." He snapped the canopy over its corresponding corner post so hard, in hindsight he was shocked it didn't tear.

"It doesn't matter who you look like. You're not that kind of guy," Shane insisted, his voice low.

Screw this. He knew his friend meant well, but he was so not having this conversation. "If it's all the same to you, I'd rather not stir things up and find out."

Unfortunately, Shane's response was measured and steady, which meant Jackson wasn't going to get out of this as easily as he'd hoped. "I'd just hate to see you miss out on a really good thing because you're caught up in what your old man did over twenty years ago. Just because he—"

"No." Jackson held up a hand to cut Shane off. Enough was enough. "Look, I know you have good intentions here, I do. But with the exception of a little guilt over fooling my mother from time to time about my relationship status, I'm happy doing what I'm doing. I'm not too jaded to see that being serious works for some people, and I'm glad that it does. All I'm saying is that I don't want it to work for me, okay?" The overhead sun beat down on Jackson like a vengeful marching band, and he swiped his forearm over his sweat-laced brow.

Shane pulled the final corner of the tent canopy over the frame, knotting the ties into place with a series of smooth tugs. "Okay," he said. "My mistake."

The hitch in his dark eyes as he focused his glance on the finished canopy suggested that Shane's remorse was genuine, and Jackson shifted at the sudden pinprick of guilt left in its wake.

"No worries, man. You want to help me anchor these stakes in the ground? I'm starving over here," he replied, trying a grin on for size. The hollow feeling that invaded his gut every time anyone brought up the F-word loosened its grip, and the thought of his mother's chicken salad made the blurry image of his father even more indistinct as he pushed it from his mind.

"You? I'm shocked," Shane quipped, rumbling out a laugh that universally signaled *all is well* in guy code.

"Yeah, yeah. Pick up the pace, grease monkey, or I won't leave you any chicken salad."

Shane dutifully gave Jackson the finger, and the two laughed and joked until the tent was secured into place in the backyard. As they headed for the house, still jawing back and forth, Jackson couldn't help but run a hand over the ache that had settled right beneath his ribs.

The one that had nothing to do with food.

Chapter Seven

"If either one of you tells my sisters I said this, I swear I'll deny it. But seriously? This party's not half-bad."

Jackson rocked back on the heels of his work boots and surveyed the crowd dotting the lush expanse of his mother's backyard. Waning early-evening sunlight poked through the leafy canopy of trees overhead, scattering hushed, golden tones of summer over the partygoers. People wound their way through the yard, clear plastic cups of iced tea or frosty beers in hand. An occasional burst of noise rose up from the horseshoe pit at the far end of the yard, usually following the resonant metal on metal twang of a ringer.

Beneath the canopy Jackson and Shane had put up mere hours ago, three wood-planked picnic tables stood at the ready, dressed up in red and white checked tablecloths like it was their Sunday best. In the true spirit of a small-town gathering, everyone had brought "just a little something" to share with the crowd, and platter after platter filled with top-secret family recipes graced the tables in a wide array of mouth-watering down-home charm.

"You clearly haven't tried the fried chicken yet. Dig into that, and your *not half-bad* will slide right on into *I'm never leaving*," Shane said with an arch of his brow. "And don't get me started on the biscuits Lily Callahan brought from her new bakery."

"There's fried chicken? *And* biscuits?" Bellamy moaned, clutching her stomach. "When did all that get here?" Her green eyes skimmed the nearby table with a look caught between *oh yeah* and *no fair*.

"Mrs. Teasdale brought the platters out while you were helping Autumn dish up the pulled pork," Shane replied, taking a draw from his beer.

"Speaking of *I'm never leaving*. Your mother's pulled pork is to die for, Jax. Honestly, it should be its own food group," Bellamy mused.

Jackson scanned the yard, catching sight of his mother sitting at a picnic table with Dylan and Kelsey. The lines on her face seemed lighter somehow, partially erased by happiness, and he smiled at the sight.

"Yeah, she let me dig into it before I hit the grill. This might be one of the best batches of sauce she's ever cooked up."

He'd been all too happy to man the grill, flipping everything from burgers to brats and feeding the masses for over an hour as the crowd grew. Something about the deep, smoky scent of the charcoal sent all of his neurons into total relaxation mode, and the orange-edged glow of the coals combined with the hypnotic hiss of the meat on the grill just hammered the whole perfect-day thing home for him.

"Hey, when was your last Jenna sighting?" Jackson asked, jiggling his brows playfully at Bellamy as he fished around in a nearby cooler for a beer. As soon as he and Shane had finished with the tent, Jackson had made up his mind to stop worrying about the whole faux-girlfriend thing for real. His mother deserved to be happy, and if that meant a little sleight of hand on his part, then it was worth it just this once.

"By now she should be on the road, but with the spotty cell service up here, I can't catch her to find out when she left.

These mountains can reduce a 4G iPhone to a technologically savvy paperweight in about two seconds flat," she sighed. "I know she feels horrible about having to get here so late. Her boss doesn't normally pull a Cruella Deville, so something awful must've gone down at work for her to have to go in today."

"It's all good," Jackson replied with a wave, and he meant it. The atmosphere buzzed with the happy chatter of neighbors catching up, eating, and laughing. The air seemed electrically charged with the down to earth goodness that fit Pine Mountain like a flawless puzzle piece, and Jackson drew in a big breath of it, letting it rush through his chest. Man, on a night like this, he felt almost anything was possible.

"So where's this girlfriend who's going to make an honest man out of you?"

Except maybe that.

"Wow, Brooke, you don't cut any corners, do you?" Jackson asked drily, covering his grimace with a sip of beer.

"When it comes to giving you a hard time, I pull out all the stops," his sister said with a grin. "So, really. Where is this mystery girl? I'm starting to think you made her up."

"Huh?" Jackson sputtered, sending beer on a straight shot to his windpipe. Shane whacked him on the back with one hand, covering up what was surely a smart-assed snicker with the other.

"Jenna had a work emergency, but don't worry. She'll be here," Bellamy assured Brooke with a genuine smile, while Jackson proceeded to cough up what felt like a vital organ. God damn, his lungs were on fire.

"Wow, little brother. You okay?" Brooke balanced her daughter on one hip, juggling a huge bowl of potato salad in her opposite palm as she peered at him with concern.

"Wrong pipe," he gasped, finally managing to clear his throat and stand upright.

"Hey, Brooke. Let me take that for you," Shane offered, swooping in for the distraction. From his expression, it was clear he meant to get the scoop—so to speak—on the potato salad, but Brooke didn't skip a beat.

"Thanks, doll." She handed off her daughter with practiced ease, while Shane gave up a look that would make a deer in headlights burst with pride. His *help me out, please* garnered zero results.

"You have to admit, you deserved that," Bellamy murmured with a quirk of her lips, and turned to coo at the baby, "Yes he did. Didn't he?"

Shane held the baby as if there was a live grenade beneath her Pampers and pigtails, and Jackson laughed.

"Come on, dude. Hailey's not even old enough to be that squirmy yet. Just don't drop her and you're all good." He took the bowl from his sister and wedged it next to a platter of confetti-colored fruit salad, his stomach perking to life with the prospect of round two.

"Okay, hotshot. You want to show me how it's done, then?"

"Oh, no." Brooke's long blond ponytail danced behind her, brushing her shoulders as she shook her head. "I have plans for this one. It seems we're running way low on ice, and Mom wanted a couple gallons of ice cream to go with Bellamy's pies. Now that you're done on the grill, think you can manage a run to Joe's?"

"Hello, for apple pie à la mode? I think I can swing it." Jackson reached over and plucked his niece from Shane's stiff embrace, tickling her round baby-belly with just enough pressure to make her squeal with glee. "And for the record, they can smell fear."

"Show off," Shane groused, but he looked more relieved than irritated.

"You know it." Jackson returned the baby to Brooke's

outstretched arms. "I'll be back. 'Til then, could you please not eat all the potato salad?"

"Only because I'm saving room for pie," Shane retorted as Jackson made his way through the yard.

After a bit of creative maneuvering, Jackson managed to get his truck free from the throng of vehicles parked on the grassy shoulder leading up to his childhood home. The lingering smell of charcoal from the grill wound its way through his open window, reminding him of the smoky flavors of the burgers he'd flipped. The way the grill marks had formed perfect charcoal outlines across the thick patties, the bright, hearty color of the garden-grown tomatoes, the soft, fluffy pillows of the perfectly toasted potato rolls sandwiching it all together . . . ahhhhhh. The whole thing had been pure bliss.

Jackson leaned back in the driver's seat, his mouth watering even though he'd eaten barely a half an hour before. The sexy rasp of a familiar voice ribboned through his memory, unfurling and spreading out in his mind.

And you have yourself an experience . . . Carly whispered, hot in his ear.

Oh, hell.

Even though he hadn't seen Carly since the morning of their accidental kiss, the thought of her sure had made itself at home inside his cranium. In fact, thoughts of her were popping up with such unnerving frequency that Jackson had pretty much stopped trying to fight them. What harm could a little daydreaming about a pretty girl do in the grander scheme of things?

You mean aside from the hard-on you're sporting like the banner at a homecoming parade?

Well shit. He needed something dull to dwell on, and he needed it quick. A stack of ho-hum papers, neatly bound with a two-inch metal clip à la the Jaws of Life, caught his eye from his passenger seat, snagging his attention with perfect timing.

If reciting random excerpts from the *Pennsylvania Building Code* couldn't get his mind on the straight and narrow, nothing would.

By the time Jackson pulled into the parking lot at Joe's Grocery, his recollection of residential building codes for outdoor storage enclosures was fresh as a daisy, and his XY parts were in a much more cooperative mood. He did a quick visual assessment of how many bags of ice would fit in the cooler he'd stashed in his truck bed and sauntered into Joe's. The place was a ghost town.

"Hey, Joe. Not a lot of people on account of the holiday, huh?" Jackson grabbed a cart and auto-piloted it in the direction of the frozen food.

"Everyone's at your ma's, from what I hear. I'm actually closing up shop in a couple minutes." Joe gave a friendly grin from behind the deli counter. "But go ahead and grab whatever you need and let me know when you're ready to check out."

"Don't worry. I'll be quick."

It was a little eerie to have the normally bustling store to himself, and Jackson started to whistle as he made his way toward the freezer cases in the back of the store. Some old tune had been stuck in his head for days now, and he couldn't seem to place it, let alone get it out of his mind. The oddly familiar notes rolled off his tongue, threatening to drive him batty, but he shrugged it off as he cut through the dried goods aisle to get to the ice cream.

A flash of movement and sudden stillness caught his eye, and he stopped midstride next to a display of long grain rice. A girl, maybe sixteen or so, stood on her tiptoes, her back to him as she reached for the top shelf. A long, dark braid snaked between her shoulder blades, and her arm seemed frozen above her, stopped short by his sudden presence.

"Oh, here. Let me get that for you," Jackson said, sliding a box of funny-looking pasta from the shelf. The heady smell of wildflowers filled his nostrils, and he dipped his head to look at the young woman in equal parts confusion and excitement. In the breath before she turned around, Jackson realized that he'd made a critical error based on the girl's petite stature.

She wasn't a teenager at all. She was a woman—*the* woman—that he hadn't been able to stop thinking about all week.

And she looked furious.

"Are you making fun of me?"

The question popped out of Carly's mouth and seemed to hang in midair for a ten-second eternity before Jackson blinked and took a step back.

"Am I . . . huh?"

Carly crossed her arms, undeterred by the way Jackson's white T-shirt hugged every hard plane of his chest like it was custom-sewn for his gorgeous muscles.

Okay, fine. So she was mostly undeterred. But he wasn't so good-looking that she'd let him pick on her.

"Are you making fun of me?" she repeated, taking the box of orecchiette from him and tossing it into her basket without looking. No way was she buying his who *me*? act. The minute he'd rounded the aisle and seen her standing there, he'd started whistling "You Make Me Feel Like a Natural Woman," for God's sake. Even with her back turned, she'd known that the crooked tune could only be coming from one set of lips.

Why was he so determined to make fun of her? And moreover, why did she care?

"I'm sorry. I thought . . ." Jackson paused to clear his throat, and Carly was surprised to notice that his cheeks had reddened. "You're kind of small, so I didn't, uh, recognize you. I wasn't trying to make fun of you for not being able to reach the shelf, though."

Carly's eyebrows winged up. "You think I'm talking about the shelf?"

"Well, yeah. What else would you be talking about?" Damn those crinkly blue eyes. They were like lonely-girl Kryptonite, for crying out loud.

"You were whistling," she accused, eyes narrowing. Come on. There was no way he just happened to have Aretha Franklin on the brain. It couldn't be a coincidence.

Jackson let out an unnervingly good-natured laugh. "Sorry, it's a habit. I don't even realize I'm doing it half the time. Was I whistling the theme song from *The Wizard of Oz* or something?"

Carly's lips parted, and she promptly wanted to kick herself at the laugh that escaped. "I'm not that short!" she protested, trying with all her strength to muster a straight face. The harder she tried, though, the more elusive her scowl became.

A smile poked at the corners of his mouth. "Right, right. I forgot. The PC term is *vertically challenged*, isn't it?"

"I can't help it if you're the Jolly Green Giant, you know." Carly was dangerously close to actual out-loud laughter, but she gathered up the makings of a stern frown. "What are you, like seven feet tall?"

"I'm six-four, which isn't really that tall. Unless you're . . . what? Five-foot-nothing with your shoes on?" Jackson squinted down at the top of her head as if judging the measurement.

Of course he had to be spot-on accurate. She straightened and kicked up her chin.

"You just have to make fun of me, don't you?" To Carly's surprise, Jackson's expression sobered.

"Sorry. I was just messing around, but I didn't mean anything by it. I honestly didn't even recognize you until you turned around."

Oh, God. The whole whistling thing *had* been a coincidence. Carly shifted her weight from one flip flop to the other, smoothing her palms over the front of her jeans.

"No problem, really." She examined her unpainted toenails and resisted the urge to wince at her egregious lack of a pedicure. "Well, enjoy the rest of your evening, then." Carly gave an awkward wave and ducked by him, grateful for the basket full of groceries that would keep her occupied for the remainder of the evening.

"Wait."

Carly's traitorous legs halted her movement, and the box of pasta made a maraca-like noise in her basket as she jerked to a stop.

"The restaurant's closed, right? For the night?"

She nodded. "Well, yeah. It's a holiday. Plus, I guess everyone around here watches the fireworks over the lake, so even if we were open, we wouldn't do any business. But we're open for brunch and dinner tomorrow, if you wanted to eat out."

Jackson's laugh echoed through the empty aisle. "No, no. I was just thinking that if you don't have to work, I could take you to a place where you can have one hell of a food experience. Since you're into that kind of thing."

Carly's curiosity perked to life and fired on all cylinders. "But all the restaurants around here are closed."

"That doesn't mean you can't get great food," he pointed out.

Carly's mind jumped to all the private parties that took place in New York when certain hot spots were technically closed. It made sense that that kind of thing happened in other places, she supposed. But Pine Mountain? It barely made the map.

"Okay." Her curiosity guided the word right past the

brain-to-mouth filter that would've surely censored it, and she sent a couple of surprised blinks in its wake. She swung her gaze down to her basket, fervently looking for an excuse hidden between the pasta and the cans of tomato paste. Damn it, there wasn't even anything perishable to blame a getaway on! She really shouldn't let herself get distracted like this. She needed to go home to the comfort of her kitchen and surround herself with the soothing familiarity of food.

Jackson smiled, revealing teeth as perfect and white as pieces of peppermint gum, and as her knees turned to liquid, her mouth refused to do anything other than smile right back.

"Great. Just let me grab a couple of things and we can go. I'll meet you at the checkout."

Chapter Eight

Jackson wheeled his cart full of five bags of ice and just as many gallons of vanilla ice cream to the front of the store, where Carly stood twisting the handle of her paper bag in one hand. She looked like she might be daydreaming, just staring down at the red flip flops barely poking out from beneath the faded cuffs of her jeans. Man, she had cute feet, with no obnoxious hot pink nail polish or funky toe rings to mess them up. Just smooth, tanned skin and bare, pretty toes. Nice.

The ping pong match between *hell yes* and *are you out of your goddamn mind* volleyed for round two in his head, but he stuffed it down. Just because he'd asked her to swing by the party with him and he was a little enamored with her toes didn't mean anything. There were probably seventy-five people in his mother's backyard. Adding Carly as one more was really no big deal, flip flops notwithstanding.

Except that the whisper was back, the weird one that told him to feed her. Which he knew was ridiculous, except that for some stupid reason, he *wanted* to feed her.

Weird.

"Wow. That looks . . . interesting." Carly's velvety voice

knocked him loose from his thoughts, and she eyed the items in his cart as if she thought he'd grabbed the wrong stuff.

"You like that? I'm going for maximum intrigue," he replied, working up a lazy half-smile.

"Either that or you're really hot," she said, immediately turning pink.

That blush was going to ruin him. Not that it would be such a bad way to go. Jackson reached into the cart to load the ice cream on the conveyor belt and decided to let Carly off the hook for the hot comment. For now, anyway.

"So have you eaten dinner yet?"

"Ice cream for dinner is a little unorthodox," Carly said as she followed him down the line. Joe bagged up the ice cream, and if Jackson didn't know any better, he'd swear the guy's smile seemed a little bigger than usual.

"Hey, don't knock it 'til you've tried it." Jackson paid for the groceries and murmured a goodnight to Joe, guiding the cart away from the line so Carly could make her way through behind him.

"Jackson, I'm a chef. I've had just about everything you can think of for dinner, including ice cream. It goes with the whole food-experience territory."

"If eating ice cream for dinner is part of your job description, I might be up for a career change," Jackson mused, stopping to pop the tailgate on his truck.

Carly lifted a brow. "Don't be too quick to sign on. Not everything tastes as good as ice cream."

Oh, come on. This was food they were talking about here. "Like?"

"Let's just say I'm not exactly a big fan of tripe. Or ostrich. But trying everything, even the things you don't necessarily like, is part of the deal."

Jackson stopped, midswing with the last bag of ice. "First of all, I'm not quite sure what tripe is, but the sound of it kind of scares me. Secondly, are you talking ostrich, like huge bird, doesn't fly, ostrich? Is that even legal?"

Carly laughed, her whole face softening with the gesture. "Yeah, unfortunately. I'm told it's an acquired taste." She paused, glancing at his truck. "So, I'll just follow you, then?" Carly nodded at the only other car in the parking lot, a Honda Civic Jackson assumed was hers.

"You're probably better off riding with me and I can bring you back here later. It's a little crowded where we're headed, and parking is definitely an issue."

He thought of the grassy off-roading he'd had to do in order to get here in the first place. It would be tough going for Carly's Honda to make it over all of that, especially since there were still people pulling up when Jackson had left. He'd have to maneuver around a bunch of cars just to get within half a mile of the house again.

"I've got to admit, you've piqued my curiosity." She stood unmoving by the back of his truck, and pinned him with a calculating look. "Where is it exactly that we're headed?"

"Isn't part of the food experience anticipating the unexpected?" Jackson slammed the tailgate, one corner of his mouth ticking up into a smile that was quickly becoming involuntary when Carly was around. Plus, teasing her was better than admitting out loud that he'd just invited her to a celebration of impending wedded bliss.

But as much as he enjoyed messing with her, he still didn't want to put her on the spot. "If you'd feel more comfortable following me, that's okay. We can figure something out once we get there."

"Wow. You really weren't kidding about that maximum intrigue thing," she murmured, tipping her head. "You're not going to give me any hints at all?"

"Where's the fun in that?" Jackson could practically hear the gears turning in her brain. Man, she was so serious!

Finally, Carly nodded. "Okay, then. I guess I'll just have to trust you. But you should probably know that I have three older brothers who would happily avenge me for so much as a broken nail."

"Something tells me you'd be just fine on your own, but you don't have to worry. Your manicure is safe with me."

A few minutes later, she was perched next to him in the passenger seat of the truck and *The Pennsylvania Building Code* had been summarily pushed aside. Golden sunlight shafted through the leaves, flickering through the truck in rushed, sparkly patterns as they moved over the main road.

"Do you mind if I open the windows instead of putting on the air?"

On an evening like this, it seemed almost criminal to breathe in artificially cooled air rather than the sweet smell of summer. Some girls were kind of picky about the windows, though, as if the possibility they might sweat a little or get their hair mussed up was public enemy number one.

"Not at all." Carly's expression became wistful, and she glanced out the window at the trees that had grown so tall, they met the trees on the other side to form an archway over the road. Jackson lowered both windows and was instantly rewarded with the earthy scent of the leaves overhead.

"Okay, so the suspense is killing me. What's tripe?"

A tiny smile lifted one corner of her mouth. "Are you sure you want to know?"

"Absolutely." He nodded. How bad could it be?

"It's the stomach lining of a cow."

That bad. Jackson could count on one hand the number of times he'd lost his appetite, but this definitely made the list. "Sorry I asked."

Carly shrugged as if tripe was as common as table salt. "To be honest, if you knew what went into some processed meats, you'd probably feel the same way about hot dogs." The breeze coming through the window loosened a strand of hair from her braid, and it danced around her face, framing her big, brown eyes. He resisted the urge to tuck it behind her ear, arching a brow at her instead.

"You cannot blaspheme against hot dogs on the Fourth of July. It's totally un-American." His mind zipped to the two loaded chili dogs he'd had for lunch. Please, God, he thought. Let some things stay sacred.

Carly chuckled. "Oh, I have nothing against a good hot dog. I'm just saying that sometimes ignorance is bliss."

Jackson thought about it for a second, watching the leaves *whoosh* by in an emerald green blur rinsed in the lowering sunlight. "Did you know what the tripe was when you ate it?"

"Not the first time, no. It was my first year of culinary school, and we were studying different ethnic cuisines. I had this classmate who swore his *nonna* made some of the best rustic Italian food on the planet." Carly shifted toward him, moving her hands to accentuate the story. "Coming from one hell of an Italian family myself, I knew I had to experience this phenomenon firsthand."

"Sounds innocent enough." Actually, it sounded like some damn fine dining as far as Jackson was concerned. He could put a hurt to some eggplant Parmesan.

"That's what I thought, too. The spread was unbelievable. I mean, this woman pulled out all the stops—antipasti, pasta fagioli, two different vegetarian dishes plus a veal Parm that was to die for. This lady was the real deal," Carly affirmed, grinning at the memory before she continued.

"Most of the dishes I recognized in one form or another, so I never thought to ask her what was in them. I mean, I've had veal Parmesan so many times, I'd know it in the dark." Despite the breeziness in her voice, Jackson sensed a whammy brewing in the story, and he leaned toward her, listening.

"So we got to this one dish, and I had no clue what it was,

but my friend was ripping at the seams to see what I thought of it. I tried to be polite, I really did, but I couldn't get into it, let alone place what the hell it was. I'll never forget the look on his face when he looked at me just as cheery as Disney World and said, 'Don't feel too bad. I can't stand tripe either.'"

Jackson tried to hide his laugh behind the guise of a coughing fit, but it was no use. It didn't help that she'd told the story with the funniest little facial expressions, like she was reliving the memory right then and there. Carly tipped her head at him, a nonverbal *oh, really*? and he knew he was busted.

"Sorry. That's classic, though. Did you kill him?"

She turned the tables and borrowed his crooked smile. "No, I hired him. Adrian's been my sous chef for five years. Can't imagine my kitchen without him."

"The tripe guy?" Couldn't say he saw that one coming. Huh.

"The tripe guy," she confirmed with a decisive nod. "We serve his *nonna*'s recipe for calamari at the restaurant. It's one of my top five favorite foods."

Jackson's jaw popped open in shock. "You eat octopus too?"

Carly's velvety laughter filled the truck, nearly cutting him off at the knees. "Squid. Totally different species. You should try it." She looked at him as if it were completely normal to consume tentacled sea creatures, and he looked back at her as if she'd lost her mind. It sounded like the kind of thing he used for bait, for Chrissake.

"Whatever you say, Ahab," Jackson replied with a wink. No way in hell was that going to happen.

"Moby Dick was a whale, not a squid." Carly's smile still played on her lips, even though her laughter had faded.

"Potato, potahto. I don't think I trust you around marine life in general."

He guided the truck off the main road, heading toward his mother's house. The seductive smell of slow-burning charcoal rushed in through the open windows from a mile out, and Jackson's stomach perked to life with a low rumble that translated to *I could eat.* Looked like all that tripe talk hadn't put a permanent damper on his appetite.

Carly shrugged. "You never know what you might end up liking. Just a little food for thought."

He suppressed a chuckle at the irony of her words, bumping along the gravel pathway that led to the drive for a minute before letting Carly in on the joke. "Funny you should mention food, because we're here."

"We're where?" She squinted through the windshield in confusion.

"Welcome to one of Pine Mountain's best food experiences." He pulled the truck to a stop in the grassy side yard and turned his hand palm-up in a small flourish.

"But this can't be right. This is someone's house," Carly said, as if he'd surely made a mistake. "Are you even invited?"

Laughter welled up in his chest, and he jerked his head toward the festivities. "Let's just say I doubt we'll get kicked out. Come on."

Carly took a breath and tried as hard as she could to erase the bewilderment from her expression. It turned out to be an exercise in futility.

"You okay?" Jackson's door closed with a *bang,* and they circled around opposite sides of his truck to meet at the tailgate.

"Yeah, I just . . . after you said it would be crowded, I assumed we were headed to a local hangout or something. You know, a public place." She eyed the cars and trucks lining both sides of the narrow gravel driveway leading up to the house, realizing with a tiny smile that Jackson had actually been spot-on about the parking. Her Honda would've been toast on the slope of the grassy yard where they'd parked, and it was the only open space as far as she could see.

"You know what they say about making assumptions," he tsked with a wink, sliding the ice-filled cooler from his truck in an easy, one-armed movement that would've sent Carly on her ass even if she'd used both arms and brought a friend for help.

Refusing to bite even though every sarcastic fiber in her being screamed in protest, Carly replied, "So I take it this is a Fourth of July party." She pointed to the festive red, white, and blue buntings fluttering from the porch railings. The smoky, hypnotic scent of a charcoal grill going full-bore sent her straight into mouth-watering mode, and the deep draw of fragrant air kicked her appetite into gear.

"Sort of." Jackson bent down to unearth the two bags holding the ice cream from inside the cooler, and she saw his shoulders draw up with a hitch.

Oho, smartass-boy. Not so fast.

"Sort of?" she repeated, scooping up the bags while he replaced the lid with a muffled *thunk*.

"It's a family get-together." He led the way past the front of the house with the cooler in tow. Little beads of firelight glowed from within the wrought iron lanterns lining the brick walkway, casting the hushed beginnings of shadows at their feet. The buzz of voices and occasional bursts of laughter carried over the breeze from the backyard, and a group of boys thundered past them toward the grassy front lawn, Frisbees in hand. Something loosened in Carly's gut, smoothing over her with a familiar sweetness.

"Cousins or nephews?" She gestured to the boys, whose hooting and hollering carried over the air like a carefree blanket.

Jackson's grin returned. "Both. The younger one is my nephew, but the older two are my cousin's sons."

Carly's heart tugged at her ribs. "I have six."

"Sons?" Jackson lifted his brow, rounding the side of the house.

"Nephews," she emphasized, not giving him the satisfaction of putting her on the spot. "And four nieces."

"Hey, me too. On the nieces, anyway. You've got me beat in the nephews department," Jackson replied, then paused. "So it doesn't make you uncomfortable to come to a big family gathering?"

"I'm the youngest of four kids, Jackson, and I have ten immediate cousins. My family is massive. I think I'll be fine. Although you could've warned me." It felt pretty good to put the shoe on the other foot and tease him for a change, and she gave him a bump with her hip for good measure.

"It would've wrecked the intrigue, which is why you came." He nudged her right back.

"You lured me with food," she corrected. "That's why I came."

"Okay, okay. Let's get this cold stuff where it needs to go and I'll make good on my promise. Come on."

As soon as the backyard was in full view, Carly had to resist the urge to stop and stare. Paper lanterns peppered the edges of a huge, white tent canopy, soft light diffusing from the thin, white globes and mixing with the growing dusk. Beneath the tent, a small crowd of people milled around, filling their plates to the brim. Even more guests sat around small wooden picnic tables with little candles in brightly colored jars in the center. The thick, lemony scent of citronella hung in the air, mixing in with the smoky perfume of the grill to form a flawless suggestion of summertime.

A cluster of men stood, laughing and drinking from frost-covered bottles of beer at the far end of the yard, and Carly squinted at the familiar objects they were tossing toward a square patch of sand just shy of the tree line.

"Are those horseshoes?" A metallic clang resonated across the yard, followed by an enthusiastic cheer that punctuated the unspoken answer to her question.

Jackson glanced over his shoulder, which was still as wide as a doorframe and oh-so muscled beneath the white cotton of his T-shirt. "You've never played horseshoes?"

"The closest thing I had to a yard was my grandmother's garden, which is a six-by-six plot of dirt in Brooklyn, surrounded by bricks and buildings."

Okay, fine. So two of her three brothers had moved to the New York suburbs with their families years ago, and both had beautiful yards with green grass and fences. But Carly's space had always been in the city, either in the duplex where she grew up or in the brownstone she'd hung a FOR SALE sign on the morning she'd left for Pine Mountain. Sadness swirled in her belly, but she mashed it down just in time to catch Jackson watching her with curiosity.

"What did she grow?"

"Huh?" Carly blinked, and the images of her grandmother's garden faded as Jackson reached for the bags in her hand.

"Your grandmother. What did she grow in her garden?" The edges of Jackson's callused fingers brushed hers, streaking heat to the base of her spine, and she let go of the handles even though she didn't want to.

"Oh, um. Some flowers—Echinacea, cornflowers, star lilies. Mostly herbs and vegetables though. We ate just about everything that came out of that garden, like it or not."

Jackson flagged down a young girl with a blond ponytail and coltish, long legs on the cusp of adolescence. "Hey, Sadie. Can you bring these into the house and put them in Aunt Cath's freezer for me? Thanks, sweetheart." He chucked the girl's chin, which brought out a giggle, and he waved to her before turning his attention back to Carly. "Got something you might want to check out."

Carly's brow drew inward. "Okay." She waited while Jackson situated the cooler next to a bucket full of cheerily colored soda cans, but he didn't elaborate. It figured he was going to make her work for it. Broad shoulders notwithstanding, he could be downright frustrating. Finally, she let her straightforward nature have its way with her vocal cords. "What is it?"

"You're a total go-getter, aren't you? Always want to be doing something," Jackson said, and in spite of his laid-back smile, she flushed.

"Sorry." Being one of the only women in a male-dominated family and an even more male-dominated career, Carly's tenacity was programmed into her DNA. While her take-no-prisoners attitude earned her more respect than heartache in the kitchen, it tended to bite her in the ass in the one on one arena.

"You really should stop doing that." Jackson straightened, and his eyes glinted in the ambient light flickering out from the candles.

"I said I was sorry," she grumbled, pinkening further. Okay, so she was a little brash. Did he have to keep pointing it out like that?

"I meant you should stop apologizing, not that I don't like how you are." He gestured toward the far side of the yard, to a thicket on the opposite side of the area from the men playing horseshoes. "My mother plants a lot of vegetables herself. Her garden's just behind that cluster of crepe myrtles, if you want to have a look. I'm sure she wouldn't mind."

Carly blinked. "Oh. Sure."

Jackson guided her around the crowd on the outskirts of the vast yard until they'd reached a dirt path winding through a thick cluster of trees covered in purple and white blooms. The woody branches hung so low over the path that Jackson had to duck significantly to get by a few of them, and after a handful of steps, they were completely shielded from the view of the crowd.

"How come the garden is so far away from the house?" Carly asked, tipping her head at the clearing about thirty feet in front of them. The cool, musky scent of crepe myrtle blooms filled her nose, making her almost dizzy with their sweetness.

"My mother's flower beds are mostly in the yard, close to the house. She swears that this"—he paused to point at the waning daylight poking through at the end of the short trail—"had the best soil for growing, though, so she put the big garden out here. Personally, I think it was because she needed a little refuge every now and then from raising four crazy children."

Carly grinned. Boy could her mother relate to that. She was convinced that at least some of those times her *mama* retreated to do laundry in the quiet of the basement, there wasn't a whole lot that needed washing. "How about your dad?" she asked, curiosity growing. "Did he hide out here, too?"

Jackson stopped short on the path so suddenly that Carly had to change course to avoid crashing into him. She stumbled, and her balance threatened to take a vacation before Jackson reached out and wrapped his fingers around the bare skin of her upper arms.

"I don't have a father."

The monotone of his voice caught her completely by surprise, and she stared at him, eyes wide. "Oh, God. Did he pass away? I'm so sorry—"

"No." The word escaped through Jackson's teeth, his jaw cranked shut.

"Then I don't understand."

Exasperation flickered over Jackson's features, but his

tone remained hollow. "What's not to understand? I don't have a father."

Deep in her gut, Carly felt an old ache prickle to life on an even older memory, one that was so faded around the edges that it was barely more than a snapshot in her mind. "But everyone has a father."

A low, needful current of energy ran between them, and Jackson dropped his gaze to where his palms wrapped around her arms, fingers firmly closed around her soft skin. By the time he lifted the glance to meet hers, his crinkly blue eyes were bottomless and utterly flat.

"Not me."

Chapter Nine

Shut up, big man. Shut up right fucking now.

Seeing as how Jackson's inner voice was rarely anything other than happy-go-lucky, the sudden nasty streak was a red flag that this conversation needed to stop, pronto. Christ, he'd been an idiot to open his mouth in the first place.

"The garden's right through here." He dropped Carly's arms and ducked through the last of the tree branches, mere steps away from the open air of the garden. Even though he knew it was rude, he moved ahead without waiting for her. Guilt pricked at him, palpable on his skin, but he continued to walk away.

"Jackson, wait."

He took a step, and then another. No way was he going to talk about this. He didn't care how sexy Carly's laugh was, or how pretty she looked when he teased her into blushing. She was out of her mind if she thought he was going to go the Dr. Phil, get-in-touch-with-your-feelings, Kumbaya route over his daddy issues. Especially since the issues were *non*issues. And he barely even knew her, for Pete's sake!

"Hey!" Her voice unloaded like a firecracker, which—given the date—would've been ironic enough to make

Jackson laugh if he hadn't been so stunned. Rooted to his spot, all he could do was turn halfway around and gape at her. Carly's eyes flashed, liquid bronze and pissed off, but her words were steady and quiet.

"Look, you don't seem to like apologies much, so I'm not going to make any. Clearly, you don't want to talk about your father, which is fine by me." He didn't see her so much as feel the heat of her as she made her way toward him on the path. When he turned to face her fully, there were only a scant couple of inches separating their bodies.

"So this can go one of two ways. Either we can forget it and still have a good time, or you can drive me back to my car in the world's most awkward silence. It's up to you, but quite frankly, I'm hoping we can forget it."

"You are?" he blurted, too surprised by her moxie to say anything else.

"Yes. I'd like to see your mother's garden, and plus, I'm hungry." Carly's eyes flicked upward, meeting his with a no-nonsense stare. "So is that okay, or do you want to just call it a night?" Her voice lifted with just the smallest hint of gentleness, but her gaze didn't budge.

Good *God* she was hot.

"No, I . . ." Jackson stopped and drew in a breath to clear his head. The air smelled like wildflowers, heady and fresh, although he'd bet even money that it had nothing to do with the adjacent garden. The last thing he'd been expecting was for her to get all rational about the whole thing. Weren't women supposed to try to get you to talk about your feelings and stuff? He blew the breath out in a slow exhale.

"I'm really sorry. I wasn't expecting you to bring up the subject, and it threw me for a bit of a loop. That still doesn't excuse the fact that I acted like a jerk. Truce?"

"It doesn't seem very fair that you get to apologize when I don't, you know."

He cracked a smile, testing the waters. All of this serious

stuff was giving him the sweats. "Okay. I'm not sorry for being an ass."

She smiled right back, her full lips parting just enough to make Jackson swallow hard.

"I accept your not-an-apology."

And even though he couldn't believe it, that was that. Carly slipped around him on the path, her flip flops sounding out a muted *snick-snick* against the dirt as she headed toward the warm grass at the clearing's edge. It only took him two strides to catch up to her, and there was just enough room for them to walk side by side, although he took up twice as much space as she did. Try as he might, there was no way he could help staring at her a little bit.

The edges of her lips twitched upward into the faintest hint of amusement. "What?" Either her observation skills bordered on the side of freakishly good or his stare was just that obvious. He lowered his eyes, staring at the scuff marks on his Red Wings to avoid coming off like a total weirdo.

"You're not like most women, that's all."

Ouch. What was he, channeling his inner Fabio or something? That had come out sounding like the world's worst pickup line. Jackson opened his mouth to backpedal, but Carly was too quick on the draw.

"Wow," she breathed, stopping at the edge of the garden.

He nodded. He really did deserve to be called out on that one. "Okay, in my head that wasn't quite so cheesy. What I meant was—"

"Not you," Carly laughed. "Although you're right. It was pretty bad. I meant wow, this garden is unbelievable," she said, scanning the large rectangular plot with awe.

Saved by the bell peppers. Jackson swore on the spot that he would never grumble about helping his mother in the garden for the rest of his natural born life.

"Yeah, it is really pretty, isn't it?" Even though he'd seen the garden no less than a million times—hell, he had tilled two of the three garden beds himself just after puberty—the sight of it in full bloom always made him grin.

Three separate rectangular beds graced the open space of the garden area, all slightly raised and surrounded by rough-hewn, wood beam borders. Strips of dark grass divided the space like lush, green carpet runners, extending around the beds in neatly trimmed paths. The area was walled in on two sides by a stretch of thick boxwoods that easily reached Jackson's chest, their imposing height softened by the varie-gated celadon and cream leaves of the hostas springing up from the ground like botanical fountains before them. Dense vines and open-faced blooms of gently climbing clematis snaked over the length of fence that Jackson and Dylan had put up along the long edge of the garden opposite where he and Carly stood, a Mother's Day present from five years ago.

"Oh, you have watermelons!" Carly leaned forward to peek at the far edge of the first bed. "We never had enough room for anything like that. And these tomatoes are gor-geous. There must be six different varieties out here," she crowed, eyes glittering.

"Seven. My mother got hooked on different kinds— heirlooms, stuff like that—one year when I was in high school, and just can't seem to resist planting them. Not that I'm complaining, because I could eat fried green tomatoes all day long," Jackson replied, starting to amble down the swath of grass separating the first two beds.

Carly wandered after him, taking it all in. "Yeah, we always had a couple different varieties too. Nothing like this, though. God, I wish I could get my hands on a place like this for the restaurant." She paused midstride, one foot halfway lifted off the grass. "Are those cherry tomatoes *purple?*"

"Ah, black cherries. They're my favorite, although she grows the Cherokee purples too."

"Now those I've seen before." Carly pointed to the cage with fat, plentiful Cherokee purple heirloom tomatoes in various stages of readiness, some still celery-green, others already blooming into their color like a summer sunset. "And most of these others, too. But I have to admit, these cherry tomatoes are a bit of a mystery to me."

He leaned in and twisted a few of the much smaller black cherry tomatoes from their sturdy vines, the dark, miniature globes still warm from the sun. Although he'd eaten them countless times, the flavors still burst on his tongue like they'd never been there before, and he popped the tomatoes into his mouth one by one to savor the rich sweetness in each bite.

"Do you want to try some?" He motioned toward the vines that hung on like strong, velvety fingers, dangling the jewel-like tomatoes from the leafy crowns.

Despite the whole kid-in-a-candy-store vibe she had going on, Carly hesitated. "I wouldn't want to impose." She looked at the tomatoes—the whole garden, really—with a strange kind of reverence, and something rippled low in his gut, the tiny whisper that begged him to take note even though his brain insisted the whole thing was totally off the wall.

Feed her, it said.

"Once, maybe ten years ago, I came down the path to haul away a bunch of branches that had fallen in a nasty rain storm, and after I was done, I stopped to check on the garden. I meant to take a quick look for any damage and head back up to the house, but these little buggers just kind of called out to me, you know? Before I knew it, I'd eaten every last one of them, right off the vine." Jackson laughed softly. He had no clue what made him think of it, but the memory unfurled in his mind like table linens fresh off the line, as if it were only hours old rather than an entire decade ago.

Carly's laugh was spun sugar, sweet and indulgently good. "Jackson, there have to be fifty or sixty cherry toma-toes between these two plants," she said, as if she'd heard wrong. "You ate all of them?"

"Yeah, my mother couldn't quite believe it either. Until I

walked around holding my stomach for the rest of the day, groaning like an idiot."

"Too much of a good thing," she affirmed, and it wasn't a question. "Was she mad?"

"Nah. This garden produces way more than my ma can eat, so she ends up sharing most of it anyway. Even the neighbors get more than they can eat, so I don't think she'd really mind if you wanted to try a handful."

Carly eyed the plant, running her fingers along the edges of the wiry vines. Her hands were small, but far from delicate, and a thin, white scar slashed its way across her left index finger. Jackson frowned at the faded line, wondering how she'd gotten it.

"Okay then. But I promise not to pick the entire plant clean," Carly said with a twist of her lips, her movements careful and deliberate as she freed a small handful of tomatoes from the vines.

"Once you taste them, you might change your tune, but suit yourself."

With her left palm cupped beneath the tiny mountain of purplish-red fruit, she plucked one from the pile, rolling it between the fingers of her right hand before taking a bite.

"Oh. *Oh*," Carly mumbled, immediately popping another tomato into her mouth. "God, that's good." She squeezed her eyes shut, as though she was trying to commit the flavors to memory. The tiny crease in her forehead that usually rested just between her brows smoothed out, and she released a barely-there sigh that Jackson was sure she hadn't been aware of. Of course he heard it loud and clear, and it shot through him with swift intention. Destination: the center of his lap.

Shit. Shitcrap*shit*! How was he supposed to manage a casual conversation with her now that he had the anatomical equivalent of the goddamn Empire State Building in his pants? Jackson winced and adjusted his jeans, thankful that—for the moment at least—Carly's eyes were still closed. He shifted behind her on the premise of picking a few more cherry tomatoes, fervently praying for a thought that would distract him from the sensual thrill on her face.

"These are unbelievable," Carly murmured, still chewing. "I must've hit twenty different farmer's markets when I planned the menu at La Dolce Vita. I can't believe I've never seen them before. They must be pretty unusual. Either that or difficult to grow."

Crap! She was turning around to look at him, and he needed to lose this hard-on, quick. Jackson hauled in a breath and sent one last *down, boy* message to his metaphorical junkyard dog. Food, food. Right! Get her to focus on the food.

"So, uh, how would you prepare them? You know, if you were going to put them in a dish."

The distraction worked. Carly's eyes went soft, and she looked dreamily at the two remaining tomatoes in her hand. "Well, they're kind of sweet, so I'd want something to offset that, but not overwhelm it. They're complex enough to stand up to arugula in a salad, with some grilled balsamic chicken for the protein. Then I'd add some cucumber to cool it down and make it taste like summer, a little simple vinaigrette to keep it fresh and let the flavors sing, and I'd have myself a dinner salad. Simple, but still hearty. Just like the tomatoes."

Mercifully, the distraction went both ways, and most of the *I want that* sensation migrated from Jackson's pants to his stomach. "Wow. I'm not usually a salad guy, but that sounds pretty good. You just made that up after eating them once, huh?"

Jackson had only eaten these tomatoes out of hand, and while putting them in a salad made sense, the way she'd connected all the flavors to make the pieces form a whole just blew his mind. Not to mention leaving him hungry.

"Well, I'd have to find the tomatoes first, but it's promising that your mother can grow them locally. I might be able to get a line on them from one of the growers in Riverside. Their farmer's market is pretty big. Of course, then I'd have to play with everything to make sure it worked."

Carly popped the last two tomatoes in her mouth before continuing. "But it'd be fun. The flavors are great. Perfect for the season." Her stomach sounded off with an echoing rumble as if to agree, and the ensuing laugh that spilled out of her made Jackson close the distance between them as if his feet were on auto-pilot.

"Are you hungry?" Looked like his arousal wasn't going to let go of him quite yet. In the back of his mind, Jackson knew that this should matter. But everywhere else, it simply didn't.

"A little." Carly lifted her chin to look him straight in the eye, even though he'd bent toward her enough to be definitely suggestive. Her teeth grazed her lower lip in a tiny nibble that did nothing to steady him.

"I promised to feed you," he said, unmoving. Funny how it sounded familiar even though he was sure he'd never said it to her before.

Feed her.

"Uh-huh." But rather than break eye contact or move, Carly kept her face tilted up despite the fact that their mouths were close enough for him to feel the heated exhale shuddering from her body.

Jackson bent to erase the space between them just as she pressed up on her tiptoes to kiss him, a mad rush of urgency and wildflowers, and all thought went out the window. There was no hesitant tenderness, no holding back in this kiss, nothing but heat and raw desire in the way her lips opened and her tongue twined with his. Sparks danced under his skin as he answered the kiss, cradling the back of her head and burying his fingers where her braid met the cool, sweet skin of her neck.

He broke away from Carly's mouth to trail kisses across the curve of her jaw, pausing just under her ear. The taste of her, provocative and unlike anything he'd ever experienced, exploded on his tongue, and it caught him like a one-two punch.

"God, that's good." All it took was the echo of the words she'd spoken mere minutes before to light Jackson's body with need. He returned to her mouth, intending to kiss her again, but he found her bottom lip firmly ensconced between her teeth. Carly released it with a throaty sigh, squeezing her arms around his shoulders with strength that both shocked him and turned him way the hell on.

Jackson pressed a kiss to the corner of her mouth. "Don't."

"Don't what?" She pushed her hot palms against his chest as she drew back to look at him. Uncertainty colored her features, but Jackson was quick to reassure her.

"I like it when you talk to me. Don't hold back." He dipped his face to hers again, running his teeth ever so gently across her bottom lip to coax her mouth open. After capturing her pleasured gasp, he moved down the column of her neck, nibbling, kissing, tasting.

It wasn't going to be enough.

As if she could read his mind, Carly whispered, "Again. Kiss me again."

With her words barely out in the open, Jackson's instincts took over. His arms shot around the back of her ribcage, unstopping as his palms skimmed her hips, then spread around the back of her jeans. With a swift yank—did he pull, or did she jump? Jackson lifted her off the ground, holding her lithe body against his chest. She locked her legs around his waist, angling her hips against his with agonizing sweetness, and his knees almost buckled from how good the friction felt.

"Well, if you insist," he said, trying to hold onto what little control he had left. Part of him screamed to slow down, to take his time and savor the slide of the denim between them in all the right places, the fall of her hair on his hands as he cupped the back of her neck then moved his hands lower over her body. But a deeper-seated part of him broke free, demanding and pulsing with heat.

Gripping her hips with tight fists, Jackson moved to the small shed at the back corner by the fence line. No way would they both fit with all the tools crammed inside, so Jackson maneuvered Carly up against the rear outside wall of the structure, hiding them from sight. At least it would provide cover from anyone who might stumble through the garden, and he used his hips as leverage to keep the seam of her body crushed against his with delicious, white-hot pressure.

"Jackson." Carly's voice ripped through him, and his erection strained against the juncture of her thighs as she trailed greedy kisses below his ear. Propelled by hot urgency, he thrust against her, pushing her back into the shed even harder and cupping his hands beneath her bottom to hold her up.

She tugged his shirt upward from the waistband of his jeans in response, and suddenly nothing stood between her touch and his body except for a whole lot of bad intentions. He thrust against her again, without thinking, holding her fast against the wall. Christ, he'd never wanted anyone so much, right *now*, and every last part of him hummed with its own altered gravity. He reached around Carly's arms to pull her closer still, but something wet and sticky snagged his attention just enough to make him look . . .

His hand was smeared with blood, and it wasn't his.

"Jesus!" Jackson hissed, and his heated thoughts clattered to a stop. He lowered her with quick efficiency, his heart slamming in his chest for an entirely different reason than just a moment before. "Carly, you're bleeding."

Holy hell, what had he *done*?

"What?" She staggered as if surprised to have her feet beneath her again, her expression wrapped in startled confusion for a second before his words seemed to sink in. "No I'm not, I'm . . . oh. Ow."

Jackson blanched at the crimson smear trailing down her right arm, and he swallowed hard before capturing her wrist with a gentle turn to get a better look. Carly twisted to stare at the angry four-inch scratch on the back of her upper arm, blinking a few times before she swiped at it with her other hand and winced. "I guess I scratched it against the shed."

Icy tendrils spread out in Jackson's chest. Had he seriously pinned her against the shed that hard? What the hell had he been thinking?

Well the answer to that one was a no-brainer. He hadn't been thinking at all. She was *bleeding*, for Chrissake. All because he'd lost control of himself.

"That's more than a scratch. We need to get it cleaned up." Jackson's voice was pure gravel in his throat, and he forced himself to take a step back from her. It wasn't lost on him that even in the summer air, he felt noticeably cooler without her near, but he couldn't risk being close enough to catch the heady scent of flowers in her hair, or worse yet, touching her again.

"It's nothing. It doesn't even really hurt," Carly protested, the crease between her brows set in a deep V.

"Still. It could get infected." Damn it. "I shouldn't . . ." Jackson stopped and raked a hand over his crew cut, mashing down on the sensation threatening to rise from his gut and take over. "I shouldn't have done that."

In the decade and a half since Jackson had left puberty in the rearview mirror, he'd never once lost control with a woman. In fact, he'd made it a point to stay detached for this very reason. It was dangerous, and he wouldn't put himself—or anybody else, for that matter—in a position to be hurt.

Jackson pressed his lips together hard enough to make them smart. Even with the best of intentions, he'd managed to blow right past the too-far line with Carly.

And it wasn't the first time he'd ignored reason with her, either.

"That's twice now that you've kissed me and called it a mistake." Carly's expression was blank, her smoldering heat dimmed down to nothing in the span of a breath.

He started. "What?"

"Last week, you apologized for kissing me, and now again you're saying you shouldn't have done it. What else am I supposed to think, other than you're sorry you did it?"

Jackson stared at her. "I didn't mean that kissing you was a mistake. I just shouldn't have let it get, you know. Out of hand."

"Oh." The reply came so softly that he almost missed it. Carly digested his words, and her lashes cast dusky shadows over her cheeks when she looked up at him a minute later. "It *was* pretty out of hand, wasn't it?" The smallest hint of movement flitted over her lips, lifting the corners of her lush mouth.

Wait a second . . .

"Are you making fun of me?" he asked, incredulous. Didn't she realize what he'd done?

"You have to admit, you kind of set the precedent there." Carly shrugged, but there was no mistaking the gleam in her eyes. "Plus, you look like somebody ran over your dog. Honestly, Jackson. You didn't hurt me on purpose."

"No," Jackson replied slowly. "I didn't." At least that much was true.

But it didn't change the fact that it had happened anyway. He'd hurt her without meaning to, all because he couldn't control himself.

"You're being an awfully good sport about it," Jackson said, finally feeling his pulse drum down a notch. It really *had* been an accident, albeit an unacceptable one. Now he just needed to get her cleaned up. It would put more distance between them, at least.

"You sound disappointed. Truth be told, I'm not really the kind of girl who freaks out at a little bit of blood."

He guided her briskly around the side of the shed, back toward the path. "Not even your own?"

"Obviously not." They walked in silence for a few steps before she tacked on, "Seriously, though, my arm is fine."

"You'll just have to humor me on this one. I insist." Jackson primed himself for an argument. He'd only known her for a week and a half, but it was plain that she was tough as gutter spikes.

"Okay. If it makes you feel better, then by all means, patch me up. But after that, I'm getting what I came for."

His eyes widened, and he stumbled in the thick grass. "You are?" Oh, hell. He could barely resist her the first time. No way was he going to be able to do it again.

Carly slowed next to him. "Yeah. Food experience, remember? I'm starved."

Smooth. Real smooth. Of course she meant the food. "Right, right, absolutely." Jackson led the way back through the crepe myrtles. As they passed by the food-laden tables under the tent, it was impossible not to catch the sheer longing on Carly's face, and the urge to feed her returned. Well, maybe they could stop and grab the world's quickest slice of apple pie. After all, it was the Fourth of July. Plus, if he got her something to eat, maybe his inner voice would shut up and he could figure out a graceful—and quick—way to take her home before she got hurt again.

Jackson turned to ask Carly if she wanted a to-go plate on their way to the house, but before he could get more than a word past his lips, he was interrupted by a very familiar, very female voice.

Chapter Ten

"Chef di Matisse?"

It took Carly a full minute to recognize the voice behind her as belonging to Bellamy Blake. Instinctively, Carly swept a hand over her braid, only to discover it was way more disheveled mess than tidy plait.

"Hi, Bellamy." Carly patted a few chunks of hair into place at the nape of her neck, and the movement revealed a crepe myrtle bloom tangled by her ear. She fumbled to dislodge it, flinging the tiny purple flower behind her back as she pasted a smile on her face. Out of the corner of her eye, Carly caught Jackson's unnervingly sexy smile at the gesture, his crinkly sky-blue eyes so warm they were almost liquid.

Okay, maybe the friends-with-benefits thing wasn't such a bad idea, after all. Clearly, the heat between her and Jackson was strong enough to put most chemistry experiments to shame. The kiss they'd shared against the shed was living proof of that. How complicated could a little mutually beneficial sex amongst friends be, anyway?

Jackson reached out and plucked another paper-thin blossom from her hair, his fingers brushing against her skin as he dropped it into her palm.

Screw complicated. She was on fire for this guy.

"Oh my God, what are you doing here?" Even in the dusk of the postsunset sky, Bellamy's shock was plain.

A laugh snuck up on Carly, and she couldn't keep it under wraps. "I know this might surprise you, but I do actually get out of the restaurant from time to time."

Although Bellamy was pretty tough in the kitchen and didn't really seem like the blushing type, her cheeks flushed at Carly's teasing.

"Oh, no, no, I just meant . . ." Bellamy paused. "I didn't know you knew Jackson, that's all," she finished, giving Jackson a look that all but yelled *ahem!*

"Well, we only met, ah, recently." Carly shot a quick glance at Jackson and did a little cheek-flushing of her own, praying that the cover of dusk kept anyone from noticing. She wasn't exactly the blushing type, either, but the memory of exactly how they'd met made Carly glad he hadn't mentioned it.

"Last week," Jackson confirmed, easing into a blazingly enticing half-grin.

Carly managed to steady her expression. She could handle grace under pressure in the most weeded of kitchens, for God's sake. Surely she could handle one teensy smile from the guy without coming undone right there in front of God and everybody. Her blood pulsed through her warmly, her girly parts ready to pick a fight with her rational brain. "I ran into Jackson at the grocery store a little while ago, and he invited me to come out for something to eat. We met last week when he rebuilt my deck."

A dark-haired guy with what looked like permanent five o'clock shadow stood next to Bellamy, and Carly heard a flash of Jackson's voice from last week in her kitchen, talking about his buddy, Bellamy's boyfriend.

"*You* were the deck rebuild last week?" Five O'clock Shadow's brow popped in surprise.

Carly's smile faded into confusion, and after a breath, she realized Jackson's grin had slipped, too.

"Yeah," she replied, drawing the word out slowly, like a question. "A tree fell on it in that nasty storm." Carly had the impression that Jackson had built hundreds of decks. He sure looked at ease swinging a hammer at the bungalow, and the results were incredible. So why was that a big deal? Unless . . . oh, crap. Jackson might not have told Bellamy about their little tête a tête, but that didn't mean he'd been equally tight-lipped with his buddy.

Jackson stepped in, all-American smile dialed up to the most laid-back setting. "Carly, this is Shane Griffin. I told him about the job I was doing out at your place last week. You know, how the tree came really close to hitting the house and how I had to jackhammer the posts out. I must've forgotten to mention the connection, with you being Bellamy's boss and all." A tiny hint of something odd flickered in Jackson's glance as his eyes passed over Shane's, but it was gone so fast, Carly couldn't even be sure she'd seen it, much less identify what it had been.

"Yeah, it must've slipped your mind," Shane said, a faint glimmer lingering in his expression before he broke into a natural smile. "Well, it's nice to meet you, Carly." His warm handshake made her relax and she broke into a smile.

"You, too." Despite her earlier protests to the contrary, the back of Carly's arm squalled in pain at being used for a meet-and-greet. It was so ironic that the little cuts always managed to hurt the worst.

As if Jackson could read her mind, he gestured to the limb in question. "I was just taking Carly back up to the house. She, uh, scratched her arm pretty badly." His eyes skimmed over her with that ultraserious look again, and even though she was tempted to make a face, she held back. It wasn't like she'd severed the damned thing, but whatever.

The hero complex was one of those guy things she'd never understand, although she supposed it could be worse.

If she hadn't gotten the cut, she might be undressed in the great outdoors right now, for example.

"Ouch." Bellamy eyed the scratch. "How'd you manage that?"

Gooooooood question. "Oh! I, um . . ." The more Carly scrambled, the more vivid the recollection of actual events became in her mind, until the kiss was all but screaming through her again.

"Pricker bush," Jackson intervened, smooth as freshly rolled pie crust.

Carly blinked, lost in the wake of his quick thinking, and the look that flashed between them hung on for just a fraction too long. "Yup. A big one."

"You know, you should get Autumn to check that out. It looks kind of nasty," Bellamy ventured, and Jackson's expression brightened.

This couldn't be good.

"You know what, that's a great idea. My sister Autumn is a nurse." He lifted his head to scan the crowd, which wasn't difficult since he was a good four inches taller than pretty much everybody in the surrounding area. "Ah. There she is. Hey, Autumn! C'mere," Jackson called out, beckoning to a pretty blonde sitting at a nearby picnic table. The woman hopped up and started to weave through the crowd.

"Honestly, it's fine. It barely even hurts," Carly lied. In truth, the stupid thing stung like nothing else, but since her arm was still attached, making a big deal out of it seemed silly.

"I'm not taking *no* for an answer, remember? Plus, the faster you get that cut cleaned up, the faster we can eat. Personally, I'm dying for some apple pie. That is, if there's any left." Jackson glowered jokingly at Shane, who released a shrug and smirk combination that suggested their friendship ran deep.

"You snooze, you lose, my friend. Sadie never even made it to the freezer with that ice cream."

"Oh, please. I made six pies. There's plenty left." But Bellamy's scolding couldn't hide the proud little smile tugging at her lips.

Carly's mouth watered at the thought of food. That bowl of minestrone she'd had at the end of the lunch shift might as well have been a week ago.

"Hey, little brother. What's up?" The pretty blonde sauntered over, and Carly was all but smacked in the face with the family resemblance.

"I need you in a professional capacity for a sec."

"You're not going to ask me to tell that story about the guy who swallowed all those goldfish again, are you? It gets kind of old after the hundredth time."

Carly bit back a sound between a snicker and a shudder. She'd seen and eaten a lot of things, but she had to draw the line at live domestic marine life.

"Actually, I need you to take a look at my friend Carly's cut." He moved close enough so that she could smell the crisp, masculine scent of his skin, like just-cut timber. It was a damn good thing Jackson's sister wouldn't be taking Carly's pulse, because she had a funny feeling that zing in her veins wasn't in the normal resting range. Especially when Jackson cradled Carly's arm as if it were a rare artifact, wincing as if the cut was on his own arm instead of hers.

"Oh, sure." Autumn turned toward Carly, her smile becoming a notch more serious. "Whoa, that's a whopper." Her forehead creased into a V as she squinted over the cut.

"It's really not a big deal," Carly said. The words might as well have been tattooed on her forehead, she'd uttered them so often in the last hour.

"Mmm, I'm gonna beg to differ with you on this one."

Autumn cupped Carly's elbow, examining the cut closely. "Shane, be a doll and run up to the house for Mom's first aid kit, would you? There are some leftover steri strips in there from when Tucker took that dive out of the tire swing last fall."

Carly's gut squeezed. "I didn't even feel it happen."

Autumn patted her shoulder. "Don't worry, the steri strips are just a precaution. If I thought you needed stitches, I'd send you off to the ER. Although you'll need a tetanus shot ASAP if you did this out here."

Jackson stiffened next to her, and Carly let out an internal groan. That was something she hadn't thought of. As much as she glossed over the various cuts she garnered along the way in the kitchen, the last thing she wanted to deal with was a big-deal infection from a cut she got from being outside. "Okay," she agreed.

Autumn examined the cut for another minute before Shane returned with the first aid kit, and while she turned to rummage for supplies, Jackson dropped his gaze to Carly's.

"I feel really bad about this," he said so only she could hear him, and she noticed the lines around his eyes that normally formed creases of laughter had gone deep with seriousness.

"It was an accident." Carly's answer was hushed but firm. He opened his mouth to argue, but then Autumn swung her attention back to Carly's arm, and the words just disappeared.

Even though Carly was technically right, Jackson still felt like the world's biggest miscreant for pushing her against that shed. Yes, she'd been a willing participant—Christ, the fact that she'd matched his hunger and intensity from the word *go* had been half of what turned him on so much in the first place. Still. Next time, he'd have to make sure to figure out a way to rein in his overeager libido.

Next time? If there was a next time—he'd just be more careful, and he'd be damn sure to stay away from the freaking shed. After all, it was no big deal to kiss a girl a couple of times, even if those kisses had been packed with enough electricity to power up an entire city block. They were only kisses. He'd done it plenty of times without losing his mind.

Autumn tipped her head at Carly in a measured glance, examining her face as closely as her arm. "I know this is going to sound crazy, but have we met? You look awfully familiar," she said, swabbing the cut with an antiseptic wipe.

"I don't think so. I've been in Pine Mountain for six months, but I haven't gotten out much because of my job. I moved here from New York," Carly added, her face slightly strained.

Well, sure, that cut probably hurt like hell. Renewed guilt pushed through Jackson, and he squashed it down. He must be crazy, thinking there could be a next time with her. That cut was evidence enough that the two of them together fell squarely into the very-bad-plan category.

"Carly's my boss. She's the head chef at La Dolce Vita," Bellamy said.

Autumn gasped, a steri strip poised over Carly's arm. "Oh, no way. I've seen you on TV. You're Carly di Matisse, from *Couples in the Kitchen*. I love that show!"

Jackson bit back a laugh, waiting for Carly to correct the mistake. A TV show? Really? Sure, Carly had worked at some swanky New York restaurant, but come on. Not everyone who came from the Big Apple was a celebrity. Plus, she seemed way too real for that, fancy chef status or not.

"You've seen my show?" Carly's mouth opened in surprise, and Jackson couldn't help but feel like her mirror image. What was she talking about?

"Heck yes, I've seen your show. I caught it last year when I was up in the middle of the night feeding my youngest. They run all kinds of local cable around here after the late night talk shows sign off. It's better than infomercials, that's for sure."

"You have a cooking show?" Jackson blinked, trying to register the thought.

Carly nodded, a swath of hair falling free from her braid and tumbling across her cheek. "It wasn't glamorous or anything, just a low-budget cable TV deal. I can't believe it ran all the way out here."

"In Philly, too," Bellamy chimed in. "I've seen every episode."

"Are you serious?" Carly froze in place, and Bellamy nodded her answer.

Holy crap. He'd known Carly must be a good chef; after all, those scones had been unbelievable, and she sure seemed to know what she was talking about in terms of food experiences. But a freaking TV show?

Autumn dropped her voice a notch and leaned in toward Carly with a conspiratorial waggle of her brow. "So I have to know . . . are you and Travis really married?"

Jackson's eyebrows shot upward just as his jaw *thunked* open, but his vocal cords were torqued shut. Carly was married? As in, *we registered for pots and pans, I now pronounce you man and wife, married*?

No fucking way.

"Well, yes. Technically," Carly replied after an eternity, her eyes flickering over Autumn's before zeroing in on the grass beneath all of their feet. "But we're in the process of getting a divorce."

A faint buzzing sound resonated in Jackson's ears as his sister fumbled with an apology and Bellamy immediately changed the subject to food. Jackson nodded dumbly and pretended to listen, but all he could hear was the white-noise *whoosh* of his blood moving through his ears, firmly pushed by his pounding chest.

From the look on Carly's face, whatever was going on between her and her ex—Trenton? Truman? Anyway, whatever was going on wasn't a done deal. As in, not only was the ink not dry, but the writing wasn't even all the way on the wall. If Carly was in the middle of a divorce, chances were that she harbored at least some emotional baggage over it. She'd want someone who could hold her hand through the whole thing, not somebody whose only desire was to stay in let's-just-be-casual-and-make-out-while-we're-at-it mode. Was making out even kosher? Christ. Legally, she was still somebody's wife.

Wife.

God damn it, Jackson should've known this was a bad idea to begin with. Enticing kisses or not, it was in both their best interests for him to forget about her, period. After all, not only had he lost control of himself to the point of drawing blood, albeit accidentally, but legally she was still Mrs. Somebody Else.

Forget being a bad idea. This was getting downright insane.

Jackson started to form a polite yet definite cut-and-run in his head, but a squeal of female happiness coming from the direction of the side yard blanked his thoughts. Before he could even see what hit him, Jackson's arms were full of a tall, lush-bodied honey-blonde whose lips were planted firmly over his.

Carly tried not to stare as a leggy stranger gracefully loped across the yard to lay a kiss on Jackson like they were the only two people at the party—hell, maybe even the universe.

"Loveyducks! Sorry I'm late, but work was just awful! I've missed you *so* much," the woman crooned, kissing Jackson again before releasing his lips to settle against him in a perfect fit. She looked like a photo shoot waiting to happen, from her shampoo-commercial tresses to her adorable kitten-heeled sandals, complete with French pedicure and sparkly rhinestone accents. Carly's stomach twisted tighter than her fists before dropping toward her own unpolished toes.

Jackson blinked in shock. "Jenna. I, uh . . . wow, I thought you might be a while longer." He snaked a reluctant arm around the woman, his smile stiff as over-whipped egg whites, and Carly fought the urge to throw up.

How could she have fallen for this?

"Nope! I went as fast as I could so we could be together." The woman beamed up at him like he'd invented the wheel. Or kiss-proof lipstick, which she was evidently wearing.

"Wow, it took you long enough. Was 295 a parking lot or what?" Bellamy hugged her friend and made a quick round of introductions to both Carly and Jackson's sister while Jackson stared a hole in the grass beneath his feet.

"Oh, Jenna!" Autumn leaned in to hug the woman, who miraculously managed to keep herself glued to Jackson's side while hugging his sister back. "I'm so pleased to finally meet you. You must be something special. Jackson's usually so secretive about his girlfriends."

Secretive enough to sneak around in the garden, cheating with the first available idiot who happens by?

She was such a fool. Jackson might've been infuriating, albeit in a totally sexy way, but the last thing she'd pegged him for was a snake in the grass. Of course she'd never suspected Travis of being a cheater, either, and look what that got her. Had she seriously been desperate enough to wrap her legs around Jackson's waist? Clearly, her ability to judge a person's character had left the freaking building.

"Oh, I wouldn't have missed this for the world." Jenna smiled an ear-to-ear stunner like the pages of *Cosmopolitan* magazine had just spit her out. She nuzzled Jackson's neck, and wrapped her slender arm around him even tighter as she launched into some story about how not even a work emergency and holiday traffic could keep her from her man.

Jackson stood stick-straight next to his girlfriend—ugh, the word itself stirred a groan in Carly's chest—and she couldn't tell which of them she hated more; him, for pulling the wool over her eyes so seamlessly, or herself for considering sleeping with him, even casually.

Either way, she needed to get out of here. Now would be good.

Autumn and Jenna were entrenched in getting-to-know-you mode, and Jackson stood between them with a tight smile plastered to his face. Carly felt a tiny stab of sympathy for his girlfriend, who despite the fact that she was ten degrees from humping his leg, actually seemed pretty nice. Still, Carly wasn't about to air out Jackson's indiscretions right here in the middle of a family gathering. She'd rather forget that stupid, steamy kiss and get on with things, thank you very much. In fact, she'd rather get a freaking tetanus shot than stand here and be made a fool of.

Wait a second . . .

"Well, I hate to eat and run, but I think Autumn's right. My last tetanus shot was a dog's age ago, so I'm going to zip out to that emergency clinic in Bealetown. Just to be on the safe side."

"But you didn't eat," Jackson said, his voice stilted.

"I'm all set, thanks." She worked up her biggest smile-for-TV face. Local cable or not, she still had *some* skills. "And thanks for patching me up, Autumn."

"No problem at all, hon. Just tell whoever's working the clinic that Autumn Mackenzie sent you, and that they'd better be nice with that needle."

Carly shuddered, but the thought of a needle was nothing compared to the prick standing across from her. "I will."

She'd turned to duck through the crowd, the tightness in her chest already unraveling in relief, when Jackson's baritone stopped her dead in her tracks.

Chapter Eleven

"Wait!"

A wave of hot relief spilled over Carly, making her chest hitch right along with her steps. What the hell was *that*? She should be relieved to get out of there, not happy that Jackson had called her back after only two steps.

Traitorous girl parts.

"Yes?" Carly mentally patted herself on the back for the fact that on the rare occasion she didn't embody grace under pressure, she could still fake it with the best of them. The rubber sole of her flip flop squeaked against the lawn as she turned back to look at Jackson. He raised his eyes, but didn't quite manage to meet her gaze, landing his focus on the vicinity of her chin instead.

"You need a ride back to your car. I can take you."

Well, crap. She'd forgotten her car was sitting in the parking lot at Joe's Grocery. Jackson unwound his arm from Jenna's waist and dug into his pocket for his keys, causing panic to bolt through Carly's veins. She didn't even want to be out in the open with him, much less in the confined space of his truck.

"No." A streak of color and sparkly silver light popped like a hot kernel in the distance, mercifully distracting everyone from the hard, unwavering syllable that had just passed from Carly's lips. "I mean, you'll miss the fireworks that way. I'll just call my roommate and have her come get me."

"It's really not that far," Jackson argued, his eyes glittering.

"All the more reason it'll be a piece of cake for me to get a ride," Carly insisted right back. Although Sloane would certainly grill her for details all the way home, Carly had zero doubts that her friend would come get her.

"Are you sure?" Bellamy asked, green eyes clouded with concern. "Maybe—"

"Let me take you," Jackson repeated, the words coming out like he was strangling in quicksand. Jenna's forehead crinkled, and the added attention to Jackson's insistence pushed Carly even harder to stand her ground.

"No, thanks. My ride will be here in ten minutes. Maybe less." She took a step backward, then another. No more distractions. She was out of here.

"See you tomorrow, Bellamy. Have a great night, everybody."

This time when Carly turned to walk away, Jackson did nothing to stop her.

Whoever coined that old phrase about the best laid plans was probably laughing his ass off right now. Carly squeezed her eyes shut, blocking out a dusky view of the front yard.

In her haste to get out of Dodge, she'd forgotten that cellular service was hopeless on a good day in the mountains. Her iPhone was as useless as a chocolate teapot way the hell up here in God's country, not to mention the fact that even if she could use it, she still had no clue where she was or how to get to the bungalow from here. Carly released an exasperated breath, but refused to even think about heading back to the house behind her.

"Come on, cell phone." She tapped the screen with a gentle caress. "Give me a signal. Just for a few minutes, whaddaya say?"

Not even a flicker. Carly muttered a curse in Italian before shoving the stupid thing back into her pocket. A burst of pink and white light bloomed high over the back of the house, a brightly lit peony against the velvet sky, and she stopped to think.

If everyone was down at the lake watching the fireworks, maybe she could sneak back into the house, just to use the phone. She wouldn't be breaking and entering or anything, just slipping in unnoticed for a quick call. Even if she couldn't figure out how to get Sloane here to pick her up, maybe she could call a cab or something.

News flash, stupida! *They don't do cabs up here in Pine Mountain.* She pinched the bridge of her nose between her thumb and forefinger, refusing to believe she was out of options.

"Come on, Carly. Think," she whispered, taking out her worthless iPhone to give it one last try. There had to be something. There had to be . . .

"Do you need some help?"

Carly shrieked at the male voice coming from her right, dropping her cell phone with a skitter and balling both fists into a fighting stance. She wasn't about to go down like an extra in a B-grade slasher flick, no way. Forget that the deep, disembodied voice had offered to help. Didn't Ted Bundy do the same thing to all of those poor, unsuspecting victims of his, too? Carly cocked her arms tight against her shaking body, primed to take a swing, and scanned the shadowy yard to locate the source of the voice.

"Whoa! Carly, relax. It's me. Shane," he clarified in a rush. A golden-orange pop of light illuminated the yard from overhead, and the concern on Shane's face was obvious as he creased his brow at her from a few paces away.

"Holy shit! You scared me." She slanted her gaze at him as the darkness settled in again.

"Sorry. Everyone left to watch the fireworks, and Jack—well, they were all worried that you'd be waiting by yourself, so I figured I'd come keep you company."

Carly stiffened. "I'm fine all by myself. Great, actually."

Well, *that* took stones. Jackson was pretending to be worried about her? He couldn't seriously think she'd stick around for another clandestine kiss while his girlfriend's back was turned. She huffed out a breath at the thought.

"Listen, Carly . . ." Shane trailed off, and a purple and white starburst flashed overhead. "I know this is none of my business, but things here . . . well, they aren't really what they seem."

Carly froze. So Shane did know about the kiss from last week. Otherwise, why would he be trying to save face for his friend?

"They seem pretty cut and dried to me," she replied with finality. "And to be honest, I'm not really too interested in a bunch of lame excuses. It's not worth my time." In the back of her mind, she could hear Sloane's teasing voice from a few weeks ago. *Jaded, party of one . . .*

Yeah, well, jaded was a whole lot better than duped. No way was she sticking around to hear Jackson try and sweet talk his way out of things.

"Right." Shane paused for so long that Carly thought he'd let it go, but then he spoke again. "Jenna's not Jackson's girlfriend."

"Ex-excuse me?" Carly shook her head in shock, certain she'd misunderstood. "How's that?"

Shane blew out a slow breath. "Well, you'll have to ask him for the whole story. But it's not what it looks like."

For a second, something unidentifiable and warm trilled through Carly's chest before understanding squashed it, trampling through her brain like a wet dog on a white carpet.

"Oh, I get it. He sent you to try and smooth things over, make me believe that this was all just a little misunderstanding. Well, tell Jackson not to worry about it. The kiss wasn't even all that good."

Carly had eaten some crazy things over the course of her thirty-one years, but nothing tasted as burnt or brittle as the lie that had just tumbled from her lips. She swallowed hard, but it did nothing to improve the state of her taste buds or her mood. "Look, I'm sorry. I think it's best if I just go."

Shane nodded and took a few steps toward her to scoop up her phone, which lay belly-up in the grass in front of her flip flops. He regarded her for a minute that felt like it lasted for ten, as if there was something on the tip of his tongue he just couldn't manage to set free.

"I know better than to mess with a woman who's got her mind made up. For what it's worth, though, he really is a decent guy."

Yeah, right. And she was the queen of England. "We'll just have to agree to disagree on that one."

Shane's eyes glinted with amusement beneath another burst of light, courtesy of the fireworks show overhead. "Oh, come on now. You could humor me. Seeing as how you owe me a favor." A mixture of heartfelt honesty and gentle teasing wrapped around his words, and she stared at him through the settling shadows.

"I owe you a favor?" Carly echoed.

"Yup. For taking you back to your car." Shane flipped his keys in his palm, his grin obvious in the next pop of rainbow-hued colors overhead.

Carly let out a low oath. She'd almost forgotten about being stranded all the way out here in Serial Killer country. "That's blackmail, you know."

"I prefer to call it externally motivated consideration," he ventured with a crooked smile. "What do you say?"

"I can get a ride," Carly asserted, but it came out like a question that had no answer.

"If that's what you want." But rather than leave her to it, he simply stood on the front lawn.

The truth was, Shane was the quickest means to an end, and right now, she wanted that end so bad she could taste it. "Fine. Consider yourself humored. Are you parked close by?"

Carly could've sworn he muttered something about a barracuda under his breath before he ushered her through the yard. As he led her toward his truck, she wondered if he'd spotted her concession for the lie it was.

The cheeseburger sitting on the no-frills, white ceramic plate in front of Jackson was less dinner than work of art. Sesame seeds lay scattered across the golden-brown bakery roll, dotting it with just enough texture to balance out the soft bread beneath the toasted exterior. The thick, brown edges of the grilled-to-perfection patty escaped the confines of the roll, draped in a slice of bubbly cheese. The heady, charcoal smell of the burger mingled with the salty, warm scent of the hand-cut waffle fries piled gloriously high on the side of Jackson's plate. A burger from the Double Shot was one of Jackson's biggest pleasures in life, a thing of beauty unparalleled not just in Pine Mountain, but in all of King County.

He couldn't even manage to take one bite without wanting to be sick.

Jackson raked a hand over his crew cut, silently stuffing down the lack of appetite he'd been wrestling with for the last four days. He had a sneaking suspicion the reason for his malady wasn't so much a *what* as a *who*, but hell if he was going to go there now that all was said and done.

Except part of him wanted to go there. And not a little bit.

"Hey. Sorry I'm late. The tranny in that Camaro that

came in last week is killing me." Shane slid onto a bar stool and eyed Jackson's burger with all the reverence it deserved. "Man, that looks good."

"Help yourself," Jackson said, sliding the plate over.

Shane promptly looked at Jackson as if he'd tried to give away his kid. "Okay, that's just not right. What gives?" His laugh was a cross between nonchalant joking and what's-on-your-mind, but Jackson wasn't in the mood for either.

"I ate a really late lunch." Jackson signaled the redhead behind the bar and ordered a beer. When in doubt, a tall, cold one could always take the edge off.

"Bullshit. I've seen you put away one of Lou's burgers on a full stomach more times than I can count. What's going on?" Shane pinned Jackson with a dark stare.

So much for not going there. The bartender sashayed her way over, her bottle opener sounding off in a muffled clink against the lip of the amber glass as she liberated the cap from his bottle of Budweiser.

"Nothing's going on." Maybe if he peppered the conversation with terse one-liners, Shane would lose interest or change the subject. It wasn't like they tended to sit around and talk about their feelings much, anyway.

"Have you talked to Carly since I took her back to her car on Saturday?"

Or not.

"No." The word came out sounding harder than Jackson intended, causing Shane's brow to lift.

Great. Just what Jackson needed was the Spanish-freaking-Inquisition over this. Nothing had even happened.

That's kind of the rub, though, isn't it?

After Carly had left the party—and who could blame her, really—every neuron in Jackson's brain had screamed at him to find her and explain. He'd been knee-deep in formulating a fast excuse to follow her through the yard when it struck him like a steamroller on steroids.

Letting Carly leave was the perfect way to cut ties with her before things went from seriously hot to seriously heavy. She was married, for God's sake, and he sure as hell didn't want to go down that road. Plus, it was pointless to start something he wasn't going to finish. Better to just let it fade out now, even if the method left him looking like a jerk.

Jackson shifted in his seat, the unforgiving wood of the bar stool making his back ache. There was something else, something dark and suggestive that lurked in the back of his mind and refused to let go. Carly was the only woman he'd ever wanted so much, that he'd lost control trying to have her.

And so he couldn't pursue her. Plain and simple.

Despite his actions and all the nasty little neuroses that fueled them, the thought of not seeing her safely to her car on Saturday night had rankled big time, to the point that Jackson had pulled Shane aside not two minutes after she'd walked away to ask him to do it. God love him, Shane had driven Carly back to her car, no questions asked. It was the last they'd spoken of it. Until now.

"Are you planning on seeing her again?" Shane propped his forearms on the bar and dug into the cheeseburger without fanfare.

Even though he hadn't come right out and admitted to Shane that anything had really gone on, clearly his buddy could read between the lines. And since those lines all pointed to the past tense, anyway, refuting the facts just seemed insulting.

"I don't think so." Jackson took another draw from his beer, making a face at the bottle as he swallowed. American beer wasn't supposed to go down like motor oil, but whatever. Everything he'd touched to his lips lately had tasted terrible.

Shane chewed for a minute before continuing. "Look, if you want to drop the subject, just say so. But from where I sit, it looks like it might do you some good to air it out."

Jackson bit back the urge to compliment Shane on his skirt. Truth was, the whole thing was weighing him down like a truckload of wet cement. It might not be his usual style, but throwing the story out there for Shane was a far cry from getting all touchy-feely. Christ, at this point, he'd do anything to stop feeling like a jerk and get his freaking appetite back.

"You remember that storm we had a couple of weeks ago, right?" Jackson started, taking a deep breath. Twenty minutes, two Cokes, and the full story later, Shane pushed back from the bar with a low whistle.

"Gotta hand it to you. The word *easy* just isn't in your vocabulary, is it?"

Jackson scrubbed a hand down his face, realizing he felt strangely better having told all. Not that it mattered much. In the end, the result was still the same.

"Nope. It's probably for the best that she hates my guts," he said.

Shane slanted a hesitant glance his way. "Yeah. I tried to tell her the truth before I drove her home."

"You *what?*" Jackson couldn't tell whether he should be pissed or relieved. On second thought, pissed was rarely worth it between friends. "What'd she say?"

"Let's just say hating your guts is in the right ballpark. She thought I was covering for you to smooth things over, and she was pretty adamant, so I didn't push it. Sorry if I overstepped my bounds, man."

"No big deal. Like I said, it's probably for the best," Jackson said slowly.

"But you like her." It wasn't a question.

"Yeah." The reply sent a shockwave of surprise through Jackson, although whether it was because he meant it or because he'd said it out loud, he couldn't be sure.

"So, what? You're just going to avoid her, all because you acted like a total ass on Saturday?" Shane picked up the one remaining waffle fry from the long-since decimated plate and popped it into his mouth.

"Thanks for the ego boost," Jackson muttered, sliding his empty glass back over the bar.

Shane ran a hand over his stomach in an appreciative gesture, pushing his plate next to Jackson's glass. "Don't mention it."

Jackson supposed he had the dig coming. He really had been a total ass. And the worst part was, the charade with Jenna had gone off without a hitch. His mother had beamed with happiness that could be seen from outer space every time she looked at him, a delighted kind of relief swimming over her features that he hadn't seen in years. Never mind that Jackson had been eating the guilt over it ever since the first hint of a smile had crossed her lips.

And he hadn't been able to eat anything else since then.

Shane cleared his throat in a quiet rumble. "Have you thought about a good, old-fashioned sincere apology?"

All the air *whooshed* from Jackson's lungs in a moment of clarity that made his skin prickle with sudden awareness. His gut perked to life, sending the first message of want in four days to his brain.

Feed her.

Clearly, Jackson's lack of appetite was making him loopy. Still, the impulse filtered through him, shaping itself into an idea with each pass through his system, and it made him hungry. Apologizing to Carly was a far cry from diving headfirst into a relationship with her, after all. While he knew the latter would never happen, the former was starting to have merit, with both his conscience and his stomach. Plus, she'd said herself that she wasn't looking to stay in Pine Mountain long term. How serious could it get if she wasn't even going to stay?

His brain tumbled in thought. Carly might introduce Jackson to her right hook for his troubles, but Shane was right. She deserved an apology, a really self-deprecating, sincere-right-down-to-my-toes admission of wrongdoing. And he only knew one way to pull that off.

"Shane, I'm gonna need your help. Are you game for just one more little deception?"

Chapter Twelve

"That salmon's going to be like the fucking Sahara if you don't get it off the grill, and I do mean right now," Carly snapped over her shoulder. "And where's the lemon dill sauce? Come on, people. We're not going to fill the house with cold food and slow service."

"Yes, Chef." Bellamy plated the salmon in efficient movements, offering it to her for approval while Adrian finished the dish with the satiny, butter-yellow sauce. Carly's hands flew over her work station as she added crisp-tender spears of steamed asparagus and roasted fingerling potatoes to the plate, wiping an errant dollop of sauce from the edge of the dish before sending it out the door with the server. She pulled the next ticket from the queue, barking out orders and plating the next round of dishes with speedy precision.

"Chef di Matisse? There's a, uh, problem with the dessert menu." The look on Bellamy's face suggested that she'd drawn the short straw in the news-delivering department.

Carly's shoulders knotted together like one big sweater of nasty tension, and she hissed a breath through her teeth. From the minute they'd sent out the first cover tonight, things had been going south. One of the dishwashers hadn't shown up for his shift, which meant getting everything from clean flatware to proper serving pieces in a timely manner was like getting blood from a stone. Due to an ordering mix-up with the liquor distributor, the bar was nearly out of the restaurant's most popular pinot noir, which went flawlessly with just about everything on the damned menu. And her pastry chef, while he could practically spin gold from mere butter, was unreliable as hell. Carly got the feeling she was about to find that out—again.

"What?" Carly turned as Adrian sent a plate of Seafood Fra Diavolo her way for its out-the-door inspection, and she tucked a wedge of toasted garlic bread on the side of the deep-bellied dish, admiring the orange pop of tomatoes next to the shell-pink of the shrimp. A loud crash snapped Carly's head up from the front of the line, just as Bellamy blurted something about the pastry chef not making enough peach cobbler before he snuck out early for the night.

"Fix it!" Carly hollered, moving toward the more pressing issue. Thankfully, it turned out to be a jammed door on one of the dishwashers, all bark and no bite. She returned to the pass, snatching another order from the queue. Two more orders came in, one right on top of the other, and plates left the kitchen with their servers just as fast. Another five minutes of more pressing issues passed before Carly could address the peach cobbler—God, she could kill that pastry chef. She turned and nearly ran into Adrian.

"Taste this." He had the fork in her face so fast that she could either open her mouth or wear whatever was on it, and out of instinct, she took the bite. Dense, buttery crust burst against her tongue, followed by the sweet taste of nectarines in a light syrup that danced through the back of her mouth in a smooth, summery glide.

"What is *that?*" Carly asked, the demand losing its punch as she shoved another bite in her mouth.

"Sunshine here took it upon herself to solve your dessert

problem," he said, grinning at a wide-eyed Bellamy, who held a saucepan in one hand.

"You said . . . you said fix the peach cobbler thing, so I figured nectarines were close enough. I just made a quick reduction with simple syrup and some spices and put it over the shortbread in the pantry. It's not cobbler, but . . ."

"It's brilliant. Plate it with some crème fraiche and send it out." Carly called out the order in her hand before turning back to Bellamy, a wry smile on her lips for the first time all week. "It's replacing the cobbler on the menu for the rest of the night, so get ready to make more of that sauce. Nice work."

Mercifully, the rest of the service went without a hitch, although it drained Carly's energy down to fumes. Her arm was still sore from her weekend escapade, and although she hated to admit it, her ego hurt even worse. That tetanus shot had been nothing in the face of reality.

She'd been conned like the world's biggest sap. Yet again.

Yeah, well, not anymore. Carly pulled the last ticket for the night out of the queue. Oh, thank God. Calamari was something she could do in her sleep.

"You want me to take that?" Adrian's hazel eyes darted to the ticket in her hand, but she moved down the line to one of the lowboys, pulling out the labeled containers of ingredients.

"Nope. The kitchen's pretty much broken down anyway." She nodded to the other work stations, all of which were clean and empty, the last of her line cooks having checked out for the night a few minutes before. It was a rarity that Carly wasn't the first one in and the last one out, a self-imposed high standard that all but married her to her job. She put the milky, opaque calamari in a bowl, tossing them evenly with batter before checking the temperature on the deep fryer. At least the kitchen was faithful.

"So you want to tell me why you're in such a foul mood?"

Adrian replaced the containers in the lowboy, breaking down the last station with practiced ease.

Carly blanked the frown from her face, but of course Adrian had seen it. An unexpected trickle of melancholy squeezed her stomach tight against her ribs, and she ladled the calamari into the basket of the deep fryer with a shaking hand. "Not really." God, the whole thing was ridiculous. It had been a couple of kisses, nothing more. She really needed to get over herself. "Why, am I that bad?" Despite the knot in her belly, a tiny smile moved across her lips. It felt hollow, but at least it was a start.

"A loaded question if I ever heard one. I just know you." Adrian pulled a pristine white plate from the stack at the pass and met her at the deep fryer. "You think too much and it's going to wreck that hard head of yours."

Carly snorted and put the tawny rings of flawlessly fried calamari on the plate, piling it high and plating it with her secret-recipe dipping sauce before sending it out with the server. "You're such a sweet-talker. Really." But Adrian was right. Wallowing in what had happened with Jackson wasn't going to make it any different. She needed to let it go, just like everything else. "Come on, *gnoccone*. Help me finish cleaning up, would you?"

Adrian laughed in a hard burst. "Did you just call me a big dumpling?"

The grin that found its way to Carly's face was long overdue. "I believe I did."

"You're the boss," he grumbled, but the smile beneath his darkly stubbled jaw was obvious. They fell into step together, trading jibes and jawing about whether the Yankees had a shot at winning the pennant until the kitchen was well past clean.

"Um, Chef di Matisse?" Bellamy poked her head into the kitchen from the pass-through to the dining room just as

Carly took one last swipe at the stainless steel counter with her dish towel.

"Hey, Bellamy, I thought you'd gone home. Excellent work tonight." Carly popped the top button on her whites and ran a hand over the blue and white scarf keeping her braid at bay.

A look of pleasure flashed over Bellamy's features, but it was quickly replaced by hesitance. "Thank you. I, ah, just wanted to let you know that there's a customer still in the dining room. He's asking to see the chef."

Carly stiffened. Gavin, the restaurant manager, was supposed to handle all complaints. If anything came back to the kitchen, it went right from Gavin's hands to hers, no exceptions.

"Is there a problem?" she asked. Something about this didn't feel right.

"Oh, no, no. The server said he just wants to compliment you on the food."

Carly's shoulders shifted in a slump of both weariness and relief. On occasion, she'd go out to the dining room to greet a customer, although it was usually one of the resort execs or some other VIP. Usually Adrian went for civilians, mostly because she couldn't be spared from the kitchen.

"Whaddaya say, Ade? You want this one?" While it was good PR—not to mention a lovely ego boost—to go out into the dining room when someone came offering praise, what Carly really wanted was to go home and soak her aching feet until they resembled prunes. "Pretty please?"

"Oh, no." Adrian's gravelly laughter cut through the kitchen. "As you can see, there are no weeds in the kitchen." He gestured to the back of the house, which was sparkling clean and silent. "It's your name on the menu, *gnocchella*."

Carly's mouth popped open. "Tiny dumpling? Seriously?"

"You started it. Go, bask in the adoration of your fans. I'll catch you on the flip side, Chef." Adrian didn't even bother to hide his amused smile as he sauntered toward the service exit that led to the back parking lot.

"The customer's at table twelve. Goodnight, Chef," Bellamy murmured as she ducked back toward the dining room, the swinging door making a thunk-*thunk* as she disappeared.

Carly smoothed a palm down her jacket, which other than being splattered with a little bit of lemon dill sauce, was in fairly decent shape. She took a deep breath, letting it press against her ribs before exhaling in a slow puff. Five minutes of meet-and-greet and then she could go home and put this crummy day—hell, the whole crummy week—behind her.

God, she really wished the ache in her chest would take a hike. It was bad enough her feet were killing her. If she wasn't careful, she'd have a full-bodied mutiny on her hands. Of course, the ache in her chest had nothing to do with the breakneck pace of her job or the arduous hours spent in the kitchen.

Nope. That could be attributed to a certain broad-shouldered, blue-eyed con artist whose kiss she could *still* feel on her lips, despite numerous teeth scrubbings and half a bottle of Listerine.

It really had been a hell of a kiss.

"Get over yourself, di Matisse," she grumbled, nudging the door open with one shoulder. Earth-moving kiss or not, Jackson Carter was a thing of the past.

Jackson sat back, shifting his frame against the polished wood of his chair, and drummed his fingers on the sage green tablecloth beneath them. The dishes had been cleared and the check taken care of, but unlike everyone else who'd enjoyed a late dinner at La Dolce Vita, Jackson's mind wasn't on heading home. He'd waited until the end of the dinner shift on purpose, and with the exception of a couple people still straggling at the bar, the place was finally empty.

Bellamy appeared from the back of the restaurant, making his pulse tap along with his fingers. She dipped her chin in a definite nod, blonde curls bobbing from their haphazard ponytail, before disappearing through the front entrance.

It had taken some doing on both his and Shane's part to convince Bellamy to play along with his apology strategy so he could avoid getting the manager instead of Carly. Admittedly, the appreciative-customer ruse was pretty weak, but it was unlikely that Carly would come out if she knew he was the customer, and waiting for her in the parking lot seemed less apologetic and more scary-stalkerish. So lame pretenses and a little misdirection would have to do the trick, at least to start.

The ironic part was, the minute he'd crossed La Dolce Vita's threshold, Jackson's stomach had roared to life with all the subtlety of a stampeding bull. Everything on the menu had piqued his interest, even the stuff he'd never heard of. In the end, even though the idea of calamari made him wary at best, he'd ordered what he'd come for. It might be the only way Carly would listen long enough for him to at least apologize.

Okay, so she was probably going to tell him in no uncertain terms to go to hell as soon as she saw him sitting there. The mere glimmer that she might hear him out had been enough for his stomach to get on board, but strangely, regaining his appetite wasn't the top item on his agenda.

He owed her the mother of all apologies, even if she threatened to throw him out on sight.

Jackson glanced at the back of the restaurant. If she didn't show up, he couldn't apologize, and if he couldn't apologize, he'd be right back at square one. No kisses, no sexy banter, no desire to eat.

Feed her.

Before he could even contemplate where on earth that

strange voice was coming from—was he that crazy from lack of food?—Carly appeared at the back of the room, dark eyes scanning the nearly empty restaurant. Jackson ducked his head, examining his empty table with sudden interest. Man, she looked good with that pretty blue scarf pulling her hair away from her face. He watched surreptitiously until she got about ten paces away, then jerked to a stop on the glossy hardwood floor.

"You . . . *you* asked to see the chef?" She stood perfectly straight, her bright red clogs rooting her to the spot.

Jackson nodded and bit the bullet. "I wanted to compliment you on the calamari. It was incredible." He gestured to where his empty plate had been, which was kind of stupid since the waitress had taken it ages ago.

"I thought squid wasn't your thing," she replied, her tone arctic.

"I was wrong. About lots of things." Jackson's gut tightened, but he forced the words out before she could reply, or worse yet, flee. "Carly, listen. I wasn't completely honest with you, and I'm really sorry."

She opened her mouth to protest, but he held up a gentle hand to halt her words. "I'm not going to make excuses. I know it looks, uh, pretty bad."

"Pretty bad," Carly echoed, crossing her arms over her chest.

Way to point that out, his inner voice snapped, but Jackson took a deep breath. He wasn't here to make excuses or talk his way out of this. He might've gotten himself into this mess with a series of fibs, but it was time to own up to the truth.

"Yes. It's not what it looks like, but that doesn't really change the fact that I gave you the wrong idea and pissed you off." Jackson paused to let Carly send a you-got-that-right look in his direction, which she did in spades, and then he continued. "So I thought I'd take what you said to heart, about how you never really know what you might like. I took a chance on the calamari, 'cause I was kind of hoping you might take a chance on hearing me out. What do you say?"

Carly stood perfectly still for what felt like an ice age. Finally, she took a couple steps toward the table to look him in the eye. "Shane said Jenna's not your girlfriend."

"She's not. See, the thing is . . ." Jackson paused for a breath. She'd let him get this far without decking him or calling the authorities. Might as well go for the whole enchilada.

"It was my younger brother's engagement party. I would've been fine going without a date, but my ma . . . well, that's kind of another story. She's got this crazy idea that if you're not in a relationship, you're not truly happy. So I just asked Jenna to embellish our friendship to make it look like we were dating. I didn't know I was going to run into you, and that we'd . . . well, you know . . ."

Jackson broke off and shook his head. Man, he was botching this big time.

"So everything with Jenna was just for show?" Carly's expression was neutral enough to make Switzerland green with envy.

"Yeah. I know it sounds pretty stupid. But that's the truth."

She tightened her arms across the front of her jacket, but didn't say a word. The eerie stillness of a place normally bustling with noise and movement unnerved him, as did her lack of a response. Finally, he had to admit defeat.

"Yeah. Anyway, I'll go now. The calamari really was good. Great." Jackson tossed his napkin onto the table, wondering if it was humanly possible to be a bigger oaf.

"You pretended to have a girlfriend so your mother would think you were happy?" Carly's arms loosened from her chest and fell to her sides.

"Yeah."

"Can I ask a stupid question?" She took another step

toward him, and it brought her close enough for him to see the dribbles of sauce on her chef's jacket, along with the double knot of the apron slung low across her waist.

Jackson nodded, frozen in place. "Sure."

"If you wanted your mother to think you were happy, why didn't you skip all the bullshit and just be happy?"

The answer hit him all at once. "I was happy. In the garden, with you."

Somewhere in the corner of his mind came the dark little reminder that she was going through a divorce, but oddly enough, it didn't matter. Maybe tomorrow it would, or next week, or next month even, but that seemed incredibly far away and unimportant.

Jackson wanted to kiss her again right *now*!

"It took a lot of nerve for you to come down here," Carly said, her brown eyes widening to reveal tiny flecks of gold around her irises. Christ, she was beautiful. And her tone was telling him in no uncertain terms to get out.

"I understand." His gut twisted, but he pushed back from the table and stood up. "Thanks for listening." He turned toward the front entrance of the nearly-deserted restaurant. Well, that had been an exercise in humility.

"I accept your apology."

Jackson stumbled to an ungraceful halt. "You what?"

Carly's lips edged upward in the faintest hint of a smile. "I have a mother too, you know. Though I wish you'd just told me from the beginning, I understand what you did, and I believe you're being honest. So I accept your apology."

Holy. Shit.

"I . . . I don't know what to say."

Carly laughed, and the sound burned through him like brushfire on dry kindling. "Say good night. We're closed, and my feet are killing me. Plus, Gavin will throw you out if I don't, and he's not as nice about it as I am." She gestured to a guy in an expensive-looking suit tallying receipts at the bar. As far as Jackson could tell, he was the only other person left in the whole place.

"Oh. Oh, right. Are you on your way out? I could walk you to your car," he offered, still stunned.

"Okay."

By the time Carly retrieved her bag from the kitchen and said good night to the restaurant manager, Jackson had regained enough of his faculties to at least stop babbling. The cool night air kicked into a breeze around them, ruffling Carly's scarf.

"So you really liked that calamari, huh? Or was that just to humor me?" She slid a cautious glance at him, one that told him he wasn't entirely off the hook yet.

"I don't kid about food. The first bite was a little rough, but as soon as I tasted it, I knew you were right." They headed toward her Honda, which was only a few spots away from his truck in the now-deserted lot. "Any chance you'll tell me what's in that dipping sauce? It might've been the best part."

Carly laughed. "It's a di Matisse secret. I could tell you, but I'd have to kill you."

"Ouch. Well, I'll have to settle for just eating it, then." Jackson's stomach rumbled in approval, apparently getting reacquainted with the notion of actually wanting food. "Are you the only person who knows how to make it?"

"You are persistent when it comes to food, aren't you?" Carly asked tartly, but her smile was obvious even in the shadowy light cast off from the restaurant behind them.

"Well, yeah, but that's not why I'm asking. I was just curious if you ever get a night off. You know, let someone else run the show so you can get a break. Does that ever happen?"

She paused. "Mondays. I usually have Mondays off."

"And what do you normally do on Mondays?"

"I cook."

Jackson's laugh came from deep in his chest. Somehow, her answer wasn't shocking. In fact, everything about her was so uncomplicated and real that the next thing out of his mouth was surprisingly a no-brainer.

"What do you say to shaking things up this week and eating instead of cooking?" While tonight's mission had yielded check marks in both the appetite and sexy banter columns, it would probably be pushing the limits of his luck to go for the trifecta and kiss her. Asking her out was the best compromise he could come up with on short notice, even though seeing her again entailed yet another risk. But hell, his stomach was back on board, and she seemed pretty no-nonsense when it came down to it.

When he'd told Shane he liked her, he'd meant it. All he had to do was keep it under control, and they'd be fine.

"Are you asking me out?" Crickets sang in an endless hum in the background, and Carly's keys jingled softly in her palm. Far in the distance, heat lightning flashed like a silvery blanket being snapped across the sky, but none of that quite made it into his brain as clearly as the woman in front of him. A crooked smile took over his face, and his words tasted like dessert as he spoke.

"From here on in, there aren't going to be any pretenses between us. I'm asking you out, Carly di Matisse. What do you say?"

Chapter Thirteen

"Tell me you said yes!" Sloane cried, staring at Carly over the rim of her coffee mug. Several birds took flight from a nearby branch in the backyard, zipping through the morning sunlight at the harpy-like pitch of Sloane's voice.

"You're disturbing the wildlife." Carly jutted her chin toward the tree line, trying to mask the smile playing on her lips. She'd probably go to hell for torturing her best friend like this, but the opportunity was too good to pass up.

"Carly."

The word was a warning, and Carly didn't wait for the flash of narrowed blue eyes that would surely accompany it. "Okay, I give up. I said yes." She sent her grin into her coffee cup rather than broadcasting it across the yard. It had felt all too right to say yes when Jackson had asked her out last night, a thought she'd been both wrestling with and basking in for the last nine hours.

"Gotta say, the humble apology is a pleasant surprise. Not a lot of men go for that," Sloane said, her voice tinged with awe.

"Tell me about it. But he was sincere, and it's not like I don't get the mom thing. It seemed stupid not to accept his apology."

When it came right down to it, Carly wasn't really the type to make men squirm. Dancing around the truth seemed pointless, and as much as it made *her* squirm, the truth was, she liked Jackson. The fact that she could practically feel his hands on her every time she looked into his crinkly baby blues didn't hurt, either.

As if Sloane could hone in on Carly's brainwaves, she let out a suggestive laugh. "Right. I'm sure you forgave him to clear your conscience. You little tart."

Carly busied herself with her coffee. "Yeah, that's me. Totally tarty."

"So where's he going to take you?"

"I don't know," Carly admitted, taking in a deep breath of fresh air and dappled sunlight. "He's going to call me later in the week."

"This is so unfair. Your first date since the big D and I'm not even going to be here to harass you on your way out the door." Sloane frowned and took a sip of coffee, leaning back in her lounge chair with a pout.

"Yeah, rough life you've got, jetting to New York to do a couple of high-profile book signings. You're all over the map, *cucciola*."

"Maybe next time I go, you should come with me," Sloane said, her trademark sass noticeably absent.

A tiny frisson of unease trickled through Carly like ice water on hot skin, but she tamped it down, unwilling to bog down her good mood with thoughts of the city. Visiting would only remind her how much she missed it, not to mention that she really didn't need any guilt from her mother. No, she couldn't go back until she could stay, so there was little point in dwelling on it.

"And miss all the fun here? Plus, you'll be swamped with publicity stuff. That's what you get for being a *USA Today* best-selling author."

"Yeah, yeah," Sloane murmured, her Brooklyn accent

curving over the words in a hard snap. "Well, I wouldn't want you to miss your date with Contractor Man, that's for sure. Hey, if I play my cards right in the city, maybe you won't be the only one around here to get some sugar this week."

Carly's coffee made a beeline for her windpipe. "Who says I'm getting anything?" Jeez! Was there no progression to the whole friends with benefits thing? She and Jackson couldn't possibly end up horizontal right out of the gate, could they?

"What'd you think, you'd be playing Scrabble with the guy? Getting laid is kind of the point of having a bene-friend, sweetie." Sloane's lips curled into a cat-in-cream smile. "I thought you liked Jackson."

"I do, but give me a break. The first date seems kind of abrupt, don't you think? I mean, how many times do you go out with a whatchamacallit before *you* sleep with him?"

Sloane tipped her head, sending a swath of black hair over one eye. "That's not really a fair question. I mean, it de-pends on how well I know the guy."

"How do you know none of them is your peacock, then?" Carly crinkled her nose, trying to keep the terminology straight in her head.

"Jesus, woman. Get your birds straight. It's a swan," Sloane laughed. "Repeat after me. White bird, long neck."

"Whatever." Carly's grumble—and her question—were cut off by the sound of the phone ringing from beyond the screen door.

"Who the hell would call us at 9:15 on a Thursday morning?" Sloane wondered out loud, sending a frown to the back of the bungalow.

"We're getting an early food delivery today at the restau-rant. Gavin said he'd handle it, but our produce distributor is hit or miss in the reliability department. I told him to call me if there was a problem."

Carly hustled through the door and reached for the phone. One batch of rotten produce or bad seafood would be enough to sink her entire dinner service, and it wouldn't be the first time she'd had to send someone to Joe's Grocery to clean out their stock just to stay afloat. Carly scooped the phone to her ear, poised for bad news.

And bad news was exactly what she got.

Fifteen curse-filled minutes later, Carly sank against the sofa, squeezing her eyes shut over hot, angry tears. A truckload of rotten vegetables would've been a red-carpet gala compared to this.

No way. Just no way.

"Good God, Carly. You look like death warmed over. Moldy veggies aren't that tragic, are they?" Sloane asked, making her way inside with concern.

"That wasn't Gavin. It was my divorce attorney. Travis refused to sign the final papers outlining the distribution of joint property." The words were hollow and awkward as they spilled from her mouth. Surely this was a nightmare and any minute now she'd wake up, heaving with relief.

"What? Can he even do that? You guys already split everything when you left," Sloane said, sitting next to Carly on the couch.

"Apparently, he's claiming things weren't distributed equally and fairly, and some items of 'sentimental value' haven't been accounted for." She paused to rake a hand through her hair. Travis had been so much talk and so little action over the course of their marriage that she hadn't actually expected he'd go through with his threat to drag out their divorce.

"Travis has a shriveled up raisin instead of a heart. What sentimental items could he possibly be talking about?"

"My attorney has a list. She said it's mostly stupid stuff, like the Best Hits of Steely Dan CD I gave him for Christmas in 2010 and a quilt we got as a wedding present. Like the damned thing is an heirloom or something. It came from Target, for God's sake."

"Bastard." Sloane swore, putting a much-needed arm around Carly. "He's not getting away with this. We'll go through all your stuff, right now. It shouldn't be too hard to find what he's looking for and get him off your back. Whatever we can't find, we'll just replace. Hell, I'll buy him a hundred Steely Dan CDs if it'll make him crawl back under his nasty old bridge."

Despite Sloane's attempt at humor, the tears Carly had kept at bay finally breached her lids and streaked down her face.

"It's not that easy. Travis picked things he's alleging can't be replaced, knowing full well I don't have a clue where half of them are. I can argue that I don't have whatever I can't find, but the paperwork to sort it out is going to take forever. And that's not even the worst part."

"There's more?" Sloane's hand froze, midrub on Carly's back.

She nodded, blowing out a shaky breath as she wiped her face with the back of her hand. "Apparently, he's petitioning to contest the divorce itself, saying he wants to try counseling in an effort to reconcile."

Sloane coughed out a bitter laugh. "Like that's going to happen!"

"It's all a ruse. I can still proceed with the divorce because I filed on grounds of infidelity, and it'll be granted. Travis can't make me go to counseling. My lawyer will file a motion for something called . . ." Carly broke off to read what she'd written down on the pad by the phone. "A default judgment, and that'll be that. But the hearing will take a while to schedule, and then I'll have to go to New York once it is."

"That's not so bad. At least you know you'll win," Sloane said with optimism.

Carly shook her head. She had to hand it to Travis. He must've earned an advanced degree in underhanded scheming to have come up with this part.

"Yes, but you're missing the bigger picture. What Travis wants is to wear me down, not win me back. The grapevine in our neighborhood is thick, Sloane. All he has to do is whisper this to the right people, and my *mama* is going to catch wind of it." Carly shuddered, all the feelings of bliss she'd woken up with shredded down to dust.

A sympathetic smile washed over Sloane's face. "Honey, don't take this the wrong way, but you're thirty-one. And it's not like your mother doesn't know you're getting divorced."

"No, but she's the only woman on the planet more stubborn than I am, and she wants me to reconcile with Travis. And even though you and I know it's just on paper, he's going to do all he can to convince her that he wants me back." Carly blew out a defeated breath and threw her head back against the couch cushions.

"Which means that between the two of them, my life is about to become a living hell."

Jackson palmed the handles of the double-bagged Chinese takeout and reached across his passenger seat to grab a familiar, timeworn box. His plans for the evening were a bit of a gamble, but after tossing around the usual hangouts, keeping it simple seemed like the best way to go. Carly had been agreeable to staying in when he'd called her earlier that day to firm things up, so he relied on the two things he knew would appeal to her.

Good food and healthy competition.

Sauntering up to the bungalow, Jackson took in the low-slanted shadows of early evening, enjoying the fact that the heat from the week before had broken into cooler, typical mountain weather for July.

"Hey." Carly stood in the doorframe, her chestnut-colored hair tumbling down the back of her pale yellow tank top in loose waves, and Jackson promptly forgot his name.

"You didn't let me ring the bell," he blurted, and she gave a soft, throaty laugh he felt down to the soles of his shoes.

"Sorry. I'm hungry, and your Chinese food precedes you." She gestured him inside, and he followed her into the bungalow.

"Okay, your sixth sense for food is starting to freak me out a little bit." He slipped the box to an out of the way side table before proceeding to the kitchen. Carly was good and all, but come on. Not even she could smell Kung Pao chicken through a frigging door made of solid oak.

A flash of mischief flitted over her face. "The name of the restaurant is on the bag." Carly smiled as she took it from him and hoisted it onto the smooth granite countertop.

"Oh, right." Of course he hadn't noticed that. "Well, I wasn't sure what you'd like, so I got a couple of things. There's no tripe, though, so you don't have to worry."

"I'd say I'm grateful, but I bet that's for you just as much as me." She unloaded the cardboard cartons on the counter, lifting a brow after unearthing the first three. "Either you like a lot of leftovers or you're planning on feeding a family of ten."

"What can I say? I'm a hungry guy." He moved beside her at the counter, popping the cartons open to see what was what, looking at her with an impressed yet wary expression when she dug a pair of chopsticks out of the bag and pulled the paper wrapping off.

"You know how to use those things?" He eyeballed them with doubt. Shouldn't they come with directions?

Carly nodded, peering into a carton of Lo Mein. "I take it you're a fork and knife kind of guy."

Jackson looked down at his hands. While they were large enough to carry bundles of roofing tile with practiced ease, maneuvering two skinny little sticks through his food without making an unholy mess seemed highly unlikely. "Yeah."

She padded over to a drawer by the coffeepot to get him a fork, and Jackson realized with a pleasurable start that she was barefoot. Same cute feet, same bare toes. Damn it, more than just his stomach was bound to perk to life if he didn't knock it off.

"Here you go. Do you want a plate, too?" Carly scooped up the carton of Lo Mein and paused, chopsticks hovering over the glossy noodles.

"I take it you're an eat-from-the-carton kind of girl." He gestured to the container in her hand.

The look on her face said it all. "Guilty as charged."

"Doesn't that mess with the food experience?" Jackson asked, poking through the carton of beef broccoli with the fork she'd given him.

"For takeout, it kind of is the experience. There's something fun about it, you know? A little indulgent, a little forbidden." Her eyes went wide before zeroing in on the food in her hands. "But you're welcome to a plate if you'd like."

Forget takeout. The innuendo was sweet enough to eat all by itself, even though he suspected she hadn't heard it until after it had left her lips. "No thanks. Eating from the carton's fine by me."

"I didn't even know Pine Mountain had a Chinese restaurant," Carly said, shifting the subject and lifting a perfectly rolled bite of noodles from her chopsticks to her mouth. Jackson forced himself to focus on the carton in his hand, spearing a stalk of broccoli with so much enthusiasm that he nearly punched through the cardboard behind it.

"Are you kidding? Aside from the resort, there's The Sweet Life Bakery, the diner on Main Street and the Double Shot. That's pretty much it for Pine Mountain, proper. If you want Chinese food, you have to go to Bealetown, although the place in Riverside's better."

Carly laughed. "Wow. You drove to Bealetown for this? I'm honored."

"I drove to Riverside for this," Jackson corrected, tipping his head at her. "I told you, the food's better."

"You take your Chinese food pretty seriously." A smile teased at the corners of her mouth, which sent Jackson's appetite due south.

"I take all food pretty seriously. Along with a few other things."

Carly's head snapped up, dark locks tumbling over her shoulders. "A few other things?"

Jackson was going to be in for one hell of a long night if she kept biting her lower lip like that. He nodded, willing himself to stick with the plan for the evening.

"What do you say to a little friendly competition?" Jackson asked, reaching for the box he'd tucked away on the side table while Carly had been unloading the Chinese food.

Carly's face creased in confusion for a second, but the ear to ear smile that followed it told Jackson that he'd been right on the money in appealing to her headstrong side.

"I'd say you'd better gear up. I'm about to kick your ass."

Chapter Fourteen

After five stress-filled days of back and forth with her attorney and six shifts at a restaurant where the dining room was filled to the gills, Carly thought nothing could ease her tapped-out mood. But as she eyeballed the faded box Jackson had opened up over her coffee table, she realized she was wrong.

"I'll have you know I never lose at Monopoly," she said, stopping to snag a bite of the beef broccoli before she put the carton on a tray next to her Lo Mein. The spicy tang of ginger sauce danced across her palate as she chewed. Jackson hadn't been kidding about the food being good. It was easily on a par with what she'd grab from her favorite place in Chinatown.

"Prepare to go down in flames, sweetheart," Jackson retorted, but his words were more teasing than threatening. "What do you want to be?"

Carly made her way to the living room with the tray and slid it to the carpet next to the table. "Oh, nice. You have an original set." She plucked the tiny silver thimble from the box and put it on GO. Of course Jackson chose the race car. Typical guy move.

Macho or not, he was still goin' down.

"Yeah, I'm old school. That Mega Edition junk just tarnishes a good game." He started sorting through the stack of brightly colored bills in the bottom of the box. "This is the set my brother and sisters and I played with when we were kids. I figured it would be more fun than watching a plain old movie."

She nodded over her shoulder as she returned to the kitchen for a couple bottles of water. "We played Monopoly a lot, too. My brothers used to cheat and give me twenty dollars instead of two hundred for passing GO. They were ruthless." Carly grinned. God, she hadn't thought of that in ages.

"I thought you said you always won." Jackson put a neat stack of bills on her side of the board before starting to count out his own.

"My father caught my brothers short-changing me every time I passed GO. But instead of punishing them once, he taught me how to strategize and work the board instead. After that, none of my brothers could beat me no matter how hard they tried."

"It sounds like your dad is a smart man."

A tiny pinch of sadness stuck in Carly's throat, but she swallowed it with a bittersweet smile. "He was. He died five years ago."

Jackson's eyes flickered darkly. "I'm sorry."

"Thank you." The silence stretched out between them in a thick beat before Carly blinked away the memory and took two water bottles from the fridge.

"Well, believe me when I tell you there's nothing quite as humbling as having a sister gloat over you. I bet your brothers didn't mess with you after that, huh?" His sober expression had been replaced with a more comfortable, curious look.

"Not at Monopoly, anyway," she said, her gaze catching

on the six-bottle wine fridge perched in a corner on the countertop. "You want a glass of wine?"

"To be honest, I'm not usually a wine guy. But if you've got something that pairs well with total domination in the Monopoly arena, I might consider a change of heart." He tried—unsuccessfully—to hide his smirk in the carton of beef broccoli.

"You're going to eat those words, mister." Carly slid a bottle of Riesling from the fridge and uncorked it with a practiced hand, pouring two glasses before sauntering back to the living room with a confident swagger.

"Nice food reference. Do you ever leave work at work?" Jackson took the glass she offered him, the pale golden liquid shimmering against his hand. Finally, he'd asked an easy question.

"No." She sat down cross-legged beside the coffee table and scooped up the dice, rattling them around with a muted click in her palm. "I look at food the way I look at life. It's pretty much impossible to separate the two, so I don't bother trying." Carly tipped her glass at him and took a sip. The semi-sweet bite of the wine slid down her throat with ease.

"And how do you look at life?"

She was all too aware of his eyes on her as she rolled the dice and moved her game piece to Vermont Avenue. Carly found a time-creased fifty-dollar bill in the neat stack Jackson had left for her and handed it over before answering.

"I think life should be simple, a reflection of what really matters, so I like to use ingredients that keep things uncomplicated. Then I can rely on honest flavors, evocative smells, and warm presentation to create an experience people will remember."

Jackson snagged the property card from the bank and passed it over, tipping his head at her. "So it's not just about the food."

"No, it's the bigger picture. I want people not just to remember the dish, but the feelings that go with it, if that makes sense."

"Ah. And that makes it personal. So food and life really do go hand in hand."

"Exactly." She took another sip of wine, admiring the lingering sweetness it left in its path. "How about you? How do you look at life?"

He let out a chuckle sexy enough to create an unfair advantage. "I'm pretty easy to please. Life's too short for anything else."

Right. Because just what her libido needed was more encouragement.

"So you're a go with the flow kind of guy," Carly replied, watching Jackson roll the dice.

He moved his token around the board, the corded muscles in his forearm pulling taut over the bones beneath as he reached across the table to put the money for Pennsylvania Railroad in the bank. "Sure. Most of the time."

"I might be jealous," she said, reaching for her carton of Lo Mein. "In my line of work, going with the flow only gets you trampled."

"Oh, come on. You probably have to adapt to a lot on any given night, right? I'd say that counts as going with the flow." Jackson took a sip of wine, regarding the glass with a surprised glance that translated to *not bad*.

Carly smiled, spooling more noodles over her chopsticks and taking a bite before scooping up the dice. "I'm adaptable, sure. But I can't afford to be mellow about it, and I definitely can't be easy to please. It's part of what makes it so hard to be a woman in my line of work."

"How do you mean?"

"In the kitchen, when a man is demanding, he's considered ambitious. When a woman expects perfection and won't settle for anything less, she's just a bitch." Carly shrugged, snapping up Kentucky Avenue and tucking the card next to her neatly divided stash of play money.

"Sounds like you have high standards." Jackson rolled the dice and landed next to her on Kentucky Avenue, both groaning and laughing as he counted out the rent to settle his debt.

Carly held out an expectant hand, trying to press her gleeful grin into a gracious smile. "If I didn't have high standards, I'd still be chopping onions for stock at the end of somebody's line."

"Is that how you got this?" Jackson trailed a roughened fingertip along the scar on her index finger before dropping the Monopoly money into her palm, and the unexpected contact sent a shiver down her spine.

"Oh." The breathy little gasp that pushed its way up from her chest was downright embarrassing, and Carly dropped her hand to the coffee table in an effort to cover it up. "Uh, yeah. Well, not onions, but you've got the right idea. I was cubing a butternut squash one day and slipped. I ended up with seven stitches."

A flicker darted over his blue eyes, darkening them for a split second before it disappeared. "Sounds like it hurt."

"To be honest, I was kind of more pissed that I'd wrecked the dish I was working on." That squash had been one of the most gorgeous items at Greenmarket that week. Bleeding all over it had been a travesty.

"You're pretty tenacious. And before you apologize, I mean it as a compliment."

Carly rolled the dice, trying to ignore the heat in her cheeks. "Sorry," she said, the apology auto-piloting its way out of her mouth anyway.

"Too bad your tenacity won't keep you out of trouble."

Jackson's drawl combined with an unmistakable glint in his eye, and Carly couldn't tell if she was more confused or turned on. "What do you mean?"

She followed his gaze down to the game board, where she mentally tallied the number of squares to her next landing spot with a groan. He leaned toward her, forearms propped over his muscular thighs, and grinned.

"I'm no expert, but it looks to me like even ambitious girls can go directly to jail."

"Eight, nine, ten . . . haha, that's Boardwalk, my friend. Pay up," Carly crowed, giving Jackson a firm nudge with her bare toes. He groaned and shook his head in disbelief.

"You're kidding, right? When did you put a hotel on the damned thing?" Jesus, she was absolutely relentless.

Who knew it would be such a freaking turn on?

Carly arched a brow at him, giving up a tart smile. "I used the money I took from you when you landed on Saint Charles Place last go-round, remember? That'll be two grand, please. Cash only."

Well, crap. "As much as I hate to admit it, I think I'm toast." Jackson reached out to count his dwindling stack of bills, knowing he was going to come up short. "I only have fourteen hundred. Looks like you win."

Not that he was surprised. Aside from her little stint in jail, Carly had run the board from Baltic to Boardwalk for the last hour and a half, and the three glasses of wine she'd had in the process only served to heighten her good-natured trash talk as she proceeded to wipe the floor with him.

"I told you not to mess with me," she said with a hot little smile, starting to pick up the houses and hotels from the board and put them back in the box.

Just because she'd won didn't mean he was going to let her have her way entirely. After all, a man had his pride.

"Oh, no you don't." Jackson reached out and caught her midscoop, curling his hand around her wrist. "Loser picks

up. House rules." The firm push of her pulse danced against
his fingers, but he didn't loosen his grip.

"It's my house, remember?" What her words lacked in
heat, her body made up for in spades. He let his hand sweep
around the thin curve of her wrist before letting it go.

"Yeah, but it's my game. Plus, I insist."

Her eyes glittered darkly against the glow of late-evening
sunlight setting in the windows behind her, but she didn't
argue. Throughout the course of the game, they'd talked
about various safe topics, like music (she liked classic rock),
sports (he'd have to overlook the Islanders thing for now),
and hobbies (she kept meaning to give yoga a try). But the
whole time, he'd been unable to shake the little voice in the
back of his mind, the one that made him think he was surely
going nuts because they'd had dinner together right on this
very spot not even two hours before.

Feed her.

"So are there house rules that say I can't put away the leftovers, too? Sitting here doing nothing isn't really my speed."
Carly's velvety voice jarred him out of his reverie.

"Fair enough," Jackson said, shaking off his weird inner
voice in favor of the here-and-now. "But only because there
are no dishes to do."

Packing up the rest of the game in a couple easy moves,
Jackson joined her in the kitchen a minute later. The overhead light illuminated the room with warm coziness, making
her look even more at ease in a space where she clearly already belonged. He watched Carly's relaxed gestures as she
popped the tops closed on the cardboard containers, straight-
ening everything into an orderly row.

"So do you create all of your own food experiences?"
He'd intended the question as casual conversation, but was
startled to realize he'd been thinking out loud more than anything else.

"I cook every day, if that's what you mean." Her bare feet

whispered over the floorboards, making a soft *shush-shush* sound as she made her way to the fridge with the cartons.

Jackson measured her with a steady glance, finally giving voice to the thought that had been niggling at the back of his mind all night. "I was curious if anyone ever cooks for you."

Carly shrugged, and the rustle of her hair over her shoulders sent up the intoxicating scent that went straight to his gut. "You brought takeout." She gestured to the food as she put it in the refrigerator.

"True. But I didn't make it." As soon as the words left his lips, the meaning behind them seemed to uncoil in his brain. He really hadn't fed her after all.

"I taste lots of things that other chefs make, but that's mostly to tweak them."

"That doesn't count. I'm talking about somebody making something just for you. You know, giving you the whole experience." Something in Jackson's chest thumped to life at the wide-eyed flash of Carly's stare, and his words felt reckless as they formed in his mind. "When was the last time someone fed you rather than the other way around?"

"I don't know." Carly's words escaped her on a murmur barely louder than a whisper. The innuendo threaded through the air like a provocative suggestion, so heady that Jackson could imagine its flavor in his mouth, so seductively good that he wanted Carly to taste it too. She looked up at him, her pretty brown eyes brimming not just with want, but with need.

This woman was starving for something, and he wanted to give it to her.

"That hardly seems fair. Maybe we should fix it." Jackson closed the space between them with a bold step, guiding her back against the refrigerator, so close he could feel the hot exhale of her breath as she released it on a sigh.

"How . . . how would we do that?" Carly pressed her palms against his chest, sending a shot of lusty energy all the way through him. He lowered his mouth to her upturned face, brushing his lips along her jaw and down to the sweet skin of her neck.

"Do you want me to show you?" He pulled back to look at her, putting the slightest space between them even though his body screamed in protest. No matter how badly he wanted her, he wasn't about to start something she didn't want him to finish. Carly stared up at him, her gaze dark and unwavering, as she whispered her reply.

"Yes."

In one swift move, she wrapped her arms around his shoulders, lifting up to meet his mouth with hers. Jackson responded with seamless ease, parting her soft lips as he kissed her, teasing her tongue with light, tentative strokes. Carly arched up into him, wordlessly demanding more, and it forced a groan from his chest.

"If you keep that up, your kitchen's never going to be the same." He cupped the back of her neck to expose the golden-brown curve of skin leading down to her shoulder.

"I do my best work in the kitchen." The rasp of her voice, thick with desire, and the suggestion that went with it made Jackson bite down on his lip to keep from ravishing her right there against the appliances. He dug deep, steadying his breath with considerable effort.

"The bedroom might be better suited for what I've got in mind. You asked me to give you the whole experience, and that's exactly what you're going to get."

Chapter Fifteen

As she crossed the threshold of her darkened bedroom with her heart slamming against her breastbone like it was considering a jailbreak, Carly was absolutely certain of only one thing.

Propriety and progression could take a hike. She wanted Jackson Carter so bad she could taste it.

"Carly." He stepped in and wrapped an arm around her ribcage, bending to capture her mouth in a scorching kiss. His tongue slid over hers, tempting her mouth open with relentlessly tantalizing dexterity that made her wonder what else he could do with it.

"Oh, God," Carly breathed, realizing belatedly that the oath was out loud. Jackson trailed kisses to the rim of her ear, then the sensitive skin just behind it. She let out an involuntary moan, and he pulled back to let his mouth hover over the warm spot beneath it, blowing on her damp skin with just enough pressure to elicit another heave of her chest.

Jackson's lips parted into a smile over her neck. "You're not making it easy for me to take my time, you know."

Carly's cheeks flushed, but only some of the heat was from pleasure. "Sorry," she breathed into his shoulder. Those wanton sighs probably *had* been over the top, but he felt so undeniably good that they'd escaped without her permission. She pressed her lips together in a vow of silence.

He took a step back, and her body betrayed her by shivering at the loss of contact. Muted light from the kitchen filtered down the hallway in faint strands, creating just enough illumination that she could make out the intensity of Jackson's stare. His blue eyes glittered over her face.

"No apologizing. I like it when you talk to me, remember?" He traced two fingers across her bare collarbone, the skin beneath them tightening in awareness and want. The callused edges of his fingers created just enough friction on her already aching body to draw a whimper from her throat, and he hooked a thumb beneath the strap of her tank top to slide it from her shoulder.

"Jackson." Carly whispered his name with a throaty breath. Even in the low, barely-there light, she could see the wicked intentions in Jackson's half-smile. Dropping his hands to hers, he led her through the golden shadows to her bed, sitting on the edge to face her. The gleam in his eyes became downright intoxicating as he opened his knees to make room for her body, wrapping his thick arms around her and trailing kisses along the soft cotton covering her belly while she stood weak-kneed in front of him.

"Keep talking." He edged the hem of her tank top over her belly button, following the path of the material with his tongue, and Carly reached down to curl her fingers over the rise of the fabric.

"I want this off." The words flew, uncensored, from her brain to her mouth, but Jackson didn't give her any time to feel self-conscious about it. He wrapped his fingers around hers, guiding her shirt up.

Kissing the exposed skin of her belly, Jackson murmured, "Anything else?" The rub of fabric on her tight, aching nipples was nearly excruciating, and Carly gave a sharp exhale as he lifted her top all the way off her shoulders.

"This too." Carly ran her fingers under her breasts to the front closure of her bra, and once again, Jackson's hands met her halfway. He ran his hands over the thin, white satin, cupping her breasts with firm fingers and sending a hard thrill all the way through her. Without pause, he slipped his thumbs over the hard peaks of her nipples, stroking her with slow attention, and Carly gripped the breadth of his shoulders in approval.

She arched into him, his breath heating her already sultry skin, and he opened the clasp between her breasts with a swift twist. He laved attention first on one breast, then the other, with both his fingers and mouth. Every tight ministration, every gentle touch that followed, shot rising heat to the juncture between her thighs, until Carly was certain she wasn't going to be able to trust her legs to hold her up.

As if he could read her mind, Jackson cradled his palms around her back, teasing the hollow of her shoulder blades as she arched into the warmth of his mouth. Hooking a leg around her body and using his hands for leverage, Jackson swung her to the bed, facing her side to side for a surprisingly tender kiss.

"You're driving me crazy," he murmured, breaking from her mouth to return his focus to her breasts, flicking his tongue over the bud of one nipple while she groaned in encouragement.

"I think you've got that backwards." Carly laced her fingers around the back of his head to hold him fast. Oh, God, if he didn't stop, she wasn't going to stop, and that meant . . .

She was on the cusp of the very first orgasm she hadn't had to work for.

Jackson lifted his head, his mischievous grin as palpable as his touches. "Backwards can be fun, too." He ran a fingertip around her navel before placing a kiss at the top of her breast. Something raw and desirous sprang all the way through her, filling her in a needful rush, and she scooped her hands beneath his arms to pull his mouth back to hers.

"I like you here." Carly slipped a hand to the tight press of their side-lying bodies and skimmed her palm down Jackson's chest, resting her fingers on the waistband of his well-worn Levi's for just a second before yanking his shirt over his head. The sweet friction of skin on skin sent a shockwave through Carly, and when Jackson hissed out an audible breath, a wave of pleasure coursed through her on its heels. Emboldened by his response, she brushed her hands over the hard muscles in his chest, exploring the fold of his shoulder and neck with her greedy kisses.

Jackson threaded his fingers through her hair, tightening them as her kisses migrated lower. "Carly," he ground out, his voice a husky demand. She longed to trail her hand up the hard line of his thigh, to make him say her name with that reverent, needful tone over and over. She dipped her fingertips low against the inseam of his jeans, brushing them slowly to the top of his button fly. Her movements were heavy with desire, and she stroked him with one hand while working the buttons on his jeans with the other.

"I thought I was supposed to be giving *you* the whole experience," Jackson bit out, catching her hand in his.

Carly raised her eyes to meet his heavily-lidded gaze. "You did say that backwards could be fun," she pointed out, borrowing his maddening smirk.

She barely had time to register the provocative smile Jackson dished up in return before his arms were around her, rolling her body away from his with just enough force to make her both breathless and wildly turned on. Gripping her hips from behind and propping her on her side with his chest to her back, he slid a hand over the seam of her jeans to tease her with a hot, unyielding stroke.

"Do you want to find out?" With his arm slung low over

her hips from behind, Jackson freed the button on her jeans, guiding her zipper all the way down. The tip of his tongue edged over the slope of her shoulder, and the brazen heat of his mouth made quick work of Carly's control. She bucked backward into his hips, pressing her backside into his rock-hard erection with a moan.

"Yes. God, please yes."

Jackson didn't hesitate, lowering her jeans until the only thing between his hands and the slickness of her core was a pair of dark red panties.

"No white cotton today?" He settled behind her, rubbing his thumb over the waistband at her hip.

"No." Carly flushed with embarrassment. She'd had to rip the price tag off the ones she was wearing, and they'd been in her drawer for over two years. Comfortable or not, no way was she going to risk another sighting of those horrible granny panties. Jackson snaked his arm around the curve of her waist, delving past the front of the waistband to slide his fingers against her sex, and everything but pure, uncut lust disappeared from Carly's brain.

"These are just as hot. In fact," Jackson's hand moved sinuously around her hip and down the outside of her thigh. "I think you should keep them on."

In a flash just as fast as the one that put him behind her, Jackson scooped Carly's legs apart to hook her ankle around his knee. Pressing his chest in a tight fit to her back, he reached around her again, his fingers coaxing aside the seam at her inner thigh to push into her aching core.

"*Oh.*" Carly's gasp shuddered through her, reverberating in her chest before escaping from her lips. Jackson cupped his palm against her, alternately testing her depths and teasing the sensitive skin above in flawless rhythm. Every cell in her body sizzled to life, demanding more, and he wordlessly delivered, playing her as if she were a priceless instrument.

Carly rocked against him in time, each thrust like a tightening of strings, as he coaxed her closer to release. The rasp of his fingers dared her to climb higher still, until with one last sweep and thrust with his hand, she finally tightened around him to tumble over the edge of her orgasm.

When Carly's reckless cries subsided into heavy breathing, Jackson shifted her to face him, placing the soft hint of a kiss on her mouth. The tenderness of the kiss did nothing to offset the raw desire already burning back to life in Carly's body, and the familiar need swirling through her core surprised her. With still-trembling hands, she reached down to free the rest of Jackson's clothes while he slipped her panties from her hips. Still facing her, Jackson ran a hand down the curve of her breast, skimming the flare of her body to rest on her hip.

"You are unbelievably sexy," he said in a gruff voice, thick with want. "But we don't have to do this."

Carly lifted her gaze to his, eyes wide with shock. Even though he was barely visible in the deep shadows of the room, she recognized the desire banked in his eyes, and it filled her yet again with certainty.

"Oh, yes we do." She leaned in close, placing her lips on his and her hands on his body, down the hard line of his chest and past the corded muscles of his belly. She followed the fine dusting of hair from his belly button, trailing her palm lower until she reached his cock, stroking him slowly. Nothing had ever felt so sinfully delicious and yet so right at the same time, and Jackson exhaled a hot breath into her hair.

"Christ, I can't think when you do that." He arced into her palm with a groan. "Come here."

Carly didn't stop her ministrations, using her free hand to guide Jackson onto his back while still caressing him firmly with the other. "You're awfully bossy in bed."

In one deft move, she slung a leg over his lap to straddle the cradle of his hips, resting her body low over his belly.

She leaned forward, letting the tips of her breasts brush against his hard chest, and his mouth stole the groan from her lips as they kissed.

"That's creative," Jackson grated as he broke from her lips.

A cat-in-cream grin bubbled up from the depths of her chest, spilling out on a sigh. "I'm good at creative, remember?"

"And I'm good at safe," he answered, gently rolling from beneath her to retrieve a condom from his wallet. She sent up a silent *thank God* for his resourcefulness, and the sentiment becoming personified as he returned to the bed and pulled her close.

"Now where were we?" Jackson lay back, scooping her easily toward him as if they'd never parted. He thrust his hips against hers in a tantalizing push, making her thighs quake in anticipation.

"Right . . . there." The glide of his body against hers drove Carly to a slow rhythm, and the feel of his cock close to her heat made everything under her skin prickle and hum with desire. She arched forward, angling her core over him inch by inch, until he filled her completely.

"Oh." Carly's groan shock-waved through her entire body before it dissipated, and she was so caught up in the feeling of raw electricity in her veins that for a long second, she couldn't move.

Jackson released one hand from where it rested on her hip, brushing his fingers across Carly's face in a tender sweep.

"Are you okay?" A streak of worry ribboned through the look of passion on his face, catching in her chest, and holding on with tight fingers.

"I am very okay," she whispered, bracing her hands on either side of Jackson's body and rocking against him in a slow thrust. His hands found her hips again, and he steadied her balance while arching into her. The friction and intensity of how he felt inside her brought out everything from a shiver to a moan, and Carly reached them all with delicious variation. Jackson guided her hips in perfect rhythm, and the pressure building at the spot where they were joined took hold of her body in an unrelenting wave. Every one of her muscles squeezed tight to hold onto the sensation of pure pleasure coursing through her, and Jackson thrust even deeper in reply.

"Carly." He grated out her name on a rough breath, locking his hands around her backside in a desperate grip, leaving no space between the hard angle of his hips and the lush curve of her own. Quickening the pace, he thrust against her in a movement so unforgiving and sinfully hot that Carly thought she'd die from the ecstasy of it. Jackson's fingers tightened further, guiding her over his length and back again, until he arched into her in a tight shudder, holding her fast and calling her name.

Time hung in the air, suspended in the shadows of her room, and Carly folded herself over Jackson's chest, utterly boneless. Her limbs were heavy with the feeling of being totally sated, but as the haze wore off, the wheels of her mind began to perk to life.

What was she supposed to do now? Lying here with Jackson was nice—he felt strong beneath her, and the warmth of his skin coupled with the slowing rhythm of his breath was even better than nice. Still, should she say something? Thanking him for the two unbelievable orgasms he'd just given her seemed strange, even though she was grateful as hell. So what was the etiquette for this kind of thing?

Thankfully, Jackson took charge by shifting her to his side and nestling her in close. His stomach let out an enthusiastic grumble, and Carly drew back in surprise.

"Are you hungry?" She propped herself up on an elbow, furrowing her brow at him in the dark.

He hesitated. "Who, me? Not at all." In a bid to prove him wrong, another growl echoed from Jackson's midsection, and he covered it with a hand as if to shut it up.

"Seriously? You're a horrible liar." Unable to help it, she started to laugh. "If you're hungry, you should eat."

He stilled, eyes flicking over hers. "Well, yeah, but I thought . . . I mean, I'm supposed to . . . well, I can hold you for a while first. If you want."

Carly pressed a smile between her lips. She might not have much in the way of social graces, but feeding somebody . . . now that was something she knew how to do.

"Tell you what. Why don't we warm up some of those leftovers, and then we can watch TV on the couch. You can eat and hold me at the same time. What do you say?"

A mischievous smile worked its way over Jackson's lips, and he shook his head before sitting up to give her a quick, tender kiss.

"You had me at leftovers."

Jackson leaned into the metal belly of a 1968 Pontiac GTO, both palms splayed on the driver's side quarter panel, and gave Shane a quizzical what's-next glance. All things being equal, he could do a hell of a lot worse than helping Shane finish a tune up on a Friday evening.

Although considering how he'd started his week, the ending seemed rather anticlimactic. Literally.

"Hey, can you hand me that wrench so I can pull these spark plugs?" Shane jutted his chin at the toolbox on the floor between them. "And by the way, when were you going to tell me you slept with my girlfriend's boss?"

Jackson sputtered, midreach. "Well, I uh . . . what makes you think I slept with Carly?"

Shane shook his head, moving a couple steps closer to retrieve the wrench himself, delivering a wry smile on his way. "The shit-eating grin you've been wearing since you had dinner with her is kind of a dead giveaway. Plus, Bellamy said Carly's been in a great mood all week. It's not much of a logic leap from there."

At the mention of his perma-grin, Jackson tried to smooth his expression, but it was a total no-go. He'd been smiling like a fool all week, and with good reason, too. As it turned out, warmed up leftovers were sexier than he'd bargained for, inciting a return trip to Carly's bedroom for round two before he'd finally kissed her good-bye just after one in the morning. It had been well worth the lack of sleep, even when he'd been tasked with the mind-numbing job of putting up drywall for nine hours straight the next day.

Jackson gave in and let his smile eke out. "Okay, fair enough. You win. Just don't tell Bellamy." The last thing he wanted was to make things awkward for Carly at work. Plus, he and Carly were barely seeing each other. No reason for the whole world to make a big deal out of it.

"Please. Bellamy's no dummy. She said with how Carly's been acting, she either got laid or won the lottery. Since Carly hasn't quit her job, we're banking on the sex."

Despite his surprise at Shane's straight-to-the-point response, Jackson had to chuckle. "Hey, for the record, I'd bet my next paycheck that even if Carly did win the lottery, she'd keep her job." He spun the wing nut that held the GTO's air filter in place to loosen it.

"Valid point. Good mood or not, I bet she still runs that kitchen like it's a military base at DEFCON One."

Jackson nodded in agreement—after all, Carly herself had said she couldn't afford to be laid-back, no matter what the circumstances. He had no reason to think she'd change her colors in the name of excellent sex.

And damn. It really had been excellent.

"So I take it you're going out with her again?" Shane's question yanked Jackson back down to planet Earth, and he blinked at the grimy air filter in his hands, shaking his head a few times before tossing it in the trash bin.

"Dude. I know it was impulsive to sleep with her, but give me a little credit, here. I'm not a one night stand kind of guy."

"So did the two of you make plans, Don Juan?" Shane flipped back, not breaking stride with the spark plug in his hand.

Jackson paused to mutter a choice suggestion about where exactly Shane could shove his Don Juan, but then his grin got the best of him again. "I'm taking her fishing on Monday."

Shane arched a dark brow. "You're serious."

"As a tax audit." Jackson sauntered to the workbench for a new air filter.

"And here I thought you liked her," Shane said. Jackson stiffened ever so slightly, knuckles tightening around the cardboard box in his hands.

"We're not getting married or anything, if that's what you mean." Suddenly, it took effort to keep the laid-back edge in his voice, but he shrugged once, covering up the streak of unease.

"Most girls would rather be skinned alive than go the worms and rod route, that's all." Shane's voice was easygoing enough for both of them, and Jackson relaxed. It was just a trip to Big Gap Lake for the day. He went all the time.

"Yeah, Carly's definitely not most girls." Jackson laughed. "She's the one who actually suggested it."

Shane's jaw dropped. "Get out of here."

"I shit you not," Jackson promised, holding up one hand in solemn oath. "We were talking about things to do in Pine Mountain, and she asked me about the lake."

Specifically, Carly had asked him if there was anything edible swimming in the lake, to which he'd answered "define edible." Sure, there were some decent dinner options lurking in the water, but they were a lot harder to catch than most of the other critters that would snap at any bait on a line. Those were the ones you had to worry about.

"Why on God's green earth would she want you to take

her fishing? It doesn't seem like something a lifelong New York would want to do."

He lifted a shoulder in a noncommittal shrug. "She wants to go on a research mission."

"Sexy." Shane grinned, rolling his eyes.

"Oh, fuck you." Jackson's laugh hammered home the complete lack of heat in his words. Truth was, as soon as the request to go fishing had crossed Carly's lips, despite the reason behind it, he'd found the whole thing *very* sexy. "She wants to check out the opportunities to use local ingredients at the restaurant. You know, make the food experience more personal by adding regional flair."

"Putting regional flair on a twelve-ounce pike is like putting lipstick on a pig, Jax. Some of the fish in that lake are pretty scary. You've said so yourself." Shane dropped his wrench into the toolbox with a *clang* and hooked a thumb through his belt loop.

"That's why I'm taking her, dumbass. She wants to see if there's anything worth looking for, but she's never been fishing so she doesn't know where to start. We're just going to give it a try and see if we can come up with some bass or maybe a catfish."

All in all, Jackson really couldn't have asked for a better deal. Pretty girl, relaxing pastime. What more could a guy want?

"Sounds like it's right up your alley." His eyes darted over Jackson with an odd expression that was gone before he could reply. "Thanks for the help. Buy you a beer for your effort? Bellamy's on dinner service until eleven."

Jackson nodded, his thoughts drifting to Carly at the mention of the restaurant.

Feed her.

His head jerked up with a start, and the words that had been absent all week rattled around in his mind like they'd never left.

Chapter Sixteen

Jackson maneuvered his truck over the winding driveway leading to Carly's bungalow at about the same time the sun crested over the horizon through the trees. Few things in life were as pretty as a mountain sunrise, and he eased the truck to a stop and got out, taking a long second to enjoy the view from the top of her driveway.

"Hey." Carly's voice, sleep-laden and sexier for it, took him completely by surprise, and he jerked toward the spot where she stood on the porch.

"Are you ever going to let me ring the bell?" Jackson asked, cursing himself for spouting out the first thing that popped into his head. Damn, she looked cute in her broken-in jeans and red hoodie, with all of those dark, beautiful waves of hair piled up on her head in a knot. She made her way down the walk, a steaming travel mug in each hand and a small picnic basket in the crook of one elbow.

"You're welcome to ring the bell as much as you like, but if you wake Sloane up, it's your funeral." Carly handed him one of the mugs and buried a yawn in her fleece-covered shoulder before returning her arm to her side. "Girlfriend is a little uptight about her beauty sleep."

"Thanks." Jackson toasted her with his cup. "And some

of us get up this early all the time, you know." He walked Carly around to the passenger side of the truck to open her door.

"I can't help it if you're clinically insane," she said, stifling another yawn and climbing in. "Speaking of which, aren't you supposed to be at work right now?"

Jackson laughed, walking around to climb behind the wheel before answering. "Going to work makes me clinically insane?" He rolled the windows down by habit, and the ensuing breeze toyed with the loose tendrils around Carly's face as he pulled out of her driveway and started down Rural Route 4.

"Your charm is no good with me before ten AM." She lifted a brow, probably in an effort to look menacing, but she was too damn pretty to pull it off. "You're avoiding the question."

He sent an intentionally lazy smile in her direction. "Did you just call me charming?"

Carly's jaw tightened over a frown, which struck Jackson as more adorable than anything else. Holy shit, was she tough. She opened her mouth, presumably to retract her statement about his charm, and he cut her off with a grin.

"Okay, okay. Technically, I didn't take a day off. My boss, Luke, had some stuff he was going to take care of on Saturday, but I did it instead. He's covering for me today to make up for it."

Her narrow gaze softened. "You really didn't have to do that just to take me fishing."

"Are you kidding? Luke was so grateful to sleep in on a Saturday, I think he considered giving me tomorrow off, too. And if you want to have a shot at catching anything worth eating, then yeah. I really did have to do it. Morning's the best time to catch fish around here. Too late in the day and the tourists get loud."

Carly laughed, a magical sound that popped him right in the gut. "I'm sorry, I wasn't aware fish had ears."

"Not all animals need ears to hear. When there are a lot of people on the lake, water skiing and tubing and whatnot, most fish don't tend to stick around. The disturbances in the water along with the higher temperatures later in the day send them packing." He paused to take a sip of coffee. Bold, rich flavor filled his senses, and he drew back, impressed. "Wow, this is insanely good."

Carly laced her fingers around her own travel mug, a satisfied smile on her lips. "Thanks. It's a special blend from Jamaica. A little tough to get, and kinda pricey, but if you're going to get up this early, you might as well have something that'll kick-start the hell out of your day."

"What'd you do to make it taste so good?" Jackson took another draw, inhaling as he went. The second sip didn't disappoint, either, all deep and earthy, and he savored the smooth aftertaste on his tongue.

"It's fresh-ground, but other than running it through a French press and adding a little sugar and milk to offset the strength, I didn't have to do much." Carly closed her eyes and inhaled, the curve of her breasts rising up to meet the open V of her hoodie, and every one of Jackson's nerve endings sizzled to life.

She exhaled, slow and sweet. "It also doesn't hurt that we're drinking it on a gorgeous morning with fresh air pouring in through the windows, you know?" A long strand snapped free from the knot on her head, bringing the smell of wildflowers with it.

Forget the coffee. The scent of Carly's hair, the way she made something as benign as a fleece hoodie look so utterly sexy, the jolt of heat that coursed through him like raw electricity . . . now that was worth waking up for.

"Right." Jackson laughed as he made the turn toward the docks. "I forgot. Everything's an experience."

Carly smiled over the rim of her coffee mug, and her fresh-scrubbed face and big brown eyes ganged up on his libido in a move that he'd swear was unfair, except he liked it too much to complain.

"Life's an experience. You might as well eat good food on the way."

Carly eyed the small, pristine boat moored to the dock with sinking uncertainty, her knuckles going white around the wicker handles of her picnic basket. This was not the kind of experience she'd had in mind.

"You didn't mention we'd be going on a boat," Carly said, her vocal cords threatening to betray her casual façade. She shifted her weight against the silvery, weather-worn boards, watching Jackson step aboard the boat in a seamless transition from dock to deck.

"It's pretty much impossible to catch anything you'd eat in water this shallow, so I asked my brother-in-law if we could borrow his boat for the day. Why, is that a problem?" Jackson paused, his blond brow furrowed in concern.

Carly eyed the lazily bobbing boat in a standoff, grateful for the cover of her sunglasses on the off chance it could sense her fear.

"Nope," she lied. How the hell was she supposed to know you couldn't fish off the perfectly good pier jutting out from the end of the dock, and that Jackson's brother-in-law had a boat just right for the job? Her desire to use local resources felt far less emphatic than it had when she'd started tossing the idea around in her head a few weeks ago.

"You want a hand?" Jackson put the fishing poles and supplies they'd picked up from the bait shop down on the deck by his feet, turning to give her a crooked smile on his way back to standing.

"Sure," Carly replied, feeling anything but. "So, um, what

kind of boat is this, exactly?" Her inner voice willed him to answer with something along the lines of *the kind that's physically impossible to sink*.

"It's a nineteen-foot Bayliner with a 150-horsepower motor." He reached out, presumably to help Carly on board, but she rooted her feet to the dock and passed over the picnic basket in an effort to stall. It figured her one fear in life would rear its ugly head. How had she not seen this coming? Nineteen feet was downright miniscule for a boat. The Staten Island Ferry could probably eat ten of these little things for breakfast. And she wasn't even crazy about the ferry.

Jackson cleared his throat in a gentle rumble, and Carly was startled to realize he'd stepped back off the boat to stand next to her on the dock. "You've never been on a boat before, have you?"

She crossed her arms over her chest, a trickle of sweat beading between her shoulder blades even though it wasn't all that hot out.

"For your information, I have," Carly corrected, her chin lifted high. "Just . . . not one this small."

"Ah. I take it you're not a fan." Jackson's trademark smirk was conspicuously absent, and she exhaled in a slow leak.

"I don't like being right on the water, that's all."

But rather than tease her or give her a hard time, he just gestured to the boards beneath their feet. "So you're okay on the dock."

"Well, the dock is anchored to the ground. Plus, the water's not so deep here." Carly pointed to the shoreline, where a tall swath of reeds poked up from the bottom. "I just . . . I feel more comfortable knowing where the bottom is."

Stupid, irrational fear! Why couldn't she be afraid of thunderstorms like Sloane? At least that made sense—natural disasters were way scarier than plain old watercraft, for God's sake.

Jackson took a step toward her, so close that there were barely inches between them, and she inhaled fresh soap and morning sun, intoxicating on his skin.

"I want to show you something on board the boat. After you see it, if you don't want to go, we can fish off the pier."

"But we can't catch anything off the pier. You said—"

He leaned in and kissed her, firmly but without force, and she was so shocked that all she could do was kiss him back. He lingered on her bottom lip for just a second before dropping his chin and lifting her sunglasses.

"I know what I said. Now shut up and come look at this so you can decide what you want to do, okay?"

All Carly could think in the instant that followed Jackson's words was that she really wanted him to keep kissing her. "O-okay."

With her brain too wrapped up in lust-tinged shock to cry out to her legs in protest, she followed Jackson to the edge of the dock. He boarded the boat with ease before turning to grasp both of her shaking hands, and she placed her feet in his footsteps as she slowly boarded the boat. They were mere feet from the dock where she'd stood without fear just a minute ago, the same clusters of lakeside reeds waving lazily from their anchors in the murky bottom. She could do this.

Probably.

"Great. Why don't you have a seat for a second? I have to start the engine for what I want to show you, but I promise we won't leave the dock."

She nodded her agreement, and Jackson guided her to the bolted down passenger seat before sitting behind the wheel, pulling a key with a funny-looking foam keychain on it out of his pocket. He slid it into the boat's ignition, starting the boat with a low growl.

"This is a fish finder." He gestured to a square screen that looked startlingly like the GPS in Carly's Honda. She narrowed her eyes at it, confused.

"Okay." She drew the word out like a question, and Jackson pointed to the corner of the screen, continuing in that completely laid-back way that made the knots of tension in Carly's shoulders moderate in spite of her unease.

"It uses sonar to show an image of what's under the boat. It's not an exact picture, like a photograph, but it gives you a really good idea of what's down there based on the shape and density of things." He pressed a couple of buttons, adjusting the screen to show her a series of colorful blobs.

"Those are fish?" she asked, incredulous. There were a jillion waves and colors on the screen! This lake was loaded with fish, right here at the dock. They had to be able to catch something from dry land . . . or at least dry dock boards.

Jackson chuckled, and it rippled through her without permission. "No."

Carly pursed her mouth into a tight line. "Then why would you show it to me?"

"Because that's the lake bottom. See? You can see the layers of what's beneath the boat, all the way to the ground. It even measures how deep it is, right down to a tenth of a foot."

He pointed to the numbers in the corner of the screen, and the grainy picture popped into relief in Carly's mind. It really was the bottom of the lake, with a different color representing the varying thickness of what lay beneath them on the lake bed, and a dark, floating space for the water in between.

"So, I can look at this and see the bottom at any given time?" Her innate fear of being out in open water screeched at her that it didn't matter, they could still sink like a stone, but her curiosity let the question out of her mouth anyway. Jackson wouldn't drag her off in a boat that wasn't structurally sound; plus, the lake wasn't *that* big. They'd still be able to see land, even if they went pretty far out.

Jackson grinned, an unnervingly lopsided, endearing

smile that lit up her belly with warmth. "Yup. And bass don't like deep water, anyway. They stick pretty close to the shore, in the grass where it's nice and cool. We'll probably do most of our fishing in about ten feet of water."

"Really?" Okay, ten feet wasn't so bad. And she liked that close to the shore part. "If they like it so close to the shore, how come they don't hang out here by the dock?" The stubborn part of her really wanted to get back on those boards so her feet could celebrate the solidity of dry land. But her curiosity kept her tethered to the middle of the boat.

"I told you, too loud. We have to go out around the far edge of the lake, into the eddies a bit to find quieter ground. Unless you want to stay here." He shrugged, a gentle lift of his shoulders that told her he really would stay if she wanted to.

The sun shone down over the opaque water, thick green like sea glass, sending little sparkles of gold over the low waves. Carly felt a sudden reckless desire to stay on the boat, to look her fear in the face and tell it, "not today." She slid a glance at Jackson, filling her lungs with air so fresh she could taste it on her tongue.

"Okay, Gilligan. But keep the Fish-o-Vision where I can see it. And make it quick, would you? Before I change my mind."

Jackson maneuvered the Bayliner through one of the quieter eddies on the lake, happy to find it unoccupied by other fishermen, or anyone else for that matter. They had a good couple of hours before the tourists would come through and booger things up with pontoon boats and jet skis, making it all but impossible to catch anything. He killed the motor and reached down for his tackle box, propping it on the seat behind him.

"So does this thing have an anchor, or what?" Carly asked, still a little pale from the ride across the lake. All in all, for someone who was afraid of being on a boat but too stubborn to say so, she'd been a trooper, especially when he'd hit open water and had to crank up the speed to get them across the lake.

"Of course it has an anchor. But we're not going to use it. Not until I'm sure this is where we want to stay, anyhow." He pulled a lure out of the box, the metal hook on the end glinting in the morning sun, and reached low for one of the fishing poles he'd stowed in the storage compartment by his feet.

"We're just going to float?" Carly sounded less than thrilled at the idea. Man, she didn't like to give up control for anything, did she? He grinned and shook his head, threading the lure onto the monofilament and drawing it tight.

"Yup. We'll be fine. Trust me."

Carly paused, still sitting firmly in the very center of her seat. The water sloshed in quiet rhythm around the sides of the boat, a slight breeze keeping the temperature cool but pleasant. After a minute, when they hadn't capsized or run aground or been swallowed alive by the Loch Ness Monster, she shrugged out of her hoodie and slid a few inches closer to the side of the vessel, peering over the edge.

"It is pretty nice out here." She turned her face up to the sun, the cotton of her snug white T-shirt emphasizing her luscious curves in the bright light, and Jackson barely missed running his finger through with the barb at the end of the lure. Christ, Carly even made sitting still look hot. He needed to distract himself, otherwise he wasn't going to escape with all ten digits intact.

"So, fishing," he said, clearing his throat. "There's not a whole lot to the actual process. Casting's the hardest part, and I can do that for you." Her lips curved down in an I-don't-think-so frown, and Jackson recanted. "Or I can teach you how to do it." He handed over the fishing pole he'd just baited.

"So how come you're not using real worms?" She peered at the plastic lure on the end of the line.

"Don't sound so disappointed. Different fish bite on different things. We're going to try our luck with these first. If all else fails, there's live bait in the cooler."

Carly nodded. "Okay."

Jackson's libido gave him a healthy nudge and two thumbs up. Carly was definitely the only girl he'd ever met who hadn't made a face at the mention of worms. Man, her boldness was sexy.

Her casting skills, however, were pretty abysmal.

"Well, you've, um, kind of got the right idea," Jackson said the third time through. In truth, they were lucky no one had lost an eye or taken a header into the lake, but he didn't want to discourage her efforts. "You sure you don't want me to start the first one out for you?"

Carly chewed her bottom lip, which sent his pulse into an absolute frenzy of oh-yeah. "Well, maybe just to start out," she agreed, passing him her fishing pole.

He cast the line just short of a bank of reeds before returning it to her waiting hands. "Now just turn the reel slowly, like this." Jackson reached around her petite frame with ease, covering her hands with his own and rolling the handle of the reel in a slow draw. "And if anything pulls back, holler."

"I can do that." Carly glanced up at him over her shoulder, her ear brushing against his chest as she turned her head. "Thank you."

"Sure." Reluctantly, he stepped back to bait his own line, standing next to her as he cast. The morning was nothing short of stunning, and after a while, Carly got the hang of casting well enough to manage with only a little help. They fished in comfortable quiet, lulled by the gentle sloshing of the water against the boat, and Carly's face relaxed into a serene smile. Surely, there weren't many things in life better than this.

"I'll bet you don't get this kind of quiet in New York." He inhaled a deep breath of sunshine and mellow bliss. The handful of times he'd ventured into Philly, he'd made it all of six hours before the noise drove him bat-shit crazy. Carly's languid expression disappeared, covered over by a stony façade, one that caught his full attention.

"No. You don't."

Jackson was silent for a minute that lapsed into several, casting and reeling in on a gradual draw before repeating the process once, then twice. "Still homesick," he said. It wasn't a question, but she answered him all the same.

"Yeah." Carly stood, moving nothing but her gaze as she watched him cast, the monofilament whizzing in a tight, silence-slicing hiss over the boat. Her own line lay slack in the glassy lake, and after a minute, she slowly reeled it in.

A strange knot of tension squeezed Jackson's ribcage like a legion of rubber bands, flexing around him and forcing him to ask the question rambling around in his mind. "Don't take this the wrong way, but what's keeping you here? I mean, if you miss it that much, why don't you go back?"

Carly's laugh was a hard, humorless burst. "Go back to what? An ex who'll stop at nothing to use me to further his career? Or maybe a rumor mill that sees me as second-rate in spite of all my hard work? And don't even get me started about my mother." She raised her chin in a defiant jerk. "Everybody keeps saying I should go back, but they don't understand. I don't have anything I can go back to."

He swept a long glance over her, the tranquil beauty of their surroundings so at odds with the sadness on her face.

"You feel like airing it out?"

Ahhh, stupid question. Carly wasn't one of those touchy-feely types. She was too tough for spilling her guts. He opened his mouth to tell her to forget it when he caught the strangest expression on her face.

"You know what? I think I do."

Chapter Seventeen

"Let me make sure I've got this right. Your husband is emotionally blackmailing you to sign a contract for a TV show just so it will make him look good, and your mother wants you to reconcile with him to save your soul?" Jackson propped his sunglasses over the crown of his head to pin Carly with a shocked, sky-blue stare. It was the first thing he'd said in about twenty minutes, and she suddenly felt a lot lighter for having put the last seven months into words.

Even if those words had basically amounted to Jackson's paraphrase.

"That about sums it up." She moved her gaze back to the bottle-green water before sitting down in her seat and wrapping her arms around herself.

"So you see why I'm stuck? My mother has already called me four times, and that was just this week. We keep having the same conversation, over and over again," Carly sighed. "I don't blame her, necessarily. I think underneath it all, she only wants me to be happy. But Travis has her snowed just like he does everyone else. Despite any good intentions she might have, it's impossible to get her to see my side of things."

"That sounds familiar." Jackson gave his reel a tight yank, and she wondered if maybe the line was tangled in the reeds.

"It does?"

He nodded. "My mother would be a lot happier if my life included some things that it doesn't, too. I'm happy being who I am. But she doesn't see my bigger picture the same way."

"That's a perfect way of putting it, actually," Carly agreed. "Okay, yes, I'm a little homesick, but at least I have a job out here. I'm running my own kitchen, on my own terms. And the experience will make me that much better when I do go back to New York, so it's worth it. I've just got to get through this crap with Travis first."

A muscle ticked in Jackson's jaw. "Yeah, he sounds like a real prize."

"It sounds trite, but I was young and stupid. He charmed the hell out of me, and I fell for it hook, line, and sinker." She paused, letting out a chagrined laugh as the unintentional pun registered.

"You get one bad fishing reference per day, so this time, I'll let you slide," Jackson drawled, resetting his lure with an easygoing smile. He turned to cast, the hypnotic whir of the fishing line sliding over the reel just as it had for the last half hour as she'd talked. It was oddly relaxing, and the just-right combination of sunshine and lakeside breeze on top of it seemed to reach down and pull the tension right from Carly's shoulders. Which was nothing short of a miracle, considering the topic of conversation.

"So what now? I mean, your lawyer said you can still proceed with the divorce, right?" Jackson asked gently enough, but she still had to fight back a wince before answering.

"Yeah, that part's pretty cut and dried. I filed on solid ground, and there are people who can corroborate Travis's affair." The word tasted bitter, like coffee that had been on the burner for way too long. "Sloane and I managed to knock about half the stuff off the list of things he wanted back. I'm convinced he already has some of the other stuff, but is claiming he doesn't just to drag the whole thing out. At any rate, my lawyer filed the paperwork showing I complied in a timely manner, but there are no guarantees the judge will move to proceed. So for now, he's getting what he wants."

Frustration bubbled in Carly's chest, pushing her thoughts right past her brain-to-mouth filter. "You know what sucks about it the most? I actually believed in marriage and happily ever after once. I thought Travis and I were going to take the culinary world by storm and live out our dreams, but instead I just got taken for a ride."

"Better that you found out when you did, rather than further down the line," Jackson said, but she shook her head in a tight swing.

"What would really be better is if I'd never believed in it in the first place." Carly's words echoed over the lake, sending a ripple of disquiet up her spine. God, she really was jaded. But if she'd never fallen for Travis's empty promises she wouldn't be in this mess.

Jackson reeled his fishing line all the way in, lifting it out of the water. Instead of recasting, he put the fishing pole down carefully and came to sit next to her on the bench seat across the back of the boat.

"Maybe. But you can't change that now, so there's really no point in worrying about it."

Carly sighed, leaning against his sun-warmed frame slightly, and he wrapped an arm around her shoulders to pull her closer. The tough, land-on-your-feet part of her brain told her in no uncertain terms to end the embrace. If she wasn't going to indulge in a pity party for herself, she sure as heck wasn't going to let someone else throw one, either. But as she melted against Jackson's body, absorbing the lull of the boat and the steady calm of his chest pressed to her side, she felt a smooth wave of comfort roll through her, filling up even the tiniest places.

And she didn't want to let go.

"Easy for you to say," Carly mumbled into his T-shirt, nestling closer. "You're not the one getting divorced from the world's slickest egomaniac."

Okay, she really needed to stop feeling so sorry for herself. She shifted, fully intending to let go and put her game face back on, but Jackson surprised her by holding her even closer. He leaned into the corner of the bench seat, pulling her back to his chest, and chuckled into her hair.

"Nope. But that doesn't mean I can't help you out a little while you are."

Carly's insides tightened, flooding familiar heat down into the seam of her jeans. An image of Jackson, face passionate as he rolled his hips into hers, flooded through her mind.

"You are rather helpful," she murmured, letting him brush his lips against hers in a slow stroke. Her body relaxed into the hard lines and angles of Jackson's arms, and she went liquid as he kissed her thoroughly before pulling back to give her a sleepy, seductive smile.

"Just a little food for thought."

In the end, although the idea of peeling every inch of clothing from Carly's hot little body right there in broad daylight was enticing as hell, Jackson forced himself to pull away. As badly as he wanted her, getting caught in the altogether by some unsuspecting tourist family—or worse yet, the local Coast Guard—was just a bad plan. Plus, what she needed most was a shoulder to lean on. The rest of his anatomy would just have to wait. He commanded himself to overlook her slightly puffy lips, saying a silent prayer of thanks when she retwisted her sensually mussed hair into a tidy knot on top of her head.

"Hey, are you hungry? I brought lunch." Carly brightened

as she reached for the picnic basket he'd tucked away in the oversized storage console. His stomach burbled in interest, an audible rumble that made her laugh. Christ, he wanted to eat that sound instead of whatever she'd packed, just take it in and swallow it whole so he could have it inside of him.

Okay, right. He needed some sustenance, because clearly, he was losing his mind.

"I'm always hungry. What've we got?" He stood behind the wheel of the boat, maneuvering back upstream a bit. They'd managed to drift pretty far down into the eddy, and Autumn's husband Chris would be right pissed if Jackson ran his boat aground, no matter how pretty the woman distracting him might be.

Carly's face lit up even further as she rummaged through the contents of the basket she'd moved to her lap. "Italian pasta salad, brick sandwiches, and oh! Amaretti for dessert." She waved a cellophane bag of buttery-brown cookies with a flourish.

"I'm sorry, did you say brick? As in, give me some mortar and I'll build you a house, brick?" Jackson killed the engine, having gotten them far enough upstream that he could easily drift for a while without being in the way of passing watercraft.

"Relax, I'm a chef, not a stonemason. The sandwiches are made with cold cuts—sopressata, pepperoni, and capocolla, to be precise—but in order to fit all of that plus the Provolone, the roasted red peppers and the greens on there, I had to hollow out some of the bread and put bricks on the sandwiches overnight. The weight compresses the ingredients slowly, without mashing them to a pulp."

Jackson's brow hiked up at the surprising heft of the sandwich she passed his way. "Jeez. This thing must weigh two pounds." His taste buds joined his stomach in a jig of sweet anticipation.

"Yours probably does," Carly agreed, taking out another sandwich that was half the size of the one in his hand.

He laughed. "My appetite precedes me, then?"

"You're the one who said you're always hungry." She laughed as she passed him a bottle of water. He sprawled comfortably next to her on the bench seat, leaning in to place a kiss on the apple of her sun-warmed cheek.

"Thanks for feeding me. You didn't have to."

Her hands skittered to a stop over the propped-open basket. "Just like you didn't have to rearrange your schedule to take me fishing, you mean? Bringing lunch was really the least I could do."

Jackson wanted to answer her, but he was suddenly too busy contending with the explosion of spicy, smoky flavors having a party in his mouth. Each bite brought a slightly different combination of hearty richness from the meats and mild sweetness of the red peppers. He might not know the fancy names of the herbs she'd used to give it that final kick of over-the-top goodness with each swallow, but that wasn't going to stop him from enjoying them to the hilt.

"Wow." The word was a muffled grunt more than anything else, and Jackson spent another minute eating before finally pausing to speak again. "The red pepper goes great with the cold cuts. Even the leafy stuff tastes really good." He stopped to examine the layers of the sandwich in between bites, noting the different colors and textures in each component.

"See, now you're learning. It's all about balance. All three meats are bold, but each in its own way. The sopressata's smoky, the capocolla's spicy, and the pepperoni's a little of both. But then the veggies and herbs cool things down, while the balsamic and olive oil work their magic with a smooth bite. Plus it's filling as hell, so I figured you'd like it. Even with the leafy stuff," Carly laughed.

The wheels of his brain kicked to a slow, steady turn as

he thought of all the ingredients. "So you really think using local ingredients could make stuff like this even better? I mean, Pine Mountain's not exactly known for its . . . well, anything, really."

But Carly shook her head as if to disagree. "Using local ingredients makes sense, and you'd be surprised what you can find, even in rural locations. Take your mother's garden, for example. With a plot that size, I could go a long way toward making unique daily specials with ingredients I know are at the height of freshness. The only hard part is getting started. Well, that and getting funding."

Jackson paused, his sandwich halfway to his lips. "There's a huge nursery and farm out in Bealetown, where my ma gets a lot of annuals and starter plants. It's only about thirty minutes from here. If you wanted to start a garden, that'd be a great place to get seedlings."

He'd been to Brooks Farm countless times, hauling everything from flats of petunias to strawberry plants to the crepe myrtles lining the garden path for his mother. Jackson could find the place in his sleep. "I could take you if you want to check it out."

"Really?" Carly's eyes danced with fiery warmth, the excitement on her pretty face so obvious it all but reached out to pinch him. "If I could come up with a solid business plan and get my hands on the resources from somewhere that close by, I might just be able to get resort management to approve a garden on the premises. God, could you imagine how incredible it would be if I could get my hands on fresh produce like that every day?"

Her hands fluttered to emphasize her excitement, and not even the sun overhead could hold a candle to the wide, bright smile parting her lips. "I mean, we'd still have to use our distributors, but not nearly as much, so it would cut costs on that end. Although start-up might be a problem. And I'd need quite a bit of space for a project like that. Still . . ."

Her murmur tapered into a look of deep thought, as if she was so caught up in the ideas that she'd forgotten she was spinning them out loud.

No two ways about it, Carly's enthusiasm was catching. Jackson stared at her, fascinated, his thoughts pattering together in a steady stream of *hell yes*. He leaned in, brushing his hand across her knee to capture her attention.

"There's that field across from the west gate, adjacent to the side entrance of the restaurant. It's got to be almost an acre of wasted space," he said, estimating it in his mind's eye. "It's partially blocked from view by the grove between the resort and the west-side hiking trails, and the ski slopes and villas are all on the other end of the complex. You really couldn't ask for a better place for an on-site garden. It's even on the same side of the resort as the restaurant."

Carly chewed her bottom lip, a streak of uncertainty taking the edge off her smile. "Yeah, but even so, once you factor in a professional landscaper, a contracting company for the actual labor, and at least one full-time gardener to oversee maintenance, the price tag might be more than the resort is willing to consider. I'd need one hell of a business plan to convince them to do it, with the research to back it up. It would take months of trial and error before I found someone with the know-how to help me plan something like this."

She had a point. Jackson knew from experience that neither the knowledge or the execution came easy—or cheap. Shit, he'd helped his mother set up her garden from scratch, and it had been a labor of love, both physically and financially.

Jackson sat up straight, his thoughts clicking against each other like dominoes being knocked down by the flick of a finger.

"If research is all you need, then today just might be your lucky day."

* * *

Are you out of your ever-loving mind? This is the most insane thing you've ever done, bar-fucking-none!

Jackson had to admit, his inner voice might have a point.

When he'd blurted out the idea of hooking Carly up with his mother to talk about planning a garden, it had seemed benign enough. But then the genuine flush of excitement on her face morphed into full-on delight as they made their way back to the dock to put their plan into action, and he realized—too late—the gravity of what he'd done.

He was taking the woman he was dating to meet his mother. On *purpose*.

Okay, but they were going to talk about tomato cages and tillers, so how big a deal could it be? After all, garden planning was in a totally different hemisphere from wedding planning, and it wasn't as if he and Carly had anything serious going. Plus, with everything she'd told him out on the lake not even three hours before, Jackson was pretty sure getting hitched was in the very basement of things going through her mind.

Strangely, his inner voice didn't argue.

"Are you sure your mom won't mind us dropping in on her like this?" The concern in Carly's voice carried over the breeze coming in through the wide-open windows of his truck, and his gut panged to life at the sound.

"Knowing her, she's probably in the garden right now anyway," he replied. "She usually goes out to pick vegetables in the afternoon. It's how we used to know what was for dinner."

Carly's face, sun-kissed from spending the better part of the day on the boat, bent into a thoughtful smile. "Yeah, my grandmother used to do that too. You never knew what you were going to get," she laughed. "But I can't complain. She grew eggplants like nobody else, and eggplant Parmesan was the first thing I ever cooked all on my own."

"Let me guess. You were eight at the time." Jackson watched the loose tendrils of hair blow around her face like a dark, riotous halo.

"Eleven," she corrected. "And let *me* guess. By the time you were ten, you'd already single-handedly designed and built the deck in your mother's yard. Or did you build the house, too?"

His laughter filled the truck. "We didn't even live here when I was ten, smartass."

Carly's sardonic grin slipped, her forehead creasing into a little V over the bridge of her nose. "You weren't born in Pine Mountain?"

Shit. *Shit.* Jackson swallowed hard, all traces of laughter swallowed up by the rush of wind coming in through the open windows. "No. I was born in Harrisburg. It's west of Philadelphia." The vague memory of a small, cramped row house flickered through his mind, like a movie being run on one of those ancient reel-to-reel projectors.

"I'm sorry, I just assumed you'd always lived here." Carly's voice matched her surprised expression, but Jackson didn't move his gaze from the windshield.

"We didn't come to Pine Mountain until I was eleven." Well, they hadn't moved so much as escaped, but he really wasn't in the mood for semantics.

"Oh," Carly murmured. She was probably waiting for him to talk about it, but there wasn't anything he could say that would change things. Talking about it now was useless, and taking a trip down memory lane was as far from his wish-list as you could get.

"Parts of when I was a kid were a little . . . rough. I'd rather not talk about it." It was as much as he'd ever volunteered about his childhood trauma to anybody, but even the one-liner sounded heavy in his ears. Jackson braced for the questions she was surely working up anyway, the ones he'd have to evade because he sure as hell didn't have the answers to them, and everything he did know, he wasn't about to share.

Except Carly didn't say anything else. The silence between them stretched out, and the tension churning through him lost its steam. He pulled off the main road, navigating the narrow lane leading back to his mother's house as he'd done a million times before, trying to think of something to say. Hell, Carly probably thought he was a jerk of epic proportions for tight-lipping it after she'd been so open about her own past, but nobody wanted to know the details behind those years he'd stuffed into the dark corners of his memory. Truly, he'd give anything to be able to forget them himself.

"Okay."

The single word made his head snap up, and he stared at her in disbelief. "What?"

Carly lifted her sunglasses to measure him with an unassuming stare. "Look, remember what you said earlier, about helping me out while I was going through all of this stuff with Travis?"

Jackson nodded dumbly, and she continued. "Well, just because I felt like talking about it doesn't mean everybody works that way. So if I can return the favor and help you out by *not* talking about things, then that's what I'll do."

Holy. Shit. For a second, Jackson thought he might be in love with her, until he realized he didn't do that kind of thing.

"So you don't care that I don't want to talk about it?"

"If you did want to talk about it, would you tell me?" Her eyes flashed in the bright sunlight pouring in through the window, like whiskey in the bottom of a crystal glass.

"Yeah." The answer startled the hell out of him, but it was true. Carly was a no-bones-about-it kind of girl. If he was going to blab about his past, she wouldn't give him a bunch of psychobabble crap. She'd be a good listener, in theory. In practice, he was sure he wouldn't find out, but still. *If* he was going to go that route, he couldn't think of anyone better to do it with.

The edges of her lips kicked into a smile, more kind than seductive, but it stirred a warmth in him all the same.

"Then no. I don't care. If you change your mind, you'll tell me."

Funny thing was, as he sat there all dumbfounded and amazed and slightly turned on, Jackson knew she was right.

Chapter Eighteen

As Carly followed Jackson along the winding path through the crepe myrtles, her brain spun like a blender going full-tilt. She'd always dreamed of a project like building an on-site garden, but the lack of resources to actually make it happen—not to mention the massive premiums on what little real estate was available in the city—made it nothing more than a pipe dream. While using local resources to supply restaurants with everything from produce to protein was increasing in popularity, most places had to set a realistic radius in order to make it work. Sure, produce from one hundred miles away was fresh. But if she could get it from a hundred feet away? It would be priceless.

"So there are three plots out here, right? Are they all the same size?" Carly's brain whirred along, ticking off lists of vegetables in silent, rapid-fire succession.

"Yup. Fifteen by twelve. And then there are the two raised beds with blueberries and sugar snap peas and a few other things, depending on my mother's mood each season." Jackson grinned expectantly over the broad expanse of his shoulder, and Carly's lips popped open in surprise.

"There are two other beds?" How on earth had she missed those?

Jackson's grin turned wicked. "Over on the opposite side of the shed."

Well, that explained why she hadn't seen them last time. Her cheeks prickled, but the laugh swirling in her belly refused to stay put. "I see. So those are over by the fence, then?"

The memory of thickly climbing clematis unfurled in Carly's mind, like a lush canvas of sapphire and pink blooms floating on a dark green sea, and she forced herself to use it to blot out the image of Jackson pushing her against the shed, kissing her until she'd forgotten she had knees. As pretty as the climbing vines were in her mind's eye, it was no easy task.

"Mmm hmm. They're side by side, a lot closer together than the three bigger plots." He pulled back a low branch, moving aside to usher her into the clearing. God, the space was just as gorgeous as it had been the first time, all verdant leaves and soft, inviting textures, and the fresh scent of foliage and sun-warmed earth hung in the air like a whispered suggestion.

"What was your mother in the mood for this season, besides berries and peas?" Carly's curiosity perked, and she swung her head toward the fence line for a peek.

"Why don't you ask her?" Jackson jutted his chin toward the shed, pausing for just a second before cutting a path through the emerald-colored grass on the perimeter of the garden. A tall, thin woman wearing a wide-brimmed straw hat stood in profile at the entryway to the shed, reaching up to take something off one of the shelves tucked inside.

"Hey, Ma. You still having trouble with the doors on that thing?" There was a tinge of something odd in Jackson's voice that Carly couldn't quite place, but then it was gone, replaced by his easygoing smile as he closed the space between them and bent to hug his mother hello.

"Oh! What a nice surprise." The expression on her gently-lined face, right down to the sudden glimmer in her cornflower-blue eyes, clearly showed her pleasure at the impromptu visit. "You didn't tell me you were coming by," his mother tsked without chagrin. Her gaze halted on Carly, but the happiness in her eyes didn't budge. "And with a guest, no less."

"That's me. Full of surprises." The genuine affection they had for each other was as obvious as the grass under Carly's feet, and her gut did a roll-and-twist maneuver that ended in a dull ache right beneath her ribs.

Jackson cleared his throat and continued. "Right. So this is Carly. She's the head chef at La Dolce Vita. You know, down at the resort."

A knowing smile bloomed on the older woman's face. "I'm familiar with the resort, Jackson."

He nodded with a sheepish grin, but took the subtle jibe in stride. "Carly, this is my quick-witted mother, Catherine Carter."

A smile twitched at the corners of Carly's lips. Her father used to tease her the exact same way. "It's nice to meet you, Mrs. Carter." Carly extended a hand, but Catherine bypassed it and surprised her with a warm, quick hug.

"You, too, sweetheart. But call me Catherine." She took a step back and arched a pale brow at her son. "So what brings the two of you out my way this afternoon? Surely you have better things to do than sit around in the garden with your old mother."

Jackson glossed over her wry comment with charm so honest and genuine, it seemed as much a part of him as the color of his hair. "As a matter of fact, that's exactly what we came out here to do." He gestured to Carly, who took his lead and ran with it.

"I've been putting together some ideas for a project related to my work at the restaurant, and if you don't mind, I'd love to talk to you about your garden."

She launched into a condensed version of the plan that

had been flying through her mind for the last couple of hours, enthusiasm infusing her words even though she put some effort into trying to seem neutral. Carly could feel Jackson's eyes on her as she told his mother about her philosophy on food and what she ultimately wanted to do at the resort, and her ideas spilled out of her mouth on wave after wave of pure excitement. She hadn't been this truly energized over a project since she'd started at Gracie's, and the renewed enthusiasm guided her words out into the open, fragrant air of the garden.

"So if there's any way you might be able to help me out with your expertise, I'd be really grateful," Carly finished, sweeping a hand toward the rows of vegetables in various stages of readiness. Catherine regarded her for a long minute, her kind, blue eyes dancing as she shifted her gaze to Jackson.

"Well. When you said you were full of surprises, I suppose you really meant it." She slipped a basket from a shelf in the shed and passed it to Carly, gesturing to the garden with a reverent smile. "Come on, sweetheart. The best way to learn about planting a garden is to get your hands on it, so we'll start there."

Catherine looped her arm through Carly's, and Carly caught the tail-end of the look she exchanged with Jackson over her shoulder. "There's some leftover tuna casserole in the fridge if you're hungry. Help yourself." Catherine's smile covered her face from ear to ear, making her look more like a schoolgirl than the mother of a grown man.

"Carly and I are going to be a while."

"Okay, seriously? That was the most incredible day I've had since . . . God, I don't even know when!" Carly clutched the stack of notebook pages she'd scribbled over the course of the evening to her chest, turning to look at Jackson from the passenger seat of his truck. "Your mother is one of the most amazing women I've ever met."

Jackson chuckled, a smooth, rich sound that snuck through the dark cab of the truck to melt Carly's insides with its sexy warmth. "I think the feeling's mutual. She was just as excited about planning a garden at La Dolce Vita as you, and that's really saying something." He nudged Carly with an elbow, and the contact made her insides squeeze with delicious tightness.

"Well, there are no guarantees the execs will bite, but this will go a long way toward presenting a strong plan. I think we really have a shot at this." Carly straightened the copious notes she'd taken as her conversation with Catherine had drifted from the garden to the farmhouse table inside the kitchen. Two hours, a pitcher of sweet tea, and eight pages of chicken scratch later, Carly had more than enough down on paper to serve as a springboard, and not all of it had come from Catherine.

"Thanks for calling Luke to get those contracting estimates. I wouldn't have known the first thing to ask about a project like this." She tipped her head at Jackson, squinting through the velvety darkness to make out the chiseled line of his jaw.

"I was only on the phone with him for half an hour. No big deal." Jackson's shoulders hitched into a nonchalant shrug, as if the phone call had been effortless. In reality, he'd taken two pages of notes himself.

"It would've taken me twice as long, at least," she insisted. "I owe you big time."

Carly leaned back in her seat, cool night air rushing through the open windows. The last traces of purple bled through the sky at the tree line, and the first hint of starlight began to scatter and blink to life overhead. She drew in a deep, contented breath, letting it swirl around in her lungs.

Her stomach made a sound vaguely akin to that of a charging rhinoceros.

"Whoa! Hungry much?" Jackson laughed, brows lifted.

She had no choice but to admit it—she was starving. "Sorry. With everything going on, I guess we didn't eat."

Jackson rubbed his free palm over his midsection. "Speak for yourself. You should've had some tuna casserole."

Carly's stomach gurgled again, and she pressed her hand to her side in an effort to shut it up. Hello, body betrayal! God, couldn't her organs at least be graceful about it? "I know, and your mom offered twice. I was just too excited to eat."

"And now?"

"Now I could eat enough for the two of us." Her stomach jerked against her ribs in a bid for obvious agreement.

"Holy crap, I'd better feed you stat, then." A funny look crossed his features, but she couldn't make it out in the dark. "You up for something a little unconventional?"

They were in the middle of the Blue Ridge Mountains, for God's sake. Most people up here considered Mexican food unconventional. "I've had just about everything you can think of, remember? I mean, I'm up for basically anything right now, but I don't think you're going to have much luck if you want to surprise me."

Even in the near-dark, the irony on his face was plain. "Oh, I think I might."

When they pulled up to a quiet, two-story apartment building ten minutes later, Carly stood 100 percent corrected.

"Is this . . . do you live here?" She blinked as Jackson opened the passenger door for her and waited for her to jump down to the night-cooled pavement.

"Yup. It's nothing fancy. As a matter of fact, since I wasn't really expecting to do this, I'm really kind of just hoping it's passably clean. But this is home." Jackson led her to the neatly landscaped courtyard and up a flight of covered outdoor steps.

Carly blinked, still not quite registering his intent. "So did you need to come and grab something before we go eat?"

Jackson stopped short, flipping his keys. The metal on metal jingle played against the cup of his palm, and he glanced at her, thoughtful. "Actually, I've been thinking about what you said last week. About how you always cook but nobody feeds you." He paused on the threshold, eyes dark blue and steady on her face, and something nameless and frighteningly good broke free to spread out in her chest.

"I'd like to change that. Right now!"

Carly's wide-eyed surprise never failed to take a potshot at Jackson's gut, and right now was no exception.

"You . . . you want to cook something for me?"

Christ, it only topped the list of things he wanted to do to her. The urge to put his mouth on hers and not stop kissing her until they'd both had their fill screamed through him, just as it had for much of the evening. But something dared him to override it, to listen to that voice in his head that told him to feed her, even though it didn't make any sense. He closed the space between them with only a few inches to spare, skimming a palm up her forearm before letting it rest on the angle of her shoulder.

"Well, that all depends. Do you want to let me?"

The heat of their bodies so close together colored her cheeks with a flush that swept down the column of her neck, and it took every last ounce of control Jackson had to keep his mind on feeding her. But then she nodded, and it steadied his resolve. He slid his key into the lock, saying one last prayer that there wasn't a legion of dust bunnies standing sentry on the other side.

Carly followed him through his apartment, which was mercifully clean enough, taking it in with a curious glance. "So what's on the menu?"

Good freaking question. Jackson's culinary skills were

limited to mac and cheese from a box and the occasional spaghetti with frozen meatballs, neither of which was bound to impress her in the least. "I'm a man of intrigue, remember?" He did a mental tally of the items in his fridge and gave an inward groan.

Feed her.

Oh, sure. He had to possess a little dictator for an inner voice, and a useless one at that. Feed her what?

Carly's lush mouth tilted into a smile that rendered Jackson's legs useless. "Is that code for 'I don't know yet'?"

Of course she'd frickin' figure him out. "It's actually code for 'I haven't decided yet.'"

"We could order something if you want. Or I could just take a look in the pantry and throw something together. I really don't mind." She moved through his postage stamp of a kitchen as if on auto-pilot, but Jackson caught her midstep on her way to the narrow pantry door. He pressed her body against the counter with one hand on either side of her curvy hips, loosely trapping her in place.

"I know you're used to being bossy in the kitchen. But we're not on your turf this time." All of a sudden, his lack of confidence in his culinary skills faded to black. He couldn't resist the magnetic heat of her, drawing him closer, and he dipped his mouth to the curve of her neck. "So are you going to let me do this for you, or not?"

The keening sigh that crossed her lips made him want to take his inner voice and lock it in the closet, but when Carly nodded, he forced himself to take a step back.

"Yes," she whispered, looking up at him through shadowy lashes.

"Okay." Jackson pulled in a breath to steel himself, knowing that his dick was about to be righteously indignant about his brain's decision to cook first and kiss later. He was going to have to wing his way through the kitchen, no easy task in front of a professional chef.

Right. Time to rely on distraction. At least until he could

figure out something passable to make. "We're going to do this my way, which means no cheating. No helping of any kind. In fact," Jackson murmured, reaching down to take her hands in his. "No watching, either. Not until it's time to eat."

"You're kicking me out of the kitchen entirely?" The fire in her stare told Jackson to tread carefully, but he refused to back down.

"No. I'm creating a food experience. You're the one who said you need to rely on all your senses. If you don't see what I'm doing, you'll have to use everything else that much more." He led her around to the narrow breakfast bar where he ate all his meals, cupping his palm beneath the wooden ladder back of one of the bar stools resting there.

"Twist a girl's words, why don't you." Carly made a face at him as he turned the chair to face away from the kitchen. In spite of her grousing, she climbed up to sit on the stool with her back to the counter. "At least tell me what you're going to make."

"Please. If I was going to tell you, I'd let you watch."

He had to admit, there was something incredibly sexy about distracting her this way. Falling into the old habit of teasing her felt twice as good with a seductive edge, but not even that was good enough to deter him from the task at hand now. He'd promised to feed her. Even if the best he could come up with was the can of Manwich sitting in the back of his pantry, Jackson was going to throw everything he had into making it an experience.

He turned to face her, stepping in close enough to sense her breath hitch beneath the white cotton riding the swell of her breasts.

"And no peeking, either. If I think you're cheating, I'll be tempted to blindfold you."

With that, he brushed his lips over hers in the barest of tastes before turning to walk away.

Chapter Nineteen

"You're not going to give me any hints at all?"

Jackson couldn't tell if Carly sounded more miffed than curious, but neither one made him want to tell her what he was up to. Not that he really knew. He sauntered through the kitchen, which amounted to three good steps, and propped the pantry door open.

"Nope." He whistled good-naturedly, trying to cover up the distinct possibility he was in over his head. Come on, he thought. He might not be a gourmet, but he wasn't a total dolt, either. What would he want to eat if he were sitting in that chair?

. . . *I like to use ingredients that keep things uncomplicated* . . . Carly's words from the night they'd spent in the bungalow threaded through his mind, and the idea slammed into him with all the subtlety of a three-hundred pound wrestler. If honest flavors, evocative smells, and warm presentation were on Carly's wish-list, Jackson was about to make her the meal of a lifetime.

Either that, or she'd laugh him out of his own kitchen. But it was better than nothing, and at this point, he needed something. He reached into the belly of the pantry, unearthing a sparse handful of things. Man, he hoped this didn't backfire.

Carly cleared her throat, a soft thrum of rich tones that

threatened to undo him from across the room. "How about a small hint? Just one ingredient."

"You don't like to play by the rules, do you?" It was easier to rebuff her now that he had a plan, and he moved to the counter a few steps behind her to untwist the plastic bag in his hands.

"It's not cheating if I ask and you tell me," she said, turning her stubborn chin so he could see her in profile.

Jackson was next to her in the span of a breath, the bag left on the counter, forgotten. "I'm not going to tell you. Now behave, or I won't be able to finish and you won't eat."

He curved his mouth into a smile, hovering just over the shell of her ear. She smelled like wildflowers and faded sunshine, but he resisted the urge to taste her skin before going back to the kitchen. One taste wasn't going to be nearly enough, and he already wanted to bury himself inside her as it was.

"I can't just sit still." Carly's protest trembled on her lips, but not with fear. Desire, provocative and pure, folded around her words, and Jackson traced the steadfast line of her jaw with one finger.

"You forget, I'm a contractor. I don't exactly have a four-course meal up my sleeve, so this isn't going to take very long."

Despite the protest from just about every one of his parts, Jackson returned to the kitchen and pulled two thick slices of white bread from the bag on the counter. He dropped them into the open-mouthed slats of the toaster and lowered the lever with slow pressure to try to mask the sound.

She stilled, a lone ribbon of dark hair cascading from the loose knot on her crown. "I like simple, remember?"

Jackson thought of his plan and chuckled. "Good."

Carly sat up straight, ear cocked toward the kitchen, and it occurred to him that she really was using her other senses to try to figure him out. The refrigerator huffed as he opened it, a near-noiseless breath of cold air filtering out to greet him, and a few more ingredients joined the pile on the counter. The efficient snap of the toaster was a dead giveaway—one he couldn't avoid, unfortunately—as was the warm, yeasty smell emanating through the kitchen a minute later.

"You're making toast?"

"There's no breakfast in your future unless you spend the night," he teased, hoping to stop her short with the innuendo.

Bingo. Carly sat up even taller, her spine a beautiful plumb line. "Oh! Well, I was just . . ."

"Cheating," Jackson supplied, sliding a knife from the utensil drawer. It wisped quietly across the golden bread as he layered the ingredients with measured precision, tawny and thick on one side, dark and sweet on the other.

"Sorry," she mumbled, clearly not. Damn, she was cute when she was irritated.

He pressed the two pieces of bread together, marrying the parts to create the whole. The creation in front of him was the very definition of simple, but it seemed strangely perfect in its own right, as if he'd been meant to feed her like this all along. He folded a paper towel beneath the plain blue dish, sliding the whole thing toward her on the aging Formica countertop. Leaning forward on his elbows, Jackson propped his body across from hers at the breakfast bar.

"Don't be. I'm done."

Slowly, Carly turned around, swinging her body to face him. The walls of his apartment seemed to press into his ears as he waited for the plate in front of her to register with her brain.

"You made me a PB and J?"

He swallowed. "Yeah. I know it's not fancy, but . . ."

"It's *perfect*."

Carly's eyes flicked, liquid bronze and reverent, over the plate in front of her before she scooped the toasted, crusty bread up in both hands. "Oh, you buttered the toast. Brilliant."

Jackson blinked his eyes once like a camera shutter, committing the unabashedly sensual image of Carly's face to memory. The lone curl that had fallen from the knot on her head now played across the swoop of her cheekbone, softening her expression even further, and she lifted the sandwich to her bow-shaped mouth. She closed her eyes, mahogany lashes creating shadows on her face, and inhaled deeply.

"Ohhh, God it smells divine." Her stomach growled—not a ladylike "ahem," but an out and out snarl, as if it had teeth. Something about the visceral reaction made Jackson want to lay waste to the flimsy counter between them, and he gripped the edges of the chipped Formica hard enough to make it creak. An apologetic blush crept across Carly's cheeks, but he headed her off before she could say a word.

"Don't say it." The gruff edge to his own words surprised him, but Jackson didn't relent. "If you're hungry, eat."

When she reluctantly nodded, his inner voice almost passed out with joy.

Carly opened her mouth and took a huge bite, a fact that would've impressed Jackson if he hadn't been so electrically turned on by the look of sheer joy on her face. The lines of her sun-kissed jaw worked on a delicate, determined hinge, and when she released a faint moan of pleasure, it was all he could do to let her keep eating.

"This," she mumbled, covering her mouth with one hand as she finished chewing, "is so good it should be illegal." Her next bite sent a dribble of grape jelly down the curve of her hand, but Carly either didn't notice or didn't care. She ate recklessly, her expression leaving no guesswork as to what was going on in her mind.

Jackson laughed, the low rumble filling him to the brim. "You're giving me too much credit."

She took another bite, and he watched her, completely mesmerized.

"Hmm-mmm." Carly's protest was more in her eyes than her words, and she shook her head for emphasis. "It's total comfort food." She licked the streak of jelly from her hand, and Jackson's libido went berserk.

"I'm glad you like it."

A streak of want blazed a path from his chest to his gut before heading even further south. There was zero chance he was going to last much longer on this side of the narrow breakfast bar. Jackson forced himself to stop looking at the tiny smudge lingering in the corner of her mouth. Christ, he'd give his left arm to be grape fucking jelly right now.

Carly snorted, which was probably no easy task with a mouth full of peanut butter. "Like it? I think I want to marry it." She took another bite, and Jackson promptly burst out laughing. Hell if she hadn't timed that tension-buster with perfect ease.

"I should've known you'd take your comfort food seriously." He pulled himself away from her long enough to grab a glass from a nearby cupboard, pausing briefly at the fridge on his way back to the breakfast bar.

"That's because this is serious comfort food." Her eyes crinkled in happiness as he poured her a glass of milk. "I have to admit it. You nailed the food experience."

"With a PB and J?"

She popped the last edge of the crust into her mouth, nodding with a grin. "Oh, yeah. It was just what I wanted— simple, feel-good food. Perfect for today, actually."

Something about her words broke through the tough surface layers of Jackson's consciousness, shooting past the red flags and warning signs to tickle his brain. How good he felt, just standing there in the kitchen watching her eat, should've made him wary. Hell, if she'd been any other woman, he'd have cut and run weeks ago. But there was something about her, so easy and pure, that made wanting to be near her a foregone conclusion.

And for once in his life, Jackson didn't want to fight it.

"There's not much by way of dessert," he apologized, watching her brush the crumbs from her hands. The scar on her finger flashed in an angry, white-hot line, and Jackson reached out instinctively to capture her hand in his.

"Oh, that's okay, I don't . . ." Carly stopped, eyes shuttering closed as he stroked her palm with both of his thumbs. Her hands were so small, yet so sturdy and real, and a rush of hot lust swirled around in his belly as she curled her fingers into his.

"I don't want dessert." Her voice was a honeyed murmur, one that drove into Jackson's bones and blood, filling him completely with something he couldn't name.

"What do you want?" He rounded the meager expanse of countertop that separated them without letting go of her hand. The smooth skin of her palm, the roughened calluses on her fingertips, her short, unpolished nails, all of it reached low into his gut and turned him on from the inside out.

"I want you." Carly stared at him, unblinking. Honest. Real.

He didn't think twice.

Their mouths joined with equal hunger, both seeking and finding all at once. Jackson cupped the back of her neck, threading his fingers in the dark fall of her hair to free the knot over his hands. He parted her knees with his body, releasing her from the kiss for just a breath.

"You can have me later. I'm taking you first."

The crush of her chest against his was wicked and hot, and he gripped her hips hard with both palms to pull her to the edge of the bar stool. He came within inches of losing his cool when she wrapped her legs around his waist, the friction of her jeans and everything that lay beneath bringing his hard-on to that fine line between intense pleasure and throbbing pain.

"Jackson." Carly's voice was thick with desire, daring him not to stop, and he considered ripping every stitch of her clothing off right there in the kitchen. The perfect components of their perfect day, the way he felt so easy and good around her, how maddeningly sexy she was just sitting there, all of it came together in one fine point of powerful need.

In a blur of movement, their bodies entwined, Carly's arms clinging to his shoulders, Jackson palming her curvy ass to lift her from the chair. He made his way to the darkened shadows of his bedroom in urgent strides, but as soon as he crossed the threshold with Carly in his arms, time spiraled out and slowed down. Something unfolded from deep within his chest, and he fought the urge to undress her as fast as possible, willing himself to slow down instead.

If he was going to take her, he needed to do it right.

"Close your eyes." Jackson's voice was husky, almost a growl. He itched to touch her, to slide his tongue across the hollow of her collarbone, dig deep into the heat between her thighs, but instead he tamped his urgency down to lay her carefully on his rumpled bed. Carly's eyes, wide and glittery in the moonlight spilling in through the cracked-open blinds, found his.

"What?"

Jackson braced himself on his forearms, suspended right over the crescent of her ear. "Close your eyes, Carly."

Surprise flooded through him, followed by a quick pulse of greedy want as Carly's eyes drifted closed. He slanted his lips over hers for another lingering taste before dipping into the skin on her neck, that soft spot behind her ear that made her arch up off the bed, the angle of her jaw. Jackson sampled and tasted, taking his time in some places, moving emphatically in others. Her shirt, the lace-edged bra beneath it, her jeans—he removed all of it as he dove into her like a feast, teasing her heavy breasts with his tongue and the backs of his fingers, caressing the silky skin of her inner thigh, stopping everywhere in between.

"You taste incredible," he murmured, laving the rim of her belly button with attention. Carly squeezed her eyes tight, her hair splayed over the stark white pillowcase like ink spreading through calm water. Jackson stared at her, memorizing her face, the subtle notes of her skin, her willingness. All of it.

"You're killing me," she whimpered softly, cresting upward as he slipped his eager hands beneath her hips. A streak of want rode through him, edgy and sharp, and he nudged her knees apart to thrust against the cradle of her hips with his own.

"The feeling is mutual." The barrier of his jeans and the cotton, hip-hugging panties she wore made him want to tear both garments to shreds. Carly returned the thrust in equal, excruciating rhythm, eyes flying open to look at him with a tenacious smile curving over her mouth.

"What are you going to do about it?"

Just like that, Jackson's resolve disappeared. Pushed by the need to feel Carly's skin, hot and soft under the hard strain of his chest, his hips—Christ, *all* of him—he undressed in a fast tangle of cotton and denim, assisted by Carly's eager hands.

"Jackson, I've been dying to feel you inside me. Please." She dug her fingers into his shoulders with an unexpected bite. He slid the panties from her hips in one smooth draw, exposing her tawny skin, and took a condom from the nightstand drawer before returning to the bed. He knew he should wait, should tease her to the edge with his hands, push her over the line with his mouth, but he couldn't. The raw desire to be inside of her was so overwhelming, it wouldn't be ignored.

Jackson wanted her right *now*!

As if she could read his mind, Carly reached down to where he knelt in the open arc of her hips, stroking his cock with flawless pressure.

"You're driving me . . . crazy, you know." He bit out each word, nearly losing his mind with each slide.

"Really?" She slipped the condom from his fingers with her free hand, her ministrations becoming more purposeful with the other. "Tell me again."

Confusion cut a jagged line through his lust-fogged brain. "What?"

Carly propped herself up on her palms, eyes glittering. She widened her knees around his body, inviting him in. "I like it when you talk to me, too. So tell me again. Tell me I'm driving you crazy. Tell me whatever you want."

"I just want *you*."

The words were barely out of his mouth before Jackson was inside her, plunging deep into her body, seeking her very core. They fell back against the pillows, every sinuous movement making him want the next one all the more. He whispered in Carly's ear, listening to her breathy sighs and sharper, rough-edged cries as she rocked beneath him in slow, deliberate response. With each arch of her hips, his words became more gravelly, pushing past his vocal cords on husky breath.

She rose up to meet him, faster and harder, and Jackson took her mercilessly to the edge and pushed her straight over. Only when Carly had gasped out his name and clasped her knees around his hips with a liquid shudder did he let go, following her into a pleasure that swallowed him whole.

They lay together, still, nestled in a skein of bed sheets and shed clothing and complete, sated bliss. Half-afraid he might crush her with his body weight, Jackson moved to Carly's side and drew her in tight to his body. The other half just wanted to hold her close and not move until absolutely necessary.

"You're unbelievable, you know that?" Her sleepy murmur was a confection, sweet and perfect and somehow just right for the moment, and Jackson chuckled into the wild spill of her curls as she nestled against the curve of his shoulder.

"You're not so bad yourself."

The intense release, the hushed shadows, the unabashed beauty of Carly's face as she looked up at him—all of it came together and settled into his brain like it belonged there. The whole thing should've sent him into panic mode, but he was too sedate, too happy with Carly in his arms, to even think about letting her go.

"I guess we're even, then." She nipped his ear and settled back in the niche of his body with a contented sigh.

It doesn't have to be serious. It could be just like this.

Jackson let the suggestion weave its way through his mind, spreading out over the rest of him as they lay together in the quiet. A lazy smile twitched at his mouth, and he tipped her chin up to place a soft kiss on her lips.

Just like this.

Chapter Twenty

"Special de-liv-e-reeeeeeeeee."

Sloane sing-songed her way across the cherry floorboards of the kitchen, depositing a UPS envelope on top of the pile of paperwork Carly had amassed on one end of the breakfast bar. God, she really needed to carve out space for a desk or something. Three weeks' worth of extensive research, highly detailed garden plans, and contractor estimates took up a lot more space than she'd thought they would. She shuffled aside the latest copy of the project proposal in favor of the newest arrival.

"Oooh, I've been waiting for this." A flush of tingly excitement thrummed through Carly's veins as she zipped the envelope open in a trail of fine cardboard dust. "It's the final plan that Jackson and Catherine and I put together with Owen Brooks."

Carly had been shocked to discover that the owner of Brooks Farm and Nursery was only a few years older than she was. His passion for simple, organically grown produce had been clear from the minute she and Jackson had set foot on the farm, and Owen's knowledge had gone a long way toward getting her proposal on solid ground. Solid enough that resort executives had told her to proceed with a detailed proposal after she'd pitched the basic idea.

Solid enough that if she played it just right, she might actually get the funding.

"Ah. Your boyfriend sure does do nice work." Sloane peeked over Carly's shoulder, sighing at the beautifully sketched details on the sheet in Carly's hands. "These plans are gorgeous."

"Jackson's not my boyfriend," Carly argued without heat, tipping her head at the plans. "But yes. The garden is beautiful."

Sloane arched a brow and padded to the coffeepot, the rich aroma of just-brewed French roast teasing its way through the midmorning sunshine.

"Please. I've seen the way you two look at each other. It would be pretty disgusting if it weren't so freaking cute." She leaned over to top off Carly's coffee before tucking the carafe back on its perch on the burner. "Face it, doll. You have surpassed gimme some sugar territory. Jackson Carter rocks your socks."

But Carly didn't budge. "We're friends. We have fantastic sex. We enjoy each other's company. But that's all that's going on, Sloane."

A slide show of events from the night before flashed through her mind, and she tucked her naughty grin into her coffee cup. Fantastic was really quite the euphemism. The man could blow her mind with his bad intentions.

And he had done just that for the last three weeks. A *lot*.

"Mmm. You've slept in the same bed with Jackson almost every night for the better part of a month, and he's pretty involved in this project you're up to your eyeballs in. Not to go all Devil's Advocate on you, but are you sure mixing work with pleasure is a good idea?" Sloane pushed her choppy black bangs from her face to peer at Carly over the counter, but Carly met her best friend's knowing look with one of her own.

"Have you looked at these plans? He's incredible at what he does, and Luke's contracting estimates for the labor are more than fair. Just because I'm sleeping with Jackson and we spend a lot of time together doesn't mean things are going to get complicated." Carly gathered the pages in front of her into a neat pile, tapping the edges on the breakfast bar with a sharp rap. The last thing she needed was to mess things up by getting serious.

Sloane nodded, her expression turning wary. "Hey, speaking of complicated, your mother called yesterday afternoon."

Carly clenched her jaw, the muscles by her ear tightening to a twitch. "Yeah, she left a message on my cell while I was at work. It seems Travis is getting desperate." Ugh, talk about something she'd rather not deal with at nine-thirty on a Friday morning. Okay, or ever.

"Aww, is he cranky that the judge denied his request for counseling?" Sarcasm dripped from Sloane's words, her Brooklyn accent hardening around the already rough edges.

"Probably. But my lawyer's handling all of it, including Travis's temper tantrums and power plays. I'm just trying to get on with things." In truth, between work, the garden proposal, and hanging out with Jackson, she'd barely had time to think about Travis. Unfortunately, that wasn't a two-way street. At this rate, she'd never be rid of him.

"So what's with your *mama* calling, then?"

Carly blew out a sigh. "My mother just happened to run into him at the Our Lady of Mercy Church social a couple of days ago."

Sloane made an unladylike noise without apology. "Are you kidding me? Travis is Satan's hand puppet. What was he doing at church?"

"Gracie's did the catering, which may or may not have

been coincidental." The hairs on the back of Carly's neck prickled. She hated being so cynical, but she wouldn't put it past Travis to have orchestrated the whole thing to suit his purposes. He had to be getting desperate. "At any rate, my brother was there and he said Travis laid it on pretty thick with my *mama* before he intervened."

Sloane grinned and toasted Carly with her coffee mug. "I'd have paid to see Dominic tell Travis to take a hike. Good for him."

Carly shrugged. At one point, she might've cared about seeing Travis get his comeuppance, but right about now, that would take energy she just couldn't spare. "At least the judge said we can move forward with the divorce. Although the whole my-stuff, his-stuff thing is proving to be every bit of the pain in the ass we thought it would be."

Sloane propped her elbows on the counter and dropped her chin to her hands, thoughtful. "You know, I'd have thought Travis would've dropped the *Couples in the Kitchen* thing by now. No offense, but it's not like you guys were on the Food Network or anything. Why does he still want you to sign on for the show so badly, especially when you already told Winslow no way?"

Carly rubbed a hand over her sternum, pushing her coffee mug aside. Talking about Travis was like instant heartburn. Or maybe that was heartache. At any rate, she'd had enough.

"Who knows why Travis does anything. He's probably just trying to unnerve me. But it doesn't matter, because it's not going to work."

Much. God, she just wanted the whole thing over with.

But Sloane didn't relent. "Still. Something about it doesn't pass the smell test. Do you think maybe—"

The electronic *ring* of the house phone bleated to life, interrupting Sloane and painting Carly with a fresh coat of dread. The caller ID confirmed her suspicions, but she knew from experience that putting off conversations with her mother only made things worse in the end.

"Hey, *Mama*." She cradled the receiver to her ear, smiling softly at Sloane's sympathetic glance. Sloane waggled her fingers before heading down the hall to her room, giving Carly the space she was bound to need to get through the call.

"What, you're psychic now? You know it's your mother calling by divine power or something?" Her mother's voice needled over the phone line, and Carly silently wished her coffee had something stronger in it than milk.

"Sloane and I have caller ID, Ma. It tells you who's on the other end, remember?" Carly looped through the living room with barefooted purpose, looking out into the sunstrewn yard as she paced by the windows along the back wall. Her mother still had a phone with a cord, for God's sake. It figured that caller ID wouldn't be in her repertoire, although Carly had told her mother about it a bunch of times.

"Listen, I'm sorry I missed your call yesterday. I was at work." Technically, Carly had just been shooting the breeze with Adrian about the plans for the garden, but she'd let the call go to voicemail anyway. Having an argument with her mother about her marital status—or impending lack thereof—just hadn't been on her wish-list for the day.

"Hmph. And how's the restaurant? You still working all those crazy hours?" A tinge of genuine concern colored her mother's question, and it softened both Carly's mood and her response.

"Not so much anymore, so you don't have to worry. And the restaurant is great. I'm putting together a proposal for a really exciting project, actually. If resort management approves it, we'd get to build an on-site garden. Like *Nonna*'s, only a lot bigger." The thrill Carly felt every time she thought of the garden coursed through her, and she grinned as she sank back into the couch cushions, unable to contain her happiness.

"*Nonna* doesn't have a garden." The confusion in her mother's voice was clear, and it startled the smile from Carly's lips.

"Not now. I meant the six-foot plot she had in Brooklyn before she moved to Manor House." Carly sat up straight, pressing the phone to her ear a little tighter. "*Mama?* You remember the garden, right?"

It had been seven years since her grandmother had left that apartment in favor of assisted living, but still. *Nonna* had loved that garden like she loved her kids, for God's sake. They'd all spent time in the tiny courtyard space.

"Of course I remember it, Carlotta," her mother replied briskly.

Something odd that she couldn't place made its way to Carly's chest, pressing against her bones with a subtle yet definite presence. Dominic had said she'd gotten forgetful lately. Much as Carly didn't want to admit it, her mother was in her sixties. Becoming forgetful was part of getting-older territory.

Carly cleared her throat gently. "Is everything okay?"

A pause hiccupped between them, filling the air with unease before her mother answered. "It would be, if you'd come home to work things out with Travis."

Wow. She'd walked right into that one, hadn't she?

"We've been through this before. I'm not getting back together with Travis." In an effort to avoid the subject entirely with her mother, Carly had purposely kept the most sordid details of her divorce mum from her family. Hashing them out wouldn't change the whole breaking-a-sacrament thing in her mother's eyes anyway. "I don't want to talk about it."

"Pssht! You're too stubborn for your own good. He wants

to make things right, Carly. He told me himself. Why can't you at least give him a chance?"

Heat bubbled through Carly's veins like a bottle of champagne that had seen one shake too many. "Because there's no point." Maybe if she kept it short and simple, her mother would relent.

"No point! He loves you," her *mama* accused.

Carly should've known better about her mother easing up. "Travis loved my skills as a chef, *Mama*. He loved my marketability. And as soon as he was done using them to climb the career ladder, he cheated on me. The only person he loves is himself."

"You're being dramatic. If you're having trouble, you could go to counseling. But divorce? It's so final."

If only. "I'm being realistic, not dramatic. This is the best thing for me."

"You're not giving it a chance. If you'd just ―"

"No." The tension in Carly's chest shoved her words out on an angry tide. "I'm done talking about this. I don't care what Travis says, or what you think. It's not up for debate. It's my life, Ma, and you need to butt out so I can live it!"

Silence snapped over the phone line in a hiss of white noise before her mother took a deep breath. "Well. Since there's nothing to say, I'll hang up now."

Carly pinched the bridge of her nose between her thumb and forefinger, wishing she could reel her harsh words back in for a do-over. Her mother's intentions were good, and this bullshit with Travis wasn't worth the bad blood. "Look, I―"

"Oh, no. You've made it clear you don't need me or my opinion. Good-bye, Carlotta."

The phone clicked once and went dead.

Carly stared at the phone for a full minute before replacing it hollowly on the charger. She and her mother had a history of butting heads, but it had never gotten this bad.

"You okay?" Sloane poked her head into the living space from the threshold of the hallway, concern on her porcelain features.

"Yes. No." Carly thrust a hand through her hair, wincing. "My mother's still pissed about Travis. She'll get over it." She silently added *I hope* to the end of her statement. God, Travis was slicker than snot to charm her own mother into believing he still loved her. The weasel.

"Oh, honey. You want me to make you a cup of tea? It's still kind of early." Sloane canted her head toward the kitchen, blue eyes offering reassurance.

Carly shook her head. "No, thanks." She eyed the phone. Jackson was overseeing a kitchen remodel in one of the McMansions down by the lake, and was probably up to his tool belt in countertops and cabinetry right now. As much as she wanted to hear his voice, calling him was bound to interrupt his work day. She'd have to shoot for the next best thing. "I'm going to head to La Dolce Vita and mess with some recipes, maybe flesh out a few more details for this proposal before I turn it in at the end of the week."

"Okay. Come find me if you change your mind, *cucciola*."

Carly padded down the hall, the last glimmer of happiness from her early morning gone like smoke in a wind storm.

"We've gotta stop meeting like this, or people will talk." Adrian flashed a crooked, stubble-covered grin from the doorway to the kitchen, reaching up to turn his timeworn baseball hat around. Carly rolled her eyes, but couldn't stop a tiny grin from bubbling up on her lips.

"Ha-ha. Smartass." She glanced up from the gremolata on her cutting board just long enough to pin him with a wry look.

"Better than being a dumbass. Man, those lamb shanks look all right." Adrian came closer, turning his attention from the food to Carly just a little too fast for her to cover the stress of her morning. "You, on the other hand, look like shit."

"For the record, that's probably not the smartest thing to say to a woman holding a big, fat knife." Carly finished chopping the parsley and garlic mixture and bent down to the lowboy to grab some lemon juice, but Adrian didn't budge.

"Is Travis still giving you a hard time?" His words were dark and thick, like molasses that had been in the bottom of the jar too long.

"It'll blow over." She reached into the huge stockpot to give the lamb shanks a nudge with a wooden spoon. They'd been braising for an hour, and the savory aroma coming from the pot lifted the edge of Carly's sour mood.

"He called me."

The wooden spoon clattered to the floor tiles with a colorful splash of red wine reduction, but Carly barely noticed. "He *what?*"

A frown bent the corners of Adrian's mouth, and he shifted his frame against the stainless steel counter of the work station in front of him. "He called me a couple of days ago. Tried to manipulate me into sweet-talking you back to him."

"Jesus. What'd you say?"

Adrian's hazel eyes flashed with a hint of satisfaction as he arched a brow toward the brim of his baseball cap. "I told him to fuck straight off and hung up on his sorry ass, just like I did when I left Gracie's to come here with you."

Carly blinked, still in shock. "I don't know what to say. I'm sorry you keep getting dragged into this mess." God, Travis's audacity knew no bounds!

"It's not your fault, Carly. But he's getting desperate. You ever stop to think about his ulterior motives?" Adrian moved over to the sink at the back of the kitchen to wash his hands, but his attention never left her.

"What ulterior motives could he possibly have, other than to make my life a living hell just because he can?" Carly released a heavy sigh into the stockpot. Would this emotional carousel ever stop spinning?

"I don't know, *gnocchella*. You tell me. Because something about this doesn't sit right."

Carly's frown was interrupted by the huff of the swinging doors leading out to the dining room. Gavin, the restaurant manager, tipped his chin at Carly in a serious nod.

"There's someone here to see you. I told him you were prepping for the day, but he insisted." A cool look covered Gavin's features, and Carly's heart jackhammered in her chest.

"Do you know who it is?"

"Huge guy, says you're working together on a project. Do you want me to tell him you're busy?"

The jackhammer in her ribcage turned gleeful. "No, that's Jackson. You can send him back." Carly ran a surreptitious hand over her braid while Gavin disappeared through the doors, eyebrows lifted.

"You're letting a stranger come into the kitchen?" Adrian's jaw was somewhere in the vicinity of his knees. "Have you lost your mind?"

"We're not open, relax. Plus, he's not a stranger. He's—" Carly stopped short at the sound of the doors *thunking* open. Jackson peered into the kitchen with uncertainty, but his blue eyes crinkled when he saw her. Carly had never been so happy to lay eyes on someone in her whole life.

"Hey. Sorry to barge in on you like this, but I came out to take some more pictures of the proposed garden site for Luke and I saw your car in the lot. I don't want to bother you, though." Jackson's eyes skimmed over Adrian, who had stiffened into watchdog status at her side.

Carly laughed and made her way over to him like she was a magnet and he was crafted of solid steel. "Don't be silly.

We're not open for hours." Instinctively, she lifted up on her tiptoes to press a quick kiss to his lips. After a stutter-step of surprise, he returned the favor, and Carly felt her crappy morning recede into bad-memory territory. "Come on in."

"Wow, it smells great in here," Jackson murmured, wearing his trademark easygoing smile. Adrian folded his arms over his barrel chest, and Carly bit down on her lip. Maybe that kiss hadn't been the best idea right off the bat, but Adrian would just have to suck it up.

"Jackson, this is my sous chef, Adrian Holt. Adrian, Jackson Carter. He's the contractor I told you about." Of course she'd failed to mention the whole I'm-sleeping-with-him thing, which she'd known would ruffle Adrian's big-brother-esque feathers.

Jackson extended a hand. "Good to meet you, man. Carly's told me a lot about you."

Testosterone prickled through the air as Adrian gave Jackson a once-over before shaking his hand. "Looks like she hasn't told me enough about you." Their eyes locked, neither man making a move, but neither one standing down, either.

Carly rolled her eyes and angled her body between them, putting a hand on Adrian's forearm. "Behave, *gnoccone*. He's fine." She pasted a sweet smile on her face, a clear sign she meant to kill him later, and turned toward Jackson. "Are you hungry? I can make a batch of calamari and we can go over the final plans. I'd love to incorporate the new photos in the presentation."

Jackson's eyes flicked a hard glance over Adrian, but he relented with a nod and smile. "Sure. That sounds great. I'll just go grab the camera from the truck."

"I'll meet you in the dining room."

"Okay." Jackson paused, giving Adrian one last look before passing through the swinging doors. Carly ducked down to retrieve some ingredients from the lowboy, but Adrian caught her by the elbow, midcrouch.

"I've got this." His voice was gruff, but his eyes flashed with sincerity.

She creased her brows. "Are you sure?"

"Are you?" Genuine concern had replaced the hard edge to his words, and it made Carly's lips twitch into a grin.

"It's not serious," she replied. "I'm fine. He's fine."

Adrian shook his head, but conceded nonetheless. "If you say so. But if you change your mind . . ."

"You'll be the first to know," Carly promised, putting a container of calamari on the counter. Wiping her hands on her apron, she turned to head into the dining room, but Gavin appeared in her path before she could get to the door. Although he was always serious, something about the troubled look in his eyes stopped Carly dead in her tracks.

"Whoa. You look like you just saw a ghost."

A muscle in Gavin's jaw tightened, but he didn't lower his gaze. "There's an urgent call for you on the house phone."

Fear spurted through her brain, freezing her into place. "What? Who is it?"

"It's your brother."

Chapter Twenty-One

As soon as Jackson recrossed the stone-tiled threshold of La Dolce Vita, he knew something wasn't right. Carly stood at the bar with the phone pressed to her ear, and although her back was to him, her shoulders slumped forward in a clear sign of nothing-good. Her sous chef stood right next to her, eyes full of the kind of wary concern that people only reserved for bad news. Jackson's stomach knotted in unease, a feeling that shifted to out and out fear as soon as he heard Carly's muffled sob.

"Okay, I'm coming. Just . . . tell her . . ." She broke off, presumably to take a breath, but her voice still shook as she finished her sentence. "Tell her I'm on my way. I'll meet you at the hospital. I love you, too, Dom." She stood for a minute, unmoving, before lowering the phone to the bar in front of her.

"Carly? What's going on?" For a big guy, her sous chef's voice had gone awfully quiet. The look on Carly's face nearly dropped Jackson's knees out from beneath him, and her words matched her wooden expression.

"Dominic said . . ." She paused to squeeze her eyes shut before choking out the rest. "I think my mother had a stroke."

Jackson moved without thinking, stepping in close. "God, Carly. I'm sorry."

Carly's eyes found his, flashing with a streak of intense emotion before going blank. "I, um. I have to go to New York. Right now." Her voice was so shell-shocked, it sounded like an echo.

The thought of her making a drive like that after such horrible news all by herself put Jackson into high alert. "You shouldn't go alone." He dug into his pocket for his keys.

"He's right." Adrian agreed gruffly, although he didn't look happy about it. "I'll take you back."

Jackson's instincts growled to life, but the panicked look on Carly's face stopped the choice obscenities in his head from rolling off his tongue.

"You can't. I need you here." Her eyes went wide, imploring, but Adrian didn't budge.

"Screw here. The restaurant isn't as important as getting you home."

A muscle in Jackson's jaw twitched hard, but he managed to bite down on his severe irritation. While the idea was appealing as hell, picking a fight with this guy wouldn't help Carly right now.

"Adrian, *please*. Friday's our busiest night, plus we're booked all weekend. I need you in the back of the house, and I can't leave unless I know everything here is taken care of." Carly's ragged plea cut Adrian's protest to the quick, but he didn't back down entirely.

"Okay, I'll stay," he agreed, clearly hating the concession. "But take Sloane."

"Sloane's on a deadline," Carly argued, shaking her head. "I'm perfectly capable of driving myself back to the city."

Adrian frowned. "Carly—"

Jackson's words were out of his mouth without thought. "I'll take her."

Both Adrian and Carly turned to stare at him, although with very different expressions.

"I'll be fine." There was zero fire in her argument, though, and Jackson refused to relent. No freaking way was he letting her make that drive all alone.

"Come on. Why don't you call Sloane and ask her to pack you a bag so we can just swing by and grab it on our way down the mountain. With any luck, we'll get to the city before rush hour gets nasty."

For a second, Carly didn't move, and Jackson mentally prepared round two of his defense. But then she gave a slow nod.

"Okay. Yeah. I'll just be a second."

The restaurant manager, who had been silently waiting nearby, passed her the phone without preamble, and Carly took it with a hollow glance and moved down the bar to call Sloane. Jackson palmed his keys, figuring he could call Luke from the road to let him know he'd be gone for a couple of days. Rescheduling that kitchen job by the lake would be tight, something Jackson would likely pay for with some twelve-hour days when he got back, but he didn't care. He shifted to look at Carly, but the view was immediately blocked by the menacing glare of her sous chef.

"I don't like this."

Wow. Talk about throwing it all out there. Too bad for him that being intimidated wasn't on Jackson's agenda, no matter how big the guy was.

"I'm okay with that," Jackson replied smoothly. Although he kept his tone purposely neutral, his meaning seemed to get through loud and clear. "Look, we can have a pissing contest over it when I get back. For now, I'm just worried about Carly, and I'm pretty sure you are too. So what do you say we skip the pleasantries, huh? She'll be safe with me."

Adrian served up a hard stare, and as much as Jackson hated to admit it, the guy looked junkyard-dog mean. Carly slipped a hand over her braid and passed the phone back to the manager, who murmured to her in a low, reassuring tone.

"If you mess with her, I will kill you with my bare hands. Are we clear?" Everything about the delivery of Adrian's words told Jackson he meant what he said. Jackson narrowed his eyes, but didn't consider flinching.

"Crystal."

He turned on his heel to walk Carly out the door.

Jackson shifted his weight, trying for the billionth time to find a good fit between his frame and the driver's seat of Carly's Honda. His discomfort came in a distant second to his concern, though. One glance at Carly hammered his worry home.

Other than to punch the address of the hospital in Brooklyn into the GPS on her dashboard, she'd been completely still for the two hours they'd been in the car. He'd turned off the radio and encouraged her to close her eyes, maybe get some sleep, but she'd politely declined. Not wanting to up her stress level with small talk that would've been forced anyway, Jackson kept quiet. If Carly wanted to talk, she would. Her stony silence weighed on his mind like a pallet full of bricks.

"Looks like we're about halfway there." After two hours of nothing but the white noise of being on the road, Jackson's words sounded amplified, but Carly didn't flinch. She kept her eyes on the blur of trees outside her window as she nodded absently.

Finally, he asked, "Are you okay?" Hello, stupid question! Of course she wasn't okay. Man, he was bad at this, but the look on her face was killing him, and he'd do anything to change it. Including ridiculous inquiries, apparently.

"I'm fine."

He glanced at her for just a second, confused. "You're fine?"

Carly tightened her fingers around her T-shirt, arms crossed over her chest as if she were protecting herself. "Yes, but if you need to stop, that's okay."

He shook his head, returning his eyes to the faded asphalt in front of them. "I don't need to stop." Silence rushed at Jackson's ears for a few excruciating minutes before he continued. "I guess I meant do you want to talk about it."

"Oh. Well, I don't really know much, other than what I already told you."

"Right. Your mother was having lunch with her church group, and she got really confused," he prompted. Maybe talking about it would make her feel better. Wasn't that what women did?

"Yeah. She couldn't remember why she was there or what day it was. One of the ladies with her got really concerned and called my brother, who told her to call 911. Once she got to the hospital, they started treating her for a stroke. That's pretty much all I know."

It was the same story she'd told him on the way to the bungalow, in almost the same words.

"What did Dominic's last text say?"

Carly steadied her gaze on the passing roadside. "They're doing a CAT scan and a bunch of other tests . . . an ECG, I think? They want to monitor her heart and look at her arteries. One of my brothers will call if anything changes, but for now, we just have to wait, I guess," she said before lapsing back into silence.

"It sounds like she's in good hands," Jackson offered, hoping it wasn't lame, but Carly only nodded. Christ, he felt helpless.

They drove the rest of the way in basic quiet, interrupted by two updates from her brother, which yielded little information other than what they already knew. Once they got close to the Holland Tunnel, Jackson pulled over at Carly's suggestion so they could switch places. Her knowledge of the city was definitely better, and although he'd have done it, city driving made him twitchy as hell. She maneuvered the clogged streets with ease, and after twenty minutes, she pulled into a three-story parking garage to fit the Civic into a spot that his truck would've eaten for breakfast.

"The ICU is on the third floor." Carly sat in the driver's seat on a ten-second delay, as if she wanted the words to settle in before she moved. Jackson's stomach ached, low in his gut, and he reached for her hand to give it a squeeze.

"Okay. Do you want to go find your brothers?"

Despite the dark circles smudged beneath her tired eyes and the worry etched on her face, she was still beautiful. "There's a waiting room up there. I remember from when my dad . . ." Carly trailed off, the silence in the car swallowing her words. "Anyway. That's where my brothers are."

She clutched his hand, unmoving, and Jackson held it tight, staying just as still.

"You just let me know when you're ready."

Carly's eyes flashed over his, frightened and bright with tears.

"Thank you."

Guilt flooded through every part of Carly's body, taking special care to stop for an extended stay in her chest as Jackson ushered her through the whispered hiss of the automatic doors leading into Memorial Hospital Center. She'd been here a handful of times—once to get the stitches in her finger, then again five years ago when her father died—and it looked and smelled exactly as she remembered it.

Like a pleasant cover-up for very bad things.

"Looks like the elevators are down here." Jackson

pointed toward a long, gleamingly tiled hallway with his right hand, his left still firmly twined around hers. For some strange reason, an image of his brother-in-law's boat popped into her head. She and Jackson had never used the anchor the day they went fishing, but it had been comforting to know it had been there, in all its gunmetal glory, waiting.

She needed it now.

Wordlessly, they got on the elevator, and the ride to the third floor took both forever and not long enough. The doors trundled open, and Carly forced her feet to move to the nurse's station in front of her.

"Excuse me, I'm looking for Francesca di Matisse," she told the scrubs-clad nurse behind the desk. The woman gave one efficient nod, but her eyes softened as they fell on Carly's.

"She just went for her MRI. Are you related?"

"I'm her daughter."

Her only daughter. The one who picked a fight with her just this morning. The one whose last words to her were full of anger.

Please, God, don't let that be the last thing I ever say to her, Carly begged silently.

"Dr. Moreland can give you an update when your mother's MRI is done, but it shouldn't be too long. There's a waiting room at the end of the hall. I'm sure you'll see some familiar faces in there." The nurse paused to offer up a smile, and Carly's heart lurched in her chest at the thought of seeing her brothers.

"Thank you."

Mercifully, her feet had the one-in-front-of-the-other thing down pat. She auto-piloted over the industrially clean linoleum, and Jackson kept time with every step as they followed the corridor and rounded the corner to the waiting room.

The space hadn't changed in five years, right down to the outdated magazines on the tastefully simple end tables, and Carly fought the wave of nausea that washed over her at the sight of the faded green carpet and nondescript watercolors on the walls. Her brothers all sat in various states of discomfort, eyes fixed on the muted TV mounted to the wall, until they saw her standing in the doorway.

"Carly!" Her oldest brother, Vince, was closest, and he had her in a bear hug before she'd even crossed the threshold. "It's good to see you, *cucciola*." Nine years her senior, Vince's dark hair was shot through with threads of silver, making him look like an Italian version of George Clooney. Carly held him tight, sending her muffled greeting into his shoulder.

"Hey, Vin." She squeezed him, letting him kiss both her cheeks before repeating the greeting with her middle brother, Frankie. "I got here as fast as I could."

Dominic rose from his seat, folding her into an embrace, and Carly had to fight the urge not to cry extra hard. Of all her brothers, she was closest to Dominic, who currently looked as grave as she'd ever seen him.

And that was when their father had died.

"Hey, you. You just missed Daniela by ten minutes. The baby was getting cranky, and she had to run to pick up the boys from the neighbor's anyway. But I'm glad you're here."

Something unspoken hung in Dominic's words, and he hugged her too hard, too long. The mention of her sister-in-law and nephews made Carly's heart lift with fondness, only to tighten and ache harder as she thought of the matriarch who held them all together. She unwound her arms to look her brother in the eye, just in time to see him catch sight of Jackson standing in the doorway. Dominic's brows sailed upward in surprise, but he said nothing.

"Dom, this is Jackson Carter. Jackson, these are my

brothers. Dominic, Frankie, and Vince. Jackson's a friend of mine from Pine Mountain. He drove me back."

Dom's brow popped even higher, and he extended his hand. "Nice to meet you. Thanks for getting her home safely."

"No problem at all." Jackson went the requisite rounds with handshakes and how-do-you-dos for all three of her brothers, taking their hard, assessing stares in stride.

"Why don't I head out to find the cafeteria while you guys talk?" Jackson moved toward the hallway, but his eyes were on her. "I'll bring you back a sandwich, okay?"

Carly's heart stuttered against her ribs. "No, don't go. Not yet," she amended, startling everyone in the room, including herself. She grabbed his hand and cut her gaze to Dominic, steeling her resolve. "How is she?"

Dom's chocolate-brown eyes settled on hers, hesitant. "We only got to see her for a couple of minutes."

"Talk to me, Dominic. I'm not a baby." She worked up her best I-mean-business stare. "I want to know," she said, her voice betraying her with its waver. Frankie shot Dominic a look she couldn't decipher, but he shook his head and answered her.

"There's not much to tell. She was pretty out of it, both when she got here and when we saw her, but the doctor said her symptoms have been improving, which is a good sign." Dominic steered her toward a chair in the waiting room, and she sank into it even though her back still ached from being cramped in the car for four hours.

"So she definitely . . . she definitely had a stroke, then?" Carly's throat closed around the words. She should've been more patient this morning on the phone. Damn it!

Dominic paused, but he gave it to her straight. "It looks that way. But the tests will give us a better idea of what we're looking at, okay?"

A woman wearing a crisp white coat over her pale blue

scrubs poked her head into the room as if conjured by Carly's need for answers. "Hello, di Matisse family. I've got an update on your mother." The woman's kind expression ratcheted Carly's anxiety down a notch. A small notch, anyway.

"Carly, this is Dr. Moreland. She gave us the first update when *Mama* was admitted a couple hours ago." Vince nodded at the woman, who offered Carly a handshake that conveyed both warmth and efficiency.

"I'm glad you're all here. I've had a chance to take a look at the CAT scan and the ECG and I have some good news. The CAT scan doesn't show any bleeds in your mother's brain, and we've ruled out atrial fibrillation. Her confusion has lessened significantly since she's been admitted, as has the weakness in her left arm. I think what we're looking at here is a TIA."

Carly blinked hard, but Vince stole the words from her brain and gave them a voice. "Okay, so what does that mean?"

Dr. Moreland smiled. "A TIA is a neurologic abnormality similar to a stroke, but it resolves a lot faster. It's a good thing, in that it's not as damaging as a stroke. However—" She paused to level a serious look at all of them, lowering her voice. "The next seventy-two hours are going to be critical for her. Ten percent of people who experience a TIA will go on to have a full-blown stroke."

"Jesus," Dominic breathed. "So what can we do to prevent that from happening?"

"About half of those strokes happen in the first day or so after the TIA, so we'll keep her here to monitor her condition. After that, we'll take a look at the best medications to keep her risk as low as possible. It's likely she'll need to alter her lifestyle a bit to ensure she's doing all she can to stay healthy, but there shouldn't be any long-term damage as a result of the TIA."

"As long as she doesn't have an actual stroke, you mean."

Frankie's quiet assertion flattened the air in Carly's lungs like a sucker punch.

Dr. Moreland nodded. "Yes. She's not out of the woods yet, although the prognosis is promising. I'm on until eight, and I'll keep you posted with any new test results. We've sedated her so she can rest, but you're welcome to go in one or two at a time to sit with her for a while."

Carly's brain scrambled as she tried to process, then reprocess the doctor's words, so she almost missed the last thing the doctor said before she turned to head down the hallway.

"As a matter of fact, Ms. di Matisse, your mother has been particularly adamant about wanting to see *you*."

Chapter Twenty-Two

Carly stood, completely still and terrified, on the threshold outside of ICU Room 5. The walls facing the hallway were all glass, but someone had drawn a set of pale curtains with a smudgy gray pattern over the length of the windows, blocking the view inside. Presumably so her mother could rest.

Her mother, who might still have a stroke.

Oh, God. How much of this had she brought on with that ridiculous argument?

"Ms. di Matisse?" Dr. Moreland stopped short as she rounded the corner and caught sight of Carly on the threshold, hand frozen to the door handle. "Is everything alright?"

"Oh, yeah. Well . . . no." Carly's gut churned like sweet cream butter. "I, um. I had a fight with her this morning. I don't . . . I don't want to make things worse, you know?" She twisted the hem of her T-shirt in one clammy fist.

"A lot has happened between this morning and now," Dr. Moreland replied, her expression softening a notch. "It wouldn't surprise me if she had other things on her mind when she asked to see you."

Carly shifted her weight, uncertain. "The fight was kind of a doozy. Do you think . . . I mean, if I go in there and she gets upset, could she have another one of those, what are they called? TIA's?" God, hadn't all of this crap with Travis caused enough pain already?

"A TIA is a neurological disorder, Ms. di Matisse. The one your mother had this morning would've happened no matter what. The argument didn't cause it."

"But it probably didn't make it better," Carly argued.

Dr. Moreland smiled and shook her head, her short gray-blonde ponytail swishing from side to side. "I've found that arguing rarely makes anything better." She paused, eyeing the curtain drawn over the wall of glass. "Listen, your mother does need to rest, and no, she shouldn't be stressed right now. But she has been asking for you. Why don't I take you in, and you can sit by the bed for a few minutes. We'll take it from there."

Carly's eyes burned, dry and tired. She reached out automatically for Jackson's hand, her face prickling when she came up with empty air.

Right. Dr. Moreland would have to do. "Are you ready?" She nodded. "Yeah."

Carly let go of the door and let Dr. Moreland gently glide past her, the same professional-grade rubber clogs that Carly wore in the kitchen making a familiar whisper against the floor. Hundreds of miles away, Adrian was in the middle of running a dinner service in a restaurant that had her name listed on the menu as the head chef.

It all seemed so far away.

"Knock, knock." Dr. Moreland paused for a split second before brushing past the curtain, and Carly could now see that the smudges were in fact hummingbirds. "I brought you a visitor."

Carly lifted her chin to look at her mother, and fought the urge to shrink back in shock. Her mother, who was a petite woman to begin with, looked downright child-like in the hospital bed, surrounded by scary-looking machines and equipment. Her face was drawn and tired, her dry lips cracked. The hospital gown framing her too-thin shoulders gaped at one side, showing her collarbone in stark relief against skin as pale as the bed sheets. Carly stumbled forward, grasping for some semblance of strength along the way.

She missed by about ten city blocks.

"Hey, *Mama*," she croaked, lurching to an awkward stop next to the bed.

"Carlotta," her mother whispered, a wan smile flitting over her lips. "You look like hell."

Carly's laugh was more of a strangled mew. "Thanks."

"So Dominic . . . called you," her mother rasped, laying her head back on the pillow. Carly's eyes skimmed over the hummingbirds on the curtain by her mother's bedside, trying to focus on something other than the ominous-looking jagged lines on the monitor by her head and the tubes snaking from her stick-thin arm.

"Of course. He's in the waiting room with Vin and Frankie and . . . yeah," Carly fumbled. "We're all here." She propped her hip against the bed, afraid to put all her weight on it even though her mother barely took up half the space. Dr. Moreland caught Carly's eye and gave her a tiny nod of approval before slipping past the curtain, shutting the door with a barely-there *click*.

"Well. I suppose I put a crimp in everyone's day." The words, which normally would've been delivered with trademark di Matisse zing, sounded suspiciously vulnerable.

"Don't worry about that. Just concentrate on getting better, okay." Carly scooped up her mother's hand—God, when did she get so *frail*—and gave her a tiny squeeze.

"I have . . . things I want to say to you," her mother said, but her voice trailed off in exhaustion.

"Shh, *Mama*." Carly steeled herself. Screw what Dr. Moreland had said about the TIA happening no matter what. Carly wasn't about to bring her mother one step closer to a stroke by rehashing their argument. Why hadn't she kept her big mouth shut in the first place? "We can talk later, okay? I'm not going anywhere. For now, you need to rest."

"Mmm." It was as close to a concession as Carly had ever heard from her mother. Whatever was in the IV dangling above the bed must be the good stuff. "Later, then."

Her *mama* drifted off, and Carly buckled down on the overwhelming urge to curl up next to her in the bed and cry herself to sleep.

Jackson glanced down at the untouched bowl of chicken noodle soup and crinkly package of Saltines in front of Carly. After spending the last three hours doing the emotional merry-go-round of switching off with her brothers while their mother slept, Carly looked absolutely wrecked.

"I know it sounds trite, but you really should eat." Out of everything in the cafeteria, the soup had seemed the most comforting. And since he'd had two bowls himself, he knew for a fact it wasn't half-bad.

"Isn't that my line?" Carly asked without cracking a smile. She sighed in a slow, steady breath. "Sorry. I'm just tired. And not very hungry."

"Do you think you could do me a favor and just take a bite or two? I promised your brothers I'd get you to eat something. And to be honest, being on their bad side isn't a concept I'd like to explore." He teased her gently, and she finally lifted the edge of her lips in the tiniest of smiles.

"My brothers know better than to think you can get me to eat if I'm not hungry." But still, she dipped her spoon into the broth, giving it a half-hearted swirl.

"Well then maybe you could humor me just this once."

Jackson watched with relief as Carly took a couple tentative bites of soup. She peeled back the cellophane on the crackers, and Jackson found himself thinking he'd get her a thousand more packages just like it if it would erase the look on her face right now.

"I'm glad your mom is resting. The doctor sounded really hopeful," Jackson said, hoping the reinforcement of good news would boost her mood a little.

Carly nodded and gave a soft demi-shrug. "Yeah. She's pretty out of it from the sedatives. I really only talked to her for a few minutes." She put her spoon down and leveled him with a serious stare. Christ, seeing those pretty brown eyes so full of deep sadness was killing him.

"We can come back first thing in the morning. I checked, and ICU visiting hours start at ten."

"Okay, yeah." She sat stoically for a minute, as if the four bites of soup she'd taken had sapped her strength rather than replaced some of it. Not knowing what else to do, Jackson reached out to wrap his fingers around hers, resting their entwined hands on the timeworn Formica table next to her tray.

Her eyes flickered with emotion, but it lasted for less than a second. "Thanks."

Jackson opened his mouth to answer, but was interrupted by the gentle-yet-definitely-masculine rumble of a throat being cleared behind him.

"Well. I just lost twenty bucks." Carly's oldest brother, Vince, lifted an eyebrow at the discarded wrapper and Saltines crumbs on the tray. "I didn't think you'd eat. Not even for the big guy."

Jackson moved to let go of Carly's hand, but she gripped his fingers like a C-clamp as she nodded her brothers into the adjacent chairs.

"Told you," Dominic replied, the barest hint of a wry smile beneath his tired expression. He flicked a glance over Jackson and Carly's hands before sliding into the seat next to her. "Hey, *cucciola*. How're you doing?"

"I'm tired. Did they kick you out already?" Carly's forehead creased in lines of concern and she pushed her tray back with her free hand, soup forgotten.

"She's been asleep for hours, so we decided to call it a night. Frankie had to head home because Gina had a night class and little Frank's been sick, but he's coming back in the morning." Dominic paused. "Have you given any thought to where you want to spend the night?"

Carly's head snapped up. "Oh. I hadn't really thought about it."

Jackson's gut jangled with realization. The day had been so crazy, he hadn't given it any thought, either.

"It's been a long day," Vince agreed, pulling up a chair. "Why don't you leave your car here and you two can hitch a ride to the 'burbs with one of us?"

She paused, her eyes skipping between both brothers. "Actually, I think we'll just stay at *mama*'s. It's a lot closer, just in case." The waver in her voice returned, full force. "Then we'll meet you here tomorrow."

Vince nailed Dominic with a brotherly look Jackson knew all too well, and Dominic shifted in his seat. "Are you sure you'll be okay?"

Carly's frown intensified. "Of course. Why wouldn't I be okay?"

Vince met her frown with one of his own, just as sturdy, and in that flash the family resemblance was uncanny. "Maybe one of us should stay with you too, then."

Jackson noticed it wasn't a question, and he stiffened against the unforgiving cafeteria chair.

Carly's unrelenting stubbornness swooped in to cut Vince's suggestion off at the pass. "I think I can handle staying at *mama*'s for one night, Vin. Plus, Jackson will be with me. It'll be fine."

Vince muttered something about that being what he was worried about, and Jackson sat up straighter in his seat in an involuntary response. Thankfully, his brain screamed the reminder that he had sisters too, and it kept Jackson's mouth clamped shut over the protest burning on his tongue.

Carly wasn't so restrained, though. "Vince. Don't be ridiculous." Her hand tightened over Jackson's, and she opened her mouth—presumably to argue some more—but Dominic gently interrupted both of his siblings before Jackson could beat him to it.

"Carly's right. It's a good idea for one of us to stay close. And if she says she's okay with Jackson, then she's okay."

It wasn't lost on Jackson that Dominic's eyes hardened over him as he spoke, but he returned the stare with equal strength. No way was anything happening to Carly while he was there. And he wasn't going to leave her.

He tightened his hand over hers. "I've got her."

Vince grunted and looked for all the world like he wanted to argue, but Carly shook her head, resolute.

"There's plenty of room at *mama*'s. We'll be fine there."

After an ear-piercing silence during which Vince didn't argue and Carly didn't back down, Dominic nodded. "Okay, then. Since that's settled, should we meet here tomorrow? It's been a long day, and we could all use some sleep."

Reluctantly, Vince nodded as he stood, pinning Jackson with a weary stare. "Yeah. Sorry. Today's just been tough."

"No problem at all. I understand," Jackson said, and he did. Hell, he couldn't even imagine what he'd do or say if it was his mother in that hospital bed. He shuddered at the thought.

Vince extended a hand to Jackson, who shook it with the silent acknowledgment that he'd take care of Carly. "See you tomorrow."

Both Vince and Dominic kissed Carly goodnight, and after they'd all parted ways, she sank back into the chair across from Jackson.

"Sorry about that. I should've figured they'd be protective, especially after . . . well . . ." Her words faded as if she was too defeated to even finish a thought, and Jackson stood, beckoning her into his arms. Getting her some uninterrupted rest was priority number one right now. The clock on the wall read 8:12, but reality made it feel more like two AM after a fourteen-hour workday in the sun.

"Hey. It's fine. Come on. Let's get you home so you can get a little sleep, okay?" He gathered her close for a quick embrace, and she peered up at him in bewilderment before blinking in recognition.

"Oh, right. You mean my mother's house." She shook her head, sliding her tray from the table to clear it on the way out.

"What'd you think I meant?" Jackson asked, taking the tray from her with ease. He deposited it at the back of the room before wrapping an arm around her to usher her out the door.

"Sorry. I thought . . . when you said *home,* I thought you meant Pine Mountain. I guess it's been a long day."

Something odd shot through Jackson's belly, startling him, yet he couldn't place it. Wow, today really must've taken it out of all of them.

"Yeah," he agreed, settling into silence that was punctuated only by the softness of their footfalls as they headed toward the parking garage.

But the feeling lingered like leaves whispering in the wind.

Jackson awoke to several things simultaneously, all of which were confusing as hell. After a few seconds of rapid-fire blinking and muddled thought, he cleared up the where-am-I, what-time-is-it issue. The clock on the nightstand in the guest bedroom glared a rather rude 2:15, and he rolled to his side to work through the next set of questions.

The side of the bed where he'd last seen Carly was rumpled and empty, and there was a terrible racket coming from the kitchen down the hall.

Jackson yanked a shirt over his head as he padded barefoot down the narrow hallway, guided by the metallic clang of pots and pans and the lilting hiss of Italian curse words. Carly stood in profile at the kitchen counter, the sleeves of her pajamas rolled tightly above her forearms. She gave the golden-yellow ball of dough under her palms a severe frown as she kneaded it, her hands flexing and releasing like a heartbeat.

She looked so overwhelmingly sad, with streaks of flour and utter, bone-numbing sadness covering her face, that Jackson's heart whacked against his ribcage with the need to do something about it.

"Hey." Okay, so it was a lame start, but it caught her attention. Carly's head jerked up, eyebrows winging in surprise toward the sloppy knot on the crown of her head.

"Oh! I'm sorry. I didn't mean to wake you up." Her hands folded over the ball of dough in a blur of motion.

"It is kind of two in the morning," Jackson pointed out gently, leaning against the doorframe. "Aren't you exhausted?"

Carly shook her head, momentarily abandoning the dough in favor of stirring something in a huge stockpot on one of the three occupied burners on the stove. "I can't sleep. Plus, we're going to need food. Especially when my *mama* comes home." She dipped a small spoon into the pot, grimacing as she tasted the mixture. "Ugh. That's not right." The spoon went into the sink with a clatter and another curse.

"Carly," Jackson started, but she halted his movement toward her with the firm lift of her palm.

"She's going to need food." She returned her attention to the stockpot, forehead creased tight. "More thyme. Yeah." She rummaged through the cabinet over her head with relentless energy.

Jackson scrubbed a hand over his jaw, weighing his

options. Sugar-coating things wasn't really his style; plus, Carly wouldn't fall for that anyway. He moved behind her to pluck the jar of thyme from the shelf, but when she reached forward to take it from his outstretched hand, he held her fast.

"I'm worried about you. You need to rest."

"Don't tell me what I need," she snapped, yanking her hand back. "My mother is going to need food when she comes home. She's coming *home*," Carly said, her voice emphatic. "I'm sorry I woke you up, but I have to do this. It's the least I can do after . . . after . . ." She trailed off on a choked sob, and realization slammed into Jackson like a wrecking ball.

Carly blamed herself for this.

"Jesus, Carly. It's not your fault." He grabbed her shoulders with the intention of wrapping his arms around her, but the coiled tension rippling beneath his palms shocked him into place. She swung around, defensive to the hilt, eyes flashing whiskey-brown and terrified.

"Of course it's my fault!" She balled her flour-covered fists over his T-shirt, but instead of pushing him away, she clung for dear life. "I did everything but tell her to permanently butt out of my life this morning! What if she never wakes up, Jackson? What if the last thing I'd said to her had been some stupid, angry thing about Travis? I never got to say good-bye to my father—I don't even remember the last thing I ever said to him, but did I learn anything from that? No! What if . . ." Carly's eyes flooded with tears that quickly breached her lids to course down her face. "What if she doesn't wake up tomorrow? What if she dies, just like he did? Then what?"

Jackson didn't hesitate, even though his ribcage felt like it had been run through a shredder. Carly's waning strength was no match for the pull of his arms, and he folded her close, as if he could absorb her growing sobs through the contact.

"You had no way of knowing this would happen."

"But it did. It did happen, and now I have to fix it. The only way I know how to do that is to cook, okay? So please let me fix it. *Please*," she begged, emotion breaking over the word and carrying more tears with it. "I don't know any other way to make this right."

For a second, he thought her grief would drag him under, but Jackson dug in deep to steady himself and hold her up.

"Okay. If you want to cook, we'll cook," he murmured roughly into her hair, and she shuddered against him, cries wracking every breath.

"Thank you." She repeated the words into his shoulder enough times that he lost count, but she didn't let go so Jackson didn't budge. Only when her sadness had run its course, her gut-twisting cries subsiding into intermittent hitches, did he pull back to kiss a damp temple and tell her the truth.

"You didn't cause your mother's stroke, Carly."

She rested her cheek on the tear-stained cotton of his T-shirt. "I know. But I didn't make life easier by shutting her out. Despite her nagging, she means well. I'm just so tired of dwelling on everything that went wrong in my marriage. But I never stopped to think that my unhappiness affects her, too."

Jackson cupped Carly's face and smoothed his hand over her cheek, catching the last of her tears with one rough thumb. "Keeping that inside must've been pretty tough." Even now, with shadows of exhaustion smudged beneath her eyes and her disheveled hair falling out of its knot, his heart ached for her.

"I'm sorry. I just—"

Jackson's fingers halted over her lips, literally shushing her even though he knew she wouldn't like it.

"I'll stay up as late as you want to help you cook on one condition." He jutted his chin over her shoulder to the controlled chaos in the kitchen, and Carly looked so shocked by his movement that she simply nodded without protest.

"Don't say *I'm sorry* to me for how you feel. Ever again." He dropped his gaze, catching as much emotion in her eyes as he felt brewing in his own. She exhaled a delicate sigh, her breath warming his fingers, but she didn't fight him. Instead, Carly reached up and curled her hand around his, holding on with a certainty that Jackson felt clear into the floor.

"Okay," was all she said.

He gave one decisive nod before turning toward the stockpot. "Good. Now hand me a spoon so I can taste this, would you please? This sauce isn't going to season itself, you know."

Chapter Twenty-Three

Carly squinted at the bright sunlight muscling its way past the aging curtains, realizing like a delayed reaction that she'd finally let Jackson carry her to bed at a little before five AM. Judging by the heaviness in her limbs, she hadn't moved much, if at all, during her four hours of deep, dreamless sleep. Carly tried to swallow, but her sandpaper lips only pressed together in a useless maneuver over her knotted throat as she rolled onto her side.

"Hey," Jackson mumbled, eyes still closed, and he snaked one tree-trunk arm over her to fit their bodies together. They were both still clad in what they'd worn the night before, and she brushed the pads of her fingers over the chalky smudges of flour on his T-shirt, feeling mildly heartsick at how they'd gotten there.

Oh, God. Had she really broken down sobbing in his arms, right in her mother's kitchen?

"It's almost nine." She inhaled the scent of pasta dough and fresh-cut wood from his skin, and he burrowed deeper into his pillow with a sleep-laden exhale.

"Mmkay." His breath tickled her neck, but she felt so good wrapped up in his arms and the bed sheets that the outside world almost fell away, forgotten.

Almost.

"I'm going to put on a pot of coffee and take a quick shower. I want to be there when the doctor on the night shift does rounds at ten." Carly shifted her weight to pull back the covers, but Jackson tightened his grip around her ribs, finally opening his eyes.

"Okay." He dipped his gold-stubbled chin to drop a kiss on her forehead, and Carly's heart stuttered in her chest. She paused, weighing the thoughts flying around in her brain and trying to snag one long enough to make it coherent.

"Thank you. You know, for staying up with me last night. For . . . holding me." The stutter in her chest grew insistent, pushing through her like one hell of a wakeup call. "For everything."

Lord, she was bad at this. But the expression on Jackson's face, so open and easy and matter-of-fact, settled her with uncharacteristic calm.

"You're welcome."

They lay together for a moment, his lips on the crown of her head, the smell of his skin so comforting and close, so inextricably connected that it hit Carly with a pang deep in her belly.

Sloane was right. Carly had left friends-with-benefits territory in the dust.

And if it didn't feel so warm and good and utterly right to have Jackson here, comforting her when she needed him most, it would've terrified her right down to her toes.

"I wish you'd all stop fussing over me. It's bad enough with the nurses and the doctors traipsing in to poke and prod. And don't get me started on what they've got masquerading as food around here. Breakfast was awful."

Carly had never been so happy to hear her mother's bitching in all her life. After a full panel of tests revealed that her mother's TIA had been isolated and there was still no brain bleed present, the doctors had given her a glowing report that ended with the prognosis of a full recovery. Of course, they'd had no idea what they were in for when they suggested she stay another day, just to be on the safe side.

"Sorry, *Mama*. But you're stuck here until tomorrow, so you'll have to make the best of it." Carly flipped the cover off the lunch tray that had just been delivered by a smiling nurse, wrinkling her nose at the pallid, over-boiled chicken breast and undercooked white rice on the plate. No way was that going to fly with her mother, not even if she was starving. Which, by the sound of things, might not be too far off.

"If you're hungry, why don't you try some of this salad?" Carly pasted a smile on her face in an effort to work up some enthusiasm for the ho-hum chunk of lettuce and colorless tomato beside the tray.

"Because it looks horrible, that's why," her mother replied, fastening Carly with a no-nonsense look. "Is it too much to ask my chef daughter for some real food? Please, Carlotta! You wouldn't eat this."

Carly laughed, her first one in what felt like a dog's age. "Okay, yeah." She caved, replacing the lid over the chicken and pushing the tray aside. "The guys are making a lunch run. I'll send Dom a message and have him bring you back a sandwich." Carly tapped her phone to life and pecked out a quick text to her brother.

"Now we're getting somewhere. Pastrami would be good, with extra cheese. And a black and white cookie. Maybe two," her mother replied, brown eyes lighting.

Carly shook her head, unforgiving, as she hit SEND and replaced her phone in her back pocket. "Uh-uh. You heard both doctors. We need to keep your blood pressure nice and low, which means you're taking a break from some of that stuff for a while. And don't give the nurse any grief about taking that medicine, you hear me?"

Her mother's physician had timed his visit to coincide with the ICU doctor's rounds a few hours ago, and together they'd come up with a game plan to keep her *mama* as healthy as possible after she returned home. While the dietary changes and the medication schedule were going to take some getting used to, they seemed like a casual stroll in Central Park compared to the alternative.

"The doctors said I'm going to be just fine," her mother argued, although Carly noted it came without the usual fierceness. "I'm good as new."

"You're exhausted," Carly answered, as gently as she could while still letting her mother know she meant business. "And you need to take care of yourself." She stood next to the bed, mercilessly rearranging the silverware on the tray until it was ruler-straight.

"There's the pot calling the kettle black." Her mother shifted her weight against the lumpy mattress. Her pillow slid behind her graying head at an awkward angle, but she paid it little mind as she leveled Carly with a knowing stare.

"What are you talking about? I take care of myself." Carly pressed one hip against the bed, bracing herself so she could lean in and straighten her mother's pillow.

"No, *tesoro mio*. No you don't. Not here." Her mother reached up to place a frail palm over Carly's heart, and Carly jumped at both the unexpected contact and at the term of endearment her father had usually reserved just for her.

"That's crazy, Ma." But even as she uttered the words, Carly knew they weren't exactly true. After all, if she'd been more careful with her heart in the first place, then Travis wouldn't have had any room to stomp all over her. And as if once-bitten wasn't bad enough, now she was risking it all over again with Jackson. While picturing Jackson cheating or lying to her was damn near laughable, it didn't mean he wouldn't end up hurting her in some other way. Plus, right up until she'd caught Travis with his chef's whites in a ball on the floor at Gracie's, she'd have found the idea of him cheating and lying just as far-fetched.

God, what the hell was she doing?

Her mother cleared her throat, bringing Carly's thoughts back to the hospital room. "It's not so crazy. Look at you."

Unease strummed up the length of Carly's spine, and she froze. "I don't want to fight about this." God, this was going to go bad quickly if they didn't change the subject. "Maybe you should get a little rest, huh?" She smoothed a hand over the thin blanket covering her even thinner mother, but her mother persisted.

"I'm not arguing with you. I'm trying to tell you. You want to get a divorce? So be it. I can't change your mind, and I'm starting to think it might be the right thing, anyway. But you need to look at the bigger picture. You need to look at *you*."

Carly opened her mouth, but no sound came out for a long minute. Finally, she managed a strangled, "You think I should get a divorce?"

Her mother made a face as if she'd bitten a lemon. "Oh, Travis is a sweet-talker, but he's no saint. He put the moves on Rose De Luca's daughter right in front of God and everybody at Our Lady of Mercy last week. Like Rose and I don't have eyes in our heads," she snorted, waving her hand in a tangle of IV tubes.

"My point is, even if you divorce Travis, you can't keep hiding from your life. These things that trouble you, they're gonna find you no matter where you live. If you want them to go away, you've got to deal with them." Her mother looked at her with absolute certainty, and Carly felt her gut plummet toward her knees. She sat on the edge of the bed next to her mother's tiny body.

"I'm not hiding on purpose, and I never meant to cut you out of my life. It's just that the restaurant business is so tight-knit—everyone knows everyone else, and they all believed Travis over me. I thought that if I could get out of the loop while it all shook out, I'd be able to come back and start fresh. But now . . ."

She trailed off, unsure how to end her sentence. Her mother was right. Simply being out of sight wasn't going to fix anything, not with Travis or anyone else. If she wanted to prove herself, she was going to have to fight for it, to earn it.

To reclaim it.

"Are you happy, living out there in the mountains?" Her mother's question was strangely devoid of judgment, and Carly's answer tumbled out before it had even fully formed in her mind.

"Yes." Her cheeks flamed at how readily the affirmation popped out of her, but she realized with a start that it was true. "I mean, I wasn't at first, but I love La Dolce Vita. And having my own kitchen is a dream come true, even if it isn't in a big-name city." Carly hedged, dancing around the six-foot-four reason for the rest of her happiness in Pine Mountain. "But I still miss it here. And you're right. I can't hide from my problems with Travis. Plus, I belong here, with you and Dom and Frankie and Vin."

"Hmph. You belong where you belong. You don't have to be right in front of Travis to deal with him, Carlotta, and that will come with time. I'm talking about taking care of *you*, eh? No matter where you are."

"Now who's the pot and kettle? Come on, *Mama*. This is a two-way street." Carly scooped up her mother's hand. "You have to promise you'll let us take care of you, too. And I need to be around for that."

Her mother muttered a curse in Italian, but a smile lurked beneath it. "I suppose I could give it a try. After all, I want to stick around to see you happy."

"I'm happy now, remember?" Carly smoothed a strand of salt and pepper hair back from her mother's face, and something odd thumped against her ribs.

"I know I'm old fashioned, and you can make your stubborn face as much as you please, but I want to see you truly happy. With a family. *And* your job," she added quickly, cutting off Carly's brewing argument about how they'd crossed into the twenty-first century. "I just want everything for you, the way your father and I had it. It's why I wanted you to give your marriage a chance." Her mother's voice, normally so full of stalwart certainty, wavered over the words.

The hitch made hot tears prickle beneath Carly's tired eyelids. She'd already risked everything once, only to end up with a failed marriage and a fragile heart that couldn't take another beating.

"I don't know if I'm cut out for that," she admitted, but her mother gave her hand a squeeze that said otherwise.

"One day, when you have children, this will make more sense to you. But for now, you'll have to trust me, eh? Just take care of you, *cucciola*. The rest will come."

Her mother's reply was summarily cut off by a familiar, teasing voice, and Carly gave her face a surreptitious wipe with the back of her hand as Dominic poked his head past the privacy curtain.

"Knock, knock. One turkey sandwich on whole wheat, lettuce, tomato, mustard, coming right up." He held up a deli bag with a flourish, and Carly's heart pattered in her chest as Jackson followed her brother into the room holding two more bags.

"*Dio mio*, Dominic! It sounds bland enough to put me to sleep. Who eats like that?" Her mother scowled, softening her expression slightly as she caught sight of Jackson.

"All of us, actually. If you have to eat well, then the least the rest of us can do is follow suit." Dominic handed the sandwich over before starting to unwrap another one just like it for himself, and Carly's eyebrows rose in surprise.

"That's a great idea. When did you get so sweet, big brother?"

"I didn't. It was Jackson's idea." Dominic's lips twitched upward, and her mother's eyes sparked with interest.

Carly cleared her throat for just a second too long. "*Mama*, this is Jackson Carter, a friend of mine from Pine Mountain." The word *friend* sounded strange in Carly's ears when she spoke it, like an ill-fitting shoe, but then Jackson was moving forward to greet her mother, saying how good it was to see her feeling better, and the moment was gone.

They shared a quick, pleasant lunch together full of talk about Dominic's kids and Carly's garden project, and although her mother tired out more quickly than Carly would've liked—God, she still looked so fragile—the conversation had been the least stressful in recent memory. They switched off with Frankie and Vince, stopping off at the nurse's station for a quick update, and for the first time since Carly had picked up the house phone at La Dolce Vita, she allowed herself a sigh of pure, unadulterated relief. She glanced at Jackson, who was laughing that easygoing, good-to-your-toes laugh at something Dominic had said, and her brain zeroed in on her mother's words.

"*. . . I just want everything for you, the way your father and I had it . . .*"

Suddenly, Carly's relief felt like the calm before a hurricane.

"Are you sure you're okay to drive? I really don't mind." Jackson eyed Carly warily, although he was starting to learn not to push his luck with her. She was all hands on deck in the feisty department, that was for sure.

"Jackson, we slept for ten hours last night. Seriously, it's fine." The corners of her mouth hinted upward, and his gut flooded with relief at her happiness, as cautious as it was.

"Well, yeah, but you cooked for four hours before we fell asleep, and that was after spending the day getting your mother situated back at home," Jackson said, unable to resist teasing her a little.

"Okay, so we did have a busy day. But now that my brothers and I have a plan in place to make sure my mother takes her medicine and gets to her doctor's appointments like she's supposed to, I feel much better. Plus, her freezer is so stocked with meals, I doubt she'll have to cook for the rest of the year."

"That's a conservative estimate." Cramming all that food into the freezer had been nothing short of miraculous.

Carly nodded. "And I'll be back soon enough to replenish her supply. I've already worked out a deal with Adrian that'll give me enough time off every couple of months to squeeze in a visit. It's not ideal, but it'll work."

The unspoken *for now* hung in the air, and something turned over in Jackson's chest like a stone being lifted from wet earth. He canted his head at her, watching the sun filter through the car to catch the subtle reddish undertone in her dark hair, and the ache in his chest spread out in uneven ripples.

"It sounds like you've got it all figured out." His words came out strangely like an accusation, swirling over the weird unease that had been percolating through him ever since she'd broken down in her mother's kitchen.

Feed her.

"I hope so," Carly replied with a slow test of the water, her forehead pulling into a V of concern. "Are you okay?"

Jackson shook off both the uncharacteristic tension and the return of his weird inner voice. They'd been through a lot in the last couple of days. It was enough to really mess with a guy.

"Yeah, sorry. I guess I'm still kind of beat." He laced his fingers through hers and lifted them for a quick kiss, and the move seemed to reassure her.

"Maybe you should get some sleep. We've got another couple hours to go before we hit Pine Mountain."

"Yeah, that's not a bad idea. But wake me up if you get tired and want me to drive."

He closed his eyes, willing himself to let go of the strange sensation that something wasn't quite right. After all, spending three days in the city under stressful conditions could knock even the most laid-back townie off his game. Surely, his inner voice had missed all the taste testing he and Carly had done last night. He'd gone to bed stuffed to the gills, which for him was really saying something, and he'd seen Carly eat plenty. When they got back, he could always make her a PB and J again. Maybe that would do the trick.

But as he drifted off, Jackson had the niggling feeling that all the sandwiches in the world weren't going to send his inner voice packing this time.

Chapter Twenty-Four

Four days and forty-seven work hours later, Jackson felt like the moving embodiment of *Night of the Living Dead*. Finishing that lakefront kitchen remodel had thrown him every curveball imaginable, with everything from the custom built-ins in the pantry to the wildly expensive marble floor tiles giving him fits. Mercifully, the home owner had loved every hard-wrought detail, and Jackson had been able to sign off on yet another job well done. Even if he was totally cooked over it.

Somewhere beneath the mound of scattered paperwork and discarded sweatshirts on the front seat of his truck, Jackson's cell phone shrilly demanded attention. He fumbled the hands free ear piece into place, tapping it with a tired hand.

"Hello?"

"Wow. You sound like shit." Shane's voice carried an equal mixture of joking laughter and been-there sympathy. "I take it you finished that big kitchen job, since you're actually answering your phone."

"Signed, sealed, delivered. Thank God," Jackson added. "What're you up to?" With the breakneck week he'd just endured plus his unexpected trip to New York, it had been ages since he'd seen his buddy.

"You know the Friday night drill. Bellamy's on dinner shift, so I'm kicking back until she gets home later tonight."

Despite his exhaustion, Jackson let out a small chuckle. "You, my friend, are a kept man."

Shane laughed. "Pot. Kettle. Asshole."

Jackson gripped the steering wheel, his pulse spurting through him. "I, uh, don't think I've ever heard that version," he stammered. The stupid tight feeling in his chest—the one he'd been fighting off all week—seeped through his bones like it meant to take up permanent residence.

Shane paused. "I'm just saying I'm not the only one at loose ends on a Friday night. That's all." His words were so laid back that Jackson's unease dropped a notch. Jesus, was he tired enough to blow things out of proportion or what?

"Listen, Bellamy's been baking her face off ever since Carly hinted they're going to replace that slacker of a pastry chef. Just between me and you, she really wants to move up in the ranks. Which would be cool, except now I've got three dozen apricot turnovers sitting here, mocking me. You want to come hang out for a bit, take some of them off my hands?" Shane sounded completely normal, and Jackson managed an exhale. This jumpy stuff seriously had to go.

"Sure, but only for a bit. Carly did the final business pitch for the garden project today, but with that hellish kitchen remodel, I didn't get to talk to her about how it went yet. I want to get a little shuteye before she gets home." Jackson eased his truck through Pine Mountain's singular stoplighted intersection, heading toward Shane's cabin. "I should be there in five."

He brushed a hand over his buzz cut, popping the earpiece out on the way. Yes, the emotional exhaustion of last weekend had ganged up with this crazy job to really knock it out of him, but something else stirred deep within him that he couldn't seem to ignore.

He wanted Carly to stay in Pine Mountain. Indefinitely.

Which was bullshit, really, because the whole reason he'd let himself get involved with her in the first place was because eventually, she was going to go back to the city. She'd never made any bones about the fact that her stint in Pine Mountain was temporary, that her career, her family—hell, her whole life—was in New York. It was a perfect win-win. They could be together for the time being, and when it was time to part ways, they just would, same as all Jackson's other pseudo-relationships.

Only nothing about Carly felt forced or fake, and it was starting to worry the shit out of him when it wasn't thrilling him right down to his boots.

"Jeez, I need to get some sleep," Jackson muttered as his tires crunched through the gravel path leading to Shane's cabin. A couple of apricot turnovers and about twelve hours of uninterrupted zzz's, and Jackson would be good to go.

Five minutes later, he knew he wasn't wrong about the turnovers, at least.

"Damn, Shane. How do you live with this woman and not weigh five hundred pounds? These pastries are intense." Jackson licked his thumb in appreciation for the gooey glaze Bellamy had drizzled over the golden layers of puffed dough, eagerly reaching for a second helping with his other hand.

"You don't even want to know how often I've run the loop behind this cabin in an effort to work off her latest culinary brainstorm. This pastry chef thing is killing me, I mean it," Shane said.

"Lightweight." Jackson took another bite, the tangy apricot bursting over his tongue. "Just please do me a favor and don't ever piss her off, okay? I'd like to be up to my elbows in these things for a good long time."

"Yeeeeeeah." Shane sat up in his chair, kicking a glance in Jackson's direction that set off warning bells. "About that." He stopped long enough to let the seriousness of his look sink in before he said, "Bellamy and I are getting married."

Jackson froze, a gob of apricot filling stuck to the roof of his mouth. "You're what?" he said, trying unsuccessfully to swallow.

Shane pressed a smile between his lips so that only the edges snuck out, but it was enough. He looked happy as hell. "We're getting married. I asked her yesterday."

Shock rippled through Jackson with seismic force. "Wow. That's . . . wow. Congratulations." The words felt tight and wooden in his mouth, and he forced a smile onto his face. If any two people defied the odds, it was Bellamy and Shane.

So why did he feel like he'd just swallowed a time bomb?

"Thanks. I figured you might have mixed feelings about it, so I wanted you to hear it from me rather than Carly. I'm sure Bellamy's already told her."

Jackson's jaw clenched. "I don't have mixed feelings about it. I'm happy for you guys." Wonderful. Man, he sucked as a friend. "Really."

"That's not what I meant," Shane said, no trace of argument in his voice. "I just know that serious relationships are . . . an issue for you sometimes. That's all."

Jackson's shoulders roped over with invisible tension. "Just because it's not going to happen for me doesn't mean I can't be happy for you. I think Bellamy's great, man." He sat back against the hard wood of the kitchen chair, and although he'd meant every word with genuine sincerity, his appetite still disappeared like smoke in the wind.

"Carly's pretty great, too." Shane propped an elbow on the table, eyes flicking over Jackson's for only a second before he tore off a corner of pastry and popped it into his mouth.

"What's going on there is different." Hell if he felt like having this conversation, now or ever.

His buddy looked unconvinced. "You sure about that?"

The question rattled all the way down Jackson's spine, and he stiffened even further. "I'm not willing to find out, Shane." God *damn* it, he hated what his father had done and how it had fucked with him as a result. But what was in his blood couldn't be changed, and trying was pointless.

If he got any more serious about Carly, it would end up hurting them both.

"Look, I'm not trying to piss you off, Jax. All I'm saying is, you look happy with Carly, and she looks happy with you. Why not give it a chance? And don't give me this casual-dating bullshit. I've seen the way you look at her, dude. We both know you're beyond that." Shane crossed his wiry arms over the front of his T-shirt, his words brooking zero argument.

But Jackson wasn't caving, especially not now. "Look, Carly's not here for the long run, and despite what you think about how I look at her, I'm not interested in taking a walk down the aisle. Not with anyone, not ever. No offense," he added quickly, heading off the retort he sensed Shane brewing up. "I don't exactly have a great legacy in that department, you know? I'd just as soon not take the chance."

"Dylan's getting married, and he has the same father as you," Shane pointed out in a bold push, and something dark and ugly dislodged from the recesses of Jackson's brain.

"Dylan's too young to remember what happened that night, Shane. But I'm not." The dingy row house flashed in Jackson's memory, broken dishes on the kitchen tile, the bright red shock of blood being spit into the porcelain sink. "I remember what he did to her, and why he did it. I'll never be able to forget."

Jackson stiffened to the point of pain. He couldn't go there. He just *couldn't*.

"Okay." Shane's concession reverberated through the

quiet even though he'd offered it softly. "I'm sorry for bringing it up. I just thought . . ."

Jackson cut him off with a curt shake of his head. "I know, and it's cool. I really am happy for you and Bellamy. But what I've got has to be different. It *is* different," he affirmed, his eyes burning from fresh tension and lack of sleep.

"You're different. You're not your father." Shane's words sliced through him, separating muscle and bone, and Jackson's stark reply was no more than a gravelly whisper.

"It's not a risk I'm willing to take."

Carly tiptoed into Jackson's apartment, hooking the spare key he'd given her a few weeks ago dutifully on the nail by the kitchen phone. It was after midnight, but the response she'd gotten today from the resort's executive board coupled with Bellamy's engagement had made her persuade Gavin to crack open a couple bottles of champagne after closing. Two glasses of bubbly had been enough to send Carly's already great mood soaring over the edge into a full-fledged happiness that she hadn't felt since . . .

Well, ever, really.

A quick peek into Jackson's darkened bedroom told her he was out cold, and she squashed the tinge of disappointment swirling through her. He'd been working hours that resembled her own this week, which had clearly taken a lot out of him. Ah, well. They'd have a little time in the morning for her to fill him in, and certainly, her great mood would carry over into daylight hours. For now, she needed a shower anyhow. Going to bed smelling like garlic aioli wouldn't win her any points no matter how good her news was.

Carly cranked the shower to one step below scalding, shedding her grungy chef's whites to let the water unknot the muscles in her shoulders. Lord, that felt good, and her body quickly melted to match her mood, loose and mellow and delicious. A familiar green and white bottle caught her eye, making her grin. Jackson must've picked up her favorite shampoo on his one harried trip to the store this week.

She closed her eyes, getting lost in the smell of honeysuckle and silky bubbles as she scrubbed her hair twice for good measure. The water rolled down her back, chasing the bubbles down the drain and leaving its warmth like a signature on her skin, and she leaned into it with a sigh. After one last pass with her fingertips to ensure she was suds-free, Carly reluctantly turned from the water to slide the Ivory from the soap dish and nearly had a panic attack.

"Jesus, Mary and Joseph!" She balled her fists in an involuntary response while her heart tried its best to vault from her ribcage to the shower floor. Jackson's lazy smile registered about three seconds before she threw a punch, and he peered past the flimsy shower curtain he'd nudged aside to watch her bathe.

"No. Just me." He crossed his thick arms over his even thicker chest, leaning against the tile jamb as he continued to look at her, gaze unwavering.

"Very funny. You scared the hell out of me, you know."

"And you are very beautiful, you know."

Carly pulled back, realizing belatedly that she was very, very naked and that Jackson's smile was a lot more sensual than she'd first noticed. "I . . . um, I am?"

He nodded once, a firm tilt of his chin. "Stunning."

Her skin flushed, and even though Jackson had seen her without clothes plenty of times by now, she fought the urge to cover herself, to be less vulnerable. "How long have you been standing there?"

"A few minutes. Does it bother you?"

"No." The truth popped out of her, unbidden, despite the urge to be less exposed. "Although I'm not sure the drowned rat look really qualifies as beautiful," Carly added, twisting the wet tendrils of her hair together before letting them fall down her back. Heat flashed over Jackson's gaze, darkening his eyes to the color of new denim, and before she could register his movements, he was standing beside her under the spray.

"What are you doing? You're dressed," she said, half-laughing and half caught in shock. Water streamed down his chest, plastering his T-shirt and gym shorts to his body after about three seconds, but he didn't even blink as he lowered his mouth over her ear, sending hard ripples down the ladder of her spine.

"I'm showing you how beautiful you are. Since you're clearly unaware."

Carly's knees threatened to turn as liquid as the water rushing over them, and she pressed her palms against Jackson's chest. "Oh." Her answer quickly lost its reply status and became a moan as he edged the tip of his tongue down her neck in a delicate line, swirling over the spot where her shoulder met her body. "*Oh*. Maybe we should get out of the shower," she murmured, but he shook his head, freshly emerging stubble scratching against her wet skin.

"No." His eyes glittered, so hot with desire that Carly's argument trailed off before she could voice it again. "I want you here. Just like this. Right now!"

His mouth was on her like the sinuous blue flames dancing beneath the grates of her cooktop, delivering searing heat with every pass. Her nipples hardened to peaks, and the crush of her chest against his only served to increase her aching need. Jackson knotted his fingers through her hair, catching the wet curls and tugging to gain better access to her neck. She arched up, so eager to meet him that her want bordered the needful edge of despair until he buried his face in her neck, laying a path of greedy kisses toward her ear.

"God, I love it when you do that." Her sigh bubbled up from deep beneath her ribs.

Jackson slanted his mouth over hers, taking her lip from between her teeth with his own to coax her mouth open. "Say it again." He hovered over her, breath fanning out over her aching body, and Carly replied without hesitation.

"I love it when you do that."

With his mouth still on her like wildfire, Jackson palmed the back of her shoulders, scooping her body forward to capture her in a tight, unforgiving fit. "What about now?" He swung her back to the slick tile, propping his hands on either side of her ribcage before dipping his mouth to one breast.

Sparks shot through Carly's body, landing right between her legs with an aching, needful burn. "Yes."

But Jackson lifted his head, hovering over the pebbled tip of her nipple in an excruciating pause. Instinctively, Carly's hands laced around the sinewy muscles in his neck, and she arched up to close the space between them.

"I love it when you do that," she finished, the pads of her fingers tightening on his wet skin as he laved her breast with a hot, swirling stroke that nearly stole her knees. Oh, God, she wasn't going to last much longer like this.

As if he could read her mind, Jackson bent lower, kneeling in front of her while nudging her legs apart with the frame of his body and a very hungry, lust-blown smile.

"Anything else?" He feathered kisses low over her belly, making it impossible for Carly to form a coherent thought other than *yes*.

"Yes?" Jackson echoed, and she realized she must've uttered the word out loud. He trailed a callused finger along the crease where her leg joined together with her hip, drawing a keening moan from the depths of her chest.

"Please take me. *Please*."

For a heartbeat, their eyes connected, his honeyed lashes wet from the shower spray, blue stare so intense and piercing and full of deep want that tears heated the corners of her eyelids. Jackson looked up at her, all the way through her, and even though Carly felt lost on a sea of ripping emotions, she knew he was her anchor.

And then his mouth was on her, and she promptly forgot her name.

With his strong, steadying palms braced around her trembling hips, he pleasured her in perfect strokes, holding her fast as she writhed at his ministrations. When the delicious anticipation building at her core became a screaming demand, Carly didn't hold back, and Jackson didn't relent. Cupping her bottom to keep her close, he wrung every last gasp from her until she slid bonelessly into his waiting arms.

In her post-orgasmic haze, she vaguely registered Jackson lifting her up and tossing the shower curtain aside as if it were tissue paper. Fragments of motion made it past her senses, and the cool air met her wet skin to draw a surprised breath past her lips. But then they were in the sweet darkness of Jackson's bed, where she reached up to peel his soaked T-shirt from his body.

"I love the way you feel," she whispered, feeling a hot lick of satisfaction uncurl in her belly as Jackson flung the rest of his clothes from his damp skin.

"Carly." His voice prowled out of him, low and predatory, but she opened her knees in a wordless invitation.

"I love the way you look at me," she pressed, turning her back for a split second to take a condom out of the bedside table drawer. Her wet hair hung over one shoulder, and she peeked through the curtain of it to see Jackson's eyes trained on her every move. "Like that," she breathed, unable to keep the lust from her voice.

"*Carly.*" The inflection of her name was caught between a prayer and a warning, but she didn't heed either one. She scooted back to the edge of the bed, running her fingertips over his erection lightly enough that he hissed out a breath.

"And I love the way you say my name." Her touch grew stronger, more purposeful, as she caressed Jackson with sure, even strokes until he was fully sheathed and gasping for more. She edged forward, letting her knees list open, and with one swift, unrelenting push, he was inside of her.

"Oh, *God*." Carly arched her hips to match Jackson's thrusts, reveling in how good he felt over her, his chest on hers, their arms twined together as he made love to her in flawless rhythm. The now-familiar ache uncoiled, low in her belly, and her breath hitched into a moan as it spread out to slide over her sex in another gripping climax.

"I love you. I love you," Carly whispered, clutching Jackson's shoulders. He stiffened, canting his hips into hers with a deep shudder, gripping her hips with taut fingers. Lowering his mouth to hers, he stole a kiss from her so intense, it tumbled her already hazy thoughts, and she arced up until there was no space between their bodies at all.

Tears sprang into Carly's eyes and tracked down her cheeks, surprising her with their release. The connection she'd felt when Jackson had looked up at her in the shower was nothing compared to this, and it filled her right down to the smallest, darkest places.

It was only after he'd brushed his lips over the crown of her head and gotten up to turn off the still-running shower that Carly realized exactly what she'd said.

Chapter Twenty-Five

Luke Calloway pushed back from his contract-strewn desk, shaking his head at Jackson and grinning ear to ear.

"I've got to hand it to you, man. All the work you threw into getting us this bid is going to pay off in spades. You'll head up the job, of course, so it won't be small potatoes in the labor department. But this one's going to be the crown jewel of our year for PR. Nice job."

"Yeah. I'm glad the offer came through." He stared absently at the half-ream of paper, stamped with Pine Mountain Resort's official logo. The proposal, complete with expected timetables and detailed schematics from Brooks Farm, looked downright intimidating.

It paled in comparison to what churned through Jackson's brain as he stood in Luke's cramped office.

"Look, I know you're beat from that kitchen remodel, and I'm really grateful you're here on your Saturday morning. Why don't you take the weekend to catch up on sleep and gear up to start this on Monday? Touch base with Owen Brooks, get the schedule in place for excavation and planting, and go from there. I'll return the signed contract to the resort to make it official, and we'll be good to go." Luke shuffled the papers into a pile with a sharp *rap,* and it skittered across Jackson's nerves like sandpaper on silk.

"Sure thing, boss." He threw a smile on his stubbled face, praying it didn't look as forced as it felt. Luke, who acted like he'd just won the lottery, didn't seem to notice, giving Jackson the first tinge of relief he'd felt ever since Carly had breathed those three fateful words in his ear.

I love you.

The whisper echoed through his head as he crunched his way over the gravel drive to his truck, slumping against the driver's seat with a grunt. How the hell had he not seen this coming? With all the time they'd spent together, it should've been a no-brainer, for Chrissake, and yet Carly's declaration had blindsided him. Of course, it had scrambled everything inside of him on the way, tossing up feelings he'd lodged so deeply within himself, he'd sworn they'd never see the light of day.

Right now, they might as well be laundry on the line. Even worse, Carly had clearly wanted to talk about it when he returned to bed, but he'd gently cut her off, feigning exhaustion. The emotion in her eyes as she hesitated to lie down next to him nearly undid Jackson right there on the bed sheets, but he knew better than to go down that path. Besides, what could he possibly say?

I'd love you, too, only it would be hazardous to your health?

The way Carly had looked, so sweet and provocative and pure with her eyes closed against the spray of the shower, had stirred up a desire in him that blew past want in favor of forceful need. In that moment, he'd have done anything to have her—*anything*—and the icy fear of it, coupled with the certainty of her words as they'd made love so intensely he thought he'd never recover, told him everything he needed to know.

Leaving her was the only way to save them both.

* * *

"I am the biggest idiot on the face of the planet." Carly squeezed her eyes shut over her coffee cup, feeling the bite of the table on her elbows as she dropped her head into her hands.

"Sweetie, telling Jackson how you feel doesn't make you an idiot." Sloane tipped her dark head at Carly, the sympathy on her face plain. Carly pushed back in her chair, surveying La Dolce Vita's dining room. It was empty, save for the kitchen staff in the back and Gavin tallying receipts and checking inventory behind the bar, and Carly breathed a sigh of relief at the few hours of down time she had between the rush of lunch and dinner during Saturday service.

"Still. I can't go falling in . . ." Carly trailed off, lowering her voice to a whisper. "I can't go feeling like that about somebody. Look at what happened the last time I trusted a man."

But Sloane was ready with an eye-roll of epic proportions. "Come on. You're not seriously comparing Travis with Jackson, are you? It's apples and oranges, and the apples are rotten to the core."

"Well, the oranges could still break my heart, Sloane. And I don't think I could take it again." The admission made Carly want to bury herself deep in her kitchen indefinitely, and she crossed her arms over her chest to cover the heave of her sigh. She couldn't have kept her mouth shut, could she? Stupid great-sex endorphins!

But it wasn't her mouth, really, that she was worried about. It was the rest of her.

Namely the heart she'd just unwittingly put on the line.

"Carly." Sloane leaned in, pausing before her voice softened over her next words. "Have you stopped to think that maybe Jackson is your swan?"

Sloane's question felt like quicksand sifting through

Carly's lungs. She wasn't the type to blurt out *I love you*'s in the heat of the moment.

Yet that's exactly what she'd done.

"I don't know." Carly's voice trembled, and Sloane slid from her seat to put her arms around Carly in a tight hug. "Nothing ever felt like this with Travis, you know? Not even when I caught him redhanded and knew everything was over. I just . . . I . . ."

"It wouldn't be the worst thing in the world, *cucciola*." Sloane smoothed Carly's braid, and although she did her best to fight them, tears heated beneath her eyelids.

"It would be if he doesn't love me back," she whispered, the words sticking in her throat.

Sloane gave her a squeeze before pulling back to look at her reassuringly, and Carly was shocked to see her friend's eyes also rimmed with tears. "Oh, honey. After everything he did for you last week with your *mama?* Anybody with two eyes and half a brain can see he's nuts about you."

"Yeah, but just because he helped me out when I needed it doesn't mean he's my egret . . . swan . . . love-of-my-life-bird-man," Carly argued, wiping her face with the back of her hand.

Sloane snorted, surprisingly graceful. "At least you're getting the idea."

Carly blew out a shaky sigh. "Why can't this be easy, like following a recipe?"

"The good stuff is never easy. But if he's your swan, you'll figure it out."

Carly managed a soft chuckle, even though her heart wasn't all the way in it. "How'd you get so smart about all this love stuff, anyway?"

"I write fucking romance novels, sweetie. I'm making it up as I go."

The deep rumble of a throat being cleared startled the two women from their friendly embrace, and Carly looked up to see her restaurant manager shifting his weight uncomfortably in front of their table.

"Sorry to interrupt, chef. But there's a phone call from New York on line two." Gavin's eyes shifted to Sloane, lingering for a second before settling back on Carly, his seriousness never wavering.

"Oh, God. Is it my brother?" Carly jerked out of her chair, but Gavin stepped in with a quick shake of his head.

"No, no. The guy said he's calling from Gracie's? Said it's important that he speak with you, otherwise I'd have taken a message, since you're, ah . . . obviously in a personal meeting." He gestured awkwardly to Sloane, who fixed him with a lifted brow before turning to Carly.

"It's got to be Travis."

Carly's exhale sank like a soufflé coming from a lukewarm oven. "Probably."

Sloane set her mouth in a firm line, jamming her hands into her hips as she stood up. "Do you want me to take a message? You shouldn't have to deal with his shit right now. Plus, I'd love to have a little chat with him. After all, I'm the only person he hasn't tried to lure over to the dark side yet."

The fact that Travis had tried unsuccessfully to schmooze both her family and her sous chef in the last few weeks filtered back to Carly, but she shook her head. "Definitely not. The last thing I need right now is to stir up a hornet's nest with him."

Carly's skin prickled with dread as she tried to think. Having to deal with Travis right now would put her over the freaking edge, and considering she had a packed dinner service that would start in a mere two hours, she just couldn't handle it. "Gavin, can you tell him I'm not available, please? He's just going to have to wait until I can deal with him."

Gavin nodded, one slight dip of his sculpted chin, hesitating for just a fraction before returning to the bar.

"I hate that you have to go through this," Sloane murmured, her ice blue eyes resting on Carly's dark counterparts.

"Me, too. Right now, I don't feel like I'll ever be free of Travis." God, look at all the trouble she'd gotten herself into, following her heart like an idiot. She'd do well to remember it.

Unless, of course, it was too late for that.

Dinner service was on the downswing before Carly actually got a chance to breathe, which was fine by her. The controlled chaos of her tightly-run kitchen, complete with multi-lingual curse words slung back and forth between chefs, had forced her brain to function at a fundamental level. The steady rhythm of action smoothed the rough edges of her nerves so she could actually think. Not that she was any closer to answering the million-dollar question rattling through her brain.

Had she told Jackson she loved him in the heat of the moment, or had she truly meant it?

"Hey, chef Carly. Can I get a tiramisu on the fly? The guy at table sixteen just decided he wants dessert after all." The server asking the question gave her a sheepish look, but Carly was grateful to have one more task to keep her hands busier than her heart.

"Sure thing, Kelly."

They were slowing down for the night, and rather than holler out the order, Carly flipped a dessert plate from the cold stack and propped open the dessert fridge with her hip. She plated a healthy wedge of the dessert over strategically placed swirls of chocolate sauce. Carefully dunking a whisk in a chilled bowl of crème fraîche, Carly absently whipped it into soft, feathery peaks. The dollop she placed over the fine smattering of espresso powder curved up and over, reminding her of the graceful bend of a swan's neck.

A swan's neck . . . a swan . . .

The plate dipped in her hand, a bolt of shock arrowing through Carly with startling clarity as the tiramisu landed on the floor with a soft *plop*.

Jackson was her swan. And even if it meant putting her heart on the line, she had to get over her past in order to trust what they had and believe he'd love her back.

Carly plated a new wedge of tiramisu and quickly cleaned up her mess, heading back to the pass with a surge of settling calm. The idea of risking everything for love—again—should be scary, she knew, and yet the fear and unease Carly felt whenever she thought of how Travis had betrayed her was utterly absent in the face of how Jackson made her feel.

She loved him. Was *in* love with him. And she trusted him to guard her heart.

"I need a ribeye special medium rare and a swordfish braciole. We're moving, people. I want these folks in the dining room fed and happy and telling their friends about it, let's go!" Carly reclaimed the pass with a grin, snapping up a plate of shrimp scampi and inhaling the pungent, delectable combination of butter and garlic.

Adrian lifted a wry brow, but a return grin tickled the edges of his lips. "You're awfully happy over there." He passed her another plate of scampi, which she garnished and sent out alongside a plate of chicken marsala.

"We're nearly done for the night, and the food looks perfect. What's not to be happy about?"

Adrian chuckled, calling out in a booming voice, "Yo, Sunshine! Where's that peasant soup headed for table twenty-three? Chef Carly set the bar at *perfect*, so I suggest you get it up to the pass that way." Although he sent the holler over his shoulder to Bellamy's station, Adrian leveled a knowing hazel stare at Carly, as palpable as if he'd reached out to touch her.

"You've been pretty quiet tonight, until now. Any particular reason for your change of heart?" His hands were a flurry of motion as he situated a perfectly trimmed ribeye on the grill in front of him, ducking down to the lowboy for the ingredients for the sautéed balsamic mushrooms that went with it. Despite his movements and unerring focus on what he was doing, Carly wasn't fooled for a second about where his attention really lay.

"I had a lot on my mind, that's all. But I'm straight now. Or at least, I will be." Carly paused as Bellamy hustled two bowls of satiny golden-orange soup, brimming with just the right amount of summer vegetables, to the pass.

"Two bowls of peasant soup, up." Both smelled seasoned to perfection, and after a quick dip with a tasting spoon confirmed it, Carly shot Adrian a smile.

"Can't find anything wrong with this one," she said, nodding in Bellamy's direction. The double doors leading to the dining room *thunked* with purpose as a server whisked the soup away, leaving Gavin room to slip into the front of the kitchen.

"Someone would like to speak to you in the dining room, Chef. I told him you may not be available since we still have guests, but he said he'd wait as long as necessary."

Carly's heart pinballed inside her ribcage. "Did he give you his name?"

Gavin shook his head. "I asked, but all he said was he's a personal acquaintance. I can tell him you're occupied, if you like."

Her thoughts whipped to the way Jackson had come to see her on the sly all those weeks ago, to tell her the truth about that night in his mother's garden.

Maybe it was her turn for a little truth-telling now. She steeled herself with a deep breath. He wouldn't let her down. She'd given him a chance when he came to her with his feelings, and he'd do the same for her. Carly felt sure of it.

"Adrian, take the pass. Bellamy, tonight's your lucky night. You've earned that grill, for a few minutes, anyway." Carly watched with satisfaction as Bellamy's green eyes went as round as Napa Valley grapes on the vine. In sharp contrast, Adrian's gaze narrowed to I-don't-think-so slits.

"Something about this feels off, *gnocchella*." The gravel in Adrian's voice made his disdain clear, but Carly wiped her hands on her apron, undeterred.

"It's fine, Ade. Jackson and I have something to work out, but I mean it. It'll be fine." She squeezed his wrist, but couldn't be sure if it was for his reassurance or her own.

"If you're not back in five, I'm coming out there." Adrian snatched a ticket from the queue and barked an order at the line.

"In five, you'll be plating the last few dishes of the night. I won't be long," Carly promised over her shoulder, nudging her way past the double doors with one hip.

The dining room seated only a smattering of people, and as Carly's eyes adjusted to the ambient light from the copper sconces and overhead fixtures, she scanned the room for Jackson's familiar features. Coming up empty, she caught Gavin as he returned from checking in with the hostess.

"You said someone wanted to see me?"

He gestured toward the fireplace by the far wall. "Table sixteen. Do you want me to come get you after a minute or two?"

Carly swallowed. Sixteen was a two-top, tucked away in a cozy alcove toward the front of the house. No wonder she hadn't been able to see Jackson at first glance. "No, no. That won't be necessary. Thanks, Gavin."

Carly set her shoulders and made her way through La Dolce Vita's dining room. The idea of speaking her mind in this case was nerve-wracking to the tenth power, but even though she'd thought she had a gelato's chance in hell of ever falling in love again, Carly knew without a doubt how she felt about Jackson. And he deserved to hear it, not in the throes of passion, but out loud. For real.

Okay. Now or never. Carly worked up the words, putting them on the tip of her tongue and knowing they were right.

Only what came out of her mouth as she rounded the edge of the alcove was nothing more than a shocked gasp, erasing all the words from her head save three.

Oh, my God.

"Hello, Carly. It's been a long time."

After the ninth time his eyes glazed over, Jackson pitched his pencil onto the small desk in his apartment in disgust and gave up. So much for keeping occupied with work. Hell, his brain was in cahoots with the rest of him, and all of it was stuck on the sultry, brown-eyed beauty who had taken up residence in his every thought.

Christ. He had to end it before his organs declared mutiny. Or worse, before he decided not to end it at all.

"Fuck." He pinched the bridge of his nose hard enough to make his eyes water. Maybe it didn't have to shake out like this. Maybe Shane was right, and he could make a go of it with Carly.

Maybe he could love her without hurting her.

His mother, in a blue and white nightgown, her eye swollen shut . . . sweeping up pieces of broken dishes . . .

"It's okay, baby. Your daddy just loves me a little too much, that's all. But don't you worry about that now . . ."

"No."

Jackson stood, his chest tight with finality. He couldn't risk loving anybody too much. No matter how badly the alternative was going to hurt.

He grabbed his keys from the hook by the phone and was gone.

Chapter Twenty-Six

It took a good five or six blinks for Carly's brain to get on board the reality train, and even then, she felt like she'd been slapped with some kind of really odd practical joke.

"I know you're finishing up a dinner service, but I was hoping you could spare me a few minutes of your time." Richard Buchanan, the man who had unceremoniously fired her from Gracie's eight months ago, gestured to the seat across from him with a well-manicured hand and a self-deprecating smile.

Shock flooded through Carly on tiny electric currents, until finally, she forced her mouth to function.

"What are you doing here?" She clamped down on her lip, heat streaking to her cheeks. Functionality had very little to do with tact, it seemed, and it wasn't really Richard's fault Travis had been such a snake.

Wait a second . . .

Understanding dawned, hot and quick, and Carly took a step back in surprise. "Did Travis send you to try and get me to come back to New York to do the show?" Of all the underhanded, lowlife things to do, this one had to be the worst! The white noise of anger rushed in Carly's ears, and she vaguely felt the sting of her fingernails against her palms as she balled her fingers into fists.

"What?" His graying brow clouded in confusion. "No, I came on my own. And I'm sure my being here is independent of Travis's wishes." Richard's lip curled into a faint sneer as he uttered Travis's name, and he motioned again toward the empty chair across from him. "Please, Chef."

Whether it was curiosity or just plain gob smacked autopilot that guided her legs to the chair, Carly couldn't be sure. She tossed a quick glance over the dining room, but the crowd had thinned to the point that she knew Adrian would be fine without her.

"I've got five minutes," she lied, sitting stiffly on the edge of her seat.

"That's one of the things I always liked about you. Straight to the point." Richard's smile hinted that the words were a compliment rather than the sideways insult Travis always managed to lob her way when saying the same thing.

Carly laced her fingers together and propped them on the table, trying mightily to hide her confusion. "Something tells me you didn't come all the way from New York to check out the menu, and I do have a kitchen to break down for the night." Her words held no bite, but stood firm regardless. He *had* fired her, after all. "So how can I help you, Richard?"

"I'll get right to it. I'm not above admitting I've made a mistake, which is exactly what I did eight months ago when I let you go." His patrician features hardened into steely lines. "I want you back at Gracie's, Carly. And I'll do whatever I have to in order to make that happen."

A high-pitched chirrup escaped from Carly's lips without her permission. "Are you nuts? I'm not working with Travis again." She heard her tone only after her words were out, but she'd left decorum in the dust the minute her butt had hit the chair, anyway.

Richard's smile returned, and he fastened Carly with a

knowing look. "We no longer require Mr. Masters's services at Gracie's. I'm in the market for an executive chef. *One* executive chef. Specifically, you."

Ice water seemed to have replaced every ounce of Carly's blood, and it pumped through her veins with dizzying speed. "I'm sorry, I don't understand. Did you . . . are you saying you fired him?"

"That's exactly what I'm saying."

"Oh." Considering the circumstances, the single syllable was all Carly could force from her lips. Richard took her near-silence as a sign to start talking, and he didn't waste any time plunging into the hard sell.

"Look, Carly, after you left, it became clear who the talent was. And more to the point, who it wasn't. Between his lackluster skills and his poor kitchen management, Travis has done a number on Gracie's, and I've been running damage control for months. Business is tanking, the bad reviews are piling up, and I need a change. I need you."

"When did you fire him?" she breathed, finally starting to gather her wits. Richard was offering her a chance to go back to New York. To redeem herself.

To go home.

Richard measured her with a careful glance. "Officially? About six hours ago. But the writing's been on the wall for a few weeks now. Look, Carly, I'm well aware that the circumstances of your departure were . . . abrupt. I'm willing to make up for that."

Carly kicked up an involuntary brow. "I'm listening."

The hard sell turned into solid oak. "You'd have carte blanche over the staff. I understand Adrian is still with you here." It came out sounding like a question, even though she was sure he knew the answer already, and Carly nodded once in reply. "Well. We'd be happy to welcome him back at Gracie's, should you choose to continue as a team."

She pressed a humorless smile between her lips. Richard

was no dummy. He knew that keeping her sous chef would be Carly's number-one priority. "What about the restaurant manager?" Now this part ought to be interesting.

Richard paused, no doubt remembering his daughter's penchant for his recently fired executive chef. "Alexa has been heading up the management team at another of my restaurants for about a month now. I'm sure you'd replace her wisely."

Carly's mind flashed, tumbling with so many thoughts she couldn't keep them in line. The offer had just gone from good to great, and her chance at redemption was within reach. She could go back to the city she loved, reclaim a kitchen she'd damn well earned, and be close to her *mama* and brothers to boot.

It was almost too much to process.

Sensing her momentary hesitation, Richard jumped right back in. "All recipes you bring to the menu would be yours. If you ever left Gracie's." He stopped to clear his throat delicately before continuing. "You'd be free to take them with you and we'd remove them from our menu. Also, all final decisions affecting the back of the house, from whom we hire as dishwashers to how many pounds of Roma tomatoes we need in a given week, would be up to you. Just say the word, and you'll have what you want. *Whatever* you want."

"Whatever I want?" she echoed in disbelief. "How about salary?"

Richard smiled, this time a colder gesture that didn't reach his eyes. "While I like to think your previous salary was competitive, I understand you'd be taking on extra responsibilities as the only executive chef."

Not really, Carly thought. She'd pulled both her own weight and Travis's while they were there.

"I'd be prepared to match what you're making here at La Dolce Vita, plus 10 percent, as well as cut you in on a percentage of Gracie's profits."

All the wind left Carly's lungs on a hard gasp. "You're serious." The salary alone was one thing. A cut of the profits . . . for someone with less than ten years' experience, it bordered on legendary.

"Deadly," Richard agreed. "Look, I realize I've tossed this at you, and that you need time to think about it. I'll be at the resort for the rest of the weekend. Call my cell and we'll talk more tomorrow." He slid a crisp, white business card across the table. "Just know that while I wouldn't make this kind of offer to just anybody, it's only on the table for a short time. I need you in there, Carly. The sooner, the better. You do understand what I'm saying, don't you?"

Something loosened in Carly's chest, moving up to her throat and finally, *finally* pushing intelligent words to her lips.

"Absolutely, Richard. You've made things crystal clear."

It was only after Carly had sent out the last ticket of the service and made sure her line chefs were dutifully breaking down their stations that her conversation with Richard had really sunk in. Not wanting to risk being overheard by anyone on the restaurant staff and knowing they'd all be more than busy inside, Carly caught Adrian by the sleeve.

"I need a word with you. Privately." She jerked her head to the single door leading to the loading dock through the back of the kitchen, heading toward it without waiting for a reply.

Adrian followed, his words becoming gruff as he followed her to the dark quiet of the loading dock. "Did Boy Wonder say something to piss you off? I swear to God, if he hurt you, I'm going to—"

Realization seeped into Carly's brain in a slow leak, and she shivered against the night chill. "What? Oh, no. No, this doesn't have anything to do with Jackson." Her words prickled with the intensity of a lie, but she shook them off. One thing at a time. "Richard Buchanan came to see me."

"From Gracie's?" Adrian's eyes flashed round with shock in the moonlight filtering down from the canopy of inky clouds overhead. A thick breeze rustled the leaves in the nearby grove of trees framing the parking lot around the corner, sounding like soft footfalls, and Carly hugged herself to ward off the streak of cold it sent through her.

"Yeah." On a deep breath, she told the story from start to finish, ending with Richard's entreaty to call him tomorrow with her decision.

"Holy *shit*, Carly! This is everything you wanted," Adrian breathed, seeming stuck between excitement and disbelief. "No wonder Travis has been so desperate to get you to do the show."

The words hit Carly low in the gut, like a delayed reaction. *Of course*. Travis had to have known his career was in the balance. The favorable PR that would've come with another season of a popular show like *Couples in the Kitchen* would've been his best shot at keeping his name afloat in the job market. Without it, he'd be screwed.

Oh, the irony.

"I can't believe I didn't see it before." Feeling duped where Travis was concerned was really starting to get on her nerves, and she exhaled a hot breath into the cool night.

"You had no way of knowing Gracie's was going downhill. Occupational hazard of being out here in the middle of nowhere. In order to keep your name out of the loop, sometimes you gotta be . . . well, out of the loop yourself, you know?" Adrian's words held no trace of disdain, yet they yanked at Carly's pride. "But that's a thing of the past, baby! When does Richard want us to start?"

Carly felt a twist deep in her chest. "As soon as possible. Travis is already officially gone."

Adrian nodded, his brow folded in thought. "I could stay

here until they find a temporary replacement for you. Plus, you've got a couple of chefs here who could definitely move up the line, so your backup staff is solid. It might be a rocky transition to another head chef, but they always are. This place will manage."

Carly dropped her chin in an absent nod, the twang between her ribs morphing into a painful ache. She eyed the wide, bricked entrance to the loading dock, and the sight of the grassy lot beyond it jerked her head in realization.

"The garden," she breathed. "Someone else would have to lead the garden project." The words tasted stale and acidic, like month-old lemons, in her mouth.

Adrian cocked his head, platinum hair gleaming in a shaft of moonlight. "Just because the resort approved the project doesn't mean you have to head it up. If they want to move forward, they can do it without you. Unless you don't want them to," he finished slowly, pinning her with a knowing stare.

"What's that supposed to mean?" Great. Just what she needed. A good shot of defensiveness as a chaser to all the unease bubbling within her. Still, she'd opened her mouth, and it was too late not to follow through. "I wouldn't have busted my ass on that proposal if I didn't think it was a great project. Regardless of who heads it up."

Understanding trickled over Adrian's features in a hard splash. "You don't want to leave, do you?"

"Of course I want to leave," she snapped, even though it was childish as hell. Damn it, she just needed to think. "Look, I'm sorry. I'm just . . . I'm still trying to process it all, okay? Richard's offer is a meal ticket and a half, but that doesn't mean I can just leave things undone here."

Boy, was *that* the understatement of the year. Carly stuffed down the dread forcing its way upward in her chest. "Can you give me a little time to figure out how to do this? Please?"

Adrian regarded her with a critical stare, one that seemed to read the roiling emotions practically oozing from her pores. Damn it, why couldn't she get it together? This was the opportunity of a lifetime, one she'd have begged for less than two months ago.

And yet, when she'd been sitting there, in front of Richard Buchanan, she couldn't make her mouth form the words *yes, I'd love to take the job* if you paid her cold, hard cash. Which Richard was willing to do, and then some.

Carly had to say yes. She'd be crazy—no, check that—she'd be 100 percent, bat-shit *certifiable* not to take this job.

So why did she feel like she wanted to throw up?

Finally, Adrian spoke. "Breakfast tomorrow. Seven o'clock, my place. I'll cook, you'll talk. Now get out of here, would you? You've had a helluva night." He jerked his scruffy chin toward the parking lot, partially hidden by the brick wall and night shadows.

"You sure you've got breakdown covered?" Even now, exhausted and reeling, Carly was tempted to retreat to the comfort of the place she'd created.

"Go, *gnocchella*. I love you, but I'm not asking. You feel me?"

Carly dug into her back pocket for her keys. The stuff in her bag would have to wait in her locker until morning. If she went back to get it, she'd never leave to clear her head. "Okay, you win. I'll see you for breakfast. We'll talk."

She waited until Adrian had disappeared into the rectangle of light leading to the momentarily exposed kitchen before releasing the shaky breath she'd been holding. Carly knew she had to really think, to sort through the details and figure out what to do next, but she didn't want to do any of that.

She wanted to curl up with Jackson, just like she had at

her mother's house, and let the rest of the world fall away while he comforted her.

"Oh, God," she whispered, eyes filling with tears.

And as she stood there, alone in the dark with the best career opportunity she'd ever have laid out in front of her like an exotic banquet, Carly knew she wasn't going to take it.

Jackson stood in the parking lot at La Dolce Vita, trying to meter the frenzied rhythm of his breath. He'd come here knowing it was late enough that Carly would be breaking down the kitchen with the rest of her crew. Then she'd saunter out to the parking lot, bag slung over one shoulder, rumpled chef's whites and tired smile showing all the signs of a typical double shift. He knew he needed to leave her now, tonight, before this got any better. Worse. Whatever.

He'd been walking through the parking lot, hands jammed in the pockets of his hooded sweatshirt, when he'd heard a hushed, yet perfectly distinct voice forming his name on the breeze.

"No, this doesn't have anything to do with Jackson . . ."

Instinctively, Jackson jerked toward the sound of Carly's voice, even though he was clearly eavesdropping on a private conversation. Something about her tone, so caught up in a mix of emotions he couldn't quite place, kept him from doing anything other than listening. The sound of Adrian's gravelly voice met Carly's on the breeze, and as the conversation between them had unfolded, Jackson had had to fight off both being sick and wanting to punch a hole through the bricks to his right.

"Of course I want to leave!" Carly's words, spoken so matter-of-factly, speared through every vulnerable feeling he had for her, fraying those emotions even further. Jackson heard fragments of the rest, Carly saying she needed to think, Adrian sending her home, but all Jackson could feel was the ragged hole in the center of his chest. He'd come to let her go, to keep her safe from getting too close, but he'd never once thought she'd beat him to the punch.

Better for her to do the hitting, he thought now. Numbness spread through him like frostbite, painfully cold for just a flash before leaving a tingling sensation that barely hinted there had once been feeling. Crickets hummed their nighttime symphony, and somewhere in the distance a car engine started.

But Jackson simply felt nothing.

Chapter Twenty-Seven

Jackson forced his feet around the corner of the brick wall sheltering the loading dock from the rest of the parking lot, and Carly whipped toward the sound of his footsteps.

"Who's there?" She stood, silhouetted by the moonlight and her moxie, a few steps from the restaurant's back door. His lips wanted to curl into a smile at her feistiness, but the grim foreboding coursing through the rest of him kept them weighted down.

"It's me, Carly." Jackson approached her carefully, and she wrapped her arms around herself with a shiver as she exhaled over a soft laugh.

"You scared me! What're you doing out here in the parking lot?" She paused, shaking her head. "You know what, it doesn't matter. I'm really glad to see you."

He got close enough to catch her grimace as she shivered again, and he moved to guard her from the chill in the air so automatically that he was halfway out of his sweatshirt before it even registered.

"Here. You're freezing." Rather than wrap his hoodie around her petite frame, though, he simply held it out at arm's length. If he got too close to her, letting go would be that much harder, and he didn't have the luxury of not letting go.

"Mmm, thanks." Carly slipped into the sweatshirt, which looked more like a blanket around her slim shoulders. She lifted her fleece-draped arms to pull him in, getting close enough to touch before Jackson stopped her cold.

"I heard what you said to Adrian."

She jammed to a halt against his chest, her arms an incomplete circle around his body. "You . . . you heard everything?"

Jackson inhaled, letting the cold night air seep through his lungs. "I guess congratulations are in order. You must be excited to be going back home."

Carly stepped back. "I, um. I think we need to talk."

Gossamer-thin possibility tickled at Jackson beneath the numbness, capturing his attention and mesmerizing him for a split second before he snuffed it out. Fate had given Carly the chance to leave Pine Mountain, to go back to the familiarity and comfort of her family and her blooming career, and she'd taken it just as she'd said she would.

It was the perfect out. All he needed to do was hammer it into place and send her on her way.

Jackson forced himself to shrug. "There isn't really anything to say, is there? You've never made any bones about the fact that you weren't here for the long haul. I never thought you'd stay."

"You didn't," she replied, her raspy voice shaking across the space growing between them. "But I thought . . . I mean, last night, I said—"

He cut her off swiftly, before she could repeat the words out loud. "It's fine. It was a heat of the moment thing, just like our relationship. I know you didn't mean it."

Carly's lips parted on a tiny gasp, and she flinched as if he'd struck her. "Oh," she choked out, and everything inside of him howled that he should take it back. But then he saw the faded flicker of memory from twenty years ago, the angry splash of blood, the hastily packed suitcases, and his resolve became cement, thick and unyielding. Better he hurt her now by letting her leave than the alternative.

He couldn't hurt her the other way.

"Really, Carly. Feel free to go with a clear conscience. The resort will find someone to replace you." Jackson paused, his next words swirling burnt and bitter in his mouth. "Plus, you never belonged here anyway."

A spark of anger flared over her wet eyes, making them glitter. "I never belonged here, or I never belonged with you?"

"Both. What was going on between us wouldn't have worked out in the end. Now you can go home and start fresh, just like you wanted."

Carly stiffened, her demeanor shifting as she hardened her answer. "If that's what you think, then you don't know shit about what I want, Jackson Carter."

Their eyes clashed, hers flashing an equal mixture of sadness and anger, and Jackson knew she was telling him she wanted to stay, to be with him. That she meant what she'd said last night.

That she loved him.

If he didn't walk away from her, *right now*, he wasn't going to. They stood, unmoving, in the open mouth of the loading dock, caught up together by one last strand of possibility.

Feed her.

His lips parted, but the only thing he could hear was the twenty-year old sound of fists on flesh, and it knocked him back to reality.

No. *No.*

Jackson turned his back on her and walked away.

* * *

Every one of Carly's survival instincts shrieked before yanking her in opposite directions, and she watched Jackson's broad shoulders slump in retreat for only a fraction of a second before her feet kicked into gear.

"Jackson, wait."

He didn't even break stride, which both pissed her off and terrified her. Consumed by sparks of emotion moving too fast to identify, Carly stumbled toward him, awkwardly jerking her arms out of his too-big hoodie as she moved.

"Wait! Take your sweatshirt." It was utterly lame, but it spilled from her lips nonetheless, and she gained on him from behind as his gait finally broke.

"Keep it." His voiced strained on the terse reply, but he didn't turn around. The heavy rush of his boots echoed over the inky pavement, and in that white-hot instant, Carly's anger pulsed through her like a living thing. She rushed forward, slipping behind him with speed that would've impressed her if she'd been conscious of it.

"Damn it, Jackson! *Wait.*"

Suddenly, everything shifted to slow-motion, and Carly lunged forward to grab Jackson's arm at the exact instant he reared back to answer her. She felt the force of his body as he jerked around, emotion roiling from him in waves. Her cheekbone, right where it sloped into the bridge of her nose, absorbed the sharp crack of his elbow as it made the sickening connection with her face, whirling her all the way around. For one breathless second, she felt nothing save the loss of balance, and tried to right herself on her feet although the accidental blow had turned her nearly 180 degrees.

Then the pain slammed into her like a wrecking ball, and she couldn't do anything except crumple to the ground, the back of her head hitting the pavement with a hard *whump*.

"Oh, Jesus. Carly, I didn't see you. I didn't know you were

there." There was a shuffle of movement—feet, maybe?—and Carly tried to open her eyes to gain her bearings.

But they were already open, and the only thing she could see was a handful of white spots she was pretty sure didn't exist. She blinked, and the pain splintered into a thousand pinpricks dipped in acid.

"It's fine. I'm . . ." She trailed off, overcome by dizziness. Something hot and wet dripped over her fingers, which she'd splayed over her face by sheer instinct, and she channeled all her energy into trying to focus through the pain.

Oh, hell. Was that her nose bleeding like that?

"You're bleeding. Oh, God, you're really *bleeding*." Jackson's hollow words reverberated through her, and she tried unsuccessfully to train her vision on him. He halted into silence at the sound of the back door squeaking open, and Carly heard rather than saw how he jackknifed to his feet to run toward the sound, calling for help.

A wave of nausea surprised its way over her, pulling at the tight cords of her throat in its demand to be known. The spots multiplied and swam like frenzied fireflies, darting around her line of sight in chaotic circles and making coherent thought impossible.

Why couldn't she think?

Snippets of sound, erratic and thoroughly angry, threaded past her, but she couldn't make them out. Someone touched her face, and even though the motions were gentle, it magnified the pain in the back of her skull, and she batted at the sensation with heavy, clumsy hands. She struggled to sit up, to tell Jackson she'd be fine eventually, if she could just get that annoying buzzing noise to shut the hell up.

Maybe if she just lay down for a second it would get better, and she'd be able to catch her breath. Yeah, that would be good, Carly thought, allowing her chin to list heavily into her chest.

But then there were more hands, so many that she couldn't keep them off of her. A pair of thick, well-muscled arms pulled her close, and she gave in to the weightless sensation of being carried home.

As soon as Jackson saw Adrian's hulking form cut through the light cast from the open door, he knew he'd at least get a fraction of the hell on earth he deserved.

"What the hell is going on out there?" Adrian jumped from the edge of the loading dock to the pavement below. Jackson bent over Carly, his gut instinct telling him to take care of her, but then reality stabbed at him with unforgiving clarity.

He had no business touching her. The best way to protect her was to get far, far away.

"You need to call 911. Right now, Adrian! Do it." Jackson felt the high-pitched screech of panic sink its claws into him and manhandle him like a ragdoll, and he took a step back just as Adrian bolted forward.

What had he fucking *done*?

"Bellamy! Call 911!" Adrian yelled, even though Bellamy was right behind him in the doorframe leading back to the building. She disappeared, nothing more than a blur of blonde curls and shock, leaving Adrian to zero in on Carly with laser-like accuracy.

"Mary, Mother of God. Carly, let me see." The burly sous chef paled, his expression twisted in pain as he cradled Carly's head between his palms. Jackson's gut roared at him to shove Adrian aside so he could fix what he'd done, but the fear spiraling through him locked him into place a few steps away.

Carly wouldn't be safe with his hands on her. His instincts could go to hell.

Adrian knelt beside Carly, eyes wild but missing nothing.

"Okay, I know it hurts, but I need to stabilize your neck. Just sit tight."

He moved carefully, easing Carly to a prone position on the pavement, but all Jackson could see was the bright shock of blood blooming over her chef's jacket.

He'd become the one person on the planet he hated more than anyone else. Done the one thing he swore he'd avoid at all costs.

Oh, God, there was so much blood.

"Start talking, Wonder Bread. Now," Adrian growled through his teeth. "What the hell happened?"

"It was an accident. She was behind me, and I didn't see her, but . . ."

Adrian's head snapped up. "*You* did this?"

Every cell in Jackson's body sank with recognition. He deserved whatever Adrian was going to unleash on him, because he'd spun around with all his might, intending to hurt Carly anyway. Not physically, of course, but his words would've sliced through her all the same.

And he deserved to suffer for it.

"Bellamy! Get out here!" Adrian's bellow rent the night air with its intention, yet he narrowed his eyes on Jackson all the same. "I am going to dismember you right here on the fucking pavement, and I'm going to smile while I'm doing it."

Jackson didn't flinch. "I know."

Pounding footsteps sounded from the direction of the loading dock. Bellamy skittered to a stop in front of Adrian, who was still kneeling on the ground with Carly's head in his hands, stilling her in spite of her feeble attempts to get up.

"The ambulance will be here any minute. Oh, God," Bellamy murmured, eyes shining with fear. She whipped a towel from her apron, dropping to her knees to staunch the blood coming from Carly's nose, and Carly gave a keening cry of pain in reply. "What happened?"

His mother, standing in the doorframe in her nightgown, telling his father in her soft, yet deadly serious voice . . . "It's me you want. Leave him be." His father's eyes, flinty and mean, narrowing on her, moving to give her what she'd asked for.

"I do want you, Catherine. I love you so much, you ain't ever gonna forget it. You're mine, you hear me? Mine."

He kissed her then, slow at first, but then his father pushed her from the doorframe and slammed the door hard enough to rattle the walls. But Jackson still heard the sickening sound of fists on soft flesh, saw the blood in the sink . . . the blood . . . the blood . . .

Jackson felt Adrian's fury connect with his jawbone just as the ambulance rounded the corner of the west gate parking lot, red and white lights illuminating the scene in eerie, shimmering waves.

Or maybe that was Adrian's right hook, because holy *shit* had that hurt. Jackson hunched over, palms braced on his thighs, and a metallic tang filled his mouth like old pennies, forcing him to spit. The memory of his mother, smoothing his hair as she tucked him into the backseat of the station wagon in the dead of night filled his head, making him dizzy.

He had to get out of here.

"Get up. *Get. Up*," Adrian hissed, closing in, but before Jackson could move, Bellamy distracted them both.

"Stop it! Adrian, stop!" She looked torn between not wanting to leave Carly and trying to intervene. Two paramedics spilled from the ambulance, their purposeful strides seeming to garner Adrian's attention.

Until he reared back and caught Jackson in the ribs with another blow, and Jackson lost every ounce of breath in his lungs.

"Jesus Christ! Evan, we got a brawl here!" The female paramedic whipped past Jackson so fast that all he could see was a streak of flaming red hair before she'd inserted herself between him and Adrian with all the defiance of a thoroughly pissed off watchdog. The other paramedic already knelt by Carly, assessing her while keeping one eye on the redhead, who Jackson belatedly recognized as Teagan O'Malley.

"You good, T? I got a facial trauma here, possible concussion," the male paramedic reported in clipped, precise snatches.

"Conscious?" Teagan's eyes never left Adrian, who had stood down since delivering the body shot although he looked strung tight enough to explode.

"Looks like barely." Evan rattled off a bunch of numbers and medical terms like a rapid-fire machine gun, the last of which made Jackson clutch in silent panic.

"I need that c-spine and backboard. We need to get to Riverside, stat."

Teagan narrowed her scissor-sharp stare on Adrian. "You boys going to behave, or do I need to call my buddies at the police department?"

Adrian froze, answering her with a silent nod, although his expression suggested he wasn't done with Jackson by a longshot. Jackson straightened, still coughing, and wiped a smear of blood from his mouth with the back of an unused fist.

Teagan sprang into action, shooting a wary glance at Adrian as she turned toward Jackson. "Do yourself a favor and don't *move* from that spot, slugger."

Her hands fell swiftly over Jackson in assessment, but he resisted. "Stop. Go help her, *please*." The words escaped on a gasp, and Teagan looked ready to balk until her partner called out for assistance, clearly illustrating that Carly's injuries were more dire than Jackson's.

"Dammit. Stay away from each other, but don't go far,

I'm not done with you, Jackson. You need to get checked out," she said, running toward the ambulance.

Jackson forced himself to look at Carly, so small and fragile on the ground, as the male paramedic rolled her gently into his arms to put her on the backboard. Adrian sent Jackson a look like a death sentence, even though he didn't move.

"I'm coming back for you," he promised, and Jackson nodded in resignation.

"Take care of her first," he said, and then he disappeared into the dark cover of night.

Chapter Twenty-Eight

Carly stirred, feeling as if she'd slowly risen from the bottom of a sleepy lake.

With her head on fire.

"Jackson," she mumbled, groggy and thick. She reached a hand out, fumbling, until the fragments of the past few hours knitted together in her memory, flying at her with all the subtlety of a sledgehammer.

Jackson was gone. She'd trusted him with her heart, and he'd left before she could get a word in edgewise.

"Hey, shhh. Don't worry, *gnocchella*. Everything's fine. Get some rest, okay?"

For as long as Carly had known Adrian, she'd never seen him look so scared or so small. She blinked, even though it felt like a tactical assault on her sinuses, and focused on the spot where he sat next to her bed.

"Ugh." Her tongue was thick as paste, and she shifted against the doughy mattress even though it rattled her head enough to make her nauseous. She skimmed a hand over the faded cotton of her hospital gown, frowning at the IV poking out from a swath of surgical tape. "Did I sleep?"

"A little bit, yeah." A muscle ticked in Adrian's rough

jawline, visible even through his ever-present dark stubble. "You need more, though."

Carly ignored him, letting her frown linger. "He didn't come, did he?"

Adrian returned the favor in the ignoring department, and he one-upped her on the frown, too. "Bellamy's outside. Gavin, too. They're worried, but other than to tell them you have a concussion and the mother of all shiners, I didn't know what else to say."

Carly sank another inch into her brittle pillow. "It was a mistake," she said softly, the irony heavy in her mouth. Although the hospital staff had asked her dozens of pointed questions about the nature of her injury, she'd remained adamant. No matter what had happened between them, Jackson would never lay a hand on her in anger.

Too bad smashing her heart to pieces didn't fall into the same category.

Carly exhaled a shaky breath. "Can you just tell them I'm going to sleep? I'll call the restaurant in the morning to let them know I'm okay." Her eyes found the clock on the wall, and she realized with a slow hitch that technically, it was morning now.

"Don't worry about the restaurant, Carly. Gavin and I have it covered, okay? Just rest." He brushed his fingers over hers, as if he wanted to squeeze but was afraid of hurting her, and quietly slipped from the room.

Carly knew Adrian's words were meant to put her mind at ease, but they dredged to the surface what Jackson had said earlier, when she'd stood before him, wide-open and vulnerable.

The resort could always replace her. She wasn't a necessary ingredient, just something brought in for a temporary punch of flavor to spice things up.

Sadness clogged her chest, her eyelids trembling against the weight of the fresh tears threatening to spill down her face. She'd known—she'd *known*—that putting her heart on the line was a huge risk, and yet somehow, she'd believed it would be okay, that they'd defy the odds of her past because her connection to Jackson was different. Seamless. Right.

But here she sat, just as duped as ever.

Carly gave in to a good, long cry before drifting back to sleep.

Jackson drove the deserted roads of Pine Mountain for over an hour, aimlessly riding each one out until it dead ended, only to turn around and do the same thing on a different stretch of asphalt. He had no idea where he was headed, or that he had a destination at all, really, until he stopped driving and started walking. Even then he didn't stop until he was surrounded by the moonlit chill of the path leading through the archway of crepe myrtle.

It was odd to see his mother's garden in the thick of night, vibrant color replaced by eerie shades of black and gray. He started forward, measuring his steps on the dirt path carefully so he wouldn't trip over an errant tree root, and making enough noise to let whatever wildlife might be out here know that he was certainly bigger. Finally, the low branches opened up like a yawn, and he stepped into the clearing with a sense of relief that didn't last.

His mother stood, wrapped in her bathrobe, cradling a cup of coffee between her palms and wearing her own look of relief. "Hi, sweetheart. I'm glad you came. I was starting to get worried."

"Christ, Ma!" Jackson jerked backward, pain streaking through his bruised ribs at the sudden movement. It was a keen reminder of everything that had happened tonight, and it made Jackson's mouth feel like a sandbox. "What're you doing out here?"

"Waiting for you, of course. It seems we have something to talk about." She moved toward him, her silhouette coming into sharper focus as she nodded to the wooden bench at the far end of the rectangular plot.

Jackson's thoughts swam with confusion. "I, uh . . . how did you know I'd be here?" Hell, Jackson hadn't even known where he'd be going or where he'd end up.

"Shane couldn't get ahold of you. But after he spoke with Bellamy, he was rather concerned. I can't say I blame him."

Understanding shot through him, twining around his fear. "You talked to Shane?" Oh, God. Shane . . . Bellamy . . .

Carly.

His mother nodded. "He wanted you to know that Carly's going to be just fine. Bellamy's at the hospital with her now."

Grateful relief sparked through him, although he had no right to feel it.

Thank God she's in better hands than mine.

"Come, sit." Catherine smoothed the back of her terrycloth robe before sitting on the bench, and as strange as it was, he did what she asked.

She fixed him with a stare both serious and kind. "I know you came out here to be alone, and I'll leave you to it soon enough. But it's time we talked about what happened the night we left Harrisburg. In fact, we're long overdue."

Jackson jumped as if she'd slapped him. "I don't want to talk about it." The horrible images edged their way back, threatening to surface at the slightest provocation, and he jammed them down, just like always.

But his mother stood firm. "I know. But you don't have a choice this time, because I'm going to do all the talking."

And before he could protest, she stunned him to silence with what came next.

"Your father hit me for years, Jackson. I know you think it was just one night, that he lost control and snapped in a moment of impulse, but it wasn't that way." Catherine paused, wistful. "As horrible as it sounds, the first few times it happened, I let it go after he apologized. He was a passionate man, full of emotion. He blamed the beatings on his love for me, and I thought that he truly hadn't meant any harm. It's why I told you he loved me just a little too much. For a long time, I actually believed that was true."

"Jesus, Ma," Jackson breathed, but she held up a hand, resolute.

"Weeks would go by, sometimes months, and I'd think everything was better and he'd learned how to control his emotions, that those incidents had been isolated. But then they piled up. Something would set him off, always when you kids were in bed, and he'd get so angry. Deep down, I knew it wasn't going to stop. Both of your grandparents had passed by then, but once I told Aunt Billie what was going on, she agreed to take us all in on the spot. I thought . . ." She trailed off, and Jackson watched her in utter shock as she gathered up the strength to finish.

"I foolishly harbored the hope that maybe, if I gave your father an ultimatum, he'd love me enough to stop hurting me and we could work things out. Brooke and Autumn were at a friend's house for the night, and Dylan wasn't even six yet, but you . . . you were there."

Catherine's knuckles flashed, white and worried, around her un-sipped coffee cup. "When I told him I would leave him if he didn't stop hitting me, he didn't lose his cool or scream and holler. He didn't even try to hurt me."

Blue plaid flannel, smelling like whiskey over laundry soap, strong hands—too strong for Jackson to counter— yanking him out of bed . . . his mother in the doorframe . . .

"It's me you want. Leave him be."

"Oh, God, Ma." Jackson stared, unable to say anything else.

His father had come after him, and she'd taken the punishment by defending him. How could he not have made the connection after all this time that it wasn't passion or impulse or love that had made his father hit his mother?

It was cold, hard evil.

Catherine gave a tight nod. "I managed to keep him away from you that night, but I swore to myself right then and there I would never put my children in danger again. I told you he hurt me because he loved me too much, but that's not why it happened. Your father hit me because he was a mean, terrible man, Jackson. And it's high time you realized that despite being his son, you're *nothing* like him."

"I . . . I don't know what to say. I should've done more to protect you," Jackson whispered, his eyes tightening with wet heat.

"Oh, sweetie, oh no. Don't you see? I should've done that for you, before it got so bad." She dropped her chin into the folds of her bathrobe. "After we left, I thought your memories would fade over time. Kids are resilient, and even your sisters came to terms with our leaving after a while, although of course I never told them exactly why. Once you became an adult, I assumed you'd forgotten. You've always been so easygoing that I didn't think much of your not having a serious girlfriend. Not until recently, anyway."

Jackson jolted upright, his listening-trance broken. "Don't," he warned, more pleading than insistent. "Please."

But Catherine persisted, putting her coffee cup down on the soft grass so she could take both his hands. "Being in love with someone doesn't mean you're going to lose control and hurt them, honey. It means you'd do anything to keep them safe."

Jackson opened his mouth, ready to respond with one of his many ingrained defensive maneuvers.

Instead, everything he'd felt about Carly, from the instant he'd seen her through the screen door at the bungalow to the gut-wrenching moment he'd left her in the hands of paramedics, spilled from his lips in a torrent of emotion. Catherine simply listened, her only response being a slight flinch when Jackson described exactly how Carly had gotten hurt.

"You didn't hurt her on purpose, Jackson. You must know that," she insisted, but he shook his head, resolute.

"But I did. I may not have hit her on purpose." He stopped, nauseous at the memory. "But what I said was unforgiveable. I told her she never meant anything to me. I walked away when she needed me most."

Oh, hell. No way could he fix this. No amount of *I'm sorry* or heartfelt explanation was going to convince Carly he hadn't meant what he'd said.

Even if he shouted it from the rooftops, she wasn't going to believe what was really in his heart.

It was her, plain and simple. He was in love with her.

Catherine smiled. "She's a smart girl, honey. At the very least, trust her to give you a good listen. You might be surprised at how things turn out."

"I don't know, Ma. I think this is too big." He swallowed hard. "Plus, she'd have to be here in order to hear me out, and she's going back to New York." Jackson tried to picture the restaurant, the garden, Joe's Grocery—hell, even Rural Route 4—without Carly, but he came up painfully empty.

Feed her.

Christ! His inner voice had gone outer limits. He couldn't right this with a goddamn peanut butter and jelly sandwich.

"Far be it from me to tell you what to do, honey. But she can still forgive you for an accident, even if she's taken that job."

But the numbness had returned to Jackson's body, filling him with resignation and defeat.

"Some things you just can't fix with *I'm sorry*."

"All in all, Ms. di Matisse, you're actually a very lucky young lady."

Carly snorted, both at the irony of being lucky and the fact that she'd bet a thousand dollars the doctor standing at the foot of her bed was younger than she was. "I don't feel very lucky," she said, the words more soft joke than snappy rebuke. What she *did* feel like was someone who'd been lying on a lackluster mattress for nine hours with the headache from hell, trying to hash out some kind of a plan for her wounded body, a career that had been thrown in the blender, and her utterly jumbled sense of trust and belonging.

She didn't even want to get started on her shattered heart.

"Well, your nose isn't broken and there's no damage to your orbit. Your MRI shows nothing out of the ordinary, so other than the swelling and discomfort, I think you're in the clear."

"Does that mean she can go home?" After spending all night in a recliner two sizes too small for his linebacker-esque frame, Adrian's voice carried equal parts aggravation and hope. He'd flat-out refused to leave Carly's side, despite all her pleas for him to go home and get some sleep. Which had turned out to be a good thing in the end, because although she hadn't realized it at the time, she had needed him to help her sort things out.

As well as plan.

The doctor typed something into her electronic chart, and the sound yanked Carly back to reality just in time to see him nod. "You'll need to take it easy for the next couple of days at least. And by 'take it easy,' I mean, stay home and rest. A concussion is no laughing matter, so you'll have to limit yourself a bit. I'll send the nurse in to go over your release orders with you, but I don't see any reason to keep you here."

Carly exhaled in relief as the doctor tucked her chart under one arm and made his way to the door. "Thank you."

She'd had jailbreak on her mind as soon as the sun had risen two hours ago. God, what she wouldn't give to slip into the comfort of her own bed right now, to dive beneath the sheets and never come out.

Never mind that those sheets smelled like freshly cut wood and sweet possibility that would never again see the light of day.

"You still want me to call Bellamy and Gavin and have them meet us at your place?" Adrian asked, looking at her warily even though they'd been over things no less than a hundred times.

She nodded with calm certainty, even though it rattled her head like black-eyed peas in a jar. "Yes. They deserve to hear the truth about what's going to happen, and they deserve to hear it from me." She paused, watching him carefully. "How about you? You're good to go?"

Adrian's eyes met hers, his smoky hazel gaze telling her all she needed to know. "Let's get the hell out of here, what do you say?"

Carly waited until Adrian had clicked her door quietly shut to go make the calls to their kitchen staff before she picked up the phone by her bed.

"Yes, hello. I'm trying to reach one of your guests, Mr. Richard Buchanan." She paused while the operator looked up the room number, hesitating for just a second before saying with absolute certainty,

"Tell him Carly di Matisse is calling, and that it's urgent."

Chapter Twenty-Nine

"Don't take this the wrong way, but you look like shit, buddy." Shane crouched next to a mass of tangled cucumber vines, propping his forearms over his thighs as he offered up a steaming travel mug of coffee.

Jackson took it, but didn't drink. "Great. I look like I feel, then." He squinted through the dappled morning sunlight, his eyes dry and tired in a way that marked a serious lack of sleep and a night fraught with gut-wrenching stress.

"Have you been out here all night?" Shane sat down beside Jackson in the soft grass, his dark glance flickering with concern and brimming with questions.

"Yeah. Do you . . ." Jackson stopped, fully understanding that he had no right to ask the question burning through his mouth, but the words barged out anyway. "Do you know how Carly is? I mean, when I called the hospital a couple of hours ago, Autumn said she was fine. Sleeping, and stuff. But has Bellamy heard anything this morning?"

Shane's brow lifted. "You had your sister check on her in the middle of the night?"

"Yeah. She was on shift in another department," Jackson admitted. Christ, he wanted nothing more than to be the one to check on Carly, to make sure she had everything she needed and keep her safe.

But he'd been the one to cause all of her pain. How could he possibly protect her unless it was to stay away?

She'd trusted him, and he'd crushed her heart.

There was no taking something like that back.

Shane cleared his throat and regarded Jackson with a wary expression. "So, ah, you want to let me in on what's going on here? Your girlfriend spent the night at Riverside Hospital with a concussion, and you're sitting in the middle of your mother's tomato cages looking like death warmed over. I'm trying to figure it out, I really am, but . . ."

"I didn't hurt her on purpose, I swear to God." Jackson's words clawed their way out, emphatic and pained. "I was trying to walk away from her, to keep her safe, but . . . I didn't, and even though the whole thing was an accident, I still can't fix it. Oh, hell, Shane. I fucked this up so bad that there's no way to fix it."

He gave Shane a short version of events, and damn if the words didn't lose any of their ability to make him sick with the retelling.

"I knew there was a good explanation, Jax, and I believe you. But maybe you should be saying these things to Carly, rather than bouncing them off me out here in the great outdoors, huh?"

"I *can't*," Jackson countered, frustration jolting through him. "I'm just going to hurt her again, and I've done that enough."

Shane made a noise of disdain, but Jackson barreled on. "I mean it. I've been sitting here all night, trying to come up with the words to erase it all, but I can't. In the end, I'll still have hurt her without being able to ever make it right."

"You love her, right?" Shane asked, and Jackson didn't hesitate.

"Yeah."

"Then how about a good, old-fashioned sincere apology?"

The suggestion yanked Jackson to complete attention. "Do you think she'll listen?"

"I think you should hurry, unless you want to do your groveling long-distance," Shane said, frowning into the display on his chiming cell phone.

"What?"

"See for yourself. Bellamy just sent me this." Shane deposited his cell phone into Jackson's unsteady hand.

Am @ Carly's for a team mtg to discuss job in NYC. WTF?

Jackson's mouth went dry as he remembered the job offer from Carly's old boss, but his pulse ripped through him as he scrolled through the rest of Bellamy's text message.

She's leaving tomorrow.

Feed her. FEED HER.
In that instant, everything snapped into place with gut-wrenching clarity. Carly took care of everyone she loved by feeding them, and damn it, he loved her enough to take care of her right back. It wasn't about feeding her, literally.

It was about loving her unconditionally.

It was about telling her the truth.

This time when his instinct howled at him, Jackson listened without thinking.

"Please tell me you drove your Mustang, because I need to get down Rural Route 4. Like *now*!"

"Have you thought out how you want to do this, dude? Because Adrian is going to . . . ohhhkay, maybe not." Shane trailed off as Jackson wasted no time putting a purposeful knock dead center in Carly's front door.

"I'll get past Adrian," Jackson said, and meant it. Right about now, he'd get past ten Adrians to get two minutes of

Carly's attention. He had something to say, and he was god-damn well going to say it.

Even if she still went back to New York tomorrow.

Sloane swung the door open, her voice immediately choked with surprise. "Oh, holy shit! What're you doing here?" She boomeranged a glance over one shoulder before slipping outside to the porch.

"I came to see Carly, and I'm not leaving until I do." Right. Apparently being in love with someone meant getting pretty bossy. Jackson filed it squarely under the I-don't-give-a-shit heading.

"It's not that easy, Jackson. She's, um. Kind of busy." Sloane narrowed her eyes on him. "Plus, Adrian's here and he wants to kill you. And I really don't mean that metaphorically."

Something ripped free in Jackson's chest, and he put it in words right there on the front porch. "I know about her meeting, Sloane. I know Adrian's here, and I know she's going back to New York. But I need to talk to her before she goes, and I don't care if I've got to do it in front of everybody in that fucking room."

Sloane cocked her dark head, the strangest smile perched on her lips. "I always knew you were her swan. By all means, come on in. But I'm *so* not kidding about Adrian. Watch your back, would you?"

"I think between the two of us, we can at least hold him off," Shane said, a hard flicker passing over his eyes as he gave Jackson an I-got-your-back stare.

"Okee dokey. Don't say I didn't warn you," she murmured, ushering them inside.

From down the narrow hallway, Jackson could hear the indistinct murmur of voices locked in discussion, although it was impossible to make out the words. For a second, the realization that he was about to barge in on a professional meeting with Carly and her staff filtered into his consciousness, and it tugged at his rational thought, begging him to slow down and at least think about things.

Nope. Being in love with Carly was about as far from rational thought as Jackson was going to get. As he entered the room, he realized he liked it that way.

"I'm sorry to interrupt, but I have something I need to say to Carly."

Every head in the living room whipped around, and Adrian launched himself from his seat next to Carly so fast that all Jackson could see of her was one jeans-clad leg and her bare foot.

"Like *hell!* Sloane, are you out of your freaking mind, letting him in?" Adrian shot a withering glance at Sloane, and the guy Jackson vaguely remembered as the suit from La Dolce Vita interjected a startled *hey*! But rather than back down, Sloane jammed her fists into her hips and replied with a stare that matched Adrian's dagger for dagger.

"Watch it, Holt. I'm not an idiot. If he gets frisky, I'm sure you'll take care of it," she snapped.

"Oh, I'll take care of it, all right, but I don't need an excuse."

Adrian stepped forward with clear intention, and Bellamy levered herself up from the couch, reaching for the clearly pissed-off sous chef, which in turn sent Shane into a defensive motion at Jackson's side.

Jackson made a last-ditch attempt to keep things semicalm, stepping in the midst of everyone but still unable to see Carly herself. "I just want to talk to her. I don't care if I have to do it right here, with every damn one of you between us."

"Adrian, stop."

Carly's voice echoed, haggard and quiet and so completely sweet in Jackson's ears that it almost shot his knees out from under him. She nudged her way forward, weaving through the people in the living room, and the sight of the angry purple bruise marking her cheekbone ripped through every ounce of Jackson's soul.

But he wouldn't leave. Not this time. Not unless she told him to.

Carly set her lips in a firm line and looked up at Adrian, who was the last person between her and Jackson. "If it'll make you feel any better, we can do it Jackson's way, with you standing between us. But I'd actually like to hear what he came to say."

"Carly," Adrian started, then shook his head. "I'm not going to talk you out of this, am I?" Something strange blanketed his expression, a cross between realization and resignation, and Jackson eked out a breath of relief at her answer.

"No, *gnoccone*. Not this time."

"Thank you," Jackson rasped. A tender thread of hope pulled deep in his belly, but he stood firm, afraid to recognize the fragile *what-if*. "Look, I know I don't have any right to ask you to hear me out. Believe me, I know that. But I owe you an explanation. And an apology. And . . . well, everything."

A sliver of emotion streaked over Carly's face before disappearing into her unreadable façade. "You don't owe me anything, Jackson. You were right. What we had was a heat of the moment thing, and I turned it into something it wasn't."

"No, you didn't," Jackson fired back emphatically enough to make Adrian visibly stiffen, but no way was he backing down now. "You turned it into every amazing thing that it was, only I was too much of a thickheaded idiot to see it."

Before he could stop it, the story of what his mother had told him last night in the garden started flowing out, filled in with the details of the childhood memories that still made bile churn deep in his belly.

"So when I overheard you telling Adrian about the job in New York, I thought I could just let you walk away, and then you'd be safe. Only what I said ended up hurting you so much, and . . ." He hitched to a stop, sucking in a breath at the memory. "I never heard you come up behind me. It's not an excuse, but it's the truth. I turned around with the intention to say good-bye, but you were too close, and even though I hit you by complete accident, it doesn't change the fact that I did it."

"I know this was an accident, Jackson," she whispered, gesturing to her face.

"Well, there's more you should know." He took a step toward her, locking his eyes on hers and pouring all of his emotion into the connection. "I thought letting you go home was the best way to keep you safe, that apologizing wasn't enough. And it's not, but I have to say it anyway. I'm sorry. I'm *so* sorry for what I did to you. I'd do anything to take it back, Carly. You don't have to forgive me, or say anything. But I never meant to hurt you, with what I said or what I did."

"Did you mean any of it?" Carly's expression never wavered, and his heart did its very best to hammer its way out of his ribcage.

"God, no. I love you. I'm totally, completely in love with you. If that means I have to move to New York to be with you, then that's what I'll do. Hell, I'd move to Timbuktu to be with you. I love you so much."

A chirrup of surprise crossed her lips, and Jackson realized with a stab of anxiety that she was crying. Oh, no. No, no.

And then the faintest, most gorgeous smile he'd ever seen in his entire life turned the corners of her lips up, and he rushed forward just in time for her to fling her arms around his neck.

"I love you, too." She buried her uninjured cheek in his shoulder, and the smell of honeysuckle and pure hope was so good, he wanted to drown in it. "I'm sorry that all of this happened, too, but I love you, Jackson. I love you."

"Alrighty, people. Nothing to see here. Move along, now." Sloane wiped her face with the back of her hand before shooing everyone toward the front of the bungalow, and it was only then that Jackson remembered the five other people in the room. Everyone complied save Adrian, and Jackson eased back from Carly as the big guy crossed his arms over his chest with a hard stare.

"If this ever changes, we're going to finish what we started, you and I."

Jackson nodded. "And if it doesn't?"

"I'll get used to you. Eventually. Just don't fuck it up." Adrian lifted an eyebrow at Carly in one last wordless exchange before walking through the door.

"I won't," Jackson murmured, bending low to kiss the top of Carly's head. "I know it's going to take a while to earn your trust back, Carly, but I meant what I said. I'll do whatever it takes." He paused. "I guess I should probably let my family know I'll be leaving." The thought of moving away from Pine Mountain sent a pang through his gut, but it was nothing compared to the thought of living without Carly.

She drew back with a quick curve of her lips. "It's only a couple of days, Jackson. Although I'd love it if you'd come with me anyway."

"What are you talking about? Bellamy's text said you were leaving for New York tomorrow," Jackson stammered.

"Oh, I am. You see, a lot has happened in the last couple of hours. Once Richard Buchanan officially fired Travis and offered me the job at Gracie's, Travis knew he had no leverage left in our divorce and that he'd been beat. He agreed to sign the paperwork to make it official as soon as possible. Which, as it turns out, is the day after tomorrow. So that's why I'm going to New York, but I'll be back Tuesday night."

"But . . . but what about the job at Gracie's?" Jackson's blood chilled. "Do you not want me to move with you?" Oh, hell. Maybe that was too much for her. After all, trust wasn't earned overnight.

"Oh, no. I mean, yes." She stopped, rolling her eyes and

then wincing at the movement. "What I mean is, while I'd love for us to move in together, I'm not leaving Pine Mountain."

All the oxygen in Jackson's lungs turned to sand. "What?" he gasped. "But the meeting . . ."

"I wanted Bellamy and Gavin to know I'd been offered the position in New York, in case they heard it through the grapevine. But I also wanted them to hear straight from me that I had turned the job down," Carly replied.

"Why would you do that?" Jackson breathed, not sure he'd heard her correctly.

"Because ever since Travis left me, I've been terrified to trust. But what I didn't really get until last night was that I had to trust myself first, before I could put my faith in anybody else. So I finally listened to my gut, but it just told me what I'd known all along." She stopped and gave a tiny shrug before continuing. "I belong here now. Pine Mountain is my home."

Jackson's inner voice burst to life, and he grinned as he pulled Carly close. "You know what my gut is telling me?"

A rare giggle escaped from her throat. "That you're hungry?"

But right then and there, Jackson finally got what all the fuss was about, and he answered honestly.

"That we should get married."

"Wait . . . did you . . . are you . . ." Carly blinked, but he brushed a finger over her stunned lips.

"I want to feed you PB and J when you're hungry, and I want to hold you in our bed when you're sad. I want to be as serious with you as serious gets. I want to spend the rest of my life with you, if you'll have me. What do you say?"

"Yes. Yes, yes. *Yes!*" She circled her arms around his shoulders, and he lifted her seamlessly into his arms just as she jumped to meet his embrace. As he leaned down to slant his lips over hers, there was only one thought in Jackson's mind.

He and Carly were a perfect fit.

Recipes

Carly's Bolognese

Ingredients:

- 1 Tablespoon olive oil
- 1 medium onion, diced fine
- 2 stalks celery, halved lengthwise and sliced thin
- 1 large carrot, diced fine
- 2 cloves garlic, diced
- 1 pound ground beef
- 1 pound ground pork/bulk Italian sausage
- 2 fresh bay leaves
- 1 teaspoon dried Italian seasoning
- 2 cans (28 ounces each) crushed tomatoes (organic preferred)
- 1 can (14 ounces) diced tomatoes
- 1 cup beef broth (half and half with water is fine for lower sodium), plus more for thinning
- Pinch allspice
- Chopped flatleaf parsley (a generous handful) for garnish

In a large stockpot, warm olive oil over medium-high heat. Add onion, celery, and carrot, stirring often, until soft, adding two cloves of garlic in the last two minutes of cooking (7–8 minutes total). Gently push veggies to the sides of the pot and add meat. Using a wooden spoon, break up meat and cook until brown and crumbly (about ten minutes). Add Italian seasoning, and salt and pepper to taste.

If you've got any lovely brown bits on the bottom of the pot from the veggies, de-glaze with a splash of beef broth (red wine works well here too, and the alcohol burns off so this recipe is safe for the under-21 set!) Add all three cans of tomatoes and the pinch of allspice, and heat to a low bubble.

Simmer, uncovered for at least an hour on the lowest heat setting, adding broth and/or water to thin the gravy as necessary. When you're ready to serve (the longer you let this simmer, the better it tends to be), put this over your favorite pasta (linguine is good, as are penne and rigatoni; both stand up to the thickness of the sauce nicely), sprinkle with chopped parsley and serve with green salad, garlic bread, and lots of love! You can also use this sauce as a base for a nice hearty lasagna, and it freezes well.

Blueberry Lemon "Ugly" Scones

I got the idea of putting streusel on scones from an old recipe, but because of its crumbly texture, it can make scones look rustic, or as we jokingly say in my house, "ugly." Carly's presentation (and her delivery!) is pretty, though, and one bite of these scones will tell you that looks can be very deceiving.

INGREDIENTS:

Streusel:

 A generous ¼ cup packed light brown sugar
 ¼ cup all-purpose flour
 ½ teaspoon ground cinnamon
 2 Tablespoons melted butter

Scones:

 2 cups all-purpose flour
 ¼ cup light brown sugar
 2 teaspoons baking powder
 ½ teaspoon salt
 1 teaspoon cinnamon
 4 Tablespoons (½ stick) cold, unsalted butter, cut
    into small pieces
 1 teaspoon fresh lemon zest
 1 egg, lightly beaten
 ¼ cup sour cream

Splash of milk (up to a Tablespoon)
1½ cups fresh blueberries

Preheat oven to 400 degrees. In a small bowl, combine
streusel ingredients. Mix well and set aside (mixture will be
crumbly). In a large bowl, mix flour, light brown sugar,
baking powder, salt, and cinnamon with a whisk until well
combined. Using a pastry cutter or two forks, cut in butter
until mixture resembles coarse meal. In a small bowl, combine lemon zest, egg, sour cream, and milk. Fold into scone
mixture until just combined. Repeat with blueberries. Shape
mixture into a disc approximately 2" high (dust hands with
flour to prevent sticking if necessary). Place disc on a parch-
ment-lined baking sheet. Sprinkle generously with streusel
mixture. Cut into eight wedges and separate. Bake for 15–18
minutes until streusel gets brown and melty and your kitchen
smells like heaven. Serve to the one you love!

Jackson's Heat of the Summer Burgers

Nothing says summer like a perfectly grilled burger! Pair these with some potato salad and your favorite frosty beverage, and it's an instant party.

INGREDIENTS:

- 2 pounds ground beef, 90/10 preferred
- Salt and pepper to taste
- 1 egg, slightly beaten
- ¼ cup canola oil
- ½ sweet onion, diced fine
- ½ orange bell pepper, diced fine
- 4 cloves roasted garlic, minced
- ¼ cup breadcrumbs (pulse a generous handful of garlic croutons in your food processor to make these . . . it's worth it!)

Combine all ingredients in a large bowl, in order, with your hands. Use a light touch, but combine well. Divide into eight portions and shape each portion into a patty. Grill over medium heat on a gas grill or indirect flame on a charcoal grill, to preference. Medium 10–12 minutes, flip at the halfway point. All burgers should be a minimum of 160 degrees internal temperature in accordance with food safety regulations.

Come back to Pine Mountain
this October for Sloane's story.

Read on for a taste of *Stirring Up Trouble.*

Carly leaned forward, dropping her chin into her palms. "Maybe you just need a little inspiration." But the offer only prompted Sloane to bark out a sardonic laugh at the double entendre.

"Please. Do you have any idea how long it's been since I've had a little *inspiration?*" She hooked disdainful air quotes around the word, counting backwards in her head to recheck her math.

Wait, was it January again? Already? Jeez, no wonder her muse was pissed. "I'm sorry. Maybe that wasn't a good suggestion."

"Actually, it's a great suggestion." Sloane released her spoon with a plunk, and all the frustration swishing around in her chest burst forth in an emotional jailbreak. "Believe me, nothing would make me happier than to be earth-movingly *inspired* right now. As a matter of fact, considering the lack of inspiration going on in my life, I think I'm due for a downright out-of-body experience. Not that I've ever reached the summit of Mount O during the actual act. Nope, not me. If I'm gonna get there, I've gotta fly solo."

What a joke. She had to be the only romance writer on the planet who'd never achieved orgasm with someone else in the room. No wonder she had an epic-sized case of the writing blahs.

"Sweetie." Carly's eyes widened, coppery brown and full of astonishment. She reached a hand out, but Sloane had hit her limit. She lifted a hand right back, stopping her friend's motion cold.

"No, really. Karmically speaking, is it too much to ask for the powers-that-be to send some mind-blowing orgasms my way? I'm tired of doing all the work. Plus, it's all in the name of research. I mean, show a girl a little joy, for heaven's sake!" Sloane knew she was ranting, but blowing off the steam she'd slowly built up felt divine. "Just once, I'd like to give new meaning to the phrase *life imitates art*. After all the fumbling lovers I've put up with who couldn't find my hot spots with a map and compass, I deserve some really hot, toe-curling, religious-experience sex!"

"Um, Sloane?"

But the sinfully good release prompted her to continue without pause. "I mean it, *cucciola*. In spite of what I do for a living, I'm starting to think men who can dish up Richter scale orgasms are just a cruel myth."

Finally stopping for a breath, Sloane registered the odd look on Carly's face with apprehension. "What? Oh, God, don't tell me they really *are* a myth?"

The deep rumble of a throat being cleared cut Sloane's breath short in her lungs.

"Excuse me, chef. I don't mean to interrupt a . . . delicate conversation, but I've got an emergency I need to discuss with you."

The sound of the very smooth, very male voice over her shoulder froze Sloane into place and ignited every one of her nerve endings to a slow sizzle. Stunned, she whirled in her seat, only to find herself face-to-crotch with a pair of flawlessly tailored charcoal dress slacks. The wearer jerked backward, looking both startled and more than a little put out at her sudden movement.

Carly cleared her throat too late to hide the laugh beneath the gesture. "Sloane, you remember my restaurant manager, Gavin Carmichael, don't you?"

Knowing she should be utterly mortified and praying for a fault line in the earth to swallow her whole, Sloane threw on a cocky smile instead. Letting her gaze float slowly upward, she looked Gavin right in his stunning, melted-chocolate eyes and said the only thing she could think of.

"Nice pants."